THE SYNOD

D1799590

A Novel by Avery B. Goodman

Planetary Books, 848 N Rainbow Blvd, #780
Las Vegas, NV 89107

To be among the first to learn about the author's latest events, including book and article publications, sign up for the mailing list at:

<u>http://www.averybgoodman.com/myblog</u>

Planetary Books, 848 N Rainbow Blvd, #780
Las Vegas, NV 89107

Table of Contents

REAL FACTS THAT INSPIRED THIS BOOK

For many years, the worldwide investment bank, Morgan Stanley, told its clients it was buying and storing precious metals on their behalf. Eventually, after discovering what they believed was fraud, the customers sued in 2005, alleging that the bank had never purchased the metals. According to the plaintiffs, it was simply charging them regular storage fees for storing air in its vault. The company, eventually settled the case in 2007, for $4.4 million.[1]

There is a declassified 1974 transcript of a conversation between Secretary of State Henry Kissinger and Undersecretary Thomas O. Enders. That was three years after President Richard Nixon ended the convertibility of dollars into gold.[2] Before that, the US Treasury and its agents had always been honest about market interventions. When they wanted the price of gold down they normally openly announced and sold large quantities of gold.

Since then, the government appears to have resorted to covert action, for the reasons stated in the conversation. According to Undersecretary Enders;

"It's against our interest to have gold in the system because... We've been trying to get away from that into a system in which we can control... For a long time we... change [the price of] gold almost at will. This is no longer possible..."

Nowadays, covert government interference in the free markets is not limited to the price of gold. In 1987, President Ronald Reagan signed Executive Order 12631[3], creating the "President's Working Group on Financial Markets." The stated goal was to "enhance the orderliness" of stock, bond and commodity markets, and prevent a repeat of "Black Monday", October 19, 1987, when stocks declined over 22% in one day.

The group slowly transformed into the "Plunge Protection Team" or "PPT" for short. It consists of the Secretary of the Treasury, and the Chairmen of the Federal Reserve, SEC and CFTC. Supposedly, this group "consults" with the exchanges, clearinghouses, self-regulatory bodies, and *"major market participants" (a/k/a the big banks).* In reality, the big banks are the PPT's agents in financial markets. JP Morgan Chase holds a written contract to manage the Federal Reserve's $1.25 trillion mortgage bond portfolio. You can find the disclosed contract here:

https://www.newyorkfed.org/medialibrary/media/aboutthefed/JPMC_MBS.pdf

The net effect of the close association between the Federal Reserve, US Treasury and the big commercial banks in New York City, has been to support the biggest gamblers in the world with government money. The full faith and credit of the United States of America is now being used to backstop financial speculation gone sour. The government has become an active participant in privatizing the gains made by bank-based gamblers, while socializing their losses to the detriment of other people.

Most distressing of all, there is a room, deep underneath a nondescript office building, at 55 Broadway, the heart of Manhattan. It is remarkably similar to the "THEATRES Control Center", described in this novel. Operating in semi-secrecy, the real life control center contains a similar battery of supercomputers and monitoring stations, linking thousands of cameras and audio inputs throughout the Greater New York area. Every square inch of the city is monitored, everyday, all day, 24/7. The operation is run jointly by the NYPD and, oddly, by four of the largest Wall Street banks.[4]

As the reader may see by now, truth can be much more frightening than fiction.

1 http://www.reuters.com/article/idUSN1228014520070612

2 http://mises.ca/posts/articles/henry-kissinger-on-gold/

3 A treasure trove of other information exists at www.gata.org

4 http://www.counterpunch.org/2012/02/06/wall-streets-secret-spy-center-run-for-the-1-by-nypd/

PROLOGUE

The battle of "good" versus "evil" has continued since the beginning of time. People believe that good triumphs over evil. Occasionally, that may be true. Mostly, however, evil triumphs over itself. Evil pursues selfish goals that will inevitably put it in opposition with its own kind. Evil destroys evil to the great benefit of the world. If not for this endless battle of evil versus evil, human beings would suffer endless tyranny, anguish and despair.

I - MURDER IN THE CITY

Charlie Bakkendorf was just an innocent bystander. Neither good nor evil, he was a man filled with wants and needs, but no particular malice. He was a "vault manager" at the venerable investment bank known as "Bolton Sayres." His title, however, like most at the bank, was essentially meaningless. Charlie managed nothing. He was simply a high school graduate.

He was 32 years old, single, and lonely. For the first time in years, all of that seemed likely to change. He had only known her for two weeks, but Maria was fantastic. Her image was now etched so deeply in his mind that couldn't get her out. He was crazy about her.

He hoped that his insistence on taking her home by taxi impressed her. It was a small thing, but he thought it showed his sincerity. He smiled to himself. What had started out as a cup of coffee had expanded into a nice dinner. He would see Maria again on Saturday night.

He intended to do everything right. This time, he'd take her to one of the most expensive restaurants in New York City. That couldn't fail to impress her. After that, it would be a Broadway show. He'd buy the best seats in the house. The cost of such a lavish date might total well over $1,000, something he'd never done before, but he had no worries. For the first time in his life, he had money to burn.

He'd hit the jackpot! Two million dollars! All the money he'd ever need. A trip to the 21 Club, an extremely expensive restaurant, and a Broadway play or two wouldn't make much of a dent. Being rich might be hard to get used to. He'd been penny-pinching all his life. But, come Saturday, he'd start to spend some of his new-found wealth, and treat Maria like a Princess.

The taxi stopped when it reached the 181st Street subway station, and he took out his wallet to pay. He'd taken the taxi to impress her. But, it's hard to break old habits and there was no more point to pretense. The cab fare to Brooklyn would cost another $50, maybe even more. The subway would cost just $2.50. The choice was clear. He paid the taxi driver, got out of the car, and walked down to the subway station.

A few people milled about. Mostly it was empty. The relative quiet was a welcome change. At 6 p.m., things normally seemed more like a madhouse, and traveling in the subway made you feel like a sardine in a can. That would change for the better. He'd soon have the money to buy an apartment in lower Manhattan. From then on, he'd walk to work. Or, maybe, he wouldn't have to work.

When the train arrived, he boarded, and it headed toward Brooklyn. Station after station passed. Then, he switched lines. Less than a half hour later, he exited. After passing through another set of turnstiles, and climbing the stairs, he made his way to the street. A few lamps lit the way but, mostly, it was dark. Some light also came from building windows. The street, however, was cast in shadows.

Something was eerie in the air, and he didn't like it. Then, suddenly, as if out of nowhere, his apprehension seemed to take form and substance. A short, heavily built black man walked up on his right side. The man seemed alone. His unexpected appearance, however, was disconcerting.

Charlie's pulse rose. He didn't know the man. A jolt of adrenaline surged through his body. It wasn't every night that a stranger, let alone a black stranger, ran up to him. Charlie was no racist, but, still, the sudden appearance unnerved him. The neighborhood was mostly white.

What did the man want?

Unknown to him, the man had been there for over 4 hours, and was tired of waiting. No one by Charlie's description had shown up in the proper place at the expected time, and he was impatient to take care of business.

"You Charles Bakkendorf?" the man blurted out, with a thick ghetto accent.

Charlie wondered how the man knew his name. He did not ask that question. Instead, he said nothing, and tried to behave as if there was no one there. He picked up the pace, but the stranger had no intention of letting him get away no matter how fast he walked. The two made a strange pair, walking quickly, side by side, in the same direction.

"I'm askin' you a question, brotha'... you, Charles Bakkendorf, or not?" the man asked again, irritated.

Charlie became calmer when he decided that, if the man knew his name, he couldn't be a typical mugger. Still, who was he? He stopped walking, and turned to face his pursuer head to head. He could see the man's face, but that didn't help. In the dim light of the nearby street lamp, he tried to focus. He still didn't recognize him.

"What do you want?" Charlie asked.

"You Charlie Bakkendorf?" the black man asked again.

"Yes." Charlie replied.

The black man nodded, and stepped away.

An instant later, his white companion stepped out of the shadows. There is no more accurate way of describing that man but to say he was gigantic. At about 6 foot 9 inches tall, he towered over the two other men. A mane of long salt and pepper hair, tied up into a ponytail, combined with a thick mustache, and a bandanna, wrapped around the forehead, to give him the appearance of an aging hippie from the 1960s.

This hippie, however, was no believer in flower-power or peace on Earth. He was a trained killer. Before Charlie even realized what was happening, a garrote had slipped around his neck from behind. The giant pulled the thin nylon rope tight. Charlie struggled, desperate to slip his fingers between his neck and the thin rope.

It was impossible. He was helpless. The giant was positioned slightly behind him and to the side. It was almost impossible to even land a kick to the huge man's shin or groin, but Charlie tried to, anyway, and failed. As the rope pulled tighter, he couldn't break free, and he couldn't breathe. The more he struggled, the more oxygen he needed. The pressure was relentless. A moment more and he went limp.

The giant signaled to his black partner. Each man looped an arm underneath one of Charlie's armpits. They supported him and all three walked forward in unison in what looked like a merry band of three drinking buddies. Charlie appeared to be a man who had simply passed out. It was as if they were returning from a night of drunken revelry. At a light glance, few would have realized that he was now clinically dead.

Moments later, the little troupe reached its destination. The two men dumped their victim into the back seat of the waiting BMW, squeezing his legs into the space between the seats, and propping his body up against the seat back. The dead body sat there quietly as if sleeping.

The black man sat down in the driver's seat. The car started. The giant walked around and sat down in the front passenger's seat. After the doors were shut, heavily tinted windows made the inside of the car largely invisible. But, even had the window glass been clear, now that Charlie was propped up into a sitting position, no one would notice he was dead.

The only sign of the struggle was a deep red line across the neck of the corpse.

A good kill!

The giant took great pride in his work, and this job had been done professionally. He peeled off the mustache and the salt and pepper wig. This revealed a clean-cut face and a short, military style blonde head of hair. Reaching under the front passenger's seat, he found what he was looking for.

He pulled out one of many new metal license tags. Cameras were always scanning the highways. But, they were nothing but machines, and could be fooled. The computers linked to them could be made to see whatever a skilled man wanted them to see. But, that required sophisticated equipment. It was easier to simply change the tag.

The job nearly completed, the car drove north. Eventually, it would cross the Bronx-Whitestone Bridge and go on toward the New York Thruway. The giant knew they would pass numerous strategic surveillance points. But, the cameras and microphones would also be blind in selected spots. Thankfully, he knew where each and every one of those blind spots was.

The moment they reached one, he would stop to change the plates. With that, their identity would change also. Not that he was worried about detection. He wasn't. He was certain that the critical infrastructure had been disabled during the kill. He had made sure of that.

Two men and a corpse drove long into the night.

II - HIDING THE EYES OF A SPY

Towering above the street, in lower Manhattan, is an old office building known to the public as "One Bourse Plaza." The aboveground portion of the building is still used by a myriad of businesses, and it seems to be no different from any other large commercial building near Wall Street.

However, on July 24, 2008, even as Charlie Bakkendorf was being murdered, deep beneath New York City, the most sophisticated electronic surveillance system ever designed was active. The underground room was packed with equipment, and it was cut 90 feet down into the underlying basalt of Manhattan, where no one might expect it to be.

The workers there were a sincere lot of men and women. Mostly, they were a group of 20-somethings, under the general management of one middle-aged former soldier. The soldier, Adriano Navarro, was the system's primary architect. "THEATRES" was his personal brainchild. It was partly designed to protect the city from terrorists. But, it was also designed for the banks that ran it. They wanted to know everything about their customers, and their competitors, 24 hours a day, 7 days a week.

Three supercomputers were linked to electronic nodes, laced together by fiber optics. The network consisted of the supercomputers, and a host of secondary computers. All were linked to thousands of cameras, microphones, drones and other surveillance devices set up in strategic spots all over the city. The software that coordinated everything was the fastest, most powerful set of complex artificial intelligence algorithms ever devised. It could perform its functions faster and more efficiently than a million-man army.

Separated on a perch, above the control floor, Navarro kept watch with pride. Just a few years before, it was thought to be impossible. He could watch millions of people doing everything that millions of people do, every moment of their lives, all in real-time. He could store every intimate moment. He could recall that information instantly, at the press of a button.

The button would tell him everything about any resident of the city; place of employment, home address, the amount of a mortgage or other debts, and even the size of most people's bank balances and other assets. With the press of one button, he could know who your doctor or lawyer was, who you visited and how often, where and when those visits took place, the make and model of your car, your shopping habits, and who was cheating on who. He also knew exactly what you discussed in all of your e-mails.

The databases consisted of a collection of information so vast it was beyond comprehension. Just about every piece of personal information could be made instantly available. That information was never lost. Everything was stored, day after day, on immense hard disks, and then backed up to permanent archives. Navarro had spent a lot of time thinking about all that data, but hadn't figured out how to use it to his advantage. He knew, however, that the potential was endless.

Navarro was half Italian and half Greek. On his Greek side, his family was from Laconia, and he imagined that he could trace his ancestry back to the Spartans. He was proud to be a descendant of those ancient warriors. No one would have ever guessed him to be what he really was, for he stood only 5' 8." Size, however, didn't matter. Since the dawn of time, greater speed and agility insured that a smaller warrior could always defeat a larger one. The Spartans carried malformed infants up the nearest mountain to die of exposure. Perfectly formed babies, even when small, grew up to be warriors.

Unfortunately, the man was no longer the warrior he once was. There was a crown of gray hair around his temples, and a few gray wisps that interrupted a large bald spot in the middle of his head. His brown eyes seemed bright, but he needed bifocals to offset their gradual weakening. The doctors claimed it was "aging eye", but Navarro blamed it on the Arab sun. One more sacrifice made in the service of his country; a service not properly recognized or compensated, at least in his opinion.

In 1991, he had been a sergeant, protecting an intelligence unit near the Iranian border in Kurdistan. His unit had entered Iran covertly. The mission hadn't gone well. Someone passed on information to the Iranians. The covert nature of the mission meant that they were traveling in an old worn-out van. It offered no protection against the barrage of armor piercing missiles although, under the facade, it was a lightly armored car. Most of the squad had died instantly. Navarro survived only because of his physical position in the vehicle.

He had staunched the bleeding, and gotten out before the Iranians checked the results of their attack. He'd hidden in abandoned shacks, and holes in the ground, always in pain, crippled by his wounds. Finally, he'd limped across the border. A group of PKK Kurds, who themselves had crossed into Iraq to escape pursuit by the Turkish army, had rescued him. They'd delivered him to the secret US base nearby, and from there, he was airlifted to Landstuhl hospital in Germany.

Three months at Landstuhl resulted in repair of an arm broken in three places and a shattered hip peppered with shrapnel. No full limbs were lost, but the tips of two fingers fell to gangrene. He'd also lost muscle tissue in the right leg, and he couldn't walk without a limp. The artificial hip still hurt. It shouldn't have but it did.

He'd suffered repeated bouts of infection, which called for multiple rounds of antibiotics. The wound had been opened and closed, scar tissue removed, and the same thing repeated several times. Multiple surgeries had not eased the pain, however, even though the doctors said the shrapnel was gone. Over the years the pain had devolved into a dull constant ache.

What hurt the most, though, was not physical pain. It was the limp. It made him feel weak. He had never felt weak before. They had even judged him unfit for active duty and reassigned him to a desk job. The government listed him as having been injured in an on-base friendly fire incident. The truth had been swept under the rug, and it felt like his life had been swept away with it. He was a bitter cripple.

For Navarro, a desk job meant a move to defense intelligence and managing domestic anti-spying operations. It also meant working on Capitol Hill. Congress was a prime target of both America's perceived enemies and many of her friends. His job was to remove hostile wiretaps, and place wiretaps of his own, in coordination with the NSA and FBI. This activity was designed to counter all security threats.

Specialists in wiretapping also happened to be in heavy demand on Wall Street, especially when the particular specialist held a key position in government. His official assignment provided access to the Pentagon and to Capitol Hill. The men who run big financial firms aren't hostile to the American government. But, they want money and power. To get money and power, they need knowledge.

The financiers wanted to know anything and everything that might influence markets. They especially wanted to know about the talks going on behind closed doors. Knowing what the government will do, before it does it, makes a man rich. It doesn't matter whether markets rise or fall. Money can be made in both directions.

Navarro knew a hundred ways to tap a phone, a hundred more to bug an office. He was an expert in using wiretaps, video and audio to gather information. These skills were invaluable to the bankers.

His profitable moonlighting business continued quietly for many years. It only came to an abrupt end when a top ranking member of the House Banking Committee discovered that his office was bugged. The Congressman was enraged, and it took wrangling, intervention and a strong dose of influence to keep him out of jail. The lawyers negotiated a "no-prosecution" agreement.

In exchange for silence, Navarro would receive an honorable discharge, and enter retirement, on a full military pension. The lack of punishment made the Congressman livid, except that his opinions didn't count anymore. He'd been a thorn in the side of the banking industry for far too long. When reelection time arrived, a rush of ready cash to the opponent's campaign arrived with it, to insure a sound defeat.

Of all the investment banks, the then-President of Bolton Sayres, Todd Bolton, had developed into Navarro's best client. It was natural, therefore, that after "retirement", his next job would be with that bank. As Vice President of Bolton Sayres' internal "Reputational Risk" department, Navarro's career in private industry had started with a bang. On September 11th, 2001, he'd been on-the-job for less than a month, but amid panic and fear, Navarro's voice was clear and steady.

His "action plan" for New York City offered a solution when nobody else offered a viable plan. Bolton's CEO had backed his idea. That insured those who remembered his wrongdoing would overlook it. The plan was simple. As a key economic asset, Manhattan would be protected at all costs, even if that meant undermining its citizen's fundamental privacy rights.

A few people opposed it, but THEATRES was a steamroller that couldn't be stopped. The green light came quickly. In merely 7 years, city-wide surveillance was in place. It had access to all of America's databases, including those kept by police, prison, driver's license bureaus, Medicare and Medicaid, and even the secret CIA and NSA databases. Meanwhile, the system created its own ever more comprehensive database out of the data it collected every day.

American constitutional law protects citizens from unreasonable searches and seizures, but only when the action is carried out by government. THEATRES' management, therefore, was deliberately placed in the hands of private operators. The New York City bankers were in charge. The operators received paychecks from the banks, not from any federal, state or municipal government. Therefore, no constitutional rights would ever be violated.

Navarro's thoughts were interrupted by a pretty young woman, who entered through an open door. In her hands, she was carrying a report, bound in a clear plastic cover. Susanna Maloney was a smart blonde, 28 years old, tall, and slim with long silky hair. Navarro had picked her. Efficiency and eye candy were hard to find. Bound into one woman, the combination was a pearl of great price.

She'd been his personal assistant since graduation from Colombia University, and that meant she had 6 years of experience and he trusted her.

"The daily incident report." she announced, as she handed him the paper.

The report was automatically delivered by the computers into his "inbox", but he preferred paper. Susanna printed it out for him every day. He began quickly flipping through the pages, but he didn't have the patience to read it through. He knew Susanna would do that for him. He did little more than glimpse at each page.

Finally, he looked up and asked a question.

"Anything worth reading?"

"Nothing that needs your immediate attention." she replied.

"Good." he answered.

The algorithms were self-regulating by design. They did all the heavy lifting. They could sift through a mountain of data with no human intervention or interpretation. It didn't hurt to have someone double-check them but there had never been a time when it had proved necessary. The computers were never wrong.

He toyed with his pen, getting ready to sign the document. Old man Bolton had given it to him as a gift and it was made of solid gold. He reflected with certain nostalgia on the time the old man had run the firm. The pen was given on the first-year anniversary of his employment with the bank. The old man had died too young. The current CEO, a man named Jeremy Stoneham, was someone he worked with, but not someone he liked. Stoneham couldn't even stand in the shadow of old man Bolton.

The pen felt heavy, solid, and substantial.

"Too bad Todd Bolton didn't live long enough to see this." he thought as he signed.

Todd Bolton was the last of the long line of Boltons. The family had founded and run the bank since the mid-1800s. Childless, the man had left no heirs. Leadership had finally left the Bolton family for the first time in over a hundred years, and passed to a man Navarro viewed as little more than a political hack. Everything was changing, he thought sadly, even the "Bolton" in Bolton Sayres.

After he signed the paper, he dropped the signed report on the desk in front of him and replaced the gold pen to its home in his pocket. The woman nodded, smiled, picked up the plastic bound wad of paper, and turned to go.

"Can you bring me a cup of coffee?" he called after her.

She stopped and turned back immediately, complete with her unending smile.

"What flavor?" she asked.

He loved having her get him coffee. It wasn't politically correct. Female administrative assistants weren't supposed to bring you coffee, anymore, but Susanna didn't mind. He was sure she knew he recognized her value. Having her fetch his coffee was emotionally satisfying. His eyes wandered down to her breasts. He imagined what they would look like if the blouse were gone.

The curve of her young hips completed the picture of perfection. He had often fantasized about making love to the young woman, and for just a moment, he felt the urge again. How would she react to a kiss? What if he made love to her, right there and then, right on top of the desk?

As quickly as this moment of high libido came, it went. He had been having these thoughts since she'd worked for him. She was always on his mind. By now, he knew just about everything about her. He knew that she had just broken off her relationship with a boyfriend of 5 years. The breakup would be an opportunity for a healthy man, but not for him. A woman like that would have no need for a cripple.

The coffeemaker was the type that used little one-serve pack-cups of fresh grind. The packs came in many flavors. He could have asked for just about any variety. But, he didn't care about such things. He liked good coffee, but he drank it almost entirely for the caffeine, and not the flavor.

"Be creative..." he finally answered. "I'll leave it up to you."

The girl nodded and scurried away, as he sat quietly at his desk, staring at the control center through the glass window. About 5 minutes later, she returned, with the cup of coffee in her hand, and carefully set it down on his desk, on top of an embroidered coaster.

"Is there anything else, sir?" she asked submissively.

He shook his head, lounged back in his black leather chair, took a sip, and motioned to her dismissively. Taking the cue, she left the room. He continued stare silently at the control room and the young people who staffed it as he sipped the coffee. He'd accomplished a lot in just a few years.

All of Manhattan and key sections of Brooklyn, Queens and the Bronx were already in the net. Staten Island was patchy, but in a few months, it would also be fully equipped. He had covered all the strategic entry points to New York City, and they were already logging all car, truck and bus license plates. The cameras, although very tiny, usually took a good enough snapshot of every person behind the wheel to succeed in facial recognition. Each person was being automatically checked against a list of known terrorists and criminals.

The traffic cameras, tiny building mounted cameras, miniature microphones, and full-sized traffic cams were sending a continuous stream of data at almost all times. The data was tagged, calculated, and stored as it entered the supercomputers. Every face on the street, at the wheel of a car, and every vehicle tag number could be associated with its context.

Errors were now at less than 5%. All faces were matched against photos, medical and descriptive information contained in a myriad of bank, insurance company and government records. The data was sorted in microseconds. Intelligent algorithms did almost everything. The computers arrived at tactical and strategic assessments that would take humans days to figure out. Video and sound, however, were instantly transmitted to a human operator when a threat was identified.

The eyes of men would never see a vast majority of the video and audio feed. Instead, it was simply digitized, identified, compressed, associated with a time and place, and sent to the digital storage facility in South Dakota. It could be stored there forever. Upon demand, any of those stored images and sound could be put up on the screen. He could also track particular bank customers, love interests and rival business interests, long after the fact. Special requests for such data were not uncommon, and he did his best to accommodate them.

Navarro looked at his watch. It was 10:30 P.M., 5 ½ hours into overtime, past his usual 8 hour 9-5 p.m. shift. Normally, he worked during the day. But, today, he was staying late. Staying up late into the night didn't change his normal routine very much. He was divorced, didn't sleep well, and had few social interests. Still, he was tired, and his eyes ached.

Suddenly, there was a loud knock on his door.

"Come in..." he said.

Navarro recognized the young man who cautiously opened the door and peeked inside. He'd been expecting him. The man had an urgent nervous look as he held up a piece of paper in his hand. He was an operator whose area of assignment was downtown Brooklyn.

"What is it?" Navarro asked.

"Sir," the young man said, handing him the slip of paper generated by the computer, "I might have identified a bug in the programming. It's an error code..."

"What type of error?" Navarro asked.

"Partial system blackout, I think..." the young man stated.

"What?" Navarro exclaimed.

"No one can figure it out." the young man said. "It seems almost as if part of the system's gone down. The self-diagnostic tools are useless."

"Down?" Navarro asked.

"Partially down." the man said.

Navarro smiled. The young people were all smart, but nothing substituted for experience.

"Any idea why?" he asked, probing.

"We've got ideas, but nothing concrete." the young man replied. "The cameras and the microphones in downtown Brooklyn, specifically within four blocks of one subway station are not transmitting any data."

The young man held up a paper map of the subway system, and pointed. Someone had already circled the subway station with their pen.

"This is where the subway station is." the man said.

"Were you able to see anything at all?" Navarro asked.

"No." the man replied. "But, the computer flagged it, and tried to repair itself. The self-repair routine failed."

"Hmm..." Navarro mumbled, not paying much attention to the specifics.

"It's inexplicable." the man stated. "We're supposed to have multiple redundant feeds, and they're all down at once."

"Interesting..." Navarro said, calmly.

"First, we thought the cameras were out." the young man stammered. "But, the audio's out, too. We pinged the nodes. Both the physical cameras and mikes are operational. It's not clear, at all, why the area is blanked out. It seems to be a software issue."

Navarro shook his head, and tried to appear very concerned, even though he was not concerned .

"That's impossible." he chided.

"Impossible." the young man nodded in agreement. "But, nevertheless, it is what it is..."

"The programming has been checked something like a million times, you know that, don't you?" Navarro noted.

"We still get a blank signal." the man replied.

"When did it start?" Navarro asked.

"A few minutes ago." the young man stated. "At about 10:30."

Navarro looked at his watch. It was 10:35 p.m.. Within a short time, the computer whiz kids or the computer itself would get the system up and running, again. Time was of the essence.

"Show me what you're talking about." he requested.

Navarro picked up his walking stick, laying propped against the side of his desk, and slowly and painfully rose out of his chair, limping alongside, behind the young man, who led the way out, into the control room. A moment later, they stood at the young man's monitoring station. As expected, the monitor had a blank screen.

Navarro sat down, and adjusted the keys and the touch sensitive zoom control. The console worked like a Nintendo Gameboy. That was part of why the young kids were so good at what they did. You didn't have to know much to use it. He zoomed out until the picture reverted to a map which covered a large section of Brooklyn.

"There..." the young man suggested, pointing to a section of the display map.

Navarro zoomed into the area. He clicked on "street view", at which time the map should have disappeared, and been replaced by a video feed. The screen filled with static. It was impossible to see or hear anything.

Navarro typed the reset protocol, and waited. The subsystem computer rebooted. Since the programming was stored on solid-state drives, the reboot was almost instantaneous. But, it didn't help. Both screen and speaker were still filled with little other than static.

Navarro looked at his watch. It was 10:40. In just a little while longer, the system would come back online.

"We might need to reboot the entire system." Navarro noted. "Meanwhile, send an NYPD team to the area and a repair team also."

"Yes, sir." the young man replied. "But, it'll take at least 10-15 minutes to get physical people there..."

Then, suddenly, at 10:40 P.M., as if by magic, in the middle of the young man's sentence, the video flickered onto the screen. The scene was dark, but it was possible to see shapes and hear voices. Someone was muttering a few unintelligible words, under his breath, and it was the person, not the system, which made it impossible to understand them. Navarro clicked on the button that switched the video to infrared. The scene became clear. A drunken bum shuffled down the street muttering.

The young operator shook his head, confused.

"I don't understand it... should I still send the NYPD?"

"Go ahead." Navarro replied, smiling. "You can still send an e-mail to the programmers. We'll see what they've got to say."

III - JACK SEVERS - FIVE YEARS & THREE MURDERS LATER

In 2013, Jack Severs knew nothing about the murder of Charlie Bakkendorf, which had happened five years earlier. He was simply a young lawyer working in Bolton Sayres' legal department, and he'd received an assignment no one else wanted. That no one else wanted it, however, didn't bother him in the least. For a newly hatched lawyer, any exposure to the real practice of law is exciting, even if it happens in the middle of nowhere.

He was at work that day, at 9:30 a.m. sharp, wide-awake and jittery, after 3 cups of coffee. The drive upstate would take a long time. The car loan office was empty, but the fact that there were no people didn't mean it was closed. The entire process was automated. At an electronic checkout terminal, he typed in the information requested by the computer.

He'd been on the job about a year and a half. Before that, he was a poor law student who drove an old worn-out 2002 Chevy Cavalier. He still had that old car, but it was in such bad condition he didn't trust it for such a long trip. Driving a BMW or Mercedes was exciting. This would be the first time he'd ever driven an expensive motorcar.

The bank made it easy for executive employees to borrow such cars. It kept a fleet of them because many Manhattan-based employees didn't even own a vehicle. Taxi, subway and buses were more than enough for transport inside the City. The loaner cars were meant for bank business within a few hours' drive of the city. Technically, they were restricted to use in out-of-town bank business.

The rules were in writing. But, paper can always be bent and folded. As with most things at the bank, rules were made to be broken. High-level executives regularly borrowed the cars for nothing more than weekend trips to their Hampton getaways. Jack was not a higher level executive, but he had more clout than many. His connections were of the highest level. His wife was the daughter of the bank's CEO.

The BMW, he knew, would be a taste of the things he needed to get, someday, to make his wife happy. When they'd met, he'd been nothing more than a poverty-stricken student, and she always claimed she wasn't interested in money. He knew better. Laura was a rich man's daughter. She might play house for a while with a poor boy, but eventually it wouldn't make her happy.

He mused on the idea he'd once had about championing people's rights. As a bank lawyer, he would never do that. It didn't matter anymore. His hopes and dreams would have to wait for a while. Someday, he figured, he would fight for what he believed in, but for now he had to get rich. He strongly preferred to succeed on his own merits, but her family was always ready to help.

Charity from his wife's family wasn't welcome and he'd repeatedly refused it, much to his wife's chagrin. Still, a dogged determination to please his wife was forcing him to work at the bank. He detested the nepotism that had gotten him his job. However, there hadn't been a lot of other high-paying law jobs available. He'd resisted saying yes to the offer when it was originally made, and tried every other option. But, when he'd discovered that Laura was pregnant, he had no choice, it had seemed.

Was he happy? Did he still love her? He wasn't sure. She had changed so much. After giving birth to their baby girl, she almost didn't seem like the girl he had fallen in love with. She'd gotten so fat he wondered if the new Laura had somehow eaten up the old one. It didn't matter. His obligation was clear. He had a family to support, and he was determined to do it.

He placed his right thumb on the biometric reader. A few seconds passed. Then, the machine emitted a buzzing sound, and a tiny receipt arrived. He took the receipt and placed it into his shirt pocket. Then, he took the elevator to the fourth subbasement, where he met Leroy White, a spry 60-year old black man.

Old Leroy had lived most of his life in Jackson, Mississippi. But, now, he lived in Harlem. Leroy had finished the 5th grade but he couldn't read or write. He could only smile, work hard, and benefit from the fact that his son-in-law was heavily involved in local New York politics. His daughter had married one of the most important political organizers in New York City's black community. The bank always made a place for such people.

Despite his illiteracy, Leroy competently cared for the Bolton Sayres loaner cars. The fleet consisted of about 30 BMW's and Mercedes. He treated each car as if it was his own. When Jack arrived, he was polishing a burgundy BMW 528i. As he wiped off the last haze of wax, he looked up, saw Jack exiting the elevator door, and responded with a broad smile.

"How you doin'?" he asked, with the slow drawl of a black man from the Deep South.

"Good, thanks." Jack replied. "Here to get my car."

"You got ya paapas?" he asked.

"Yeah." Jack replied, and he handed over the little receipt that authorized him to take a car. The old black man couldn't read it, but he wasn't interested in admitting that. He pretended to review it carefully, and then nodded.

"Yep, look like evertin' in orda..." he concluded confidently.

He gestured toward the cars still parked in the garage.

"Dey all beauties. Which one you want?"

Jack looked down at the receipt.

"Don't I have to take that one over there." Jack pointed. "The one with that license plate?"

"Course you do..." Leroy replied. "I jus' funnin' with ya'"

It was the burgundy BMW Leroy had just finished waxing.

"Dat Beema my favorite..." Leroy assured him.

Leroy didn't read or write, but he knew every car that went in and out. He also remembered the face of each borrower. He handed Jack the ignition token needed to start the car.

"She drives smooth like a baby's bottom." Leroy boasted. "Yes, sir! Come Christmas time, don't you be forgettin' ole Leroy..."

"I won't." Jack promised, and he closed the door.

Leroy White continued to smile and nod, as he polished another car. It looked like he was humming a tune, but Jack could no longer hear him. The silence inside the luxury motor vehicle was golden. It had a nearly soundproof cabin.

The ignition was electronically actuated by the code transmitter in his pocket. Jack had only to press the button. The car started. He drove up several floors to street level, and then onto the streets of Manhattan. By 10:00 A.M., he was through the Lincoln Tunnel, northbound toward the New York Thruway. His destination was a tiny county courthouse in Clarkesville, the county seat of Verde County, New York.

The entire city had fewer than 20,000 inhabitants, and the county only had about 76,000. New York State, he was realizing, was much more than simply New York City. The "other" New York was the place people called "upstate." Verde County was upstate in the middle of the rural Catskill Mountains. It was a throwback to earlier times. There was no industrial development. Just mountains and valleys, lowlands teeming with farms, and highlands filled with tourists during the "season."

He glanced up at the road sign. It was time to turn off the Thruway. The surroundings were pristine, green, and pure. It was as different from Manhattan as day is from night. It was hard to believe that both places could exist in the same state. After paying the exit toll, he transferred onto State Road 23A. The road was a four-lane highway where it converged with the Thruway. Then, further out, it devolved into one lane each way, in the countryside. It was the only road he could take to get to his destination.

When he finally arrived in Clarksville, he found a parking space much nearer to city hall than to the courthouse. Even in small-town America, courthouse parking spaces are always at a premium. The courthouse was old. It was built in the mid-19th century in the old Roman-style, much like the buildings in Washington DC. Except for the fact that it was built out of reddish sandstone, rather than white marble, an observer looking from the outside might not notice a big difference between it and the White House.

He glanced at his watch. It was already past 1:40, which meant he was late. He entered as quietly as he could, gently closing the door behind him. Inside, the room was very traditional, with row upon row of wooden pews, and a large platform in the front where the judge sat. Below that, and just to the left was the witness box. Further to the left was the jury box. It was empty now. Juries are never involved in the discussions between lawyers and judges before trials. More than that, however, this was a surrogate court case dealing with a Will. That meant no jury. Such decisions were made by judges.

About ten men, dressed in dark pinstriped suits, populated the front pew. They were lawyers waiting for their turn. Each had some sort of pretrial dispute that the judge needed to decide on. Jack took a seat, a few rows back, and watched as the hearing unfolded. Two lawyers were already sitting at two large tables in front, on opposite sides of the courtroom. Facing everyone was a gray-haired man wearing spectacles.

Surrogates Court Judge Floyd Van Hewing, had been sitting on the court for almost 15 years, and had practiced law in Clarkesville for 20 years before that. Jeb Knight was one of the two lawyers at the tables in front. His office was in Kingston, a large town as upstate towns went. The other lawyers thought of him as the "big business" lawyer of the region.

He specialized in representing insurance companies. He also represented bank mortgage divisions when they foreclosed, and credit card companies against people going bankrupt. He'd been hired by someone at the legal department to represent Bolton Sayres.

Jack knew that local lawyers were the "face" of all bank related litigation that took place outside New York City. Local counsel was immediately retained for all cases. Bank executives believed, with some justification, that local judges and juries were biased against them, and that having a local representing them would help offset the bias. It didn't hurt that local lawyers worked at much cheaper hourly rates.

It was Knight's first time representing a big-league city-based investment bank. Such banks were involved in an enormous amount of litigation, although ninety-five percent of it took place in lower Manhattan. Still, Knight was keen to develop the relationship, if for no other reason than to list Bolton as his client in the Martindale Hubbell lawyer's directory.

"Your honor," Knight addressed the court.

It was his right to speak first. The hearing was about his motion, and that meant he had the burden of proof.

"As my colleague admitted, NY Code Section 3212 provides that creditors have no claim upon life insurance if the named beneficiary survives the deceased."

Judge Van Hewing interrupted him, as was always his habit.

"Doesn't that mean I have to deny your motion?" he asked pointedly.

"No, your honor." Knight insisted. "Our bank is one of Thomas Mattingly's creditors, but as you know, back in 2009, the bodies of three members of the Mattingly family were found dead in their home in Paradise. A forensic investigation proved that the cause of death of the wife and son was murder, and it was followed by the father's suicide..."

The judge interrupted again.

"Why would the insurance company pay out on a suicide?" he asked.

"The policy was purchased over two years before the suicide." Knight explained. "Suicide exclusions are active for 2 years. They're designed to stop people from taking out policies to help their family's finances by killing themselves to collect. But, after two years, it's assumed that a suicide wasn't done for that reason."

"I see..." the judge commented.

"No one disputes that his wife, Sarah Mattingly, was the named beneficiary of the policy, and that she died 2 hours before her husband." Knight continued.

"What difference does it make?" Judge Van Hewing interrupted again.

"It means the only surviving heir is Thomas Mattingly's grandson" Knight pointed out. "But, since he was NOT a named beneficiary, and New York law protects only *named* beneficiaries, the money must be paid into the estate and then to the deceased's creditors. This means..."

"It means," the judge finished the sentence, "that the boy will, in practical terms, be left with nothing, because your client will take every penny, minus administration costs."

"Maybe, your honor." Knight countered. "But, that's the law, and we're all sworn to uphold the law."

"How much is the debt?" Judge Van Hewing asked.

"The line of credit was $25 million." Knight stated. "Of that, Thomas Mattingly had drawn down $1.4 million. The appraisal on the house comes to $738,000. The remaining balance is $642,545.34. The extra amount is the award of attorney's fees, costs and expenses on the foreclosure."

"Mr. Knight..." the judge continued. "Part of this court's job is to protect widows and orphans..."

"The appraisal, I might add, is very generous." Knight noted. "The bank will almost certainly get less money on the subsequent sale... but we've agreed to take ownership at the appraised value."

The judge flipped through the file.

"I don't like taking away an insurance policy from an orphan." the judge grumbled.

"Your honor," Knight stated, proudly. "Bolton Sayres provided a line of credit of $25 million, on very thin collateral."

"Why would they do that?" the judge asked. "Why would they give out a $25 million-dollar line of credit, on collateral consisting of a farm worth only $700,000?"

Knight paused for a moment, because he had no answer. A moment later, though, he'd thought of something to say.

"But, it wouldn't be the first time the bank's helped someone achieve a dream, even at great risk." Knight stated. "That's what banking is all about."

"What dream?" the judge asked.

"Thomas Mattingly's dream." Knight said.

"Which was?" the judge asked again.

The lawyer stopped for a moment to review his notes.

"To build a ski resort, it seems..." Knight replied. "If my client is to continue helping people, it must recoup what it can. Even after we collect the insurance, we'll still have lost hundreds of thousands of dollars."

"I represented Catskill Bank of Commerce, before it was taken over." the judge grumbled. "Lending so much money, with so little collateral, is a serious violation of the executive's fiduciary duty to shareholders. You don't give away money in crazy schemes."

"We're petitioning to seize the cash proceeds from an insurance policy." Knight reminded the judge. "The shareholders would be hurt if our motion isn't granted."

"Anything else?" the judge asked.

"No, your honor." Knight replied. "Thank you."

"All right, Mr. Bennington, what do you have to say?"

Albert Bennington was middle-aged and a sole practitioner. He maintained a tiny office in the lawyer's building, across the street from the courthouse. He handled all sorts of small matters for individual locals, including real-estate sales, wills and trusts, auto accidents, and the occasional probate matter like this one. He arrived at the podium confident of himself, as he always was when he appeared before Judge Van Hewen. The man, after all, was his uncle.

Meanwhile, Jack was busy flipping through the file he was regretting not reading it thoroughly. It was an interesting case, and getting more interesting by the minute. Questions were racing through his head because what the judge said was true. No rational banker would approve a $25 million-dollar line of credit, with only $738,000 worth of property to secure it.

But, there was more to it. Jack had worked at Bolton Sayres long enough to become familiar with its business lines. It was an investment bank. It sold stocks, bonds and derivatives. One of its businesses was packaging mortgages into bonds, and underwriting them. But, it never wrote the mortgages, itself.

The firm was a high-end brokerage operation, not a commercial bank. It catered to hedge funds, private equity investors, corporations and wealthy individuals, handled their money, and regularly gave investment advice. It did not make any personal or commercial loans. In fact, official policy prohibited any assets other than those that can be quickly traded. Long-term mortgage lending was entirely alien to its business.

The only loans it made consisted of margin credit to brokerage customers. Shares of stock, bonds and commodities, in an investor's account portfolio, secured such loans. They can be sold at a moment's notice to satisfy the payments due. Commercial lines of credit, secured by real-estate, are as illiquid as you could get. They must be kept on the books for years or decades.

Jack wondered, for a moment, whether the merchant banking division could have made the loan. But, the merchant bankers took equity stakes, which meant that they owned shares in a joint venture. The idea was to eventually cash in profits by selling shares to the public. Initial public offerings produced juicy underwriting fees, and the bank, as a big investor, always chose itself as underwriter. Feeding underwriting business to the firm was the reason for the merchant banking division's existence.

There was a summary, he noticed, written by one of the firm's paralegals, and a host of other documents. Finally, he found what he was looking for. The foreclosure judgment was clear as day. The plaintiff's name was at the top of the document, as it always was. It read:

"In re: The Estate of Thomas Mattingly – Bolton Sayres Holding Corporation v. The Estate of Thomas Mattingly."

That proved that the merchant banking division had nothing to do with the case. The corporate holding company name was never used. Ventures were always separate corporations or LLCs because creating separate business entities shielded the firm's assets from lawsuits.

He looked for the signature page. It was illegible and didn't help at all. The line underneath which should have contained a neatly typed name of the authorized person who had signed it, was entirely blank. It was a mystery. Who had signed off on the loan? The only way to find out was to log into the firm's computer system. He couldn't do that in the middle of the courtroom. His laptop was in the car.

Albert Bennington spoke and the sound of his voice pulled Jack's attention away from the paperwork.

"Your honor," Albert Bennington stated, "it would be outrageous to award a life insurance to a greed mongering bank!"

Then, the man pointed to a woman sitting in the third pew.

"This young mother is a widow, made so by a terrible tragedy." he stated. "Her young and innocent child, an orphan boy, less than 4 years old, has no father. Is he to become a ward of the state? A technicality, something that certainly wasn't intended, by the legislature, gives a greedy bank and this grasping lawyer from Kingston, the ability to make a ridiculous argument. This court must not to allow this to happen!"

"Objection, your honor!" Jeb Knight called out, standing to his feet.

"Overruled." the judge barked.

"But, Mr. Bennington is appealing to emotion and suggesting that you ignore the law!" Knight continued.

"You've been overruled!" Judge Van Hewing countered.

Then, he turned to his nephew.

"Are you asking me to ignore the law?" he asked.

"Of course not." Bennington replied.

"What legal citations support your position?" the judge asked.

"The rule of fairness that prohibits unjust enrichment, and the rule of pretermission of unborn children." Bennington noted.

The argument went on and on as to why the money should be paid to the boy.

"Do you have cases or statutes that support your argument?" Judge Van Hewing asked.

"I've got our basic understanding of what is right and wrong." Bennington replied with emotion.

"That doesn't hold up on appeal." the judge muttered under his breath.

"Anything in rebuttal, Mr. Knight?" Judge Van Hewing asked.

"There's nothing to rebut." Knight replied confidently. "The law is clear. Mr. Bennington can't make a decent legal argument, because there are none to be made. The boy is not the named beneficiary in the policy. It's as simple as that."

"Gentlemen." Judge Van Hewing said, while writing notes. "I won't be deciding this today. As you know, I've ordered mediation, and I expect both sides to engage in a good-faith negotiations. Can I trust you both to do that?"

"Of course, your honor." Bennington agreed.

"Mr. Knight?" the judge asked.

"Of course, your honor." Knight replied.

The judge turned to the clerk.

"Please call the next case..."

"In the Matter of the Estate of Judson..." the clerk announced.

Jack tuned out the rest. He watched, however, as Jeb Knight and Albert Bennington gathered their papers and stuffed them into oversized briefcases, evacuating their desks, so two new lawyers could take their place.

Jack wondered why Bennington hadn't come up with something to back up what he was saying. It was usually possible to find some obscure case to support any argument. You just added a special spin, and that made for a decent argument. Bennington was a lousy lawyer, he decided.

Jack intercepted Jeb Knight before he exited the courtroom, and shook his hand.

"My name's Jack Severs." he announced. "I'm with the legal department at Bolton Sayres."

"Hi, Jack." Knight said, in a hearty welcome. "They told me you were coming. Let's talk for a moment, outside..."

They stepped out of the courtroom, and walked down the hall far enough to make sure that no one could easily listen to what they would whisper to each other.

"As I've told your colleague, Tim Cohen, this case is a slam dunk." Jeb Knight whispered.

"The judge didn't seem too enthusiastic about finding in our favor..." Jack noted.

"If he decides against us, we'll win on appeal." Knight stated with finality. "Even if the law wasn't on our side, he should have recused himself, because Bennington's his nephew."

"How about the mediation?" Jack asked.

"A formality," Knight responded, "the judge wants his nephew to make money. We won't offer anything."

"But, then..." Jack said, because he had already resolved to make a phone call seeking settlement authority. "I'm not sure why I'm here? I mean, what's the point?"

"There isn't any point, never has been." Knight insisted. "The judge ordered mediation. Corporations just have to be represented by someone, and I can't be the representative, because I'm the lawyer. So, you're here. It's as simple as that."

"It sounds like a waste of time." Jack commented.

"It might be a waste of time," Knight said. "but, it's the law."

"The mediation starts at three?" Jack asked, glancing at his watch.

"Yes."

"Where's it going to be?"

"Over in Bennington's office." Knight replied, pointing. "It's across the street, in the Lawyer's Building."

Jack's stomach was growling. He looked at his watch again. It was already 2:15. There wasn't much time to grab something.

"I'm going to grab a quick bite to eat." Jack said.

"Alright," Knight stated, enthusiastically. "I'll see you over there. Nice to meet you."

"Likewise." Jack said, returning the courtesy.

Then, the two men parted company.

Jack bought himself an egg salad sandwich and a Pepsi at the courthouse café. As he ate, he tried to contact his supervisor, Murray Sachs. If he could get authority to settle, he'd feel better about everything. Even if it wasn't much, it would be better than nothing and he felt sorry for the boy. His efforts were fruitless, however. Murray Sachs was a stickler for every rule and hated risk. He wouldn't budge without first getting authority from someone above him.

He put in a call to his father-in-law, who was the highest authority at the bank. It was a risky move, and he knew it would annoy the man. The secretary on duty had learned enough, over time, to know that he didn't want to take any more phone calls from Jack. In the end, he found it impossible to get through. With 3:00 approaching fast, he finally gave up, finished his lunch, and made his way to the mediation conference.

Bennington's office was easy to find because it was right across the street and Jack arrived only a few minutes late. The room had a basic long conference table and there were five participants to occupy it. These included Jack, Mr. Bennington, Mr. Knight, the widow Sandra Mattingly, and a court-appointed mediator. As he looked across the table, he couldn't help but notice that the widow was beautiful.

She seemed little like a widow. She was slim, clean and fresh; seemingly right off the farm. She smiled softly when he shook her hand. She had brown hair and green eyes, wide hips, and a narrow waist. Her ample breasts popped out of the low-cut dress. The girl couldn't have been over 22 years old. Since her son was 4, that meant she was pregnant at 17.

He wondered about that, for a moment. What sort of widow would dress in a risqué manner? But it had been several years since the death of her husband. No one could grieve forever. Her perfume was intoxicating and it drifted to his side of the table, as they all sat down to talk. He couldn't help feeling an intense attraction to the girl. There was something very sexy about her. He felt his groin stirring, and that made him feel guilty. How could a strange woman, on the opposite side, and a widow, no less, affect him that way?

He loved his wife, didn't he? They hadn't had sex in weeks. The endless crying of the baby kept them up at night, and Laura wasn't very interested, now that she was breastfeeding. However, mostly, it was him. The intense attraction he'd once felt had disappeared with the expansion of his wife's waistline.

As the proceedings continued, he continued to find himself sympathetic. He was attracted to the woman, and felt sorry for the little boy. Still, as an employee of Bolton Sayres, he was obliged to take the legal position of his employer. But, he entertained a strange idea. Suppose, he offered money even though he had no real settlement authority? What could they do? His father-in-law was the company's CEO. His boss, Murray Sachs, would be sure to yell and scream, and maybe even complain to some committee. But, in the end, he wouldn't be able to do anything about it. That was the beauty of nepotism. Connections meant everything.

Still, taking advantage of his connections would make him everything he despised. The nepotism that had resulted in his job with the bank, would then be further extended to continued employment. Normal lawyers ended up fired for doing such things. He wouldn't be. That made it difficult to ignore his sympathies. The fact that he could get away with it was a temptation that was hard to resist. Did he dare do something like that?

The talking went on for more than an hour, and it was getting tiresome. The woman's attorney made various excessive demands with no counteroffers from the bank. Finally, he couldn't stand it anymore. He suddenly blurted something out what he'd been thinking for most of the hour.

"On behalf of Bolton Sayres, I can offer you $50,000 maximum."

There was momentary silence. Then, the woman's lawyer shook his head in the negative. He seemed to take it as a sign of weakness. The man didn't know when to take the money and run! Meanwhile, Jeb Knight seemed to lose color in his face at even the possibility that an unauthorized offer might be accepted. If accepted, the case would be over. People might blame him. More important, it would force a recalculation of his budget. His fees would dry up earlier than expected.

The reply that followed made the man feel visibly better.

"We won't take less than $200,000." Bennington blurted out. "As you know, my client's got a very strong case, and there's no way the judge will put this family in the poorhouse."

"I'm trying to make you a fair offer..." Jack urged. "Even if the judge decides in your favor, you'll lose on appeal."

"I beg to differ!" Bennington retorted.

"You've got no case-law to back you up." Jack noted. "A plain reading of the statute is clearly against you."

By 4:30, his arguments had done no good. There was no settlement. The mediation was over. What would happen when Murray Sachs learned about the offer? The case was not important, and $50,000 was meaningless in the context of the firm's profit of $20 billion. Still, making unauthorized settlement offers seriously violated the firm's rules, and legal ethics.

Jack was back in his car looking at his watch. During lunch, he'd called a real-estate agent to set up a meeting at the farmhouse in Paradise. It wasn't originally part of the planned trip, but he wanted to see the scene of the crime. The distance between Clarkesville and Paradise was about 36 miles. Paradise was in a valley near the edge of the Catskills and it would take over an hour to go from one place to another, because of the winding roads. As he made his way there, he realized he would be late.

He couldn't keep his mind off the $25 million dollar loan. The region was beautiful, but the deal was stupid. He knew a little about skiing. These mountains were foothills. They were too low, too close to the Hudson Valley, and the regional snowfall wasn't enough to keep it white through the winter season. There was also too much competition from established resorts like Hunter Mountain, with better and higher slopes. Only an idiot would approve such a loan.

The car was finally approaching the Mattingly farm. From a distance, it was beautiful rolling acreage, set against the backdrop of three heavily forested slopes. The closer he came, though, the less attractive it became. When he finally drove up the gravel driveway, it became depressing. He could see that the fields were wild and overgrown. The picket fence was termite infested.

The house was relatively large, with over 1,900 square feet on the bottom floor alone, but it was old, built in 1886. Its wood shingles were white, but hadn't been repainted in decades. The paint was peeling off in large sections. Facing the road, on each side of the walkway, there was an overgrown lawn, with uncut grass, browned by the winter. This grass had grown so high it had gone to seed. The place had been rotting away for years.

He was late, but happily noted that no other car had parked before him. The real-estate agent was even later. He parked and walked to the door. There was a key, inside a small pouch, attached to his file, and no sign of the agent. No telling when she might arrive. He could wait outside the door until she came. But, it was a murder site. A horrifying crime had occurred here and he had come to examine the place. There was no reason to wait outside the door.

He inserted the key into the deadbolt, unlocked the door, and opened it. It was dark inside, and the air was musty. He felt around the edge of the inside wall, until he found the light switch, and flipped on the light. All furniture pieces were draped with coverings, even the mirrors. Someone had prepared the place for a long period of emptiness. Whoever did it hadn't returned for a long time.

Dirt was layered everywhere. In three years of being empty, cobwebs had grown so large that some blocked the corners of the foyer. He walked around peeking into the living room, then turned and explored. The file told him there were three bedrooms upstairs, and a master bedroom downstairs. The master opened into a hallway that ran to the kitchen. The floors were polished oak, their shine heavily worn out, covered with a thick layer of dust.

He made his way, over to the stairway, and climbed up. The wood creaked as he stepped. The place was empty in a way that felt almost ghostly. In a few moments of climbing, he was upstairs, and he used the next few minutes to glance into each bedroom upstairs, one after another. Two rooms looked like they hadn't had an occupant in 100 years. The third was a boy's room.

Unlike the two others, the boy's room looked modern, decked out in relatively new Ethan Allen brand furniture. He'd done furniture shopping with Laura, when they had first set up their apartment, and he knew it wasn't cheap. Perhaps, some of the money from the line of credit had gone into that furniture? An old baseball bat and worn-out mitt rested against the wall in one corner of the room. There were also emblems of the New York Yankees and Mets.

The air smelled very stale. Maybe, it hadn't been such a good idea to go inside. He might have been better off outside. Freshening things up, though, was just a matter of opening a window. He walked over to the window and tried to open it. It was difficult, because it seemed jammed shut. Finally, with all the force he could muster, the jam broke, and the window slid upward quickly, sending Jack staggering a step backward. His right foot took a fateful step against the edge of one of the floorboards.

The unevenness of the wood planking almost caused him to trip over and fall, but he caught himself. One of the loose floorboards seemed broken, and it was now at an angle to the rest of the floor. He stooped down to flatten it and noticed it wasn't broken. There was a tiny hinge, screwed into the long side furthest from the window. The board was essentially a little trap door that could open and close. He lifted it up all the way, and looked into what was a secret compartment hidden inside the floor.

Sitting at its bottom, between the floorboard and the scaffolding below, was a thick red leather bound book with golden paper edges. He pulled it out. There was a snap clip at the front. He dusted it off so he could read the cover. It was titled "DIARY OF ROBERT MATTINGLY" in big clear hand printed letters. Robert Mattingly was the name of the murdered father of the boy now fighting for his grandfather's insurance money.

He hesitated for a moment. This was private, and had been hidden carefully to keep it safe from prying eyes. Would he be violating someone's privacy if he opened it? Curiosity overcame hesitancy. What harm would opening the book do to the privacy of a dead man? He unsnapped the front cover easily enough, and flipped through the pages, until he arrived somewhere in the middle. He read.

"July 24, 2008

Dear Diary:

Two nights ago, near the road, we saw two men carrying a bag that looked like it had a body inside..."

Suddenly, a loud female voice from downstairs interrupted his concentration.

"Hello?" she called out. "Anybody here?"

He snapped the diary shut, opened his briefcase and slipped it inside. Carrying the briefcase, he left the bedroom where he had found it.

"I'm up here..." he called down to the foyer below, where a woman was standing.

He turned to the window he'd opened, slid it shut, then made his way to the stairs and climbed down.

"Hello." she called out.

"Hi." he answered. "My name's Jack Severs, with Bolton Sayres' legal department."

The woman was middle-aged, blonde, blue-eyed and fat, her face almost puffy in its roundness. Hidden under layers of fat, however, was a once-beautiful woman. Perhaps, she was an older, somewhat more worn version of his wife. Beauty is such a fleeting thing. Jane Simon was not only worn out by age, but also by a string of former husbands and lovers, none of whom had given her any children. Well into her mid-40s, she was unattractive, and determined not to depend on a man.

The sale of real estate was one of the few ways a woman with little education, living in a rural area, could make it on her own.

Jack didn't know why he always felt awkward about shaking women's hands. But he obliged when she offered, and shook her hand with a smile, not wanting to appear sexist. The social graces in modern America, even in rural areas, required no less. There was a little more chitchat, and a few more social pleasantries. Finally, they got down to business. It didn't take long for her to provide an estimate of the value and ease by which the place could be sold.

There was no real reason to have made the trip. He could have done everything by e-mail, fax and phone. But, the case had fascinated him and the physical form of the proposed listing contract was already in his file. During lunch, he had called the woman. A personal meeting with her, at the house, was the perfect excuse to see the farm where all the murders had taken place. The discovery of the diary, however, was far more than he had expected. He couldn't help being distracted as he spoke with her.

"We normally provide the listing contract." she muttered, before signing.

"I understand that..." Jack explained. "But, we're a bank. A big bureaucracy has big rules. You understand, of course..."

She nodded and signed.

"I'll be in touch..." she promised, as she turned and exited the house.

Jack was right behind her, and he locked the place up, and handed her the key. Then, as they both headed toward their cars, he looked at his watch. It was already getting late, and his stomach was growling again. The snack he'd eaten for lunch was too small to keep him satisfied for long.

"Is there a decent place to eat around here?" he asked.

"Paddy's Diner." she suggested. "A lot of tourists go there. It's in downtown Paradise."

By the time Jack finished dinner it was near 8 p.m.. He put in a phone call to his wife. She wasn't happy about a midnight arrival back in Manhattan. But, he could do nothing about that now.

IV - MARCUS DUNLOP IN 2008

Almost exactly 5 years before Jack Severs drove north toward the tiny town of Paradise, NY, back on March 19, 2008, a certain employee was busy in his office near the top of the Bolton Sayres Tower.

To the outside world, Marcus Dunlop would be viewed as a habitual liar, cheat, drunkard, and a whoremonger. Inside the banking Synod, however, basic values are different. There, he was a well-respected man. By 2008, at a mere 25 years of age, he was viewed as one of the Synod's best and brightest, a rising star with a fine family pedigree. The title, on his door, was simpler than his real role. It read "Quantitative Investment Analyst."

Titles were meaningless. Possession of a large luxury office suite, with a view of New York Harbor and the Statue of Liberty, was the signature of importance. His particular importance arose out of the fact that his trading software could manipulate markets. He was also the son of Christopher Dunlop, Patriarch of the powerful Dunlop banking family. They owned W.T. Fredericks Bank, which outsiders thought of as a Bolton Sayres' competitor. The truth was that the two banks hadn't really competed in years. Their business was so intertwined that, in some sense, they were merely branches of the same banking institution. At the very least, the two banks were closely allied.

Dunlop's most powerful tool was "wash trading", meaning buying and selling stocks, bonds, commodities and currencies between related entities. The related entities, in this case, were the various bank members of the international banking Synod. The banks reimbursed each other for all gains and losses, when they were trading with each other. Prices ended up bid up and down according to plan. The resulting "market price" ended up reported by the various publicly watched exchanges as if it was real. Only the highest ranked officials of the banks knew what was really going on. Because the bots could "buy", "sell" and "spoof", the Synod could create the appearance of rising and/or falling prices at will.

Aside from his job duties, Dunlop had other interests. Because his bots operated worldwide, he tended to arrive at work long before everyone else in order to check on their performance. Early every morning, before starting work, he made sure a new prostitute was waiting for him at his office. This morning's girl was busy slipping back into her tight jeans, which fit her like a second skin. She pulled them on with some effort, and fastened the silver belt buckle, slipping on her pink pullover top. After she had dressed, she ran her fingers down his chest.

"You turn me on... you, handsome man." she cooed, with a foreign accent.

The pigeon English amused him. But, she was right. He was tall, dark haired, with light brown eyes and had perfectly chiseled features. He could have attracted many women, not just paid prostitutes. But he didn't like the obligations and expectations that came with normal women.

"You're beautiful, too, baby." he said. "But, I need to work."

"Tell me vat you do, again?" she asked.

"It's too complicated..." he replied, as he took out his wallet.

Her eyes lit up at the sight of money.

"I understand lots of tings." she replied, continuing to smile and watch his wallet. "Smart girl, I am... tell me vhat you do..."

He eyed her for a moment. He had no intention of telling her anything, not even the official version of his job.

"Yes, not only smart." he said, finally. "But, expensive, too."

He counted out eight $100 dollar bills, and handed them to her, one at a time. He liked doing that. $800 was a fortune to the girl, but it meant little to him.

"You have to pay for top qvality..." she said, proudly, forgetting her prior questions. She stuffed the bills into her purse, sat on his lap again, and hugged him.

Dunlop's prostitutes commonly arrived each day, between 4:30 and 5:30 a.m.. They left, on average, 45 minutes later. He paid them the minimum fee for an hour, even though he rarely used the entire hour.

This girl was lingering past her allotted time. It was already 6:20 a.m.. High time for her to leave. Turning away as flirtatiously as she could manage, she looked back around, blew him another kiss, and waved good-bye. Finally, she walked out the door.

Good riddance, he thought!

He looked at the clock. It read 6:30 a.m.. The daily call from London would come soon. The bank kept active trading desks in London, Tokyo, and Hong Kong, and a few other less important financial centers.

A shining blue LED of Dunlop's Zephyr Cypherphone lit up on the handset, and the whistling noise startled him. The phone was one of many creations of America's Defense Intelligence Agency (DIA). It was an expensive device; waterproof and shockproof, shielded from radioactivity and electromagnetism and, essentially, indestructible.

A moment later, the phones were synchronized and ready for use. He picked up the receiver on his end.

"Hello…" he stated.

"Hello, Mark." the man on the other end replied.

"What's going on in London?" Dunlop asked.

"Nothing unusual." said Jennett. "The morning fix came in as expected."

As with many people, Jennett was a member of the family. He was Dunlop's cousin. The two men had known each other, to some extent, all their lives. When Dunlop moved back to New York, his old job in London became vacant, and his younger cousin was hired to take his place.

A lot of leeway was given to those hired through nepotism. Jennett's ignorance about finance didn't matter. What was needed was simply someone who could be trusted, and could be active during London trading hours.

"What's did the Bank of England say?" Dunlop asked.

"They said no." Jennett answered instantly.

"That's what I expected." Dunlop noted.

"What do we need them for, anyway?" Jennett asked.

"They've got to supply the physical gold." Dunlop replied. "There's always a big increase in physical demand when we do a big reduction in the paper markets. If the physical gold isn't there, the market would panic, and the intervention would fail, regardless of what tricks we play."

41

"But they said no." Jennett replied, nervously. "They said the US Treasury still has to sign location swaps."

"A location swap just means a lien on some gold at Fort Knox equal in weight to what the Bank of England forwards to us in London." Dunlop explained. "Sometime in the future, if the Bank of England has to give back gold bars to their owners, they'll have the legal right to raid Fort Knox to do it."

"Doesn't the UK own the gold?"

"No."

"Who owns it?" Jennett asked.

"Lots of people... small countries, banks, wealthy individuals..." Dunlop answered. "The standard storage agreement gives the owners a set weight in gold, but no title to particular gold bars. That means that the UK can do whatever it wants with the gold, until the owners demand it back."

"Why can't they just take the gold from Fort Knox in the first place?" Jennett asked.

"Because physically taking the gold is politically impossible." Dunlop quickly replied. "Congress would scream bloody murder."

"But what if they don't agree to the swaps?" Jennett wondered. "I've got almost all my assets riding on this..."

Dunlop smiled.

Had he ever been so naïve? It was somewhat cute but hard to believe.

"No one expects the Bank of England to supply physical gold without a swap lien." he noted. "It's just a routine thing. Don't worry."

US Treasury officials might not like swap liens, but everyone knew that it was an unavoidable part of intervening in the price of gold. Without the swaps, the Bank of England would not cooperate, and gold prices would be impossible to control.

"What I don't understand is why anyone even cares what the price of gold is..." Jennett wondered. "I mean, it's just a commodity."

"Wrong!" Dunlop exclaimed. "It's the base of the entire monetary system. If we allow gold prices to become stable and secure, people won't want US dollars, pounds sterling, yen, Euros or any other paper money. They won't buy bonds anymore. They'll just buy gold. That's why the government subsidizes us to destabilize prices."

"Suppose they won't sign the swaps?" Jennett asked.

Dunlop smiled and shook his head. The other man, of course, couldn't see him.

"With the current crisis, the dollar's being pounded and so are mortgage bonds, all sorts of bonds." he said squarely. "I wouldn't even bother waiting; I'd put my bots to work now, if my Dad wouldn't have my head for it. It's Synod policy to wait until we get a formal guaranty from the Treasury. That's what the Bank of England is waiting for too."

There was a momentary pause in the conversation.

"I guess I understand now..." Jennett said, nervously. "But, there's something else I need to tell you..."

"What?" Dunlop responded.

"I was getting nervous." Jennett admitted. "Our positions are so deeply in the red. We're losing so much money."

When a trader sells short and/or buys up put options, he is betting on falling prices. If he's right, he makes money. If not, he loses. The two men had set up a hedge fund in the Bahamas to trade in secret. They based all their trading decisions on the expectation of being able to buy or sell positions ahead of major interventions by the US Treasury. For the most part, the aim of such interventions was to reduce the price of gold.

The two men had spent the last two weeks selling gold "short" on the forwards market in London, and buying up put options. They were losing money, so far, because gold prices were still rising. However, they were set up to make a fortune once confidence in the market was torpedoed and prices finally fell like a stone.

"Of course, we're losing money on paper." Dunlop explained. "That's because we're accumulating our position. We want prices as high as possible. The higher the price, the more money we make when the price tumbles..."

"The thing is... I guess... I didn't buy the puts..." Jennett finally blurted out.

"What?" Dunlop exclaimed.

"I looked at the account." Jennett admitted. "Do you realize that we're already on the hook for hundreds of thousands of dollars?"

There was a long moment of silence. The puts in question had to be bought on London's OTC gold market, which is why his cousin was

43

involved. Such transactions were private, between two counterparties, and secure from the eyes of regulators, who monitored the open exchanges for such activity. His cousin's inexperience and utter stupidity was now going to cost a fortune. The man just couldn't be trusted with anything!

Bear Stearn, one of the biggest New York investment banks, was about to fail. The entire subprime mortgage market was about to crash and burn. That had sent the price of gold soaring. People were desperately buying gold, anxious to find a safe haven for their money. In fact, almost everyone was betting that gold would continue to rise into the stratosphere. Unlike most investors, however, the two men knew that the powers-that-be would never allow that to happen. They were betting that gold prices would go down sharply.

Dunlop was experienced enough to know that losing money on paper was a prerequisite to making a killing. That is because non-connected traders had to be convinced to buy at higher and higher prices. Eventually, with everything in place, you could torpedo the prices and collect maximum winnings. By panicking, Jennett had screwed things up royally! Even with inside information, the sharpest trader cannot sell at the absolute high or buy at the absolute low. If you did that, consistently, it would invite investigation and greater scrutiny that a trader on inside information could ill afford. Dunlop struggled to remain calm.

"You should have bought those puts..." Dunlop said sternly to his cousin, not knowing what else to say.

"Sorry..." Jennett responded.

The US Treasury would guaranty the trade this morning. The bots would use Bolton Sayres's loan desk to borrow the cash needed from the New York Federal Reserve. The Fed printed money upon request and distributed it through a myriad of so-called "loan windows".

"I was worried about being wiped out..." Jennett said, trying to excuse himself.

"How many times do I have to tell you the same thing?" Dunlop chided him.

"I'm sorry..." Jennett said, again.

Dunlop closed his eyes in frustration.

"How do you know for sure?" Jennett asked.

"For Christ sakes, our people run the god-damned Treasury and the Federal Reserve!" Dunlop replied.

Jennett sighed, understanding suddenly how foolish he had been.

"I can still buy the puts..." he suggested. "The market's open."

"It's too late." Dunlop declared. "The counterparty would sue this close to the operation. They might even push the Commission into launching an investigation."

There was a moment of silence, as Dunlop mentally recalculated his expected profits. Being extraordinarily capable in mathematics, he needed no calculator to assist him, and had the answer almost instantly. Even without the puts, they would still net millions. He stood to collect close to $11 million by June 30th, or 35 times what he'd put into the project. That was an enormous amount of money, but it was considerably less than he had been counting on. It simply wasn't enough.

"It's lunch time here, did you know?" Jennett suddenly said.

His cousin had always been fat, and was obsessed with food. He regretted agreeing to have the man to fill his former position in London. The fat man now disgusted him.

"You know Jersey's Surf & Turf?" Jennett asked.

"Yeah." Dunlop replied.

Jerseys was an American-style steakhouse, one of the most expensive in London, and was a place that many expat bankers frequented.

"I wouldn't want you to skip your meal..." Dunlop said, facetiously.

Jennett didn't notice the tone. He was too fixated on eating.

"OK!" Jennett said, without realizing how angry his cousin was becoming. "Talk to you tomorrow!"

"Yeah..." Dunlop said, trying to hide his disgust.

The call was over, and Dunlop slammed the phone onto the desk hard enough to break any normal phone. He glanced at his watch, dwelling on the new dilemma. How would he make up the difference in money? It was still only 7:07 a.m.. Could he quietly add puts at this point? No. It was impossible. It was too close in time to the operation. It would invite the scrutiny of regulators if it were done on regulated exchanges, and of the Banking Synod if he did it in London.

He walked to the door and opened it. Outside, there was a vast expanse of simple cubicles. None of the line traders had a clue. That's why none had a fancy private office. Yet, all of them would be critical to the upcoming operation, as they always were. Few would ever even guess they were participants in a massive government sponsored operation. They would simply think they were following the trading advice of a quantitative analyst.

The bots would paint a price picture, mirroring Dunlop's supposed technical reports. Independent traders and financial institutions would join the early stages. Most wouldn't even be members of the Synod. They would simply join the crowd based on momentum. They were all believers. They thought that patterns on charts are always real. They didn't understand how easy it had become to paint the tape. Detection of false "momentum" would provide the kick start needed for a successful manipulation.

A nice wad of money, printed up by the Federal Reserve, would back things up, but the well-painted chart was the key. If the paint job was good enough, it would become a self-fulfilling prophecy. With a successful market manipulation, there was always enough money to both repay the seed money used to catalyze the reaction, and to provide profits for the banks. Regulators would turn their heads the other way. Everybody understood that the banks had to profit from such events. Personal side bets, like the ones that he and his cousin had placed, however, were frowned upon.

He glanced at his watch again. It wasn't 7:30. His primary contact at the US Treasury, a man named Wolff Grubman, would call at any minute. But, why hadn't he called yet? Despite the complete confidence he tried to exhibit for Jennett, Dunlop still had fears. He was plagued with a small element of self-doubt. It had never happened before but, theoretically, if a public official mucked things up, their side bets could implode.

What was it like not to have money? He didn't know. As a boy, he'd been always been given a hefty allowance. As a man, his connections insured a job with a multimillion-dollar bonus. But what if everything fell apart?

He'd already deposited $500,000 as a down payment for a tiny Caribbean island. The full purchase price was $10 million, and he'd need a few million more to build the structures. The island would need wave breakers, a massive sea wall, and a lot more. Then, there was the mansion itself, an Olympic swimming pool, tennis courts, landscaping, and the helicopter pad. Because of the stupidity of Jennett, he wouldn't make enough to pay for it all.

He looked at his watch, again. It was 7:37 a.m. Maybe, he should he pro-actively call Grubman? What would be wrong with doing that? A lot, he decided. It would make him look desperate.

Suddenly, the phone rang, and he leaped forward to pick it up.

"Hello." he answered anxiously.

"Mark?" asked the man on the other end.

He felt a deep sense of relief. It was Grubman!

The man's specialty was currencies and his real employer was the US Exchange Stabilization Fund or "ESF", a division of the US Treasury, but his office was housed at 33 Liberty Street, the New York Federal Reserve Branch building. He was middle-aged, born and raised in Brooklyn, and since he'd never left his birthplace, his accent was still very strong.

"What's the scoop?" Dunlop asked, eagerly.

"I'm not sure you're gonna' like 'dis, but…"

That didn't sound good. Could his worst nightmare be coming true?

"What, what is it?" Dunlop asked, his hand trembling, slightly, as he held the phone.

Fortunately, the call was audio-only, so the other man couldn't see his hands.

"I jus' got off da' phone with Treasury, a few minutes ago."

Who the hell is "Treasury", Dunlop wondered? Grubman *was* the god-damned Treasury.

"Dey needs you ta' staut right away." Grubman said.

That was a relief. He relaxed and exhaled. He hadn't realized, until that moment that he'd been holding his breath.

"Excellent!" Dunlop exclaimed. "I'm set to start. I just need the cash and the gold."

"You got it," Grubman stated. "but, dere only looking for a $150 drop 'dis time. Dey wanna' prove a point but not spend too much gold in da' process."

That was disappointing.

"Anyway, you've got $460 million, fer da performance bonds." Grubman continued.

"But, that's only half of what I asked for..." Dunlop said, sounding somewhat disappointed.

"We can give you more cash, if you need it." Grubman said.

That went without saying. The Fed could print money in an unlimited quantity and hand it out in several ways. All a big bank needed was to ask. Money could be credited to electronic reserve balances simply upon request, and it could be used for anything, including manipulating markets.

The Fed's so-called "loan" windows theoretically provided only "overnight" loans. However, any well connected bank could infinitely renew any loan from the Fed. The money was essentially a gift, not a loan, and everybody who knew anything, knew that.

"The cash to buy performance bonds isn't what I'm worried about." Dunlop pointed out.

A performance bond is the money, required by a futures exchange, like COMEX, before it will allow a market participant to control a futures contract. Normally, it amounts to only a tiny fraction of real value of the commodity. Cash from the Fed was always used to pay for performance bonds. Getting awarded that cash was an essential first step in any major market intervention.

However, the bots often didn't need a lot of performance bond money. They usually did the heavy lifting using wash trading. The eight Synod member banks traded futures contracts between themselves, and they regularly reimbursed each other for losses with their own gains. It was all part of the operating agreement. But, even with this abundance of fake transactions, a substantial amount of "seed cash" was still needed in order to successfully present the trades as "real." This is because third parties can end up in-between some of the trades conducted on open exchanges. All transactions, designed to affect prices, must be conducted at public exchanges. The whole idea is to trick the public into paying either too much or too little. Private two party transactions, in London, cannot accomplish that goal.

The only check and balance to the abuse are the physical markets. In theory, you could force the price of any stock, bond, currency, or paper-traded commodity down to zero or up to infinity. With real goods, like gold, however, low prices can often cause massive increases in real-world physical demand. This can create a problem, because banks only have enough physical gold to satisfy less than about 1% of their depositors. They expect 99% of all gold depositors to either buy paper-based derivatives, or store gold in bank vaults from which it never gets removed.

The manipulators of physical commodity prices operate in an environment in which a certain price always exists, below which the system will collapse, due to inability to meet increased physical demand. The intervention and manipulation game is about finding the lowest price that won't collapse the system. Critical to making sure this is a very low price is getting physical gold guaranteed by the good faith and credit of the United States of America.

Very high prices and very low prices are both essential to the game. The point is not to create low long term gold prices that last for decades but to create high volatility, discouraging conservative investors from buying gold. That serves to push them into investments favored by paper-pedaling governments.

"It's the physical gold I need." Dunlop barked.

"You guys haven't returned one gold bar in 28 years!" Grubman noted.

"Returning gold bars isn't part of my job description." Dunlop pointed out.

"I'm just tryin' to explain what's goin' on." Grubman said.

The dwindling availability of US government gold was the primary reason prices could rise so dramatically, from 2001 to 2008. The main source of gold to slow down that price rise came from European governments. But, Europe was tired of selling off its gold, and the Bush administration had become wary of gold liens.

All the easily accessible supplies of gold were gone.

"Shrinking gold supplies are taken seriously, you know." Grubman continued.

"There's always a price for stability." Dunlop countered.

Both were standard arguments used within the small circle of people who knew about gold price manipulation. Stability justified sacrifice.

49

The government would continue losing gold from its reserves, to subsidize price suppression.

"Some are feelin' dat' da cost of intervening is getting too high." Grubman noted.

"Look," Dunlop warned, "if they're not willing to put up the gold, then we're out of business."

"You're speakin' to da choir, Mark," Grubman conceded. "but, deys' got priorities above my head."

"I understand." Dunlop replied. He was tiring of the dithering. "What's the bottom line?"

"You get tirty' five tons." Grubman muttered.

Dunlop was disappointed.

"Thirty five tons?" he questioned. "You expect me to get a $150 price reduction on the back of thirty-five tons? I've got to deal with London, Switzerland, India, and China..."

"Look," Grubman sympathized. "no one expects the reduction to hold. It's just for now, just because of all dis' stuff about banks failing and all..."

"I can't wave a magic wand." Dunlop complained.

"Look, I'm not really 'autorized to tell ya dis, but, uh..." Grubman confided, but then hesitated.

"Tell me..." Dunlop insisted.

"De has actually got 60 tons allocated." Grubman admitted. "But, I'm supposed to tell ya only tirty' five, OK?"

"No problem." Dunlop agreed, immediately. "I heard nothing from you."

There was a short moment of silence, and then Grubman continued.

"Dere's somethin' else I wanted to talk ta you about..."

"What?" Dunlop said.

"You know I always take care of my friends."

It was a strange comment for Grubman to make. He didn't consider Wolff Grubman to be a friend. He was just someone he had to deal with. The man was actually too old, too Brooklyn, and too low class to be a friend.

"You've always been a good friend." Dunlop lied.

"I always treated you right, haven't I?" Grubman added.

"Sure." Dunlop agreed.

"I always give ya some extra stuff, just like today..." Grubman pointed out.

It was true. He couldn't deny that Grubman was helpful. He was a disgusting little man, but he was unquestionably helpful.

"Yeah." Dunlop agreed.

"I'm not supposed to do dat, ya know." Grubman pointed out.

What, exactly, was the man getting at? Did he know about the front-running? The arrangement was strictly confidential. The front-man was a trusted Bahamian lawyer. Breaking Bahamian banking secrecy laws could subject the lawyer to criminal penalties, and the Bahamian government took such things seriously. The black money pouring into the country was very important to them.

"I need somethin' from you..."

Here it was. Sharing the cash with Jennett was bad enough. His cousin no longer deserved a dime, after what he'd done. But, the prospect of being forced to share with Grubman bothered him even more. The man hadn't even put any money in the pot! He felt like shouting and cursing at the top of his lungs. However, he was well aware of the fact that he was treading on thin ice. The man could hurt him badly, if he chose to do so.

So, instead, he simply said:

"Yeah, of course, if there's anything I can do for you, of course, I'll certainly do it."

"Well, I'm figuring it's about time I got somethin' fer me for a change..." the man went on.

Here comes the blackmail! Dunlop thought.

How much did Grubman think he was making on the deal? How had he found out about it?

"I've applied for a position with W.T. Fredericks." Grubman finally said. "I wanna get on ya' dad's staff."

Relief spread through Dunlop's nervous system like a soft cream soothing chapped skin. The man knew nothing!

"Of course, you've got my highest recommendation." he said.

"Tanks..." Grubman noted.

The Synod always rewarded its friends. All government servants knew that. That's why they did special favors for the banks. Inside information passed to the bankers on a regular basis. Former Treasury Secretaries and Chairmen of the Federal Reserve knew that they would get multimillion-dollar CEO positions, after government service. In the alternative, if they were determined to maintain outward appearances, such men could work for the Synod as so-called "consultants" and would be paid hundreds of thousands, or even a million dollars for a one-hour speech.

Grubman, however, was no Fed Chairman. He was but a small cog in the wheel. The Synod paid off in proportion to the importance and usefulness of the government servant while in office. The man could look forward to a cushy job, a well decorated office, and a salary in the high six figures. There would be little pressure to do anything useful. His only challenge was to find a place that would be of interest.

The idea of a man like Grubman, on his father's staff, disgusted him. Would he still be there when he came into his inheritance? No, thank God for that! Grubman was old, pushing 60, and he'd probably be dead by then. That made him feel slightly better. He finished the call and turned to his computer to check the readiness of the bots. They were ready to go. Before the end of the day, part of their accumulated portfolio would move from a big loss to a juicy profit. A few days later, all his private positions would be heavily in the money.

He glanced at his watch again. It was 7:55 a.m.

There was still a lot of reprogramming to do. He had to get to work. There would be little time for the usual prostitutes over the next few days. Crashing the gold market with 60 tons of physical gold would be a challenge, but he was up to it.

V - GOING HOME TO MANHATTAN

The drive back to Manhattan took all evening, and he arrived late in the night. Except for the security guards and a few stragglers, Bolton Sayres' Tower was empty. There was plenty of room to park the car. Although bank business is rarely conducted on weekends, every loaner car was gone. Executives, in direct violation of the written rules, had driven them to various weekend getaways. The car he was driving, he decided, might be the only one actually used for a true business purpose. He suspected that it was sorely missed by the holiday-goers.

He parked in one of many empty spots, and deposited the ignition transmitter in the "late return" box. A short side trip into a 24-hour mini-mart to buy candy, and a taxi ride home, quickly deposited him at the five-story red brick midtown Manhattan apartment building he called home. The candy, he hoped, would make her feel a little better about his late arrival. He'd learned by experience that candy or flowers were essential to soothe the savage beast inside the angry women in his life. Laura preferred candy to flowers, so that was what he normally bought for her. Ironically, he thought, although he hated the fact that she had grown so fat, he might be part of the reason.

He took the elevator up. When he opened the front door, he did so carefully, in order to make the least possible amount of noise. There was a light singing in the background, though he could hardly hear it. It was delicate yet distinctive, and he recognized it as none other than Laura. She was singing a bedtime lullaby. He walked toward the voice and opened the door to the baby's bedroom carefully. Laura was rocking little Jenny to sleep. Whether or not the baby's eyes were closed was impossible to tell, but Laura glared at him. Taking that as a signal, he closed the door quietly, and went to their master bedroom.

Once inside, he slipped off his shoes, shirt and pants, and draped them over one of the chairs. He glanced at his watch as he removed it. It was after 11 p.m., way past little Jennifer's bedtime, and a little past his own. He was physically and emotionally exhausted, and as he lay down, staring at the ceiling, he felt like falling asleep. Then, suddenly, he lost that feeling, as he remembered something.

He got out of bed, and walked out of the bedroom, back to his briefcase, which he'd put down in the foyer. He opened and took out the red diary and looked it over for a moment. Should he turn it over to the attractive widow, Sandra Mattingly, who was also executor of the estate? No, he couldn't do that. It was potential evidence in a murder case, and it needed to go to the police first.

Meanwhile, there would be no harm in reading it. He carried the book with him back to the bedroom, lay down, again, found the place he had left off, and continued to read.

> "...But, our suspicions were confirmed when the bag tore as they were carrying it, and a man's arm came dangling out. The bigger man stuffed it back in, but then we knew for sure that the two men were burying a body in the woods..."

The diary belonged to the murdered young man, the father of the orphaned boy. Whom was he referring to when he talked about "we"? Was there another witness? On the next page, he received the answer.

> "It was my first date with Sandra, and this was the last thing I wanted her to see. I just wanted to show her my special glen in the woods..."

Sandra was the name of the young widow at the mediation. Her son was the only survivor and heir to a suicidal and murderous grandfather's estate. She was fighting the bank in court. It had to be her.

He glanced at the top of the diary entry and noted the date, which was, again, July 24, 2008. But, he remembered what he had read, earlier, and it mentioned "2 days ago." That meant the events occurred on July 22, 2008.

The sound of the bedroom door opening interrupted his concentration.

"What are you reading?" Laura asked, as she walked in.

"Nothing important." Jack replied, as he put down the diary on the floor to the side of the bed.

A box sat on the dresser wrapped in a red ribbon. She pointed to it?

"What's this?" she asked.

"A gift." he replied, with a smile.

She detoured, opened the box, and extracted two chocolates, popping them into her mouth like a bolt of lightning. Candy box in hand, she walked back to the bed and climbed in next to him. There was no doubt about it anymore. He was partly responsible for her expanding waistline.

She stopped, for a moment, just shy of the bed, so he could see her for a while, in the new lingerie she'd bought at Victoria's Secret. It left little

54

to the imagination, but given her weight problem, that wasn't necessarily a good thing. She leaned over and planted a sloppy kiss on his lips, nuzzled her head against his shoulder, and looked at him with love-struck eyes.

"I can't stay mad at you, you know…" she quipped. Then, she got more serious. "You remember that we're going to the zoo tomorrow, with Jennifer?"

He hadn't remembered, but he'd learned to keep such facts to himself.

He nodded.

Her hand edged its way toward his private parts, which she began softly stroking. Apparently, that was to be his reward for bringing her the candy. He could smell the aroma of her delicate perfume, and it suddenly occurred to him she might have spent the last few hours planning this approach. No perfume, however, pleasant though it might be, could make up for the weight.

When she wanted to feel "sexy" she dolled herself up like this. She would put on a lot of makeup, expensive perfume, and dress in a sexy nightgown. The trouble was that nightgowns that looked incredibly sexy, when draped over a Victoria's Secret model, were not necessarily sexy when worn by a woman twice the size she ought to be. She seemed oblivious to the fact that clothing and makeup cannot make obesity attractive.

Laura and her mother were of the same mindset. They often went shopping together, leaving the baby in the care of a trusted old Hispanic woman, Isabel, the same Nanny who raised his wife. They would buy up ridiculous baubles, like the nightgown, in the expectation that it would somehow transform them. They would have accomplished far more by simply restricting their food intake, especially of things like cookies, cake, and candy.

How could he tell her? She broke down into tears at the slightest mention of any such realities. However, the incredible amount of weight she'd gained since he'd met her was a huge turnoff. In spite of the fact that he felt a momentary desire, arising out of the stroking of his manhood, it passed quickly as soon as he took hold of her rolls of fat. They were disgusting. Having sex with her, nowadays, felt a lot like it must feel to make love to a walrus.

Maybe, feeling the way he did was wrong. But, it wasn't a matter of right and wrong. It simply was what it was. He couldn't help himself. He closed his eyes, and imagined that he was in bed with a different woman. The strikingly beautiful young widow from upstate New York came immediately to mind. As he fantasized, his body began to function normally again.

How odd was his life becoming? Dreaming about another woman was necessary, now, in order to allow him to satisfy his wife. His closed eyes and imagination had accomplished what might otherwise be impossible. Nevertheless, the exercise was unsatisfying, and he was rather happy when it was finally over. He continued to stare at the ceiling, even as his wife was falling asleep. Then, making sure not to wake her, he slowly got off the bed, quietly picked up the red diary, and carried it into the other room.

He sat down on the sofa, opened the book, and began to read again.

> April 8, 2010
>
> "I finally told my father. What else could I have done? There's a man buried in the woods, right under our soil, and only I know. Who better to go to than Dad? Sandra isn't going to understand though..."

The story went on and on, mostly about being hesitant to tell his father about what he had seen. Jack stopped reading, and wondered.

Was the corpse still buried on the Mattingly's farm?

It was possible that the diary would change everything. The police seem to have gotten it all wrong. A dead body, secretly buried in the ground, brought the possibility of foul play by a third party into the picture. A staged suicide was a distinct possibility.

But, why the entire Mattingly family?

He flipped quickly past many pages that spoke of mundane matters. He wanted to read the parts that related to the dead body. Then, he came across another short snippet, lodged between accounts of what the man had eaten for breakfast, and how difficult it had been to milk the cows.

> *April 17, 2010*
>
> "She's angry at me for telling my father. She says I promised I wouldn't say anything to anyone, not even my mom and dad. But, I had to tell him. He's my dad. Anyway, there's nothing I can do about it now."

He looked at the wall clock. It was 2:30 A.M., the middle of the night, and he ought to sleep. How would he walk around the zoo all day in the morning? Still, he felt compelled to read more. His intense curiosity about the Mattingly family was bordering on a compulsion.

Why am I losing sleep over a dead man's diary?

He'd always enjoyed reading murder mysteries. This one was real, which made it interesting. But, his job didn't involve solving murder cases. He had to deliver the diary to proper authorities. It would be their job to ferret out the truth. The moment he handed the diary to the cops it would be gone forever.

That gave him an idea. His scanner was on top of a desk in the corner of the room. It was impossible to put the book through the page feeder, because that meant physically cutting the pages out of it. Instead, he began manually placing the whole book on the scanner, and laboriously scanning one page after another. He hoped the noise wasn't enough wake anyone. After nearly an hour, he'd scanned all the pages that had any writing on them.

He saved the finished scan to his laptop's hard disk, and onto a USB stick which he slipped into his pocket. Finally, he returned the diary to his briefcase, and went back to the bedroom. He climbed into bed and closed his eyes. He found it hard to sleep. His mind wandered, drifting back to when he'd met Laura for the first time.

She'd had been an incredible beauty, back then. He'd met her when she happened to sit down across from him at the law library. She never studied law but like many female students at UCLA, she liked to study at the law library during finals week because it was the quietest place on campus. The general public and young women in particular, erroneously believed that all lawyers were rich, and all law students would become rich. So meeting and marrying a law student meant marrying a rich husband.

Laura didn't need a rich husband. She was already richer than any potential husband could possibly be. Unknown to Jack at the same, she was the daughter of a man whose net worth amounted to hundreds of millions of dollars. However, like all young girls, her behavior tended to go along with the flow of her friends. What the other young girls thought and did, she did also. One of the things they did was study at the law library prior to final examinations. That meant she also studied there. They were impressed when another girl landed a law or medical student. That meant she was impressed also, regardless of whether she had any need to do the same.

At first, he'd been so fixated on studying his review book he hadn't noticed her. When he glanced up, he saw her. She'd worn a floral summer dress that day. The faint sweet scent of perfume had drifted toward his nose. Her hair was silky, long and brown.

Her green eyes seemed to sparkle in the light reflected from the windows. Her breasts were small, but well shaped and her tight body was lithe and tanned, perfect for a bikini. She'd looked up from her book, and immediately noticed that he was staring at her.

When she stretched and smiled, Jack understood. The unspoken language needed no words. The come-hither look has been universal to humans since the dawn of time. She was telling him, in primal body language, that she was receptive to his advances. She said it silently, with every move and every facial expression. She was screaming it without saying a word.

"Good book?" he whispered.

She giggled, and held it up so he could see the title.

"Do you think basic Physics is a good book?" she asked.

The book title was surprising. In Jack's experience, pretty girls didn't study physics and other hard sciences, like Chemistry or Engineering. Some did, obviously, but they were few.

"I see." he said.

He frantically tried to think of something else to say.

"You'd be surprised how many people like physics..." he said, finally.

"Nerds?" she had replied, giggling.

"I like physics..." he commented.

"If the shoe fits..." she said, laughing. "I'm taking physics because it's part of the science quotient to graduate. Otherwise, I wouldn't go near it. So, what are you, a physics guy?"

He smiled.

"Do I look like a physics guy?" he asked.

She pretended to think, and shook her head.

"What do I look like?" he asked, again.

"A law student." she said, immediately.

"Good guess." he said. "I've never seen you here, before, so I assume that you're not?"

"Bingo!" she agreed.

"What's a beautiful girl doing in a boring law library like this?" he teased with a platitude.

"Boring is exactly what I need right now." she explained. "I've got finals... I need to cram!"

Each unit of UCLA has its own calendar. The undergraduate college runs on the quarter system. The law school, however, keeps to the more traditional semester. That means that after the law students finish their academic year, the undergraduates are taking final examinations for the third quarter.

A funny-looking woman was sitting two tables away, and she became an unwanted participant in their conversation.

"The problem with undergraduates," the woman snapped, "is that they're not mature enough to stop making noise."

She was short, plump, and had shoulder length black hair. Her eyes were deep and black, she had pimply skin, and breasts that were that were far too big even for her round body. She was well known because she was a top student. That was especially unusual because she was Mexican-American, a group that isn't known for excelling in academic pursuits. Her name was Wilma Valdez.

Wilma's accomplishments were long. She was the President of the Females Law Society, a member of the University Senate, and a Governing Board Member of La Azteca (a Mexican Law Student Association), and a winner of the "moot" court competition. Jack judged her, however, not on accomplishments but on appearance and personality. As far as he was concerned, she was a witch. Many of the male law students shared this opinion.

The Female Law Society continued to spearhead an unsuccessful campaign to exclude undergraduates from the law library. Almost all the undergraduates who used the law library also happened to be female. They were much prettier, on average, than the female law students, which enraged the law school girls. Their formal objection was that undergraduates were immature, loud and disruptive. The real objection was that the co-eds were poaching. This truth, of course, couldn't be admitted openly.

"Wilma, chill out..." he replied.

"Flirt with your little friend, Jack." Wilma spit angrily. "You're going to fail the Bar. God! You'd think we're in a singles bar! Disgusting!"

Jack was about to say something rather nasty, but his new friend intervened before he could say anything.

"Let's go somewhere and get something to eat..." she suggested, impervious to the other woman's venom.

Confident he would agree, she packed her physics book into her backpack, before he replied.

"Uh, sure..." he stammered, as he awkwardly packed his own books.

She led the way, and he stumbled along behind her. When they passed through the library exit, onto the law school patio, she stopped, and turned to him, holding out her hand.

"My name's Laura Stoneham, by the way." she offered. "What's yours?"

He shook her hand gently. Shaking women's hands felt awkward, especially when the woman was pretty. He tried to think of something interesting to say.

"My name's Jack." he responded, because it was all he could come up with at the moment.

She giggled.

"Nice to meet you Jack." she said, still holding his hand.

Finally, he came up with something...

"Do you know the origin of handshaking?"

"No." she admitted.

They walked.

"It was originally a greeting between warriors, in the days before guns." Jack explained. "Men shook their right hand, because the right arm is normally the sword arm."

"Hmm..." she nodded.

"When two warriors met and shook hands, they weren't saying hello, necessarily, but the act meant there would be peace because neither one could reach his sword while he was shaking hands."

"Interesting..."

"So, when you shake someone's hand, it's really saying, I'm not going to kill you today..." he continued.

She laughed.

"How do you know all this stuff?"

"I've been a history buff my whole life."

"I never liked history." she admitted.

There is a campus eatery between the UCLA Law School and the Graduate School of Business Administration and it was their final destination. It was about a 3 minute walk. He tried to think of clever things to say, but it wasn't easy.

"It's undergrad finals week, isn't it?" he asked.

"Yeah, I've got three finals next week, two the week after."

"You're a busy girl..."

They arrived at the cafe, stood on line for a few minutes, and both ordered burgers, fries and a coke. A few minutes later, they were at the checkout. She reached into her purse, but Jack shook his head.

"It's on me." he said.

"You don't have to pay." she insisted. "I don't believe in that. I can pay for myself."

Being first in line, however, he took out his wallet and simply paid for both of them.

"Next time I'm paying..." she insisted.

They sat down at a table.

They talked about her final exams, the bar examination, and a host of other things.

"My dad's a lawyer..." she said, suddenly.

"Really?"

"But, he doesn't practice law." she went on. "He works for a bank."

She probably didn't realize that her father had flunked the bar examination, he decided quickly. That's usually what happened when unlucky law students became bank branch managers, insurance adjusters, Walmart store managers and so on. These days, given the huge flood of newly minted lawyers, though, even some who passed the bar also ended up in such positions. He didn't want to join that world of underemployment.

He tried to be diplomatic giving no voice to what he erroneously believed was her father's failure in life. Instead, he had simply said:

"That's interesting."

As foolish as it might now seem, at the time, tiptoeing around the subject seemed the wisest course of action. He was very attracted to her and didn't want to say anything that might offend or cause her to be distressed. The best policy was to steer clear of her father's bar examination failure.

"My goal is to become a trial lawyer. I'll fight for the little guys. For what's right and just."

"You mean, like, an ambulance chaser?" she laughed.

"No." he insisted. "Why do people think stuff like that? I'm talking about lawyers who do the right thing; who represent honest people against crooked corporations. That kind of thing..."

"You're funny." she said, giggling again.

He wasn't sure what to make of it. It didn't matter, because a moment later, she changed the subject.

"Do you think you'd ever want to live in New York City?" she asked.

"No." he replied, honestly. "I never liked the whole idea of New York City. To me it seems big, crowded and dirty. Just a crappy city, I think. The worst of all possible worlds..."

"It's where I'm from." she declared.

He suddenly realized his mistake. The last thing he had wanted to do was insult her. He should have known she was from New York City. She spoke with a slight accent. How could he have been so stupid?

"Why did you go to UCLA and not, you know, Colombia or NYU?" he asked, trying to change the subject.

"Because I'm studying acting and I went to NYU for two years. But, I want to do film. My choice was USC or UCLA. USC is in a bad neighborhood, so I'm at UCLA."

"You could have studied film at NYU..."

"It's true that NYU has a film school. But, L.A.'s the center of the film industry, and New York doesn't compare."

"You want to make films?" he asked. "Or, act in them?"

She nodded enthusiastically.

"I want to both make them and act in them. And you? Why UCLA, and not Berkeley?"

"I never applied to Berkeley. I did apply to Stanford."

"Why not Stanford, then?" she asked.

"Too expensive. Even with financial aid, I'd have hundreds of thousands of dollars of student loans to pay off. UCLA is relatively cheap. With financial aid, I'll be less than $100,000 in the hole when I graduate."

In retrospect, he wondered why she hadn't just stopped talking to him, and dropped him then and there. He had known nothing about her, back then, so he hadn't suspected a thing. Yet, in some sense, she'd been putting on a show. After all, the type of loans he was talking about must have seemed like small change to her. Yet she had played her part perfectly, giving him no clue as to her family's wealth and power.

"That's deep in the hole, isn't it?" she commented. "How do you know you'll be able to pay it all back?"

He hesitated.

"I don't know... not for sure."

She laughed, and pointed to his plate, since his burger was already finished.

"Well, no one will ever hire you to flip burgers, that's for sure, because you'd eat up all the profits!"

He hadn't realized how quickly he'd wolfed it down so he laughed with her.

More small talk followed, ranging from the weather in New York compared to California, the comparative merits of Miami vs. Los Angeles. Then, the talk continued into opinions and thoughts on a wide assortment of matters.

Finally, he asked her the critical question.

"Want to go to a movie tonight?"

She smiled, but shook her head.

"I can't. But, don't take that for a no. I DO want to go with you... just not tonight."

"Okay." he tried not to show his disappointment.

"It's finals week. If I don't do well, my dad will make me go back to NYU."

She took out a piece of paper, and scribbled something on it.

"Here," she said, handing it to him. "it's my cell number."

That night he couldn't get her out of his mind, so he called her, but she didn't answer, and didn't call back. As the days wore on, he called repeatedly. Her image was carved into his memory. He never saw her in the library again. However, finally, the day after undergraduate finals were over, she returned his call.

"Do you like Opera?" she asked.

He didn't like Opera. There was nothing more painful than sitting through 3-4 hours of people singing in falsetto. That was especially true when it was in a language he couldn't understand. However, the pain was worth bearing, he decided, if it meant he could see her again.

So, he lied.

"I love opera." he said, feigning enthusiasm.

Among other talents, Laura was fluent in both French and Italian. She understood every word. Tears welled up in her eyes during the emotional parts.

They dated almost every evening after that for almost two weeks. The cool dry summer nights in southern California bring young bodies into bloom. There was a small isolated place on Malibu beach, with a cool sea breeze. They walked, hand in hand, barefoot. The setting sun provided a colorful horizon seen from a wide but empty beach, except for the two of them.

He turned toward her, and they paused. He took her face and held it in his hands. She looked up, her lips waiting, her eyes deep pools of blue. Her nose, eyes, hair, body... were perfect. There was a faint scent of perfume about her. One hand dropped toward her waist. He could feel her tender breasts pressed against him, and he pulled her closer. She was warm, inviting, exciting.

He leaned down and kissed her, their lips melted together. Her body gave way, and the two of them melted into the sand below. Neither was a virgin, but it had been longer for her. When he finally took her, she accepted his passion as naturally as the sea accepts the rivers that spill their waters into it. It didn't take long for his seed to spill into her.

He pulled out, but too late, as some sperm had already met their target. Neither of them suspected that a baby had begun to grow in her belly.

He was exhausted and she was feeling whole again, for the first time in a long time. He slowly drifted into a light semi-sleep. But, before he could drift into a deeper sleep, she spoke again.

"Jack?"

"What?"

"Do you love me?" she asked.

He hesitated. He hated when girls asked questions like that. After a moment of thought, however, he happily realized that he didn't have to lie this time.

"Yes."

She kissed him quickly, and lay down by his side, on the sand, again.

"I have to leave for New York." she said, suddenly.

"What?" he opened his eyes and sat up.

"I should have told you earlier." she whispered. "I'm sorry."

"I don't understand..."

"I'm going for the summer. Why don't you should come with me..."

"I've got to take the bar exam."

"Afterward, then." she implored.

He wasn't sure what to say. No doubt, her parents were paying her tuition and almost all undergraduates went home for the summer holiday. He had no right to be upset. Yet it troubled him. They could talk by phone. But, disembodied voices cannot substitute for the warmth of another human body. Not even a video call on Skype would cut it. There was no substitute for the feel of her breasts, her kisses, and the soft wet warmth hidden between her slim legs. And, what if she met someone else?

"Can't you wait until after I take the Bar?"

She shook her head.

"My Dad's got all this stuff scheduled. But, I'll only be gone for three months... and I'll be back in the fall."

Three months might as well be forever, he thought to himself.

A deep sadness overtook him. But, the sadness, this time, wasn't about the fear of losing her, but about losing his parents. Everyone went home and spent summers with their families. He didn't. His parents had died in a car accident, on the Pacific Coast Highway, when he was only 11. He'd been raised in foster homes ever since. He had no family and no place to call home. No parents. No sisters. No brothers. He was all alone.

He remembered driving her to the airport in his old beaten-up 2002 Chevy Cavalier. He'd picked it up used, for $1,000, from a Japanese exchange student who was about to return to his own country and had to sell it fast. The car was imported from the rugged salty winter roads of Michigan, and had seen several owners. It was complete with rust and body holes. He'd done some of the bodywork himself. He'd also taken it in for a cheap repainting job. It looked okay now, but it was still a crappy little car, and that was ironic.

He hadn't known, back then, that she was the daughter of a very wealthy man. If he had, he might have been too intimidated to approach her and too ashamed to drive her to the airport in such a beaten up old car. But, he didn't know. Suddenly, a loud voice woke him from his half-dream state.

"Jack!" Laura shook his shoulder. "Wake up! We're going to the zoo. Remember?"

He opened his eyes, and noticed that she was holding the Mattingly diary.

"What's this, by the way?" she asked.

"It's a diary I picked it up at that hearing upstate."

"You picked up a diary?"

"It's a complicated story."

She put the book down on the dresser top.

"Well, don't tell it to me now." she said. "You need to get dressed."

VI - IMG V. BOLTON SAYRES

As of the year 2013, the Daniel Patrick Moynihan Courthouse was still the second-largest courthouse in America. It is a 27 story high monument to a dead Senator from New York, built of granite, marble and oak, and located at 500 Pearl Street, in the Foley Square neighborhood. It is the home of the U.S. District Court for the Southern District of New York, and its modern courtrooms house 60% of all the world's litigation involving banks.

Jack Severs and his colleague, Timothy Cohen were friends with a common interest. They both sat quietly at the defendant's table, alongside the more experienced attorney in charge. As members of the "in-house" legal staff, they would play no part in the courtroom drama about to unfold. Cohen was serving as Bolton Sayres official corporate representative. Severs was along for the ride, on his own time.

In-house lawyers never represent banks in cases involving big money. That is the exclusive preserve of ultra-expensive specialists. Outside counsel handles major litigation. Each attorney is carefully chosen for each case. The hearing wasn't a trial on the merits of any kind. It was a routine matter of pre-trial discovery. The discovery process, however, is a crucial part of every case.

Pretrial discovery is a dull process that is often the subject of multiple disputes between lawyers. It is a critical process because real world trial victories don't arrive in Perry Mason moments. They result from tedious and, sometimes seemingly endless hours of preparation. Over 99% of all cases are won or lost during the discovery stage.

Bolton Sayres always faced a myriad of large and small litigants. Some were suing the bank. Others were being sued by it. What made this case unique was that the bank's antagonist had considerable resources. A multi-billion-dollar corporation was suing the bank. To make matters worse, the case also involved a lot of money.

International Megatron Group (IMG) v. Bolton Sayres, had been pending for almost 2 years. The immediate issue at hand, however, was not the final trial on the merits. Instead, it was International Megatron's motion to compel document delivery. Mediation was also scheduled, later in the day, in the hope of settling the case but this hearing would address only one issue.

After word of Jack's unauthorized settlement offer in Verde County had leaked out, as expected, he wasn't fired. His connections to the top of the bank prevented that. However, he would never again serve as a corporate designated representative. Timothy Cohen held the title in this case, but also had no real authority. Authority to settle, in big money cases, always resides in the hand of outside counsel, who gets it from the top executives of the firm.

The attorney at the speaking podium had a client list that included the crème de la crème of the corporate world. His billing charges reflected that. They were so high that only such entities could afford to pay him. He was a name-partner of his law firm, which was one of the largest in the city. He represented IMG, and commanded hourly fees well over $1,000 per hour.

Despite having a legal reputation without peer, the man was not impressive physically. Short pudgy legs, a pug nose, gray thinning hair and a large bald spot in the middle of his head made him look somewhat like an elderly Hobbit in a three-piece suit. His eloquence, however, compensated for his looks.

"Your honor, my name is Dillon Higglestrom." he began with formality, even though on the off-hours, he and the judge were good friends who had known each other since their days at Yale. "I represent the plaintiff, IMG. At issue is our motion to compel production from defendant, Bolton Sayres…"

"Go ahead…" the judge said.

"My client is a large American multinational corporation." he began. "Three years ago, we made a successful bid for Pan-Euro Bank, a large European-based commercial bank. We filed a notice of intent, but the EU Competition Commission ruled that the combination would violate the fair competition rule."

"Fair competition rule?" the judge asked. "Compared to unfair competition?"

"The European Fair Competition Code is the analogue of America's anti-trust statutes." Higglestrom explained. "It's supposed to prevent companies from gaining monopoly power."

"I see…" the judge said, nodding his head. "Go on…"

"We eventually reached an agreement with the EU." Dillingham said. "We were free to buy Pan-Euro, but only if we spun off most of the existing IMG Financial's European operations. To sell them, we hired an investment bank, Bolton Sayres. Their job was to find us a buyer. After about 10 months, they found German Fatherland Bank. Bolton's executives claimed that the Germans weren't interested in the consumer loan division. We had about $800 million worth of consumer loans. They claimed they couldn't find any buyers."

"How much time was left on your selling deadline?" the judge interrupted.

"About a month and a half was left, your honor." Higglestrom clarified. "With this deadline looming, my client was desperate to sell, but Bolton claimed that the highest offer was only $250 million. They said that they finally found a group of individual "investors" who saw value in the consumer loans. It was a private equity fund that offered $450 million, a $350 million discount against face value, but $200 million more than what they claimed was the highest other offer."

"I see." the judge commented.

"My client believed that there were no other decent offers, so it sold the consumer loans for $450 million. Several months later, we learned that the fund actually consisted of the Bolton Sayres' executives who were supposed to be finding us a buyer. A month after buying the loans, they resold them for $700 million! It's obvious that they had that offer before and didn't disclose it. We took testimony from a Vice President of German Fatherland Bank. He testified that the German bank had always wanted to buy the consumer loans, but that Bolton's executives told him we didn't want to sell them. The lies allowed them to coin a $250 million profit in one month's time, in violation of all standards of common decency and fiduciary duty."

The judge raised his eyebrow. Higglestrom seemed satisfied that he had made the intended impression. He continued confidently.

"The testimony of the German Vice President led to an amended complaint. We're suing for fraud, breach of fiduciary duty, and unjust enrichment. We're seeking compensatory and punitive damages, plus attorney's fees, costs and expenses."

"That's all very interesting, but we're not here to decide the merits of the case." the judge commented. "What do you want me to do today?"

The clever lawyer had been waiting for that question.

"German Fatherland Bank's Vice President testified that he was recorded. He even kept a copy of the consent agreement, which he produced to us, and which we've marked as plaintiff's hearing exhibit "A", for identification. We ask that this exhibit be considered by your honor..."

Higglestrom turned, and walked quickly to the desk at which Bolton's advocate sat, leaving a copy with his opponent. Then, he handed the copy meant for the judge to the bailiff, who obediently transported it to the bench. The judge accepted the paper from the bailiff, and read it.

Higglestrom spoke again.

"Your honor, Bolton Sayres has possession of audio recordings of its meetings with German Fatherland Bank." Higglestrom said. "The recordings are important to proving our case of fraud and to collecting an award of punitive damages. We've requested production of the tapes, but they've ignored us. We ask for an order requiring production. If they fail to produce the tapes, within 30 days, we ask that a default judgment be issued in favor of the plaintiff, on grounds of destruction or concealment of material evidence."

Once again, everyone was carefully watching the judge's face for signs of his reaction. This time, the effort was for naught. The man kept a strict poker face.

"Anything further?" the judge asked.

"Not at the present time, your honor." Higglestrom confirmed.

Attention now focused on the other desk, where Bolton Sayres' lawyers sat, including Jack Severs and Timothy Cohen.

"What says the defense?" he asked.

James Hunter was a tall gray-haired stately old lawyer with big connections. His firm, Surrey & Clark, was one of the largest and oldest in New York. It catered specifically to the needs of the big banks. Hunter represented Bolton Sayres, W.T. Fredericks, and many other Synod members in a myriad of cases. Like his opponent, he also knew the judge, though not as well. Such personal legal connections often mattered a lot, but they wouldn't count for much in this case, because both sides were equally well connected.

It is unusual to have lawyers of this caliber forced to rely on their wits, rather than their influence. It was made even messier because this judge came from a very wealthy family. He couldn't be bought. That made Hunter nervous. Adding to it was that his opponent, despite his unimpressive physical appearance, was the scion of one of the most influential families in New York's legal community.

Despite his inner disquiet, Hunter put on an air of supreme confidence as he walked up to the podium. He placed his papers down, fiddled for a moment with his reading glasses, adjusted them, and spoke.

"Your honor, I'm not going to bother refuting each detail." Hunter began. "Suffice it to say that my esteemed colleague recites a fabric of his imagination. IMG's requests are overly broad, heavily burdensome and not reasonably calculated to lead to relevant evidence. Simply put, this motion is nothing more than a fishing expedition, where they are trying to hook onto anything that might help to support a very weak case."

"How can one specific set of recordings be a fishing expedition?" the judge asked. "I'm looking at a signed and dated release. It authorizes the recording. Why won't you produce it?"

The true answer was one that Hunter couldn't give. Bolton refused to produce the recordings for a reason. Doing so insured that the company would lose the case, and be the subject of unfavorable publicity if the matter went public.

"The release, alone, doesn't mean the recording was made." Hunter insisted. "Our records division says it doesn't exist. But, even if it did, it would be privileged under the work product doctrine and attorney-client privilege, and not discoverable."

"How can recording a meeting prior to the time of litigation be work product?" the judge asked.

"It was done to deter litigation." Hunter admitted.

"Is German Fatherland Bank a defendant in this litigation?" the judge asked.

"No." Hunter admitted.

"Then, it's not work product." the Judge concluded aloud. "How, is it covered under attorney/client privilege?"

"Numerous Bolton executives, many of whom are attorneys, were present." Hunter said.

"Mr. Hunter." The judge chided. "The fact that there happen to be people with law degrees present doesn't mean anything."

"The bottom line, of course, is that no such recording exists." Hunter insisted. "Releases are just obtained as a matter of routine."

"Your client gets a signed recording release for every discussion?" the judge asked, skeptically.

"It's often done." Hunter replied.

"Then, I'd like to see them…"

"Let me clarify… they sometimes get releases that they don't need. To find you other releases that weren't used would be extremely time consuming…"

"According to the plaintiff's brief," the judge said, "German Fatherland Bank's Vice President testified that they specifically asked him to wait while the recording devices were turned on, and then turned them on."

"Perhaps..." Hunter said, but was cut off.

"What efforts have been made to find the recording?" the judge asked.

"We've done a keyword search." Hunter explained. "The recording, if it ever existed, would be over 3 years old by now."

"If I am not mistaken, the SEC and FINRA require your client to keep redundant copies of documents for a minimum of 6 years, isn't that right?" the judge noted.

Jack was impressed. It was rare to find a judge who knew the law. Most were just party hacks, who ended up with a judicial appointment as a reward for services rendered.

"Yes, your honor." Hunter replied. "But, in a big company, even if a document exists, it might get lost over 3 years."

"If that's the case, it's still your responsibility when evidence in your custody and control is lost." the judge pointed out. "You realize that, don't you?"

"Not necessarily." Hunter insisted, grasping at straws. "You have to look at the circumstances."

"The plaintiff's brief says you refuse to search your backup tapes?" the judge asked.

"It's unreasonably burdensome, your honor." Hunter insisted. "There are countless terabytes of data, and it would all have to be laboriously searched for one alleged needle in a haystack."

"Doesn't Bolton keep a physical index?" the judge asked, drilling into the heart of the matter.

"Yes, but..." Hunter began, but was cut off again.

"I'm not convinced. Not at all..." the judge declared, his poker face gone.

It was now becoming abundantly obvious that he would decide the motion for the plaintiff.

"Your honor, this lawsuit arises out of a bad decision by IMG, which is at least as sophisticated as my client." Hunter insisted. "They should know when consumer loans can or cannot be sold. They'd like to blame others for their own mistakes."

72

"You're free to argue that at trial, Mr. Hunter." The judge pointed out. "Right now, I'm ordering you to search and find the recording, no matter how many terabytes you have to search to do it."

"We've got thousands of tapes in storage." Hunter complained.

The judge turned his attention to Higglestrom, who was sitting at his table, nodding, thrilled with the judge being on his side.

"Mr. Higglestrom, have you provided Mr. Hunter with the dates on which these alleged recordings took place?"

Higglestrom stood up.

"Unfortunately, your honor, the witness could not give exact dates, but we have specified the month. We also offered to compensate for the time it might take a group of paralegals to find the recording in question."

The judge nodded.

"Thank you." he said. "Mr. Hunter, the request isn't overly burdensome. I don't know how many tapes your client makes every month, but you're going to have to look through them. You can send an invoice for paralegal time to Mr. Higglestrom, and if there is a dispute about the time and cost, you're free to return here."

Hunter appeared crestfallen, but a moment later, he returned to keeping a stiff upper lip.

"Thank you, your honor." Higglestrom stated from the other table.

"I'm ordering Bolton Sayres to deliver the tape to Mr. Higglestrom within 30 days." the judge said. "If that can't be done, I want a detailed summary of what you've done to search. I'll want to know who did the searching, exactly how much time it took, what you looked at and so on. If it comes to that, I'll entertain the motion for sanctions."

Hunter nodded, but said nothing more.

"Your honor..." Higglestrom interjected with a smile. "May I ask that this order also describe the potential sanctions if Bolton fails to comply? Such language may help encourage the other side to find the recording..."

"I'm not making any ruling on sanctions yet," the judge said. "let them search for the tape. If it is not produced, we'll revisit this..."

"Thank you, your honor." Higglestrom stated, still pleased, though not as happy as he might have been.

The lawyers left the tables, and Jack and Timothy Cohen removed themselves into the pews. They felt no particular emotion concerning the result. They just wanted to watch as many cases as possible. The next dispute arrived, and a new set of lawyers walked up to the argument tables. They continued to watch, case after case, until lunchtime.

After lunch, however, they both sat at a long walnut wood conference table. On one side, the two young lawyers, and the more experienced counsel for the defense, James Hunter, sat quietly. On the other side, there was plaintiffs' counsel, Dillon Higglestrom, his buxom blonde paralegal, Dora, Lloyd Falton, the one of the top men in IMG's legal department, and Sam Parrington, the company's longtime CEO.

It is very unusual for a CEO to attend mediation, even in big money cases. Normally, underlings do such things. Parrington, however, had been personally involved in the negotiations that led to the sale of the consumer loans, at a big loss, and felt emotionally invested in the outcome. He was determined to see that Bolton Sayres and its executives paid dearly for cheating him.

The mediator sat at the head of the table, trying to keep the peace. Discussions had gone on for close to an hour, until, finally, Hunter played the cards in his hand.

"As you know," Hunter said. "Bolton doesn't think much of this case. But, since we value IMG as a client, we're ready to offer $30 million in full settlement..."

Sam Parrington was a tall, thin, gray haired man, about 66 years old, with a beak for a nose, and eyes as sharp as those of an owl. He was well known for his volatile temperament, and prone toward sudden outbursts. He'd spent the better part of his adult life building IMG from a small manufacturer of radiation sensors, inherited from his father, to a multinational conglomerate. He was seething over being defrauded.

So far, the man had betrayed his reputation by behaving cordially, remaining silent, and leaving most of the talking to his lawyer. That, however, was nothing but the calm before the storm.

"You're a son of a bitch!" Parrington suddenly blurted out, before his lawyer could stop him. "What the hell is that supposed to mean?"

"Mr. Parrington," Hunter said, in a measured tone. "I am simply pointing out that Bolton Sayres values you and IMG as a customer, but we..."

"Bullshit!" Parrington shot back. "If Bolton's people valued me as a customer, they wouldn't lie, cheat and steal from me!"

74

"That's an unfair characterization." Hunter said, carefully.

"Your fuckin' client stole hundreds of millions of dollars for God's sakes!" Parrington shouted. "That's the bottom line. $30 million is peanuts! It means the crooked bastards walk off with $220 million that belongs to me. You're gonna' pay the full $250 million, plus our attorney's fees and costs. I won't authorize settlement for one penny less!"

"I understand how you feel, but my clients won't pay anything near that." Hunter replied dryly. "They don't feel they've done anything wrong."

"That's, of course, because your clients have no moral compass." Parrington exclaimed. "They don't know right from wrong. They're nothing but a group of sociopathic gangsters. Banksters, let's call them…"

He turned to his lawyer.

"Let these banksters tell it to the jury!" he instructed. "Let them hand over a couple of billion dollars in punitive damages. Fuck them!"

Higglestrom placed a calming hand on Parrington's shoulder, and the man sat down, temporarily quiet again.

"Look," Higglestrom tried to explain. "Bolton's got a huge exposure here. The testimony of the German officers and directors is going to be devastating. They're angry because they also were cheated. They're all eager to testify against your bank. Once the jury finds your client guilty of fraud, other companies won't want to do business. My client is being very reasonable. He doesn't want anything more than he would have had if your brokers hadn't defrauded him. Offer us the $250 million and you can make this case go away, so long as the executives involved are fired. Anything less is corporate suicide."

The firing of the responsible executives had long been a condition of settlement. James Hunter shook his head, smiling.

"I can make one final offer to you, but I'm not authorized to go any higher." he said, finally.

"How much?" Higglestrom asked.

"$50 million." Hunter said. "And, that's it."

Higglestrom shook his head.

"No." he said. "$50 million isn't enough, and the firing of every Bolton executive involved is non-negotiable. It's an open and shut case. We'll win, hands down."

"The world has changed dramatically in the last few years." Hunter said in response. "You'll be surprised."

"What's that supposed to mean?" Higglestrom asked.

Hunter ignored the question and, instead, set his own terms for the settlement.

"We require your client to sign a strict non-disclosure clause," he stated. "and the settlement must be confidential. There are a lot of other potential litigants out there who also want to win the lottery..."

Parrington suddenly jumped out of his chair.

"The lottery?" he screamed. "Fuck you! I'll have this shit on every news channel in the country! Every newspaper! I'll destroy your fucking bank! I'll put them out of business!"

"You overestimate yourself." Hunter commented, wryly.

Parrington turned to his lawyer, visibly shaking with anger.

"We're finished talking to this fucker!" he declared, and then he stood up, and addressed his entourage as he headed for the door. "Let's go!"

Obediently, everyone on the IMG side of the table got up and headed toward the door. Just before leaving, however, his lawyer stopped, for a moment, to shake the hand of the court appointed mediator, specifically ignoring everyone associated with Bolton Sayres. The rest of the IMG delegation, however, left the room, without shaking anyone's hand.

The door slammed behind them.

There was silence, for a moment. Then, the court-appointed mediator stood up, and packed his briefcase.

"I'll file an impasse with the court." he explained to no one in particular.

A short episode of small talk followed. Then, having finished packing up his papers, the mediator shook hands with the Bolton lawyers, who were the only people left in the room, and then left. The three lawyers for Bolton Sayres were left alone. There was silence at first, and then, Hunter gathered his files, and put them away in an oversized briefcase.

Jack was flabbergasted by the whole affair. Was this some cleverly disguised negotiating strategy? If that were the case, it didn't seem like it was working. IMG's case was as strong as any he could imagine. He had read the file, cover to cover. There were a host of smoking gun documents and witnesses. All the witnesses were angry and ready to testify.

The man was unpleasant, but everything Parrington had said was true. It was an open-and-shut case. It was a surefire win for him, and a sure loss for the bank. A small group of rogue executives had carried out the fraud, and Jack saw no reason for the firm's failure to fire them. It astonished him that they were still working there.

It almost seemed like Hunter had read a different file.

Timothy Cohen finally broke the silence.

"That went well, I guess..." he said, facetiously.

Then, Jack added his own two cents to the mix.

"Parrington isn't likable, but the evidence shows that some of our people were bad actors. Given our exposure, not to mention the hit to our reputation when we lose, I don't understand why we're not settling for what the other side is asking for..."

Hunter didn't respond immediately. Instead, he finished clicking his briefcase closed. Then, he looked up, smiled, and laughed.

"I agree with Jack..." Cohen added, before Hunter said anything.

Hunter, however, just shook his head, and continued to smile.

"Not a chance." he said, finally.

"But, the case is open and shut. You must know we're going to lose." Jack pointed out.

"Who says we're going to trial?" Hunter asked, as he shrugged his shoulders.

"If you're going to make a better offer, why drag it out, and antagonize the other side?" Cohen asked. "Why not just make the offer and get the case behind us?"

"We're not making any better offers." Hunter stated, cryptically. "And, we're not going to trial, either. In fact, we won this case about 15 minutes after the discovery hearing ended..."

Both young lawyers shook their heads because they didn't understand.

"Well," Hunter said, "I should actually say that we've already 'favorably settled' the case."

77

"Were you in the same room I was?" Jack commented, brashly.

The older man took no offense. He enjoyed seeing the younger men confused by something neither of them could understand.

"Once again, boys, this case is NOT going to trial." he said. "The settlement's already arranged."

Jack couldn't help but shake his head in disbelief, and he laughed nervously.

"You and I are living in a different dimension, then..." he commented.

"No. We live in same dimension, Jack, just at different levels of expertise." Hunter insisted. "You're still a bit wet behind the ears. You don't understand how things work. But, you will..."

"Well, if you've arranged a settlement, then I'm going to nominate Parrington for an Oscar." Cohen suggested.

Hunter just smiled and shrugged his shoulders.

Jack wondered what to do. Bolton Sayres would lose badly. Decision making power was in the hands of a lunatic. He felt obligated to report the problem. Thankfully, the case wasn't scheduled for trial. He thought about his options. Who could he report it to? Murray Sachs didn't have the authority to fire outside attorneys. Even if he did, he was too weak-willed to do it.

He could approach John Farley, the head of the legal department. He could also report the matter to Laura's dad. Jack was beginning to think that her father was tiring of hearing from him. He made frequent reports of the things he saw happening at the bank that he considered wrong. The man probably would not appreciate another report.

Still, Farley was not a very pleasant or sympathetic ear. He continued to resent Jack because of the way he had been hired, which had circumvented the normal approval process. If he went over Farley's head, the resentment would increase.

Hunter found the temptation to brag almost impossible to resist. Conceit and braggadocio can often be the undoing of a man. Suddenly, he spoke again, and his words interrupted Jack's train of thought.

"You both think I'm going mad, don't you?" he asked. "Just keep an eye on the news, from this point on, over the next couple of weeks. Our fiery friend, Mr. Parrington, is about to learn a lesson."

"What?" Jack asked, confused.

"Let's just say this..." Hunter stated with scorn, "Mr. Squeaky-Clean is in some big trouble."

"What's that got to do with this case?" Jack asked.

"It has everything to do with the case." Hunter hinted cryptically. "It's just like I said. Watch and learn..."

Jack had worked almost a year and a half at Bolton, and he'd seen employees come and go. People moved back and forth between high paying employment and consulting contracts, and lower paying but politically powerful jobs at federal agencies. Still, he hadn't grasped what Hunter was trying to tell him.

The three men continued to chat a while longer, but as they packed up their briefcases, mostly it was about the weather, the Yankees, and the Mets. Finally, everyone left the conference room, and returned to their normal places of work. Jack had a pile of unfinished work to occupy his attention. After a time, he forgot about IMG and what Hunter had said.

A few days later, however, he came across an article in the Times. Sam Parrington was under investigation for failing to disclose multiple discrepancies in IMG's bookkeeping. The paper said that Parrington's lawyer had no comment, other than denying there was a legitimate basis for the government's action.

By the next day, the Journal was reporting Parrington's arrest. Shortly after that, IMG's board of directors removed him as CEO. The official position of the company was that "poor health" prevented him from continuing his job there. The board scrambled to find a successor, and a day, later, they named one.

IMG's new CEO would be Frank Colligari, a former fund manager with a big reputation as a "turn around" manager. He started his career in the investment banking division of Bolton Sayres, and managed the so-called Bolton Sayres Partner's Fund. The same private equity fund had purchased the consumer loan portfolio from IMG! He was one of the executives named in the fraud complaint.

A week before the court's deadline on delivery of the voice recording, IMG's Board of Directors approved a settlement. As demanded by Bolton Sayres, all details would be confidential for all time to come. However, as a member of the legal department, Jack was privy to the details. The amount paid would be exactly $50 million. One of the first acts of IMG's new CEO was to hire Bolton Sayres' investment banking division for a new round of stock and bond offerings.

Jack tried discussing the matter with Timothy Cohen.

"It's idle speculation," Cohen said, when confronted. "because we don't know what really happened."

"It's obvious what happened." Jack insisted. "This lawyer, James Hunter, is as corrupt as they come."

"Parrington was an asshole. So, why go out on a limb on his behalf?"

It was obvious to Jack, however, that his friend mostly wanted to justify a desire to do nothing.

"You told me, just three weeks ago, that you agreed with me. You know we would have gotten creamed at trial, just like I did"

"Maybe, I said that..." Cohen responded. "But, it doesn't matter anymore. The case is settled. Let sleeping dogs lie…"

"Crooked people like that shouldn't be allowed to just get away with stuff like this. Who does he do it to next? You, maybe? Me? If we look the other way now, we're just as guilty as he is."

"What do you want to do?" Cohen asked.

"Stop him." Jack said.

"And, how, exactly, are you going to do that?"

"By reporting it!"

"He'll never be stopped by people at our pay grade." Cohen replied. "Nobody's going to listen to our reports…"

"We can testify against him. Tell what happened. Parrington's obviously got some of the best lawyers in town. They'd probably jump at the chance to use us as witnesses..."

"Are you crazy?"

"I'm serious. If we don't step up to the plate, who will?"

"It's not my business." Cohen insisted.

"I'm going to report it."

"To who?" Cohen said.

"Well," Jack hesitated a moment, "To Mr. Stoneham, for starters. I'll need you to back up my story."

Cohen shook his head.

"No. I don't have the luxury of being married to his daughter. I need this job."

Jack was disappointed because he now saw his friend as somewhat of a coward. But, there was no use belaboring the point. He'd somehow enlist the man's help later on.

"There was something else I wanted to talk to you about." he said, after a moment.

"What?" Cohen replied.

"Remember, that upstate case I covered for you?"

"You mean the foreclosure?"

"Yeah, it's been a few weeks, and I've been so busy with other things that I neglected to talk to you. I found something up there."

"What?" Cohen asked.

Jack told him about the diary and the incident with the dead body described in it.

"You should turn it over to the Verde County Sheriff..." Cohen advised.

"I know..." Jack said. "But, how do I safely deliver it to them? I don't really have time for another trip."

"Send it by courier."

"FedX?"

"We've got a special courier who delivers stuff to Albany every day." Cohen said. "Fed X will deliver overnight, but these guys do it the same day. Or, maybe, even better, go ahead and take it to that FBI guy who's always asking us for leads."

VII – MR. STONEMAN GOES TO WASHINGTON

Jeremy Stoneham was 55 years old, but his physique seemed like that of a much younger man. It might have been partly genetic, but it was also partly due to the elaborate exercise routine he subjected himself to. Every morning, he diligently worked out, and the weight training, running on the treadmill, and stair stepping had become a part of his daily routine. He'd even gotten the company to add a private gym to his suite of offices. Nevertheless, in spite of his toned physique, the freshness of youth was long gone from his face.

His head was crowned with sparse gray hair, with a large bald spot in the middle. There were deep wrinkles in his brow and his smile lines were more like permanent canyons in his face. The black rimmed glasses he'd been wearing for 40 years had earned him the nickname "Clark Kent", and the nickname still stuck, despite the ravages of time, but he was no superhero. He did no deeds of derring-do, nor would he ever save the world.

Stoneham was simply a hard-nosed executive with a keen sense for profit. It was often said that Bolton Sayres was the savviest trading firm on the Street. Part of that resulted from the careful attention the firm paid to politics, and of all the executives, none played the political better than he did. The so-called "Great Recession" that started in 2008 had brought tough times even many financial firms. But, those with very close ties to the government had flourished. Such ties were the key that allowed Bolton to coin record profits even as some of its rivals languished and collapsed.

Since he'd become CEO, the financial press had anointed him the so-called "King of Wall Street." The premature death of the last Bolton family magnate, Todd Bolton, had crowned him with the throne about three years before. Kingship, however, came at a price. It handed him a host of problems that didn't seem royal. His ascendency resulted from an intense political power struggle following Bolton's death. Not everyone liked him, or the fact that he'd taken power. He had enemies inside Bolton Sayres and in other parts of the Synod. Some still wanted to see him burn.

He was slowly weeding out his enemies, putting his own loyalists in their place. The process would take years. Someday, he would be secure, but that would be a long time from now, Meanwhile, his position and power arose from the benefit that Bolton Sayres and the Synod gained from his extensive connections to government. That was the reason he was traveling to Washington DC. Much was riding on the trip, and many people were depending on him.

As the helicopter flew south, its chopper blades cut through the air like a chainsaw, resulting in a deafening roar within the cabin. It was so loud that it might have broken his eardrums, but for the helmet and headset. These muted the roar into background rumble, felt more by the body than the ears. Small radio transmitter/receivers in the helmets allowed free communication in an environment where the noise would otherwise make discussions impossible. With the helmet and headset, however, he could talk to the pilot with perfect clarity, without shouting.

He turned to the man.

"What's our ETA?" he asked.

"Less than 10 minutes now." the chopper pilot reported.

Stoneham nodded, satisfied.

Bolton Sayres owned several helicopters, and two private jets, but the fairly short distance between New York City and Washington DC, made helicopter the transportation of choice. Jets were useful for long trips across the country or across the Atlantic. For short trips between New York and DC, a jet would consume more time than taking a helicopter. This was because roadway congestion, and airport clearances for takeoff and landing, often caused long delays getting in and out of airports.

He was anxious about the upcoming meeting. The job of convincing the President would fall mainly to him. No one else had the close ties he had. The Synod was asking the President to sign an order opening up what remained of the US Gold Reserve to swap liens. He was one of the President's earliest and largest fundraisers. That long and close relationship could swing the decision in their favor, which made his arrival imperative.

Still, he felt awkward about it. He had to go, hat in hand, begging the President to do something that sold out the American people for the banks. But, there was no choice. The Synod had been manipulating gold prices for many years. Never had it found itself in such a mess. The New York branch of the Federal Reserve, which its people completely controlled, had always supplied enough gold for the manipulations. The material delivered directly from the Fed's underground vault, or it was delivered in London, the result of swap liens given to the Bank of England, backed by gold held at the Fed. Almost all the gold at the Fed was now encumbered by liens or had been distributed physically.

The only way to save the banks, now, was a literal "raid" on Fort Knox. It wouldn't have to be a physical raid. No physical gold need change hands, at least not right away. The Bank of England, which is also controlled by the Synod, held some 10,000 physical tons of gold in its vault. It was willing to supply the actual gold.

When and if the story ever became known, it might create a huge scandal. However, that wouldn't happen for many years, and only if the British proffered a formal demand upon the US Treasury. By then, the politicians and bankers involved would probably be dead, so they weren't particularly worried about it. If the President didn't sign off on this thing, though, they'd worry plenty.

He thought about what to say. Should he admit that refusal meant instant bankruptcy for two of the largest banks in the world? Would the President realize that the bankruptcy of those two banks, given the interwoven nature of their derivative obligations, would mean the end of the current financial system? He would have to make that very clear to the man.

Stoneham was having a hard time keeping his mind on the subject of what he would discuss with the President. His mind kept drifting off topic, and back to the unexpected arrival of his son-in-law that morning. Normally, nobody got through his secretaries. But, a temporary had been assigned from the secretarial pool, because his usual girl was on vacation. The new girl wasn't experienced enough in his personal affairs. She knew Jack was married to Laura, but from that she had erroneously assumed that he had carte blanche. His regular secretary knew better. He no longer wanted to speak with Jack during working hours, because the boy always came up with issues that were distracting and too difficult to deal with.

He'd never expected the young man to become an ideal employee. He had hoped, however, that he would eventually begin to understand the realities of the business world. That didn't seem to be happening. The complaints about Jack kept streaming in from just about everywhere in the company. Just a few weeks before there had been an incident involving an unauthorized settlement offer. The amount involved was piddling, but the boy's supervisor wanted to fire him. That wasn't going to happen, but it was still an annoying distraction.

Now, the boy had come directly to him, complaining about the actions of James Hunter, one of the sharpest lawyers the bank had on contract. He claimed the man used illegal influence to persecute the bank's legal opponents. So what? Protecting the interests of the bank was Hunter's business. The man would use his political influence to do it. That was no more than was to be expected.

Everyone cultivated political connections for a reason. Why dabble in politics if there was no advantage? Why make a campaign contribution if it wouldn't result in special favors? The people you put into office helped you, and if you put a few more dollars in their pockets, in appreciation, it greased the wheels of government. That's what politicking is all about. The boy didn't understand the game. It wasn't likely he ever would.

It had already been more than a year and a half since Stoneham learned about his daughter's transfer from NYU to UCLA. He'd expressed his displeasure, but the fact that it had taken nearly ten months for him to realize she was gone didn't help. It wasn't his fault. It didn't mean he didn't care. He just had to pay constant attention to bank business. The incident ended with Jack being hired by the bank. That got Laura back to New York.

He wished she was more interested in following him into banking. She was now a mother, but before that, she hadn't shown the slightest interest in banking or finance. She'd set her sights on becoming an actor. Now, in housewife and mother mode, she seemed to have lost all interest in working at anything at all. That was OK. But, just yesterday, she was playing with her dolls. Now, suddenly, she was fully-grown with a child of her own. How did kids grow up so fast?

He vividly remembered the disturbing dinner, when she'd come home from California. All she could talk about was the young man she'd met. The first thing he did, right after dinner, was to investigate the boy. But, his own men hadn't done a thorough enough job. He needed to know much more. He sought the help of the then-Director of Reputational Risk, Adriano Navarro, a man with an investigative operation that no one could match, but someone he'd never liked and wanted to get rid of.

Navarro was a creature of Todd Bolton. In his declining years, the old man had become oblivious to many things, not the least of which was the growing power of his protégé. Navarro had used Bolton's patronage to build a vast network of spies. They were everywhere, both human and electronic. The man's tentacles reached into every major office in banking and government. That made him dangerous. So dangerous, in fact, that Stoneham had his home and office swept for bugs, every day, just to make sure that Navarro hadn't placed any bugs.

It had been easier to deal with Navarro before he had gained the special visa from the Council. He had voted against it, but the others outvoted him. It made the man almost independent. Technically speaking, he was still on the payroll of Bolton Sayres. In reality, however, he now answered only to the Council, where Stoneham had only 1 out of 8 votes. The Council decided matters for the Synod banking cartel as a whole, and the fact that Navarro answered only to the Council, put controlling the man beyond his ability.

As much as he loathed having to work with him, when information from secret and otherwise blocked databases was needed, including expunged juvenile court cases, there was nowhere else to go. The man was a disgusting little Sicilian, but he was good at what he did. A day after receiving the assignment, Navarro had arrived in his office, unannounced, carrying a thick plastic covered report. He had dropped it on the desk, and slid it across. That had seemed like a sign of disrespect, so Stoneham had chosen not to pick it up.

"What did you find out about the boy?" Stoneham asked, ignoring the file folder.

"It's all in the report." Navarro had said.

The man was olive skinned, half-crippled, and repulsive.

The dark rings under his eyes made them look beady, and the slight downward hook of his nose completed the picture of a Mafia goombah. Stoneham would have fired him long ago, if it had been possible to do so. But, firing Navarro was out of the question. No one was in a position to replace him. There were also many, inside the Synod, who would back him in a political struggle.

Navarro ran THEATRES, the most powerful surveillance system ever designed, and had graduated from running Bolton's in-house reputational risk division, to running the secretive Synod-wide "Reputational Risk" office. Removing the man from Bolton Sayres' payroll would have elicited a laugh and a one hour delay in receipt of his 7 figure pay check. No individual bank official, regardless of his position, in the structure of the organization, had sole authority to fire a council-wide operative.

The man had to be fired by the Council as a whole, or not fired at all. It was a political matter. He tried to gather the support needed to can Navarro but the man had too many supporters, not the least of whom was Christopher Dunlop, the most powerful single individual in the Synod. Many other people were simply afraid of him. The man knew a lot about everyone, and could sink some of the most powerful people with an information release. Some said that he kept a dossier on everyone. Many of his enemies had faced harmful information mysteriously leaked into the public domain. That had destroyed marriages and careers.

"I don't have time to read reports..." Stoneham stated, roughly, "give me an oral summary..."

He'd already decided that Jack Severs was nothing more than a social climber who had latched onto his daughter for personal advancement. He knew that everything Navarro discovered would reinforce that fact. Severs was white trash. The boy wanted to get ahead by marrying well. Innocent girls from good families had to put up with men like that. It was up to their fathers to protect them.

He hadn't protected his little girl as he should have, and for that he felt a pang of guilt. She was a beautiful girl and an easy target. He'd screwed up badly by failing to pay attention. Now, if saving her meant paying big money, he was prepared to pay.

"The boy comes from a modest background, economically that is." Navarro began his summary.

Stoneham nodded. The boy was poor. His own private investigator had discovered that already. It wasn't news. He shook his head in discontent, because it reminded him of just one more thing that irritated him.

"I can't fathom why she refuses to date Mark Dunlop..." he muttered.

Bolton Sayres and W.T. Fredericks bank were the core of the Synod. Unlike the Boltons, the direct family tree of the Dunlops had not died out. Marc was the heir to a huge fortune and the Dunlop family had enough shares to maintain its power over the company indefinitely. That was in spite of the fact that the company was now one of the largest ones traded on an exchange. Of course, the Dunlop fortune, as well as his own, would shrink dramatically if the present meeting in Washington DC ended in failure.

Many might view the idea of the Dunlop heir working for Bolton Sayres, rather than his own family's bank, as ironic. It was not. It was entirely normal. A chain of obligations and agreements a mile long linked the two tightly intertwined institutions. Meanwhile, their differences complemented each other rather than conflicted. Bolton was on the cutting edge of technology, but Fredericks was a full service bank, not merely an investment bank.

As a computer whiz, the young Dunlop was a perfect fit into the Bolton Sayres' business model. His proprietary technology proved to be at the cutting edge of computerized trading and analysis. He would someday take his place as the head of W.T. Fredericks. But, for now, his talents could were more useful to the Synod, as a whole, where he was.

"Christopher Dunlop's boy is a spoiled brat." Navarro stated his views as flatly and honestly as he could. "Your daughter couldn't find herself a worse husband."

The comment surprised Stoneham. By what right did a greaseball like Navarro insult the heir to the Dunlop fortune?

"The Dunlop boy's a genius!" he countered.

That was the truth, as he saw it. The boy's self-designed trading "bots" were superior to anything else on the market. They were minting a fortune for Bolton Sayres and the banking Synod.

"He spent time behind bars..." Navarro noted.

"A few hours." Stoneham responded. "And, he was only 14!"

"He would have spent more if not for the corrupt judge the Dunlops paid off." Navarro noted. "Hacking into the FBI's website and sending out a wild virus that took down half of the computers in Europe is not a minor crime."

"He was young and foolish." Stoneham countered. "Judge Watkins simply helps straighten unfortunate mistakes. He's not corrupt."

Judge Watkins regularly straightened out many of the problems which beset the important families of New York City. He was one of several judges on the Synod "payroll." He handled juvenile cases, and key people in the Clerk's office would always make sure to assign him to the right cases. It was a mutually beneficial relationship.

"It didn't work out too well for the FBI agents." Navarro said.

"You don't go, willy-nilly, arresting young men from good families, inside their own homes!" Stoneham insisted.

"Of course, not." Navarro said, wryly. "But, I wonder if the Dunlops repaid the government for the cost of all those wrongful discharge lawsuits?"

"As I recall, old Todd Bolton rescued you from an FBI sting operation..." Stoneham countered.

That was hitting below the belt, but it seemed justified. He wanted to see the man cringe at the stab he'd just given him. But, Navarro disappointed him by preserving a poker face. He might have belabored the subject by reminding the man about his paid jobs for the Synod while he was working for the government. After all, a military man who bugs Congressional offices stoops about as low as you can go.

Instead, he thought better of it. There was no point to antagonizing the man, in spite of the pleasure of doing so. Pushing him too hard might put his cooperation at risk. Instead, he remained positive.

"Young Mark has grown into a fine boy." Stoneham said. "He's an expert in artificial intelligence, mostly self-taught. He's the best at everything he does... this boy from LA that Laura seems to prefer, couldn't stand in his shadow."

"I didn't say young Dunlop was stupid." Navarro replied.

Stoneham had introduced Laura to Mark Dunlop at her debutante ball. Both families were optimistic, but it hadn't worked out. They'd dated for a few months, and then, Laura broke it off without explanation. She even refused to tell her mother why. That was unusual. She normally told her mother everything.

"What else did you find out about Jack?"

"No family, no pedigree as you might call it..." Navarro continued. "No connections. But, he graduated from UCLA Law School."

"I knew all that already." Stoneham noted.

That Jack had graduated from one of the best law schools in the nation didn't impress him. Maybe, Stanford might have done the trick. But, for the most part, nothing outside Harvard, Yale, Columbia, NYU and the University of Pennsylvania impressed anyone in New York. Stoneham didn't particularly like lawyers anyway. Technically, he was a lawyer himself. He was still a member of the New York Bar and a graduate of NYU's law school. However, he hated trial lawyers, especially the ones who sued banks. His previous investigator had reported that Jack was dreaming about becoming one.

"He's only a student." Navarro pointed out. "How much money do you expect him to have?"

"It's always something." Stoneham grumbled. "Lack of opportunity, discrimination, drunken parents, parents who are too strict, parents who aren't strict enough. People just don't take responsibility for their own failures."

Navarro ignored the tirade and continued.

"Don't you want to know why he's poor?" Navarro explained.

"Not really." Stoneham admitted.

"He's poor because he's an orphan," he said, finally. "both of whose parents died when he was eleven."

That caught Stoneham by surprise, but he didn't respond to it, and Navarro continued.

"He grew up in foster care, juggled from family to family until he was 17. He lived in the dorms at UCLA from shy of 18 years old. He was awarded an academic scholarship, but not enough for living expenses, so he has a lot of student loans. He worked part-time at every opportunity during the year, and then full-time during summer and holidays…"

That Jack Severs was a hard worker didn't matter. Most people who tried to climb the social ladder were willing to work hard. It didn't make him feel any better about the boy. He was unknown, without family connections, from a world outside the mainstream. There was nothing good about him.

He wasn't sure how to respond to what he'd heard, so he leaped on something negative.

"Everyone who says they're poor gets a scholarship and a student loan." he noted. "That's the way it works in a welfare state."

"I said he got an academic scholarship." Navarro pointed out. "It's not based on income. He got straight A's in high school. He won a National Merit Scholarship. He had nearly a perfect SAT score. Then, he took the LSAT, and scored in the top ½% of all the students taking the test. He graduated from UCLA College, and then from UCLA Law School."

"If he's so smart, why didn't he go to Harvard?" Stoneham countered. "Most people in our legal department went to Harvard, Yale or Columbia."

"His academic record was good enough. He simply didn't bother applying."

"Why not?" Stoneham wondered.

"I don't know." Navarro admitted.

"No family, no connections, no pedigree, not even enough ambition to apply to an Ivy League law school!" Stoneham concluded. "I'd like, very much, to get this boy out of my daughter's life."

"You want me to kill him for you?" Navarro asked.

The man almost sounded serious. It was obvious, however, that he was being facetious. Stoneham shook his head.

"I just want him out of her life."

As a young boy, he'd felt the sting of poverty. He didn't want his daughter to go near it. His mother was a distant relative of the Boltons, a third cousin, twice removed. She had married low. It was for love, not money, and it had ended in a life with a lowly postal clerk. He'd grown up in subsidized housing in the Bronx. He didn't want his daughter to follow his mother's example.

"As I recall, this boy has a criminal record, doesn't he?" Stoneham declared.

That was information he thought might impress Navarro. He knew a few things from the investigation his own people had done.

"He was arrested one time." Navarro stated.

"One time is enough." Stoneham countered. "As I recall, it was assault and battery with a deadly weapon..."

"There's a back story..." Navarro pointed out.

"More excuses?" he snapped back.

"The boy studied mixed martial arts since he was 12." Navarro noted. "He's smart, he's athletic, and he's somewhat of an expert in Karate, Jujitsu, and sword fighting. A friend of his first foster family was a Karate instructor, and that's what got him started. By 16, he held three black belts. He had one in Karate, another in Jujitsu, and a third in Kendo. He'd also won a youth championship in Judo. The deadly weapons the police mentioned in the arrest warrant are his hands."

That surprised Stoneham, but he tried hard not to let the other man know. His first investigator hadn't found any of it. Juvenile arrest records were supposed to be sealed. Access was part of the reason he had transferred the investigation to Navarro. The man was obnoxious, but he could get things done. He had information sources that no one else had. That made him incredibly valuable.

"When Jack was 17, he attended a high school in one of the crappy neighborhoods in southwest Los Angeles, near Long Beach. Mostly Mexican and black, it's filled with drugs, street gangs, and crime of all kinds… you name it."

"So what?" Stoneham had asked.

"Well, here's where it gets interesting… he goes walking down the street, and sees two kids, a boy and girl, getting victimized by three gang-bangers. Two of the thugs have their blades out, and the third is busy stripping the girl of her clothing. There would have been a rape for sure, and maybe two stabbings if Jack had simply walked by and done nothing.

"But, he stopped and told the gang members to get lost. They didn't take kindly to that, so he's still got a long scar, on his left upper arm, where one of their blades sliced him. But, within minutes, all three of them were disarmed, and one had a broken kneecap, the other a broken arm and leg, and the third… the one who was going to rape the girl… he ended up lying in a puddle of his own blood, stabbed by his own knife. The blade penetrated his spine and he ended up crippled for life."

The story perked Stoneham's interest, and forced him to take notice, despite himself.

"Then, why was he convicted of a crime?" he had asked Navarro. "He sounds like a hero."

"He was a hero." Navarro replied. "And, he wasn't convicted of a crime. Whoever told you that didn't do a proper investigation. They arrested him, and took him to the hospital, where they stitched him up. The police are always inclined to arrest people when there's been mayhem. The two high school kids, who could have told the true story, ran away. When the two victims finally showed up, Jack was released and all charges were dropped."

"What about the gang bangers?" Stoneham had asked.

"They prosecuted two of them." Navarro explained. "Both were juveniles, so they got a month or two of detention The third was crippled for life, so he was given a suspended sentence. The guy's still alive, by the way, but Jack sentenced him to life in a wheelchair. His family tried to sue, but none of the usual ambulance chasers would take the case."

Stoneham picked up the report. He examined the outside cover for a moment. Then, he tossed it back down onto the desk, without opening it. He looked at Navarro again.

"What about other gang members?" Stoneham asked. "Weren't there any revenge attacks?"

"The Department of Social Services removed Jack to San Luis Obispo." Navarro explained. "I guess the distance was too far away for that scum. That's where he finished high school. He returned to LA, two years later, to attend UCLA. By then, I suppose, the gang was busy with something else."

"How is it you know all this?" Stoneham had asked. "I thought juvenile records were sealed?"

"All records, including sealed and expunged records, remain in the database." Navarro pointed out. "They're just blocked if you don't know how to access them."

"And, you know how?"

Navarro answered without hesitation.

"Of course." he said.

Stoneham made a mental note. Accessing encrypted records, from a state criminal database, without authorization, had to be some sort of crime. Maybe, he could use it against Navarro. The man was accessing records he had no right to access. Still, it was valuable to the Synod. Jeopardizing it would be sheer folly, and would not go over well. Not only that, but he wanted access to such information, himself. It was just one example of the reason so many people supported Navarro. He was the master of whispers, an invaluable source of important information.

Stoneham's thoughts turned back to the boy. He had courage, which was worth something. It wasn't worth as much, perhaps, as a fine pedigree, but it was worth something. The boy was also book-smart. You didn't get good grades and a National Merit Scholarship if you weren't. Still, he was also impulsive and somewhat thoughtless.

No sensible person would rush into a fight, 3 to 1, let alone unarmed against gang-bangers with knives. Clever people didn't play such odds. Smart people stacked the deck in their favor before taking action. The boy had won his bet, but he was also lucky to be alive. Taking on risk, with no possibility of gain, was just foolish.

On the other hand, such courage is hard to ignore, no matter how hard-boiled a man becomes. That the boy was tough meant something too. More than anything else, winning was the bottom line. He had won. No matter how old, cynical, stubborn, and set in his ways Jeremy Stoneham might have become, was also a man and a member of the human race.

Heroes impress men. It is genetic programming. Instinct doesn't rely on life experience or the degree of a man's cynicism. Stoneham couldn't help but admire Jack for what he had done, as foolish as it may have been. The same programming causes young boys to watch super-hero cartoons endlessly.

"What about his parents?" he asked with renewed interest. "What kind of people were they, before they died?"

"The father was an aerospace engineer." Navarro answered. "He worked for one of the big government contractors near Torrance, California. Mother had a master's degree in anthropology, but never used it. She was a housewife after her marriage."

Stoneham had found himself reconsidering the facts. The boy might not as bad as he thought. Still, he couldn't let Laura disappear into oblivion with a poor boy from Los Angeles. He needed to keep her in New York City. That left two choices. Pay the boy to leave or lure him to New York. Eventually, he had enlisted Laura in his plans, though she did not know it. He simply told her to invite Jack to New York, on an all-expenses-paid trip.

Jack eventually arrived in late August 2011, but lobbed another surprise when he refused to allow anyone to pay for the trip. Stoneham had viewed the secret videos, over and over again. It was obvious the boy's reactions were real. The surprise on his face, when he was picked up by a Mercedes limo, was genuine. The look of astonishment when he had lunch at the Stoneham penthouse on Central Park West, for the first time, was real.

Even after he had learned about Laura's family wealth, he refused the room that had been offered, at the Waldorf Astoria hotel, and opted to stay in the tiny Brooklyn apartment of his friend, a young Hispanic man who had moved from LA to New York City 2 years before Jack.

Of course, none of that had convinced him that the young man was a suitable son-in-law. He'd sat the boy down in private, in his library, and offered him $100,000 to walk away. At first, the boy's negotiating skills had impressed him. He assumed the price was simply higher. His higher offer, however, was immediately rejected. He had upped the ante, several times, until he'd offered $2 million dollars. It was far more than he had ever imagined he'd pay. Still, the boy refused. That's was when he backpedaled. He told Jack that the offers were just to "test" his sincerity, and the boy believed him.

The logical next step was getting him to stay. That was the reason for the job offer. It was not exactly charity. The bank was involved in a surge in litigation, and wanted to hire new lawyers to help carry the load. There were so many lawsuits that existing staff couldn't manage them all. It was easy to find lawyers, especially new graduates, who were now a dime a dozen. Every managing director and department head seemed to have a son, son-in-law, or nephew who happened to be a recent law graduate in need of a job.

The continued investigation told him that Jack still didn't have one offer of employment. He'd graduated in the top 25% of UCLA's class of 2011, but he had nothing to show for it. He'd figured the boy would jump at the chance to work for a bank. Opportunities like that didn't come around every day. Stoneham knew that working at Bolton Sayres was the dream of many Harvard law graduated. It was an opportunity of a lifetime that most young men would seize at a moment's notice. However, Jack had initially refused all the job offers.

Stoneham couldn't help but remember the boy's words.

"I've stood on my own two feet since I was eleven. I can't stomach getting my first job through nepotism. But, thanks anyway..."

Foolishness was the reason the boy had gone, unarmed, into a fight with three armed hoodlums. It was why he had initially turned down lucrative job offers at Bolton Sayres. It was now why there was a host of complaints about him. The boy was book-smart and real world foolish. That would be his undoing.

After Jack had rejected all the job offers. Laura announced that she would be returning with him to Los Angeles. That's when he secretly got her a leading role in a big new Broadway musical. To this day, she innocently believed that her superior singing and acting ability had secured her the job at the audition. That gambit accomplished its purpose. The goal was to get Laura to want to stay in New York so badly that she would convince Jack.

In the end, however, it was the pregnancy that had made the decision for them. The boy was honorable. Having learned that his baby was growing in her belly, he immediately proposed. They got married, and he'd finally agreed to take the offered job with the bank. The Vice President in charge of the legal department hadn't been too happy about that. He had earmarked the job for his own nephew. But, in the end, he had no choice but to accept orders from above.

If Jack had a more practical mind, he could have groomed the boy to be his own successor. That's what the Dunlops were doing with young Marc Dunlop. However, Jack's idealism would be his doom. It would destroy his career. James Hunter was a top lawyer and had been working for Bolton Sayres as long as Stoneham could remember. No executive in his right mind would hire expensive outside lawyers for their eloquence, or knowledge of the law. They were always hired for their political clout. Why didn't Jack understand that without having to be explicitly told?

The right connections got things done. The wrong ones mucked things up. A well-connected attorney could turn a sure loss into a winner. Hunter and his partners had gotten Bolton out of many scrapes over the years. Losing the man would be a great loss to the firm. His fees were high, more than $900 bucks an hour, but he was worth every penny and more. But, how could he explain all that to such a foolish boy?

How could he make reality acceptable to an idealistic son-in-law who understood nothing about reality? The boy was married to Laura. That meant it was essential that he have a decent job and make a decent amount of money. The Board of Directors would never allow an unrealistic fool to reach an important position, let alone lead the company. Before he could succeed, he had to learn how business was done.

Jack would never make a good banker. But, perhaps, there was another job he could excel at? Some of the other banks in the Synod still maintained old-fashioned lines of business, like credit cards, and home loans. He might fit in better there, rather than in a trading environment. There was no time to think about that, now, however. The best response, for the moment, was no response. Someday, he'd sit down, like a Dutch uncle, and explain the ways of the world to the boy. Until then, he'd find excuses to avoid the issue.

The pilot's voice broke into his thoughts by making an announcement.

"Sir, we'll be landing in about 2 minutes..." he said.

Stoneham nodded.

As one of the President's largest fund-raisers, Stoneham's helicopter would normally land directly on the south lawn. This morning, however, fifteen top financial industry CEOs would travel from New York to Washington DC by helicopter. Not all could land there. Obvious preference given to him, over others, would stimulate jealousy and cause tempers to flare. To avoid discord, the chopper landed a few blocks away.

From this secondary heliport, a black Mercedes limo drove him the short distance to the White House. The car ran so smoothly that it was hard to tell whether it was moving or standing still. He was startled when they finally arrived, the limo door opened, and light streamed into the cabin, causing him to squint in the brightness of the day.

A smiling woman stared at him through the open door, her arms in a welcoming gesture of invitation.

"Welcome to the White House." she said. "The Secretary of the Treasury is waiting in the conference room."

Stoneham nodded, and climbed out of the limo.

He was not worried about keeping the man waiting. He had known him since he'd been an intern at Bolton Sayres. About 12 years his junior, the current Secretary of the Treasury had graduated from Bolton Sayres to the Federal Reserve Bank of New York. He had served the banking cartel well over the years. Now, he would be very helpful in convincing the President to sign an order opening up the US Gold Reserve.

Most of the invited CEOs had already arrived. It was 10:30 a.m., and the meeting was set for 11:00. He knew all of them on a first name basis. Everyone was standing on the patio, shaking hands, chatting and drinking refreshments. There was still a little time. It wouldn't hurt to take a few minutes to meet and greet. After about 15 minutes of mingling and hand shaking, Tanya Sorbo, the White House's conference coordinator, got everyone's attention.

"It's time..." she announced, graciously. "Please follow me, gentlemen."

She led the group of dignitaries up the pathway through the lawn into the west wing. A few moments later, they arrived in a large conference room, decorated with Thomas Chippendale and Queen Anne style furniture. It was on the first floor, but it seemed like the top of the building, because there was a false skylight was built into the ceiling. There were also traditional paintings of two former American Presidents, Theodore and Franklin Roosevelt, hanging on the walls.

That's why former President Richard Nixon had named it the "Roosevelt room," and the name had stuck like glue. It is the most popular conference room in the White House.

The companies represented were some of the most important in the world. Eight of them were official members of the Synod. All, however, would be devastated if W.T. Fredericks' London gold operation imploded. The bank owed physical gold to other banks and insurers, and to several participants at the meeting, as well as a myriad of minor central banks. Some of the other participants were minor players in the gold manipulation game. However, like Fredericks, all of them owed gold, and none had more than a fraction of what they needed to repay their gold-based debts.

That was the dirty little secret. Almost none of the people who think they own gold actually do. First, there are a hundred of more claimants attached to every bar of gold. Second, most have signed non-allocated storage agreements, which provide an indivisible claim to the bank's general assets. They have no greater claim upon gold bars, than any simple bondholder does, but they don't know it. When and if a bank goes belly-up, non-allocated storage customers are nothing but unsecured creditors.

One clever trader had figured it out and upset the applecart. He'd bought call options on hundreds of tons of over-the-counter paper gold forwards. Such "forwards" are contracts for the future delivery of gold that trade off formal exchanges. Like a standard futures contract, however, the holder can force delivery on maturity. Instead of taking the paper profit like most speculators, therefore, he converted all a huge number of call options into gold forward contracts. Then, he demanded physical gold on maturity. The bank, of course, didn't have the gold.

The problem was that the models showed that it was not necessary to keep on hand more than 1/2% of the gold it was obligated to deliver. The only real gold in any Synod bank was the gold stored inside the New York based Bolton Sayres' vault, and there was precious little of that. Bolton, in turn, relied on the gold stored underneath the NY Fed building to meet its needs.

Frederick's flawed model predicted that the maximum gold for delivery would never exceed 1/4 of 1% of the total derivatives sold. All of it was solid stuff, based upon historical demand trends. But, trends could change and when they did, those on the wrong end could get creamed. With the blogosphere screaming and yelling about the fraudulent nature of non-allocated gold bullion storage, people were now asking for delivery of their physical gold. But, there was precious little gold to deliver. The latest demand, by the one trader, had been enough to break the camel's back.

If a ready source couldn't be found, Frederick's gold forwards would have to be settled in cash dollars. According to the law, a cash settlement was not technically a legal default. The small print contained within the non-allocated gold storage agreements allowed it. However, if it happened, the forced cash settlement would alert the public to the real situation in the gold market. The dirty truth would be on open display. Gold price manipulation would move into the light, and that was almost certain to result in a massive run on the fractional gold banking scheme at all the banks.

People would also discover that many of the gold bars that were supposed to be "allocated" – ones that they theoretically held title to – also didn't exist, or had several other owners. The immense fraud, by most of the biggest names in the business, would vaporize confidence in all markets. The contagion would spread into paper currencies and into the stock, bond, and commodity markets.

Every established financial institution, inside and outside of the Synod, itself, had a stake in stopping the financial Holocaust from happening. The matters discussed today would be a state secret for at least 50 years, but saving the world, at least the world as the bankers knew it and wanted it to continue to be, now depended entirely on the President.

The press described today's meeting as a panel discussion on jobs and inflation. Supposedly, it was part of the administration's effort to forge better relations with the financial industry. It was all bullshit. The President had excellent relations with Wall Street. He was the first black President, and the Street as a whole had enjoyed putting him in office. It often sang its own praises for having done so. Wall Street money backed him and his administration backed up the needs of the banks and hedge funds.

The only real issue at hand was gold, that glittering barbaric relic that was a biting thorn in the side of the banking industry. If the President refused to open up the gold stored at Fort Knox, the price would soar. The Synod would implode. It was as simple as that. Marc Dunlop had done the mathematical calculation and he said that it would take approximately 1,300 tons of physical gold to break the psychological back of the gold market for years to come. Stoneham's mission was to convince the President to sign off on that swaps, so that that the Bank of England would agree to put that immense tonnage at the disposal of the Dunlop bots.

Had he been in power back then, Stoneham felt sure that he would have done exactly what the Rothschild Bank did in 2004 and exited the gold market. Gold's nature as a physically delivered commodity made it a powder keg waiting for a spark. The spark had finally come with a simple modeling miscalculation. Without government help, all of the big banks and the insurance companies that relied upon them, would go bankrupt together.

The total non-allocated obligation amounted to an enormous tonnage of gold, and there was no possible way the banks could ever pay it. Minimizing the losses over a period of several years was essential. It had to start by slamming positive sentiment. Marc Dunlop claimed he could do it if he had the resources. He claimed he could have his bots run a massive bombardment of short positions that would force under-capitalized long buyers to liquidate. Essential to success, however, was a coordinated price attack. Then, the banks could begin slowly unwinding their short positions into a panicked market. To generate that panic, however, physical gold swaps with the official US Gold Reserve were essential.

The conference table was long, wide, and made of walnut, and polished to such a shine you could see your reflection in the wood. The President would sit at the head of the mirror-like table. To his right, would be the Secretary of the Treasury. Then, the Undersecretary of the Treasury would sit to his right, Christopher Dunlop, who was still the most powerful banker, despite his bank's gold troubles, would sit next to him. To Dunlop's right, was Jeremy Stoneham's seat. The rest of the CEOs followed, in order of their personal influence, the size, wealth and political influence of their particular institutions.

Suddenly, the announcement came. The Secretary and Undersecretary of the Treasury, both old friends, and the President, himself, a more recent but also dear friend, were walking into the room. In a sign of formality and respect, everyone stood up. Decorum required this outward display in spite of the fact that everyone was on a first name basis. When the President sat down, they all sat down, and the meeting was called to order.

Everyone in the room felt the pressure...

VIII - THE ODYSSEUS CLUB

The Odysseus Club is one of the premiere watering holes catering to Wall Street's 20 and 30 "somethings." It is especially good in the spring because the outside terraces open up in April. The food is tasty and reasonably priced by the usually overpriced New York standard. The place livens up right after work, especially on Thursday nights, because during "happy hour" that night, they serve half-price drinks from 5 until 8 p.m.

At 6:00 p.m. on Thursday night, Timothy Cohen found a reason to walk by Jack's cubicle. Almost everyone else was already gone but Jack was still hard at work and juggling several assignments. For all the complaints that his father-in-law might have, laziness was not one of them. He was so engrossed in his work that he didn't even notice that his friend had arrived and was leaning over the edge of the cubical divider.

"Earth to Jack..." Cohen said, facetiously. "Earth to Jack... Come in Jack..."

Startled, Jack looked up.

"Tim!" he said, surprised. "What are you doing here?"

"It's more appropriate for me to ask you, why are you still here?"

Jack turned back to the screen.

"I'm just trying to finish stuff..."

Cohen pointed to his watch.

"You know that it's after six, don't you?"

Jack nodded, but kept fixated on his screen.

"Time to quit, my friend..." Cohen continued.

"I've just got so much stuff to do, and not enough hours in a day..." Jack replied.

"That's because you do too much. You're always volunteering. What is the story with that Florida firm, anyway? And, how about that diary you told me about?"

"The Florida case wrapped up yesterday. They just wanted to settle, so we settled with them. As for the diary, I took it over to 26 Federal Plaza; to the guy we work with."

The address, 26 Federal Plaza, was the FBI building, an address that needed no further identification.

"What did he say?"

"He told me he'd take a look, but that the FBI probably doesn't have any jurisdiction. He says he'll send it to the Verde County Sheriff."

"That's exactly what you wanted, isn't it?" Cohen noted.

"Yeah…"

"You did the right thing."

"It was the most time efficient way of dealing with it…" Jack replied. "At least, I'm not responsible for it anymore."

Jack rubbed his eyes, which were aching. He's just received the new case file, and it was hefty. It was getting late in the day. According to the paralegal's summary, the SEC was taking "administrative action" against seven of Bolton's investment bankers. The regulator accused them of manipulating an initial public offering (IPO).

His job was to analyze the case more carefully than a paralegal could. It was important for upper management to know how the case would affect the bank, and it was necessary to make a recommendation as to how to deal with it. That would require writing up a short report. It was likely, however, that no one would ever read his report or, if they did, they were unlikely to care what he said in it. As one of the younger, least experienced lawyers, he had no real influence and certainly no decision-making power.

"Did they say how much the consent decree will cost us?"

"What are you talking about?" Jack asked, perplexed.

Instead of answering, however, Cohen decided to change the subject to something he found more interesting.

"Don't you know what today is?"

"Not really." Jack replied.

"It's Thursday night." Cohen stated as if the day of the week was very important.

"What does that mean?"

"It means that too much work and too little play makes Jack a dull boy!"

"Funny…" Jack said, as he smiled.

People had fun at his very common name all the time. He was used to it.

"It's happy hour at the Odysseus Club!"

Jack wasn't in a lively mood, and didn't like nightclubs.

"The more I read this stuff, the more I can't believe we've got scum like this working for us." he exclaimed, instead.

"Lots of pond scum at Bolton, that's for sure!" Cohen agreed. "Thank God for that. It keeps us employed!"

"You are getting to be intolerably cynical!" Jack exclaimed. "These cases are outrageous."

"Are they?" Cohen stated blandly. "I'm not surprised. What I am surprised at is the SEC. Normally they don't bother. It sounds like they have a directive to 'raise cash."

"What?" Jack asked.

"That IPO stuff happens all the time." Cohen replied. "They never do anything about it."

"But, our guys told some big hedge funds that if they committed to buying fifty thousand additional shares, within the first few minutes of trading, they'd let them in and out early." Jack explained.

"Standard pump and dump."

"The SEC says it was part of a scheme to force prices up, short term, at the expense of small investors in the longer term." Jack explained. "The early hedge fund buyers could pull off a coordinated exit, selling into the buying frenzy our guys create after hyping the stock."

"Oldest trick in the book."

"One of our guys actually got on CNBC, and claimed the shares were in great demand. He was talking bullshit because only the hedge funds were buying."

"They always do that." Cohen commented.

"Then, why aren't they prosecuted?

Cohen smiled.

"It's all about money."

"Money? The SEC investigation is about money, or the reason our guys conspired with the hedge funds?"

"Both..."

"What are you hinting at?"

"Look," Cohen responded. "The people have the money. The banks take it from the people. The government takes it from the banks. It's a 'quid pro quo.' You know what I am saying? They sue us and pretend to police Wall Street. We pay them, promise not to do it again, and pretend to be chastened. When you compare what we pay to what our guys steal, the crimes pay well. So, the same schemes are washed, rinsed and repeated, time and time again."

"I don't understand." Jack declared, shaking his head. "If the government wants money, why not just impose a huge fine, big enough to discourage this crap?"

Cohen shook his head in disbelief.

"Jack, I love you!" he blurted out with a smile. "You're incredibly naïve! Didn't you hear me when I said quid pro quo? The Feds will make us pay a million bucks for each consent decree. That looks like big bucks to average people. However, it's just a fraction of what Bolton, and its executives make on these deals. As bank lawyers, our job is to settle out as cheap as possible. The government needs gravy too."

"You can't possibly believe that."

"The hell I don't!" Cohen insisted.

"You're telling me everyone is corrupt? The people who did the crimes, the banks and the government?"

"Yep." Cohen said, in a tone that made it seem obvious. "The only ones who aren't corrupt are the little people who invest their hard-earned pennies into all these hare-brained schemes and, of course, guys like you."

"That's hard to believe..." Jack said, shaking his head again.

"Don't believe me?" Cohen pointed out. "You saw what happened to Parrington. Can you imagine what happens to people who don't have power and money?"

"That was a special case involving one very corrupt lawyer. I'm working on making sure he's dealt with appropriately." Jack insisted.

Cohen smiled.

"How did that little talk with your father-in-law go, by the way?"

"He's going to get back to me."

"Let's see, how long ago was that?" Cohen stated, with cynicism. "I'll venture to guess that he'll get back to you when kingdom comes, and that's only if you're lucky."

"He's going to get back to me when he returns from Washington DC." Jack countered.

"Good luck. But, then, you are his son-in-law. You might get a response. I'd just get fired."

"I don't believe that." Jack insisted.

"Believe this, Jack..." Cohen insisted. "With respect to this new case of yours... NOBODY and I mean NOBODY ever gets prosecuted unless he's either at the lowest end of the totem pole and he's being used as the fall man for something we can't deny, or when management gets pissed at him."

"If you believe that, how can you continue working here?"

"How can you?" Cohen countered.

"Because I don't believe that." Jack explained.

"Start believing." Cohen said. "Because it's true."

Jack shook his head in response.

"I'll bet I can tell you exactly what happened in your new case, without even knowing any of the facts..." Cohen said.

"OK, go ahead." Jack agreed.

"First, they pushed up prices with the help of the hedge funds." Cohen explained. "Then, to keep the stock rising, they traded the shares between the underwriters, always bidding it upward, repaying losses to one another as they happened. That's called wash trading. Our guys do it all the time. Then, they sold the over-allotment shares and used the money to reimburse the syndicate for what it spent when third parties got in-between the wash trades. When all the shares were placed with mutual funds and individual investors, maybe 3-4 weeks after the IPO started to sell, the share price plummeted. Am I right so far?"

"How do you know all that?" Jack asked.

"Because it's the same with every IPO," Cohen insisted, "That's how it's done. They create the appearance of success. The innocents don't know when to get out. The conspirators do."

"You're describing criminal acts, so I'll recommend we forward these files to the Justice Department."

Cohen shook his head, still grinning.

"Oh, please, Jack, the Justice Department isn't going to prosecute someone just because you refer the file to them."

"Maybe they will..."

"No, they won't." Cohen said, dismissively. "That FBI guy, for example, the one you gave your diary to, he assigned to us primarily to investigate the people management gets pissed at. Those are the ones who get prosecuted."

Jack shook his head in disbelief.

"You can't really believe what you're saying."

"It is what it is." Cohen conceded, with a wave of his hand. "If I could get the kind of money I make here, I'd leave, and work somewhere else. But, frankly, my friend, there are too many unemployed lawyers. I prefer to have a job."

Jack didn't know what to say. He'd lived his entire life believing in the system. The idea that the government not only allowed, but actively participated in the process of systematic fleecing small investors was shocking. But, he couldn't deny Cohen's accuracy in describing the scheme. How could he know all that without ever looking at the file? It must happen all the time. The man had worked at the bank a lot longer than he had.

"I don't need a paycheck that bad..." Jack declared.

"Maybe, not. But, then, you're married to a Stoneham... I'm not."

"That's got nothing to do with it." Jack said, defensively.

"I'm sorry. Look, I didn't mean that." Cohen apologized, and held out his hand. "We're friends, right?"

"Sure." Jack replied, as he shook the offered hand.

"Then, I'll tell you a secret. I don't intend to stay here forever. I'm just learning everything I can. When I know everything I need to know, I'll quit, and switch sides. I'll sue the crap out of these bastards. I'll shock any jury or arbitration panel simply by pointing out the truth. I'll be the terror of the banks. They won't dare face me in court, so they'll settle and I'll get rich. I'll help the little people at the same time. That's my plan. How about doing it with me?"

Jack suddenly felt a strong desire to quit along with his friend. He wanted to do exactly what Cohen described. It was better to get out now, and not wait until he became so dependent on the salary it would be impossible to quit. But, then, he was already dependent on the salary. If he ever quit, he wouldn't be able to pay the monthly rent for his flat, let alone buy food, clothing or any luxuries for his family. His wife and daughter would end up taking money from his in-laws.

Cohen spoke again without waiting for Jack's reply.

"Meantime, stop obsessing! Come out with me tonight. I'm headed to the Odysseus Club..."

With the new baby, and his wife waiting at home, Jack had almost forgotten what a social life was. Still, he would have liked a drink with a co-worker. He knew about the club, although he'd never been there. It was a well known favorite, but mostly a singles hangout, and he was not single anymore.

"I don't know..." Jack wavered. "Laura's probably waiting for me."

Would she mind? Maybe not. She'd already told him he needed to socialize more. If he didn't come home too late, she might be okay with it.

"Call her." Cohen exclaimed. "And get the OK."

There weren't even any deadlines looming. There was no reason not finish what he was doing tomorrow, during normal working hours. He made a quick call to Laura, whose initial objections faded away into a promise he wouldn't come home too late.

Then, Jack turned to his friend.

"I've got a few loose ends to tie up. Can you give me a half hour?"

"Sure." Cohen said. "You know how to get there?"

"Yeah."

"OK, we'll be waiting for you..."

Jack nodded and waved good-bye.

Then, after Cohen had left, he turned back to his computer, sent out the emails he'd already composed, and signed off. A short trip to the men's room, and about 10 minutes later, he set off by foot to his destination. When he arrived, Cohen spotted him right away.

"Jack! Over here." the man screamed out.

He was standing and motioning Jack over to the table, Jack raised a hand in greeting, walked over, and shook hands. There were two other men sitting there. The man sitting to Cohen's right looked to be a little older, maybe in his 30s, and he seemed to have a permanent smirk engraved on his face.

"This is Marc Dunlop, one of Bolton's top analysts." Cohen said. "He's worshiped by the proprietary traders... Marc, I want you to meet Jack Severs."

He shook Dunlop's hand, but felt a sense of coldness that defied explanation.

"I know about you." Dunlop stated coldly.

That was surprised Jack. As far as he could remember, he'd never met the man.

"It's nice to meet you." Jack said. "But, I thought prop. trading was ended by the Volcker rule?"

"Fuck the Volcker rule..." Dunlop exclaimed.

He turned to Cohen, shaking his head, and laughed, while pointing at Jack.

"Is this guy for real? Is he supposed to be a lawyer?"

The comment was annoying, but Jack held his tongue, and there was a momentary pause, during which no one said a word. A small brown skinned man, sitting to the left of Dunlop, finally broke the silence.

"The Volcker Rule is not yet in effect." he advised, authoritatively, with a thick accent. "The Fed delayed implementation until 2017."

"Why?" Jack asked.

"Because we asked them to." he replied. "Even when it goes into effect, however, there'll still new ways to get around it. The banks, you see, make a market in stocks, bonds and commodities. At W.T. Fredericks', for example, we never touch bank capital. We trade only for clients, many of whom are hedge funds, owned by former executives with the firm…"

Cohen officially introduced them.

"Jack, this is Sandip Gupta." he said. "He's a lawyer on the personal advisory staff of W.T. Fredericks' CEO. If there's any FINRA or SEC rule you need to know about, or want changed, he's the man to call."

"Nice to meet you, Jack." the man said, holding out his hand.

The two men shook hands.

"Sandy isn't telling you everything, of course…" Cohen said. "W.T. Fredericks' so-called 'clients' are hedge funds, but they're really just offshoots of the bank itself. They've got access to virtually all the money that the bank can borrow from the Federal Reserve. They're sponsored and funded by bank capital."

"I object to this smear upon the good name of my company!" Sandy Gupta exclaimed, chuckling under his breath.

"The banks will never stop trading, in one form or another, no matter what rule the government passes." Cohen declared. "They'll just trade around the rule."

The Indian smiled, and drank a deep swig of beer.

"Just so…" he added, satisfied with Cohen's statement. "You can call me Sandy, by the way."

"Sandy" was born in India, but he was a naturalized American. His mother, father and sister were also naturalized Americans. Their roots were in the Kshatriya caste, descendants of the Maharajas of Uttar Pradesh, a big Indian state that had once been a country in its own right.

Family connections were openly the key to success in Asia. The same was true in the western world, although in America many people, especially those in the banking industry, try to glue on a veneer of meritocracy. Nepotism and opportunist hiring based upon political connections is, was and always has been the standard of practice in both east and west. Plum jobs go to family members and/or those with the type of connections needed by the banks.

Sandip's family had immigrated to the United States when he was three and he barely remembered his homeland. His family's political connections, however, were very deep and knowing where to pull the strings in India meant everything. W.T. Frederick was a huge force in South Asia, where its hiring practices reflected the need to apply influence where doing so was very useful in securing prime opportunities to make money.

"Go ahead, and sit down, Jack." Cohen motioned.

Jack took a seat.

"I hear you're spending much of the year, now, in the Caribbean..." Sandip Gupta said to Dunlop, to make conversation.

The other man nodded, but otherwise ignored the little Indian man. Instead, he pointed to a blonde at the raw bar.

"You see her?" he announced to the others. "I'm gonna fuck her tonight. Watch and learn..."

He got up, suddenly, and pranced over to the bar, swaggering half out of bluster, and half out of drunkenness. He tapped her on the shoulder and whispered something in her ear. For a moment, the results were unclear. Then, suddenly, she turned away and left the bar, leaving him standing, abandoned. He lingered, for a short time, before making his way back to the table of young men. He sat down again, with a dejected look on his face.

Jack laughed innocently.

"I guess that didn't work out too well..." he noted with a smile.

"Fuck you!" Dunlop exclaimed angrily without smiling. "You know who I am?"

"I think so." Jack replied. "Marc Dunlop, as I recall."

"That's right. I'm a Dunlop." the man boasted. "My father's Christopher Dunlop, the CEO of W.T. Frederick!"

Jack didn't know exactly how to respond. He didn't particularly care if his father was President of the United States. The man was drunk, and had an unfriendly tone in his voice. Then, suddenly, Dunlop stood up smiling, and held out his pint of beer in an outstretched hand, ready to make a toast.

"Funny, isn't it?" Dunlop stated. "Here you are, a nobody, and here I am, a somebody, and for some strange reason, you don't know who I am, but I know exactly who you are! Something not entirely right about that."

"And, exactly, who do you think I am?" Jack asked, quietly.

"You're the man who's been banging Laura Stoneham for her money." Dunlop exclaimed, as loudly as possible. "You knocked her up, got her pregnant, and married into her fortune. Everybody knows that!

For a moment, Jack struggled to restrain himself. How did this drunkard even know Laura?

"Ha!" Dunlop growled, in a sharp laugh. "I heard she's gotten fat. That's the price you pay for all that money."

"Who the hell do you think you are?" Jack exclaimed, standing up.

"I'm a somebody talking to a nobody!" Dunlop retorted, laughing. "Everyone can see that... right, guys?"

Dunlop turned around and gestured to everyone at the table. Then, he turned directly toward Jack, and glared at him. He suddenly broke down laughing, and turned away again.

He turned back, a moment later, his finger pointed at Jack, laughing.

"Can you believe this idiot doesn't even know who I am?!" he exclaimed loudly. "Everyone in this bar knows who I am!"

"Mark..." Sandip caught a piece of Dunlop's clothing, and tried to pull him gently into his seat. "Sit down... man..."

But, Dunlop pulled violently away.

"Hey, I saw the reaction of that girl you walked up to." Jack noted wryly. "They may know you, but they certainly don't like you..."

"You think you're special, don't you?" Dunlop continued, addressing Jack again. "But, you're not. You're Mr. Nobody. But, I think it's great that Nobody is fucking the boss' daughter! You got your job by fucking her, isn't that right?"

He offered a mock salute with his right hand, and then offered the hand to Jack, palm out.

"Gimme five, Jack!" said Dunlop, continuing to laugh.

Jack's anger was visible on his face. He was already embarrassed about the nepotism that had got him his job, but to be taunted about it by a man like this made it worse. He felt like punching him in the face. His increasingly visible anger didn't slow Dunlop down one bit. The man seemed encouraged by it.

"Sometimes, I miss that wet cunt, you know," he said, "but she always liked sissies…"

Jack's hand was balled into a fist and his friend, Cohen, noticed it immediately. He turned to him, shook his head, and held up his hand as a "stop" signal.

Cohen whispered in his ear.

"Just ignore him…"

"I heard that, you dirty Jew!" Dunlop continued, now addressing his venom toward Cohen. "That Stoneham chick was once the most fuckable piece of ass in all of New York. She liked sucking me, Jack… that was her favorite thing, and she was great at it!"

He moved his hips in a manner than inferred sex.

"Oh, yeah…" Dunlop exclaimed, "I miss how she used to scream. She's such a screamer. I remember…"

Despite the difficulty in suppressing his anger, Jack responded coldly, and without emotion.

"You're drunk, and oddly, that's the reason you're still standing." he said quietly, though his face was livid.

"You hear that, folks?" Dunlop exclaimed. "He's threatening me… Me! But, this weakling is going to let it pass!"

"Asshole!" Jack exclaimed.

"Ooh, hoo, hoo…" Dunlop continued, chuckling like a madman. "There you have it. He's angry… true love! Ha! That's what I thought, too, when I was fucking her…"

He made another thrusting motion with his hips.

"We both love the same girl, Jack!" he continued. "Love the fat ass, the fat tits. Hmm…"

Jack was out of his seat, but Cohen grabbed him. He pulled him back, pointing as subtly as he could, whispering.

112

"Those two men at the tables, over there, are his bodyguards."

Jack glanced in the indicated direction, and noticed two large muscle bound men drinking beer. Neither was paying attention, however.

"If you lay a hand on him, they'll be all over you." Cohen cautioned.

Jack noted their huge size. They might be too big to easily deal with, but he soon forgot about that, as Dunlop caught his attention, again. The man made a face and then he pointed to a busty redheaded waitress. As the girl passed, he grabbed her, draping his arm around her shoulder. Then, he drew her close.

"Tell him who I am." he said to the girl.

"You're Marc Dunlop, of course." she replied.

"And, what does that mean?" he asked.

"You're the richest guy around?" she asked.

"Right!" he exclaimed, as he slipped two $100 bills down her blouse. "She loves me... don't you, honey."

The waitress smiled, and continued walking, as he held onto her for a moment. Then, she stopped, laughed and smiled.

"Sure, Sweetie!" she said.

"How much do you love me?" Dunlop asked her, just before she was out of range. "You want to come home with me, tonight?"

"You got some thousand dollar bills in that wallet?" she joked, and freed herself from the last touch of his hand, while reaching into her shirt to rescue the two $100 bills already parked there. She slipped them into her pocket, and continued walking to the kitchen with her order book.

"You see..." Dunlop pointed out. "Everything is for sale. You buy, you sell, love is no different. Understand?"

Dunlop staggered back, and almost fell backward over his chair. When he caught himself, he spoke again.

"Sit down, Mark!" Cohen said.

"Fuck you, Jew boy!" Dunlop addressed Cohen.

Then, he pointed to Jack.

"This is your boy-toy, isn't it? You're swinging both ways, now?"

"Mark, sit down, please." Sandip urged.

But, he wouldn't sit.

"Her Daddy gave you a job after you knocked her up, didn't he?" he declared, now speaking in Jack's direction.

There was no response. He nodded.

"That's what I thought..."

"Dunlop, sit down!" Cohen said.

"Jew boy..." Dunlop dismissed him. "I'm busy dissing your lover!"

"The company, I think, is getting old." Cohen said, still holding onto Jack's arm, and pulling him away from the table. "Let me buy you a beer."

As soon as Jack's back was turned, Dunlop lunged forward and tried to punch him hard, directly on his upper vertebrae. Because he was drunk, however, the blow connected with the back of Jack's shoulder. It was hard enough to cause pain, but not enough to do any real damage, other than cause the area to eventually turn black and blue.

Instinctively, Jack swung around. As Dunlop attempted to hit him a second time, he blocked the man's arm with a sideways movement of his hand. It was easy to block the blows of a drunken man. Dunlop lunged forward again, trying to hit him, but each time, his blows were easily parried. Finally, frustrated, he leapt forward with all the force he could muster, and tried an outright tackle with all his weight.

The movement registered in the back of Jack's mind. Instinctually, he pivoted to the right, in a move rehearsed repeatedly in kata practice. With his hips as the fulcrum, he redirected Dunlop's momentum forward and beyond him. The man's mass sped forward, and translated into a spin through the air, sending him flying onto the floor beyond. He fell hard on his side, the wind knocked out of him, and he was senseless on the floor.

That's when the two muscle-bound men noticed something amiss. They arrived almost immediately. One of them tried to grab Jack but he evaded the grasp. Then, the other one, larger, fully 6 foot 5 inches tall, muscled like a body builder, came up from behind, and tried to put him into a full Nelson. Jack slipped out of that. As the bigger man tried to catch hold of him, he dropped to the floor, and then, suddenly, the man's forward leg was kicked out from under him. The huge body went tumbling to the ground like a falling skyscraper.

The smaller bodyguard, who was actually only a smidgen smaller, was on top of Jack in the next moment. But, he found himself the victim of a similar fate. He flew in the air and landed down hard on the floor next to Dunlop. Unlike his ward, however, the bodyguard wasn't drunk, and he was also much stronger, both because of his size, and because, pound for pound, he was build of whalebone and muscle. He got laboriously to his feet, and got ready to try again. Jack was in a defensive stance, ready and waiting for the next move.

The two huge men were more careful the second time, and approached as a unit ready to become far more ruthless. The smaller one had already parted his jacket, and reached toward a waistband holster that held a revolver. That was when the little Indian man intervened.

"Wait!" he screamed, and courageously stepped between Jack and the bodyguard grabbing for the gun. "Enough!"

He seemed to have authority. The two huge men hesitated. Another set of large men, club bouncers, almost as big as Dunlop's two bodyguards, were also heading toward the commotion. The two bodyguards were supposed to prevent incidents like this one, and they knew they would already face trouble with the boss for having failed to do so. The easiest thing was to listen to what the little Indian had to say.

"What did he do to Marc?" the slightly smaller bodyguard finally demanded.

Their charge was still lying, senseless, on the floor.

"Can't you see he's drunk?" the little Indian explained. "They were talking and Marc wanted to say something. When he tried to reach this man, he tripped, fell and hit his head. That's all there is to it."

"That's not what I saw..." the bigger bodyguard said.

The two muscle-bound men looked at each other, confused as what to do. Notably, however, the smaller bodyguard's hands moved away from his waistband holster, and his jacket had fallen back into place, hiding the concealed weapon again.

The little Indian's words seemed to grow more authoritative, in the minds of the bodyguards, regardless of the fact that they might know what he was saying wasn't true.

"Don't worry," the little Indian said, "I will tell his father exactly how this happened, you know, how you did everything you could to protect him. Understand?"

By now, the two bar bouncers had arrived.

"What's going on?" the lead bouncer demanded, wary themselves about dealing with men bigger than they were.

"It's just a little misunderstanding." Cohen explained, and pointed to Dunlop lying on the floor. "Our friend got himself drunk, tripped and fell. And, these nice men will take him home."

Then, he turned to the little Indian.

"Isn't that right." he asked.

"Exactly so." Sandip Gupta replied.

The two sets of huge muscle bound men eyed each other with suspicion. Gupta turned to the bodyguards.

"All right, boys, let's take him home…" the little Indian said.

The bodyguards grunted their agreement. The smaller one walked over to where Mark Dunlop lay, and picked him up like a rag doll, draping him across the shoulder, and walking toward the door.

Meanwhile, Cohen slipped a $100 bill to each of the bar bouncers.

"Let's forget about all this unpleasantness…" he said, quietly.

The two bouncers smiled and nodded, while slipping the cash quickly into their pockets.

"Anything you say, Mr. Cohen." one of them exclaimed. "You're the man."

The other one nodded.

Meanwhile, the two bodyguards carried the now semi-conscious Dunlop. It was an odd sight. Two huge men, one holding what looked like a little rag doll on his shoulder, walked together to the door, accompanied by one scrawny little Indian man. The odd group made its way out and disappeared.

Jack turned to Cohen.

"I owe you some money, I think." he said, digging into his pocket to take out his wallet.

Cohen dismissed the idea with a wave of his hand.

"Buy me a beer." Cohen stated. "Better yet, I'll buy you a beer. It was my fault that all this happened."

Without waiting for the answer, he pulled Jack toward the bar.

"I didn't intend to throw Dunlop that hard..." Jack explained apologetically, when they reached it.

"Did you intend to throw the bodyguard that hard?"

"I intended to throw him harder, but he didn't cooperate."

"To be honest, I've never seen anything like it!" Cohen exclaimed.

"Instincts die hard, I guess." Jack replied.

"What instincts? Who has instincts like that? It was like watching a fucking Bruce Lee movie. What kind of Kung Fu shit was that?

Jack laughed.

"Karate, Jujitsu, and a little Judo mixed in."

"You think you could have beaten those two bodyguards, in spite of their size?"

"One of them was slow, but I'm glad I didn't have to find out."

"You've got to teach me some of that shit, OK?"

"It takes a lot of time." Jack explained.

"I don't care how long it takes. I need to learn that shit. But, now, it's drinking time!"

He sat down at the bar, and Jack sat down next to him.

"You know, Dunlop's been a total asshole since I met him, in one way or another." Cohen stated.

"Why were you hanging out with him?" Jack asked.

"Connections, my friend. I met him through Sandip, who went to law school with me. The guy is an asshole, I guess, but he's the son of W.T. Fredericks's CEO. This means he's rich as hell. It doesn't hurt to know rich people. And, when he's in a good mood, he buys drinks for everyone..."

"He called you a Jew boy..."

"Oh, I don't care about that." Cohen replied.

"I thought you said your long term plan was moving to the other side to sue these bastards?"

"Yeah, but it doesn't hurt to keep your options open. You never know what the future holds..."

"You said Dunlop works for Bolton?"

"He does. You know about the Dunlops, don't you?"

"Not really." Jack admitted.

"His family owns W.T. Fredericks. It's one of the richest families in the world."

"Why doesn't he work for Fredericks, then?" Jack asked.

"I don't know. Some of the sons and daughters of the biggest big shots make the rounds at all the banks."

"That first blonde girl didn't seem impressed."

"She's got a football player boyfriend and only goes for athletes." Cohen noted. "But, she's the exception, not the rule. That's probably why he got so upset. He's not used to rejection. He was born with a silver spoon in his mouth, and most girls want silver spoons of their own. He usually gets his way."

"Did he really date Laura?" Jack asked.

"Beats me. What beer do you want? Dark, light? I'm a Guinness man, myself."

"I don't drink alcohol." Jack replied.

"Are you kidding me? It's happy hour. Half-priced drinks!"

"A 7-Up, maybe."

"What are you a Mormon or something? It's Thursday night. I'll buy you a beer. It'll help you relax.

"7-Up relaxes me fine..." Jack countered, smiling.

Cohen laughed.

"You're a strange guy." he said, as he finally ordered a Guinness dark beer and a 7-Up.

A moment later, the barmaid gave them the drinks. Cohen held up his mug, and made a toast.

"To you, me, and getting richer than a Dunlop!"

Jack laughed, and took a sip from his 7-Up.

"Money isn't everything."

"The hell it isn't." Cohen insisted. "You're living in the center of a money empire, didn't you know that? All money roads lead to New York."

Cohen downed his Guinness in two long droughts. Jack worked on his 7-Up. Cohen ordered another beer.

"Come on! You can't drink 7-Up all night..."

Jack's 7-Up glass was only half-empty and it was a near certainty he intended to do exactly that. Meanwhile, his friend drank beer after beer.

Half-way into the third beer, they met a group of traders from the derivatives desk at W.T. Fredericks. Unlike Bolton Sayres, the other bank had all the trappings of a real bank. It had savings, lending, and credit card divisions. However, as with Bolton and the other members of the Synod, its most profitable business was selling various types of derivatives. That included interest rate swaps, futures, forwards, options, credit default swaps, and synthetic emulations of stock and bonds.

The Synod owns the market for derivatives. The syndicate makes it almost impossible for non-member banks to compete. But, the agreements that created the cartel decades ago had turned markets into a huge casino. Customers could legally place bets on almost anything, including pork bellies, iron ore, oil, gold, silver, interest rates, the tea in China, and even the weather! Weather futures contracts are listed on the biggest registered futures exchange, CME, Inc.

Control over the US Treasury, Federal Reserve, European Central Bank, Bank of England and other central banks is used to maintain tight control over such derivatives, especially of interest rates derivatives, which has always been the biggest business of all. This control allows the Synod to make certain that the "house" always wins, just as in casinos that are more traditional. The only difference is that a few wild individuals can disrupt the carefully orchestrated fix, which is something that is more difficult to do at a traditional casino.

The derivatives traders at the Odysseus Club that night were a wild bunch, a group of young people who drank heavily and partied hard. Many young adults, in and out of the financial world, foolishly pride themselves on such abilities. The inevitable drinking challenge came as the W.T. Fredericks contingent partied like there was no tomorrow. Timothy Cohen was a lawyer, and in Jack's mind that meant he ought to have known better, but he was actually just as dedicated to drinking contests as the derivatives traders.

It didn't matter to any that the next day was a workday. The crowd of over 30 people had to be entertained. The drinking contest began with 6 participants but, soon, only three serious drinkers were left, Timothy Cohen among them. The crowd consisted of lower level W.T. Frederick bankers who were good-natured in the sense they were as ready to cheer for a Bolton Sayres lawyer as for one of their own. One more shot of alcohol caused another contestant to topple from his chair. That left two, Timothy Cohen and a corpulent W.T. Fredericks banker.

The man's massive rolls of fat provided ample storage tanks. It was hard to imagine that the relatively lean Timothy Cohen could successfully compete with him. But, Cohen stayed the course, and refused to throw in the towel.

"Drink, drink, drink, drink..." the crowd urged, as two more shots of whiskey appeared in front of them.

Jack glanced at his watch. It was 11 P.M..

It was a crazy thing, but even Jack had become somewhat caught up in the festival-like atmosphere. Unlike the others, he was not drunk, and would have been happy to go home to his wife and baby girl. His friend, however, refused to leave until the contest was over. As long as Cohen went on competing, Jack was duty-bound to stay. He couldn't leave until the contest was over.

Cohen had downed 5 mugs of beer before the contest began and Jack lost count of the number of whiskey shots consumed since then. Then, there was a mutual time-out to allow the two men to stagger to and from the toilet, after which the contest began again. Cohen looked at Jack with bloodshot eyes, hand over his stomach, as he walked of the bathroom, but he refused to quit.

The horde of 20 and 30 somethings hooted and hollered like children at a ball game. Jack wondered about the spectacle. How could banks, especially venerable ones like W.T. Fredericks, entrust investor money to such people? The screaming crowd of derivatives traders had authority over $78 trillion in gross derivatives, and could potentially destroy tens of billions of dollars worth of shareholder value in seconds. Only the Synod's control over the central banks prevented such disasters.

He'd once read about an incident in London, on June 30, 2009, when an oil trader bought 7,000,000 barrels of oil, worth well over $500 million dollars, after becoming drunk. Those buys had driven the price of Brent Crude upward by more than $1.50 a barrel for no obvious reason. Finally, prices took a tumble. The man lost hundreds of millions for shareholders. But, what Jack didn't know was that the bank that lost that money was not a member of the Synod. It was simply another card player, at a rigged table.

That is not to say that the Synod's card dealers could not also make huge errors as a result of inexperience or simple mistakes. Despite the good-natured cheers, these W.T. Fredericks employees were the same spoiled brats who had imploded the world economy in 2008. They were mostly the sons, daughters, nephews and nieces of managing directors and other officials at the banks. Jack watched them, and it occurred to him they were sure to do it again. Unlike the non-member bank, nearly driven out of business by oil market losses, the Synod banks were saved from their mistakes by the world's central banks, at the expense of careful savers across the world.

"I'm winning!" Cohen insisted, barely able to keep his words from slurring into one another.

Jack came close and whispered,

"This is stupid. Let's go home."

Then, he took hold of Cohen's arm, and tried to draw him out of the chair, but it was impossible. The man would not budge.

"I'm winning!" Cohen insisted, again.

The crowd chanted again.

"Drink! Drink! Drink!" they chanted.

Another set of shot glasses, filled with whiskey, appeared on the table, one for Cohen and another for the fat derivatives trader. Both men sucked them down in one swig.

"Drink! Drink! Drink!" the crowd continued to chant.

Neither man wanted to disappoint the audience or lose the game. So, the game continued. More shot glasses appeared. They drank and drank, then drank more. Finally, the W.T. Frederick trader was swaying in his chair, and he looked as if he was about to topple. Lucky for him, however, Cohen fell first. Jack was near enough to catch his friend, but he still hit his head lightly against a hard tile sill that projected from the wall on the right hand side of the table.

Jack held onto him and pulled him upright by his elbows. Finally, he was in a sitting position on the floor. There was a loud cheer, as the

W.T. Fredericks traders lifted Cohen's fat competitor into the air. They chanted.

"Gimme an M! Gimme an A! Gimme an R! Gimme a T! Gimme an I, Gimme an N!" they screamed at the top of their lungs, in a manner reminiscent of a football game. "What does it spell? Mar-tin, Mar-tin, Mar-tin, Mar-tin..."

The young men carried their dubious hero across the barroom, in something akin to a Conga line, until they arrived at the Men's toilet, where he threw up, just outside the door. Two men carried him in. They'd done things like this many times before.

Back at the table, Jack was on the floor with Timothy Cohen.

"I think I'm gonna be sick." Cohen stated.

A moment later, he threw up too.

Jack walked him to the bathroom, where they took their position, at the toilet next to the one being used by Cohen's onetime nemesis, the fat derivatives salesman. Before being finished, each man vomited up a good part of what he had drank that night, and any food eaten, came up with it.

It was well past midnight, by the time Jack got Cohen into a cab. He virtually carried him into his midtown Manhattan apartment. Thankfully, the place was within easy walking distance of his flat. His friend had continued to have periodic convulsions of the stomach throughout the trip home. It was so bad that the cabdriver demanded extra compensation for having to clean up the backseat.

The building had no elevator, which meant he had to carry him up the stairway, all the way to the third floor. Once in his apartment, Cohen wanted to drink water, and after that, the vomiting continued, but there was nothing but water left to throw up. Did he belong in a hospital?

The one-room efficiency was tiny, only 15×12 feet. It had a pull down Murphy bed on one end, and a sofa along the length of its side. Jack pulled down the bed, and maneuvered his friend onto it. Then, he draped a blanket over him, and walked toward the door.

"Need to sleep this off..." Cohen mumbled, half conscious.

Jack got to the door, and opened it, as he exited.

"Jack..." Cohen mumbled.

"Yeah?" Jack responded.

"Thanks."

He said nothing more, for he was asleep, and after a moment of hesitation, Jack closed the door and left, locking it from the inside. He'd put in a call to Laura, earlier that evening, telling her about the situation. However, he was sure there would still be hell to pay for coming home so late. When he finally arrived, it was well after 2 O'clock in the morning. He would have suffered an intense screaming session, if not for the fact that the baby was asleep. That saved him.

IX - THE FUNDRAISER

The old Hotel St. Moritz, at 50 Central Park South, reopened in 2002, with a new name, the "Ritz-Carlton Central Park Hotel." Aside from the glamour of the old hotel, its location made it a favorite. It has a beautiful view of the park, and isn't too far from Fifth Avenue, Broadway, and Rockefeller Center. Most important, it is within easy walking distance of the Stoneham's penthouse.

It was Friday, April 19, 2013, and the hotel was playing host to the Bolton Sayres' annual gala, known as the "Bolton Benefit for the Arts Dinner." Most things about the gala were going well but, unfortunately, the weather was not being cooperative. Rain was pouring down so violently that it seemed as if God had opened a faucet in the heavens. The attendees, dressed in fine tuxedos and elegant evening dresses, avoided a drenching only because they arrived in taxis and limousines.

Jack also arrived by taxi, right after work, and he waited for his wife just outside the front door. Thankfully, he shielded from the rain by the canopy that covered the drop-off driveway. When Laura finally arrived in her taxi he greeted her, and then they walked in together. Neither of them liked such affairs. They weren't there for the fun of it. She had come to support her mom who, as usual every year, was in charge of the event.

Various NY society women stood around in circles. Big events like this one gave them an extended opportunity to do what they did best – gossiping. Rumor and innuendo fly whenever large numbers of women congregate, and this was no exception. It was flying fast. Little cliques had formed, here, there and everywhere. These were the conduits for the gossip. The truth didn't matter. As each story grew more spectacular with time, more people were around to embellish and pass it along.

Some servers scurried about, carrying delicate glasses, with a choice of champagne, white and red wines. Others carried plates filled with tasty treats, like hot steaming plates of miniature egg rolls, franks in blankets, salmon tarts, and mini-Coney Island knishes. These appetizers, Jack had decided long ago, were the only thing that made such social functions bearable.

"Oh, Jack, look!" Laura exclaimed. "Your favorite!"

She reached over to the passing waiter, who stopped to allow her to take what she wanted. As she loaded up with egg rolls, which were actually her favorite, not Jack's, she transferred one or two to him. Then, a moment later, she gulped down the rest, almost as if inhaling them. He smiled politely. He'd discussed the weight issue with her too often. Now wasn't the time to repeat it. Besides, she ignored him anyway.

"I know it's gross," she admitted, finally, "but I'm hungry..."

How had she transformed from a slim beauty less than two years before, into a matronly chunk of a woman? He didn't know. He did know, however, that the trend was going in the wrong direction. She continued to grow wider. Her face was still pretty, if a big bloated, but her body was beginning to resemble the ogre's wife in the Disney cartoon Shrek. As always, of course, she was entirely oblivious to his feelings. Sometimes, he wondered whether she cared at all.

She excitedly pointed toward a middle-aged balding man and his wife. Leon and Anna Sikovsky had immigrated to New York City in 1986 from the old Soviet Union. They had come to America in their late 20s during a visit of the Moscow Ballet and defected. Both were now successful dance choreographers on Broadway. They'd never returned to their mother country, even after it threw off communism.

Leon was also now a successful musical director. Laura pulled at Jack's arm as she nudged him in the couple's direction. When they arrived, she gave Anna Sikovsky a quick kiss on the cheek, and did the same to Leon, gesturing toward Jack.

"This is my husband, Jack!" she exclaimed, proudly. Then, she turned to Jack. "Mr. Sikovsky choreographed our musical..."

Jack knew she was talking about the musical play in which she had been cast as the lead, just before they had married.

"Dis is da boy I hear so much about, eh?" Sikovsky said.

His strong Russian accent was impossible to mistake for anything else.

He stretched out his hand.

"It's a pleasure to meet you." Jack said, as they shook hands.

"Such a handsome boy..." Mrs. Sikovsky whispered to Laura.

The level of the whisper made every word clearly and intentionally audible.

"Ah," Leon said, "dis young lady, my little Laura, vill' someday be a star. I am sure of it."

Laura beamed.

"You're too kind, Mr. Sikovsky..." Laura responded, graciously.

Another waiter passed by, and Jack helped himself to a glass of pink champagne. Then, he felt a heavy arm wrap strongly around his shoulders from behind. He glanced around. It was her father, Jeremy Stoneham. He gave his daughter a kiss on the cheek.

"Daddy!" Laura exclaimed, giving him a big hug. "I thought you were still in DC?"

"I was." he confirmed. "But, that ordeal is over."

Stoneham shook hands with Leon Sikovsky.

"Mr. Stoneham," Jack said, "I'm glad you're back."

Stoneham smiled.

"So, am I..." he said.

"How did it go?" Jack asked.

"It went well... very well, indeed." Stoneham noted. "We accomplished everything we set out to."

"That's great!" Jack said. "Now, if you've got a minute, I'd still like to talk to you about what we started to discuss just before you left..."

Stoneham shook his head, and waved a flattened hand in the negative.

"This is not the time, Jack..." he insisted.

"When is the time?"

Stoneham ignored the question. He turned to the Sikovskys, instead.

"You two are looking fabulous!" he noted. "Thanks so much for coming."

"I should tank' you." Sikovsky said, sincerely. "For all you've done in support of da' arts."

"We all do what we can." Stoneham noted, pleased with the remark.

As several new people approached, Stoneham shook more hands, and he put his arm around Jack's shoulder, again, nudging him forward. The opportunity presented by the new arrivals allowed them to politely separate from the Sikovskys.

"There are a few key people I want you to meet..." he said to Jack.

Laura had also disentangled herself from the conversation and followed a few feet behind. They were interrupted mid-stride, by a man who suddenly arrived from the left, to shake his father-in-law's hand.

The new arrival was old, with deep wrinkles and age spots scattered across his face. Most of his hair was long gone, but what little remained was gray, and covered only the edges on the sides and back. Despite his aged appearance, the man's eyes were bright, and there was no sign that his wits had slowed.

Stoneham greeted him warmly.

"Admiral Stark!" he exclaimed. "What a pleasure it is to see you again."

He motioned toward Jack.

"This is my son-in-law, the young man I was telling you about."

Newly introduced, Jack shook the old man's hand, and then the old man noticed Laura.

"Ah!" he exclaimed, smiling. "Little Laura. As pretty as ever..."

She smiled and nodded with a little embarrassment from the enthusiastic compliment. Just then, another young woman suddenly tapped her on the shoulder, and gained her attention. She turned to find out whom it was, and her eyes lit up.

Patricia Aubry was an old and dear friend from boarding school. It had been a long time since they'd seen each other. The two young women embraced, kissed, and began to chat, ignoring the three men, and leaving them in a semi-private conversation.

"Jeremy," Admiral Stark said, "I want to thank you personally, for bringing Clyde Gibbons into the loop. His middle eastern experience has been helpful, given the threats we're facing..."

Stoneham beamed, and then turned to Jack.

"Admiral Stark is Chairman of the President's Commission on Homeland Security..."

The Admiral was retired, but still politically active. The old man turned toward Jack, and lowered his voice, as if he were telling a big secret.

"Your father-in-law is a lot more important to national security than I am..."

"That's not true..." Stoneham stated, smiling with pleasure at the compliment.

"It is true." the Admiral insisted. "All the stakeholders know it. The streets are safe from terrorism, in large part, thanks to Bolton Sayres and the other banks."

Jack didn't know exactly how to respond to that.

"I don't know what to say." he admitted, finally.

Admiral Stark turned toward Stoneham.

"You haven't told him yet, have you?"

"No." Stoneham answered.

"Don't you think he ought to know?"

"I suppose he ought to." Stoneham conceded. "You do want to be in the loop, don't you, Jack?

"Well, yeah, of course." he admitted.

"Good." Stoneham responded. "But, everything we're about to discuss is confidential. Understand?"

"Jack, your company plays a much more important role in national security than you probably realize." Admiral Stark added.

What they were saying made no sense, but Jack didn't belabor the point.

"I'm happy to listen." he said, finally.

"I'll need more than that." Stoneham insisted. "I need a solemn pledge to keep everything in complete confidence. Is that agreed?"

Jack didn't like to give such pledges, because he was one of the few who tended to keep them. His curiosity, however, had grown very strong, and it was increasing by the minute. He felt compelled to agree. Otherwise, it would be impossible to resolve the mystery.

"Of course." he replied. "I would never risk national security. You know that."

"I know that." Stoneham agreed. "Still, I need your word of honor. No matter what your view is you must keep your word, and make sure everything we are about to discuss is strictly confidential. Do I have your word?"

"Yes, of course." he agreed.

Stoneham then nodded toward the Admiral.

"Let's find a place more discrete..."

Stoneham turned toward his daughter. She continued to engage in active conversation with her long lost friend. No attention had been paid to anything they'd said.

"We've got company business to discuss." Stoneham explained to her quickly. "We'll be back in about twenty minutes."

She smiled and nodded but, otherwise, didn't seem to acknowledge what he was saying. Instead, she continued the animated discussion with her old friend, ignoring the men for the most part.

The three men walked toward the exit door and out of the main ballroom into a long hallway, until they stopped at a particular door. Stoneham opened a door that unveiled a large conference room. They checked the room carefully.

"It's still safe, I'd say." Admiral Stark concluded, finally, and shut the door behind them.

Jack was not so sure. It seemed strange to discuss something sensitive enough to have him sworn to secrecy, in a publicly accessible conference room. However, the two other men seemed at ease with the surroundings and it was, after all, their secret.

"It's OK." Stoneham agreed, expecting Jack's question. "The moment that door closes, this room is soundproof. We sweep it for bugs regularly."

"You do?" Jack asked.

"Of course," Admiral Stark added. "it was swept for bugs just a few minutes ago."

The meeting with Admiral Stark, in the middle of the gala, had seemed like a surprise. However, if they had just had a room swept for listening devices, then both the meeting and the decision to reveal whatever they were about to reveal, was not happening due to a chance meeting or a decision made on the spur of the moment. It was carefully planned.

Admiral Stark lowered his voice, but didn't whisper.

"It's simple..." he began, and explained, in about 15 minutes, the broad picture of THEATRES. After he had finished, Jack was speechless.

"Not exactly what you expected?" Stoneham asked.

Words were scarce, but they formed on Jack's lips.

"It's... Orwellian." he exclaimed. "You're watching everybody, 24 hours a day, 7 days a week... everybody, everyday?"

The Admiral nodded with some pride.

"Not everywhere, not inside people's houses, not without a court order, but, generally, yes..."

Jack shook his head, in disbelief. He was shocked to the core.

"We have no choice." Stoneham said. "If not for this surveillance, New York City would be a radioactive waste by now.

"Incidentally, just to correct what may be a misunderstanding..." the Admiral was keen to add. "We are not watching. We're simply logging it all."

"What's the difference?" he asked.

"The difference is huge." the Admiral continued. "The word 'watching" implies that some human being is spying on another human being. Our system uses digital scanning. No human being ever sees any identifying information unless the computer detects a serious threat."

"Big brother is still watching." Jack pointed out. "And, that's the bottom line."

"It's a give and take, you know." Stoneham noted. "The trade is hard, but keeping America secure is a hard job."

"I don't think you've considered all the implications." Jack stated.

"Oh, we have, I assure you." Stoneham answered.

"I don't think so." Jack repeated.

"To set up the system," his father in law pointed out, "every document was signed and approved publicly. Getting the proper permits meant describing it all, in intimate detail, in public records. Potentially, all those archives are open to the public. But, there are so many other documents in there, so long as nobody points it out, nobody notices this."

"Does the mass media know?" Jack asked.

"Of course, they know." Stoneham replied.

"Isn't it supposed to be their job to point it out?"

"We have agreements…" Admiral Stark noted.

"What kind of agreements?" Jack wondered aloud.

"Oh, nothing formal." Stoneham explained. "It's just that the press isn't going to make waves, since they live here too."

"How can you silence every newspaper and news channel in the country?"

"Not just in this country…" Stoneham stated. "Ninety five percent of all the English speaking mass media is owned by just 5 major media companies. And, we own a lot of their shares. But, we don't try to silence them. They simply understand that this is for their benefit too."

"So, it's a conspiracy to keep it from the average citizen?" Jack pointed out. "You've created a spy system with tens of thousands of pinhead cameras, covering every inch of the City, and the press has agreed to cover it up!"

"Conspiracy is a harsh word." Stoneham commented. "It's just an agreement."

"That's what a conspiracy is!" Jack stated, "You've got it so no one can walk, talk, eat, drink or do anything else without being recorded, and the media is saying nothing in order to keep the issue away from public debate."

"Some bloggers have covered it." Stoneham said.

"Most people don't listen to bloggers." Jack replied.

"That's not the point." Stoneham said. "We're not hiding anything."

"Of course, you're hiding everything." Jack insisted. "If the public ever found out what you're doing, there would be a huge scandal."

"You're not getting it, son." Admiral Stark insisted.

Jack shook his head.

"What am I not getting?"

"We're at war." the Admiral explained.

"Congress is supposed to declare war, and to the best of my knowledge, that hasn't happened."

"We've got a Presidential decree." Stoneham pointed out.

"You talk about war," Jack said, "but what war? Is that the supposed war against terrorism or a war against the American people? Who programs the computers, by the way? Who stops the system from being deployed against the innocent? It could be used for blackmail. If someone disagrees with the powers-that-be, their lives can be destroyed."

"We're targeting terrorists." Admiral Stark noted. "Bad people. Not average Americans."

"Who decides what an average Americans is?" Jack asked. "It's a slippery slope."

"Any potential problems will work themselves out in time..." Admiral Stark said.

"It's also unconstitutional." Jack said, finally.

"That's where you're wrong." Stoneham replied. "The Constitution does protect against unlawful government searches. But, the government doesn't run this operation."

Jack shook his head in disbelief.

"Who does?"

"We do." Stoneham replied.

"You, personally?"

"No."

"Who, then?"

"The banks." Stoneham replied.

"Can't you see that makes it worse?" Jack said. "You've set up a privately controlled surveillance system, backed by US military technology and the full faith and credit of the United States' government. It's outrageous."

"It's been fully vetted in court and passed all the tests of constitutionality." Jeremy Stoneham pointed out. "We're talking about security. Without it, New York City would no longer exist."

"You can't prove that." Jack insisted.

"To prove it, the city would already have to be gone." Stoneham said. "So, thankfully, I don't have to. We're not in court, Jack. But, I know that what I say is true. Throw away your preconceived ideas. They come from a different day and age. Do you remember that girl you saved from being raped, when you were 16 years old?"

"How do you know about that?" Jack asked.

"I know about a lot of things." Stoneham replied. "You were 16 going on 17, but your age doesn't matter. The point is that the police were not there to help. They didn't even know what was happening. You saved that girl and her brother. What if you weren't there? What if the knife that gave you that big scar on your arm, had plunged into your heart instead? You could have been killed, you know…"

"It was a calculated risk." Jack replied.

"Whatever." Stoneham said. "But, that young girl and boy were lucky to have someone like you around to save them."

"I don't see how the one relates to the other." Jack stated.

"Simply this… THEATRES will insure that innocent girls who face evil rapists are no longer alone. Muggings will be relics of the past. Our computers can perceive and detect threats to innocent lives, and when they do, they can send out the police automatically, and immediately. It's a public good."

"There's the slippery slope…" Jack repeated. "Why not bug everybody's house? Then, cops could arrive automatically and immediately whenever people raise their voices. That might stop domestic violence. But, you'd also be stopping anyone from having a private life. It's not the kind of world I want to live in."

"Surveillance inside a residence or business requires approval by the court." Admiral Stark stated, with annoyance.

"What court approved all this, incidentally?" Jack asked.

"The National Security Court." Stoneham answered.

Jack shook his head again.

"There is no such court".

"There is," Admiral Stark said, "but appointments aren't made out in public view."

"Then, who appoints them?"

"The President, of course." Admiral Stark stated.

"Without the consent of Congress?" Jack asked.

"All the judges are already sitting on a Federal District Court or Appellate Court seat. They've already been approved by Congress, so it isn't necessary to do it again."

"If they're serving a different function, it is." Jack asked.

"That's a matter of interpretation." Stoneham insisted.

"So, you've got a secret court appointed by the President?"

"You could say that."

"Composed of hand-picked judges…"

"You expect us to simply wait for something worse than 9/11?" Admiral Stark asked.

"There are other ways." Jack said.

"There's no other way." Admiral Stark insisted.

"There is." Jack shot back. "You could register the people most likely to engage in terrorism. And, how about slowing down the immigration of Muslims?"

"Selected registration of Muslims?" Stoneham asked.

"Maybe…" Jack conceded.

"Unconstitutional." Stoneham replied.

"The Supreme Court ruled that Japanese internment during World War II was constitutional." Jack replied. "You could target nationalities, like Saudi, Moroccan and so on. I admit that registration and a national database would be unfair to some people. But, compared to this? It's a lot better than destroying everyone's liberty at the same time. If your expansion plan is approved, you'll end up destroying the privacy rights not only of the people of New York, but of everyone in America."

"What you're proposing would complicate relations with the Saudis, the Moroccans; whoever else is on the list." Admiral Stark pointed out.

"We've got valued customers in the middle east." Stoneham noted.

"This isn't about customers." Jack insisted. "It is about rights. Can't you see that anymore? You've created George Orwell's 1984."

"The Orwell book is about government surveillance." Admiral Stark insisted. "The banks run our system and they're private."

"Who paid for setting it up?" Jack asked.

"New York City contributed $150 million for construction of the operations center." Jeremy Stoneham explained. "That was matched by the Federal government. But, we pay rent on the facility, and it's a profit center for the City. We pay the salaries, utilities, maintenance, repairs, and so on."

Jack shook his head again.

"What's in it for the banks?"

"The chance to do our part…" Stoneham replied.

"It's gotta' be more than that, I'm sure." Jack replied.

"You don't get it, son." Admiral Stark blurted out. "It's about patriotism! And, so long as people keep their noses clean, they've got nothing to worry about."

"There is no such thing as a perfectly clean nose." Jack pointed out. "Everyone's done something they're not proud of."

"You don't catch bad guys playing 'footsie'." Admiral Stark noted.

"You've set up an unaccountable monster." Jack replied. "The people running it would have to be pure and incorruptible, in order to stop it from ending up as a nightmare. But, human beings are corruptible. It's in our nature. And, one particularly bad actor can destroy everything we hold dear."

"That's exactly why we need you." Stoneham stated.

"What?" Jack asked, confused.

"You!" Stoneham repeated. "I've spent hours thinking about this. It's the best way we can make use of your unique skill set and personality characteristics. I want you to run THEATRES."

"You're joking." Jack snapped.

"No joke." Stoneham insisted. "*We* want you to run THEATRES. The man who runs things now needs to retire. Many of us want him to go. As you say, someone incorruptible needs to be in charge."

Jack didn't have the words to respond.

"You're not perfect, of course, but I've never known anyone more incorruptible than you." Stoneham stated. "This system isn't going away, Jack, no matter what you think of it. But, if you run it, you could insure that what you fear never comes to pass."

"I, I don't know what to say..." Jack replied. "Except, maybe, that it's a system that ought to be closed down this very moment, not run by me."

"You don't need to make any commitment yet." Stoneham suggested. "And, when you do, the transition will be gradual. You'll come into the picture, one job at a time."

There was a pause for a moment, as Jack wasn't sure how to respond.

"We need someone we can trust." Admiral Stark added.

"Which is why, starting next week, I'm having you transferred from legal to compliance." Stoneham stated. "It'll be the beginning of your new job with the company. We'll move you, from job to job, until you learn everything you need to know, and, finally, insert you as a general assistant to the current director. Within a year, as smart as you are, you'll know enough to run the whole show."

"What happens to the current director?" Jack asked.

"He's old." Stoneham said. "Ready for retirement."

"Does he know that?" Jack questioned.

"What does it matter?" Stoneham replied.

"I still don't know what to say." Jack admitted.

"That's OK." Stoneham replied, pleased to see his son-in-law tempted by the opportunity. "It's a lot to chew on. I want you to think about all the concerns you've voiced. Remember, THEATRES isn't going away. Who better than you to make sure it will never be used for evil purposes?"

The concept of invasive surveillance was objectionable. How could he possibly accept a job running it? He felt like telling the world. The public had a right to know. However, his word was his bond. He could not break it. But, perhaps, he didn't have to choose between doing the right thing and keeping his word. Suppose, he accepted the job? If he ran the show, power would never be abused...

"I would have to study this before deciding." Jack finally said.

"We'll provide you with all the detail you need." Stoneham replied enthusiastically. "I'll have an overview on your desk by tomorrow morning."

"Your country needs you..." Admiral Stark added.

Jack nodded, but he said nothing more.

He had responded exactly as his father-in-law expected. He was not expected to agree right away. However, putting him in charge of THEATRES accomplished two of the older man's goals. First, it neutralized Adriano Navarro. Second, his daughter would be married to an important person in the Synod, even though he might never be a top notch banker.

The THEATRES' operating agreement conferred joint authority on four of the banking synod's American members. The members, however, might change, at a moment's notice, from being allies to being rivals. Whoever had control over the powerful spying system had a tremendous advantage. Every candidate had bias, because every person proposed by a CEO was sure to have some relationship with him. Critical, however, was that the individual was viewed as being his own man, regardless of his relationships. This opened the door to employing the most honest of men in the midst of the most dishonest of businesses.

Everyone who was anyone was watching Jack's progress, because of his marriage to Laura. Although he had exasperated his managers at Bolton Sayres, other banks in the cartel viewed him as an uncompromisingly honest young man, unfit for a high executive banking job. That might win votes in the Council when it came to choosing someone new to run the surveillance system.

Stoneham shook the Admiral's hand.

"It's been a pleasure." he said, well-pleased with how everything had gone.

"Same here." the Admiral replied, with a big smile.

The old man directed his attention to Jack.

"Young man, I like you..." he said. "You've got a bright future, and I know you'll serve your country well."

It was strange how the two old men talked. It was as if it was already a done deal. What would happen if he said no, as he was inclined to do? It was presumptuous for them to assume anything.

When the Admiral had gone on his way, Stoneham took Jack aside for a moment longer.

"Never express doubt about national security questions to men like Admiral Stark. Understand?"

Jack didn't, but he also didn't want to argue, and his mind was now filled with a myriad of thoughts and ideas arising out of the recent discussion. He just nodded. The two men returned to the main ballroom together. Upon entering, a man suddenly came between them, and Jeremy Stoneham's attention was distracted.

Jack spied Laura in the same place he had left her. She was still talking to her childhood friend. It was only a few paces more to get to her, walked over, and interrupted the seemingly endless conversation.

"Let's go home..." he whispered to her.

She shook her head.

"I've got to stay for my Mom's auction..."

He closed his eyes, for an instant, in frustration.

"All right. But, after that, I want to get out of here, okay?"

She nodded, and returned to speaking with her long-lost friend. Jack discovered some of his colleagues standing around in the distance. He walked over to speak with them, and while his back was turned, an unwanted visitor took his place.

Marc Dunlop was smiling like the Cheshire cat.

"You mind if I talk to Laura for a few minutes?" he asked politely.

"Of course not." the other girl said immediately, giggling.

She then turned to Laura, and pointed.

"My Mom's over there, and I need to talk to her anyway. But, you've got my new cell, so let's keep in touch…"

Laura nodded, and the girl walked off, leaving her alone with Dunlop.

"What do you want?" she demanded in a rough tone.

He shrugged his shoulders.

"Just want to say hello" he commented wryly. "Is that wrong?"

She said nothing in response. He paused a moment, then continued.

"You don't see what a loser Jack Severs is?" he blurted out suddenly.

"All I see is the jerk standing in front of me." she instantly replied.

"Face the facts, Laura." he insisted. "Leave the slums. We're both rich, so money isn't an issue, and I don't mind that you've gotten fat. I've always been in favor of open relationships anyway. You and I need to be together, if only from a dynastic point of view. Can't you understand that? Why do you keep fighting it?"

"I'm not fighting anything." She replied. "I've got a baby girl, and a husband, and you're just, well, nuts. Go away…"

"I'm willing to forgive you for saying that." he said.

"Go away." she repeated.

"Whatever caused you to go with that trailer trash, we'll work it out together." he suggested. "I don't mind the baby."

She turned toward him, furious.

"Jack flies as far above you as an eagle does above a snake."

That was about when Jack noticed. He was some distance away. He'd been distracted by the members of Bolton Sayres' legal team he was talking to. The noise in the room prevented him from hearing anything that Dunlop had said. However, he finally noticed the man's presence when he turned around, and saw Dunlop face to face with Laura. It annoyed him greatly.

He walked over immediately, and confronted the man.

"Get away from my wife!" he blurted out, on arrival.

Dunlop turned, looked at Jack, for a moment, then shook his head and laughed. Then, he turned back toward Laura, again.

"It's that he acts like a caveman, isn't it?" he noted. "That's what you like about him, right?"

Jack turned to Laura.

"Do you know this guy?" he asked.

"Unfortunately, yes." she replied.

"He's bothering you, then?" Jack noted.

"No." she said, shaking her head. "He's not bothering me. But, he's about to leave, aren't you, Mark?"

"Not really…" Dunlop replied.

Suddenly, Jeremy Stoneham scurried over.

"Ah, Mark!" he exclaimed, enthusiastically shaking Dunlop's hand. "Good to see you!"

He turned to Jack and pointed to the man.

"This is someone I've wanted to introduce you to for a long time." Stoneham said. "He's only turned 30 recently, and he's already one of our youngest managing partners!"

Jack glanced at Laura, and then at her father, but made no reply.

"He's one of the few analysts who always get it right regarding the direction of the market." Stoneham continued.

Stoneham turned to his daughter.

"Laura, have you officially introduced them?"

"No." she said.

"This is Marc Dunlop, Jack." Stoneham said.

Dunlop smiled and offered his hand. Jack chose not to take it.

"What exactly does managing partner mean?" Jack asked Stoneham.

"In the days when the firm was a partnership, it meant you had a share of the profits." Stoneham explained. "Now, of course, we're public, so it just means you've contributed exceptionally. You get voting rights on some things, and it affects your bonuses. This young man managed to generate close to a billion dollars of revenue for the firm, last year. Naturally, he's paid well."

"We already know each other." Jack stated.

"Marvelous!" Stoneham said, enthusiastically.

Apparently, the man had failed to notice that his son-in-law refused to shake the other man's hand. Paying no further attention to the two young men, he put his arm around his daughter and nudged her towards someone he wanted her to meet. As he was leaving he turned to the two men left behind.

"You fellas talk. Get to know each other better..." he said.

In a moment more, the two men were alone. There was silence for a moment.

"I don't hold any grudges." Dunlop said, finally.

That seemed conciliatory enough.

"I don't either." Jack replied, wanting to be equally generous. "You probably just had too much to drink."

"That's why you got away with it, you know..." Dunlop noted.

"Got away with what?" Jack asked.

"Attacking me." Dunlop replied.

"I didn't attack you." Jack insisted. "I defended myself, nothing more."

"The hell you didn't!" Dunlop insisted.

"You swung at me while my back was turned, and you hit me on the shoulder." Jack said.

"You've got a bad memory." Dunlop said. "But, as I said, no grudges. I rather admire you, actually."

"What?" Jack said, perplexed by the strange man.

Dunlop smiled.

"Well, here you are a poor boy; nothing to your name... plebeian you might say... not a penny in your pocket. You've done rather well for yourself. You knocked up a fancy girl, got her pregnant, and her Daddy gave you a job to save her reputation. Clever, clever boy..."

"You don't know shit!" Jack replied, carefully trying to control his growing anger. "And, you don't know anything about Laura, either."

"On the contrary, I know everything about Laura." Dunlop insisted. "I've known her a lot longer than you have. In fact, it's fair to say I know her inside and out. But, I wouldn't want to bang her now, not with all that extra weight."

"Go to hell!" Jack suggested.

The comment angered Dunlop.

"Do you know who you're talking to?" he asked.

"You told me about your daddy last time." Jack responded. "I'm not impressed. You're still an asshole, nothing more."

Dunlop false smile turned into a scowl.

"Look at you, getting all red in the face." Dunlop taunted him. "I think the cave man is planning to attack me again… right?"

"I NEVER attacked you." Jack insisted. "You fucking liar! YOU attacked me!"

"Excuses…" Dunlop stated. "They all have them, you know. It doesn't matter. Fact is, you positioned yourself well. You'll be taking a stab at that Stoneham money soon enough, I'm sure. Planning on knocking off the old man?"

"Laura and I got married for love and no other reason." Jack declared.

"Oh, yeah, love, that's right…" Dunlop said venomously. "Do you have any idea how much richer I am than you? What do you make? What? $100,000 a year? $150? $200 grand, max, I'd say. I can buy you and sell you!"

"You're an ass." Jack replied.

"I can still buy you and sell you." Dunlop stated.

"I can't be bought."

"Everyone can be bought." Dunlop replied.

"Wrong." Jack insisted.

"Bullshit!" Dunlop exclaimed.

Jack shook his head in disgust.

"Slime ball!"

"It's just price, fool." Dunlop continued to rave on.

Jack decided there was no point in continuing. The man was a raving maniac. He wasn't worth the time or effort. When he turned to walk away, however, Dunlop leaped forward and intercepted him.

"Don't get mad, Jack." Dunlop taunted. "I like you. I really do! You didn't have a pot to piss in, but you must have had a hell of a cock. Laura likes them big, you know. She liked mine, too..."

The man's taunts were finally getting to him. It was bad enough continuously questioning himself about getting his job through nepotism. Having his enemy point it out, repeatedly, made things worse. He wasn't sure what to do. He wanted to smack the man around, but that would be a mistake. Aside from causing a big scandal, and the possibility of being put in jail, Dunlop probably had his bodyguards waiting, somewhere in the vicinity.

Instead, Jack continued to walk away, but Dunlop had no intention of letting him go so easily. He trailed after and suddenly grabbed him.

"I'm not finished!" Dunlop exclaimed.

"I think you are..." Jack replied.

He stopped, turned, and pulled the man's hand away from him, twisting his wrist around into a painful but harmless wristlock.

A moment later, just prior to the moment that Dunlop would have had to fall, to escape both the pain and having his wrist broken outright, he released him.

"Fuck you!" Dunlop exclaimed, rubbing his wrist in pain. "I'm gonna' fuckin' have your ass kicked!"

Jack laughed.

"It would take another million losers like you". He declared. "And, I hope your two bodyguards are around to help you. Because, otherwise, next time you grab me, I going to break a few of your bones."

"Fuck you!" Dunlop exclaimed, but he did not grab again. "I'll fuckin' call them over if you touch me again."

"Do whatever you want." Jack said.

"You're a fucking thief!" Dunlop exclaimed. "You stole her. You fucking stole her!"

"You're mentally sick." Jack replied, now rather pleased.

He doubted that Dunlop could love anyone but himself. Laura was not the raving beauty she once was, but she belonged to him. With that thought, he walked away, and left the other man steaming.

"Watch your back, Jack!" Dunlop warned in an ominous tone, pleased with the rhyme. "It a dangerous world for you, from this moment on…"

Jack ignored him and continued walking. Soon he was too far away to hear the man's ravings. He found Laura on the other side of the ballroom, talking to someone new. When she saw him, she gestured for him to come closer. As he did that, he saw she was talking to an elderly man, who looked to be in his late 60s.

"This is Senator Collins…" she said, gesturing. "Senator, this is my husband, Jack…"

"It's an honor to meet you, Senator." Jack stated.

"Senator Collins is one of Daddy's oldest friends." Laura said.

"I've known little Laura since she was so high." the Senator noted, making a gesture with his hands inferring a tiny size. "She's all grown up now. You're a lucky young man."

"I know." Jack agreed.

The Senator turned away, and shook the hand of someone else, providing an opportunity for Jack to nudge Laura into a private conversation.

"How well do you know Mark Dunlop?" Jack asked.

Laura rolled her eyes.

"I just know him, OK?" she said.

"Did you ever date him?" Jack asked.

"For a few weeks." she admitted.

"Why?" Jack asked.

"Because our parents tried to push us together almost since we were born." she replied.

"Did you sleep with him?" he asked directly.

"What?" she asked surprised.

"Did you?" he asked, again.

"It was a long time ago…" she replied.

"Why did you stop dating him?" he asked.

"Because he's a pervert and an asshole." she replied.

"But, you slept with him, didn't you?" he concluded.

"I wouldn't have, if I had any choice." she insisted. "He forced himself. I was only 16."

"Why didn't you report it to the police?" Jack asked.

"Because… I don't know why… it would have caused a lot of trouble for my father."

Tears flowed down her cheeks, and he caught her as her legs almost gave way beneath her.

"Does your father know about it?" he asked.

She shook her head.

"Are you kidding me?" she said, finally. "And, he can never know, Jack. Don't you dare tell him!

"I just wanted to know, myself, that's all."

Her strength dissolved, even as his resolve and anger strengthened. Marc Dunlop was born rich and annoying. He was a nuisance and a jerk. Now, it was more than that. It was as personal as it could become. He hated the man; hated him with all his heart and soul. His thoughts had turned murderous. He felt a sudden desire to grab the man by the neck, and squeeze until dead. Would that be enough? No, it would be more gratifying to boil him in oil, or simply smash his head into a million pieces with a club.

"Take me home…" she said, finally.

He didn't ask her anything more. He had tortured her enough, and he knew that his own morbid thinking was unhealthy. The more she might tell him, the more upset she might become and the more murderous he would feel. There would be time to learn the rest of the story in a different environment. Her emotions and his were running too high. Leaving the gala was what any good psychiatrist would recommend. Several people intercepted them on the way out urging them to stay. That made it difficult to leave. But, after making the appropriate excuses, they left the hotel.

They caught a cab, and it brought them quickly to their nearby apartment. They took the elevator up, and walked down the carpeted hallway to their own door. Jack slipped the key in, and opened the door. Then, he flipped on the lights. The scene was shocking. The entire place was in shambles. The place was ransacked save only the walls.

Much of the damage seemed beyond repair.

X – RANSACKED!

There is nothing as sacred as a home. It is the place you turn to when everyplace else is uncertain. The safety of a home makes people feel secure. That's why psychologists say that only a small part of the pain, that a burglary brings to its victims relates to the robbery itself. The rest comes from the violation. Once burglarized, a home never feels like the sanctuary it once was. It never feels entirely like home again.

There was no evidence of forced entry. There was no evidence of any entry at all. Yet, someone clearly had entered. The results were obvious. The kitchen cabinet doors and drawers were wide open, and their contents spilled out all over the place. Pots, pans and cutlery lay there, some upright, others overturned, and a few dented. The cushions from the couch and the armchair were ripped wide-open, end-to-end, leaving bare foam open to view. All of the upholstery was in tatters. There was nothing spared.

Many cups and saucers lay smashed. Pieces of glass and ceramic shards littered the floor. Books were all over the place. Even Laura's collection of Ladro ceramic sculptures were now in pieces. The curio cabinet, where they'd been stored sat broken, on its side; its glass panes shattered. Jack motioned for Laura to stay put, outside the door, as he entered cautiously.

He glanced around with suspicion.

Thankfully, Isabel Laura's old nanny had been called in to babysit little Jennifer and they were both at the Stoneham's penthouse within a short walking distance, but far from the scene of the crime. No doubt, she was sleeping, playing and smiling, blissfully unaware of the angst afflicting her parents. The old woman would feed, bathing and play with her in a safe environment. Whatever had happened here, thankfully, was a world away from his daughter.

Could the robbers still be on the premises?

He headed first to the baby's room. The door to the room was ajar, and he carefully opened it all the way. Toys were no longer in the toy cabinet. They were scattered everywhere. Then again, the baby's toys often ended up scattered around, so that alone told no tale. The crib seemed untouched, but the rest of the room had not escaped from the damage. Pulled drawers were halfway out of the dressing table, their contents strewn on the floor.

There was something odd about the whole affair. The door was sealed when he entered, and its deadbolt had been locked. It made no sense for a burglar to lock the door after a robbery. He checked the windows, and they too were still securely bolted shut. No one could have entered through the windows or, if they did, they had managed to close them perfectly afterward.

As he exited the baby's room, Laura was still standing outside the entry door. He motioned to her again, giving the "OK so far" sign, but with hand signals, he urged her to stay outside. Then, as carefully as he could, he crept forward toward the master bedroom. If any burglar remained that's where he would be. His heart beat fast as he approached the door, and he hesitated for a moment.

Then, he grasped the doorknob quickly and plunged in, ready to dart for cover or confront whatever he might find. There was nothing to confront. There was only silence. The room was a repeat of the rest of the flat. It was a mess. Then, suddenly, he heard a sudden rustling sound. His eyes darted to the place from whence it came. The fluffy Persian cat jumped down from the windowsill. She was making the noise.

Oblivious to the destruction around her, the cat sidled up, purred and rubbed on his leg. She must have hidden during the burglary. Except for the cat, though, the bedroom was empty. The contents of the dresser drawers lay on the floor. Their clothes were also strewn about and the mattress had been sliced through the cover, revealing the springs and pads of foam inside.

Then, he felt someone suddenly touching his shoulder from behind, and it gave him a start. He swung around, ready to confront whatever was there. It was only his wife.

"I told you to stay outside." Jack chastised.

"What am I, a dog?" she asked.

Tears were smearing the mascara on her face, again, which she had fixed since he had questioned her about Marc Dunlop. She was afraid and upset; it was a stupid thing to chastise her. He turned and wrapped her in his arms, holding her in a soft embrace.

"I'm sorry," he said, "It's just that I'm on edge."

Tears continued to flow.

"We should never have rented in a building without guards." she insisted.

She had told him that, repeatedly, at various times in the past. Renting a simple flat, in an old brick building, with no door attendants or guards, was his idea, not hers. Rents in Manhattan were astronomical, and he didn't want any more help from her parents. It was bad enough that he owed her father his job. He wanted to live on the salary that the bank paid its in-house lawyers.

Meanwhile, she had insisted on living within walking distance of her parents, which meant paying some of the most expensive rents per square foot, in New York City, already one of the most expensive cities in the world. She refused to live anywhere across the river, in Brooklyn, where the rents were more reasonable. The flat was a compromise.

Even though the flat was a relatively modest 1,100 square feet in total size, it was costing almost $8,000 a month. Nevertheless, in the face of what just happened, he found himself second-guessing his decision. Had his bullheaded stubbornness put them all in danger? He walked back through the entry foyer, and relocked the exterior door from the inside, leaving the key inside the lock to insure that no one could possibly open it from the outside.

When he returned to the bedroom, she was picking things up, but tears were still streaming down from her eyes. It almost made him feel like crying himself. The last time he'd cried was at his parent's funeral. That was when he was 11 years old. For just an instant, the dam might have broken, for the first time in 14 years. Nevertheless, in spite of the disquiet and stress he felt inside, he fought with himself to show no visible emotion. He didn't want to appear weak, especially when he had to be strong, for Laura's sake, if for no other reason.

That's when he suddenly spotted a familiar white envelope on the floor. He remembered locking it up in the top dresser drawer months ago. He picked it up, and ripped it open, and his heart pounding as he did so. The $3,000 in cash was still there! Not a penny was missing! He slipped the cash into his pocket and walked back to the living room. The TV, microwave, radio, and his wife's newly bought Apple "iPod" were on the floor. Some of the stuff might be broken but none of the small pricey devices were gone.

That made no sense. Why wouldn't a burglar steal an iPod, that can be slipped into a shirt pocket?

Then, he spotted his laptop computer. It was also on the floor, but nearer to the kitchen. He picked it up, and noticed it was lighter than usual. That's when he also noticed that a part of the back cover had been removed. He flipped it over. The screws around the hard disk

149

compartment were gone. The hard disk was missing. Other than that, however, the laptop didn't appear to have been disturbed.

He stared, for a moment, confused. What did it all mean?

He shook his head.

"It doesn't make any sense." he declared loudly.

Suddenly, Laura was by his side, hugging him, and wiping the mascara from her eyes with a napkin.

"It makes sense." she countered. "We never should have rented here!"

"That's not what I mean." he said, shaking his head. "Normally, when someone breaks into a home, the purpose is robbery. Burglars steal stuff. That's what they're supposed to do. But, almost none of our stuff is gone."

She looked at him, bewildered by the new idea.

"What?"

"Can't you see they didn't steal anything?"

She looked around the flat, and picked up a ripped cushion, holding it in front of her for no particular reason. She held it there, staring, but said nothing. Finally, she put it down. Then, she turned toward him, and nodded. There was new understanding in her eyes.

"You're right." she said, finally. "My jewelry is still in the bedroom."

"This wasn't a robbery." he declared. "They were looking for something, and I think I know what it was…"

Jack rummaged through the books and papers that had fallen down.

"They stole just a few things." he said. "The hard drive from my laptop and…"

He kept searching through the books, and then, not having found what he was looking for, continued.

"… a hard copy of the red book."

"The what?" she asked.

"The red diary I brought back from the case in upstate New York." he explained. "The one you found in my briefcase."

"A hard copy?" she wondered. "What about the original?"

"I gave it to the FBI." he explained.

"The FBI?" she wondered aloud.

"Well, it talks about a crime." Jack explained. "So, I figured, I had to get it to the police. Another thing that's missing is my evidence receipt…"

They looked at each other, for a moment, silently, each wondering the same thing, but neither willing to express it.

"It's hard to believe…" he concluded.

"You think the FBI did this?" Laura asked.

"I don't know." he exclaimed. "But, who else could it be?"

Suddenly, the sound of sirens ripped through the air.

"I called the police while I was outside the door…" she said.

A few minutes later, the NYPD arrived, and detectives were busy dusting for fingerprints. When it became clear that there was no forced entry and no fingerprints but theirs, the questioning drifted to the size of their insurance policy. The cops seemed to believe that they had burglarized their own apartment! That line of questioning ended, however, with a quick phone call from headquarters. When they learned who Laura Stoneham Severs was, they dropped the idea of insurance fraud.

It took about an hour and a half of accomplishing nothing before the police left. Jack guessed that the police would never find the perpetrators. Professionals leave no clues. That evening, after a short phone call with her mother, it was agreed that they would move into her parent's place for an indeterminable amount of time.

Jack wasn't eager to live with his in-laws in spite of their lavish lifestyle. Laura had actually suggested just that when they first became married. The place was huge, and almost empty. But, he had staunchly rejected the idea. Now, the choice was out of his control. The safety of the baby was paramount. The perpetrators had ransacked the flat in broad daylight, and seemed to have no fear of the police or of detection. They left no traces. They were very dangerous people.

The Stoneham family's Manhattan penthouse was smaller than their Long Island Hamptons mansion, but it was still almost 10,000 square feet of living space, built in a high-rise building that sat on the most expensive real estate in the world. The place occupied the entire top floor of one of the few relatively new buildings on Central Park West. It

151

had a 24/7 armed guard patrol, and was protected even further by multiple security systems.

Despite all the attractions, Jack would have preferred not to be there. He always felt out of his element when he spent too much time with the Stonehams. He didn't pay a lot of attention to his in-laws, however, because he couldn't get his mind off what had happened. Whoever had trashed his apartment was involved with the murder described in the diary. Of that, he was sure. But, who even knew about the diary? He could count them on one hand. He had told Tim Cohen and Laura, but both were beyond suspicion. He had delivered the original diary to an FBI agent, Peter Barkley and gotten a "receipt for evidence." Now, that evidence receipt was gone.

Supposedly, Agent Barkley was to review the matter for possible federal jurisdiction. Because jurisdiction was unlikely, he had fully expected the file to be forwarded to the Verde County Sheriff. The upstate county prosecutors would control the matter under state law, not federal. But, when he'd called the FBI, and told them he wanted to speak with Agent Barkley, the receptionist seemed evasive. When he'd contacted the evidence office, they claimed they couldn't print out a duplicate receipt because there was no original. All record of the diary was gone.

Jack found himself second-guessing himself more than ever before. He now wondered why a detective assigned to investigate banks had become so close to the lawyers for the bank. It had a strong appearance of impropriety. Yet, everything had seemed so perfectly normal before. He should never have trusted such a man. He couldn't trust the FBI and couldn't trust the bank. He couldn't trust anyone.

The next day was Saturday, and Jack returned to his flat to pick up some things. It was no more than about a seven minute walk from the Stoneham's penthouse. He gathered the various items he wanted to take with him, and while doing so, he noticed a pair of jeans on the floor. Suddenly, he remembered! He picked the jeans off the floor, and slipped one hand into the small secondary pocket of the blue jeans. There it was. Bingo! The tiny USB flash drive, so small it had been missed!

He took it out, smiling, and slipped it into the corresponding little secondary pocket in the fresh pair of jeans he was wearing. That gave him a sense of triumph. The vandals weren't invincible. They'd screwed up. There was a huge amount of information on that little flash drive, not just the diary, but also copies of his research notes. The home invasion made it clear that the diary and, perhaps his research too, was a threat to someone. Whoever arranged the loan on that upstate farm also arranged the ransacking of his home. He was now absolutely certain of it.

The vehicle described in the diary was a BMW 528i. Bolton Sayres' loaner car fleet was composed largely of BMW 528i's. No license plate number was listed so it was impossible to connect the crime to an exact car. Theoretically, however, that problem was not insurmountable. The bank kept complete records on the car loans. Dead people could no longer speak. But, maybe, the bank's database might speak for them.

His brand new backpack was actually a disguised laptop bag. Inside was the computer he had just purchased to replace the old one. He inserted the Bolton Sayres' VPN CD, and ran the setup program. VPN means "virtual private network," an encrypted communications protocol that sets up a private tunnel between a computer and a company's internal databases. Using Bolton Sayres VPN, each employee had a set of login credentials, which authorized a level of access.

Within minutes, Jack's level of access allowed him to connect remotely to the firm's internal network. He could and did search the bank's records as easily as he might have if he had been sitting in his office. It took a while, but after about a half-hour of searching, he believed that he had found what he was looking for. He tried to download the data, but faced an error message:

SYSTEM CANNOT COMPLETE REQUESTED OPERATION

The error message repeated each time he tried to download the data. Finally, he closed the lid, put the computer into "suspend" mode, slipped it carefully back into the backpack, and left the flat. There was a small deli downstairs, where he sometimes ate lunch. It had a WIFI connection. While eating lunch, he tried the same operation. To his amazement, this time it worked without a hitch.

The records of all Bolton Sayres' BMW 528i loaner vehicles, borrowed over the past six years, including thousands of names, dates and times, were contained inside two relatively small files. He opened them, found the one that included the date he was looking for, and scrolled down the list. Employees had checked out sixteen loaner cars on July 22, 2008. Twelve were BMW 528i's, and eleven had been checked out before noon.

He retrieved the little flash drive from his pocket, plugged it into its port, and copied the files onto it. Then, he opened a folder containing the scanned copy of the Mattingly diary and copied that back to his new laptop. He wanted redundant copies this time. After nearly losing the diary, he wanted to make sure all the materials were still contained in at least two places.

He opened the images. Then, he read and reread sections of the book to confirm his memory. It described two men burying a dead body somewhere around 1 or 2 in the morning. It took about three hours, more or less, to travel by car from Manhattan to Paradise. If the man were killed in New York City, therefore, if he assumed that the killers would travel north, immediately afterward, that meant the killing probably took place no later than 10 to 11 p.m. in the evening. Since there was no talk of any putrid odors, the man couldn't have been in the trunk much longer than that. Most likely, he was killed sometime in the evening that day.

He scrolled down the list again. Out of all the BMWs checked out on September 22, 2008, most people had checked them out before noon. Only one person had checked a vehicle out late in the afternoon of that day, but it was at 5:32 p.m. That was a lot earlier than 10 or 11, but if he had planned the murder, he would have known he needed the car long before the act itself. The name was clear as day. Marcus Dunlop! The man was scum. Was he also the killer? It was evidence of the flimsiest sort, but it was something. He had his first lead!

He hadn't yet followed-up with Laura about her relationship with the man. The cascade of events had come down too fast. As angry as he had been about it, at first, he'd forgotten to do so. Yet, here he was again. The man's name kept popping up, like a bad penny. Was he also a murderer? It was easy to come to that conclusion. The man was unlikable in the extreme. He was a spoiled rich kid who had abused Laura, and behaved terribly. if he could rape sixteen-year-olds, what would stop him from turning to murder later in life?

Nonetheless, there were still gaping holes in the theory. First, what motive would the son of one of New York City's wealthiest and most politically connected bankers have for murdering simple farmers and innkeepers in upstate New York? Second, neither of the two men, described in the diary, fit Dunlop's description. He could have hired them and paid them, just like his father paid the bodyguards. There were always thugs ready and willing to murder for cold hard cash. Was that what the warning, "watch your back...", was about? Would the man try to murder him too?

It wasn't evidence that would be admissible in a court of law. There were too many wild assumptions. All those assumptions, however, fit into a tightly thought-out theory of the case. He couldn't be sure, however, that the theory, solid as it seemed to him, was not signed and sealed by his personal hatred of Marc Dunlop. There were plenty of perfectly innocent explanations for borrowing a company car that afternoon. After all, who would be stupid enough to use a company vehicle to transport a murder victim?

The key to resolving a lot of the speculation, of course, was finding out whom the victim was. If he knew the identity of that first murder victim, it would lead to some insight as to the rest of the killings. If his theory was correct, the man would be a missing person, now, from the New York City metro area. As the thought gelled, he opened a web browser window, and typed some search terms into Google.

"New York City Missing Person July 2008"

Several sites popped up on the screen, among which was the New York State Division of Police. He needed a missing person report corresponding to the day, month and year in question. He tried a few more websites, but he had no luck. The legal department also had a subscription to Westlaw, which he could easily access through the VPN. The service is one of the two main legal research portals, and it contains a complete newspaper and magazine archive, containing nearly every news story for the last 100 years.

He logged into Westlaw and repeated his search, but to no avail...

There wasn't one news article about missing persons on that date, or the day before. That made no sense. Over eight million people lived and worked in the city without even considering the suburbs. The metropolitan statistical area has almost 30 million people. Why weren't there some missing persons? Was he doing something wrong in creating his online search? If so, there was one person he knew would be able to help.

He took out his cell phone, and began to dial. Then, he stopped, midstream. Cell phone calls were too open. Talking on a mobile phone was the electronic equivalent of shouting. Anybody nearby would be able to listen to them. Without encryption, his discussions would be open to the public. He put the cell phone back into his pocket, and looked around. There were no landline phones around.

Thankfully, the old building had been standing for over 80 years. It had a payphone inside. He had already taken delivery of the package of additional information sent to him by his father-in-law, and he knew quite a bit about how the spying system worked. Based on what he'd read, it was still better to stay off the cellular system. Unless THEATRES flagged his landline call as suspicious, a human being would not be listening in.

Thankfully, the person he was about to call lived in an old building, and had an old-fashioned wired phone. Jack cashed a dollar at the counter, in exchange for quarters, dialed the number, looked at his watch, and hoped the man would be home. Then, he waited, as the phone rang.

****

Madison Avenue, between 55th and 72th Street, is one of the premiere shopping districts in Manhattan. It is the so-called "Gold Coast" of the shopping set. It contains some of New York City's priciest options, including a Giorgio Armani store at 760 Madison Avenue. Only rich people can afford that.

At the very moment that Jack had attempted to access Bolton Sayres' loaner car index, a gigantic man sporting a blond crew cut, was quietly walking out of the Armani store, with a smile on his face. The smile disappeared, however, as he was startled by the sharp whistling sound coming from his pocket. Only one thing would cause that notification, and it wasn't something he wanted to hear.

He pulled out his phone. On the surface, it appeared to be nothing more than a standard 4 inch Android powered handset; just a simple thin little box with a touch screen. In reality, it was a unique phone. Its operating system was a modified version of RuMos, military grade software developed in Moscow as an offshoot of Android. The Russians had removed the monitoring elements built into the operating system by Google. They had replaced them with modified monitoring elements that sent all data back to Moscow. But, then, US programmers removed most of what the Russians had put in, and replaced it with monitoring elements that sent the information back to New York.

As he stared at the screen, the phone flashed the symbol of a five-pointed star, inside a pyramid much like the one on the reverse side of a dollar bill, complete with an all-seeing eye. It is the symbol of the Synod. As the symbol flashed, the phone itself vibrated. There was no doubt about it. It was an automatic message from a monitoring system that his boss had set up five years before.

He touched the middle of the star, running his finger around the edges in the circle. The words flashed across the screen.

WARNING!! CONFIDENTIAL DOCUMENT DOWNLOAD REQUEST!

His finger slid, again, along the touch sensitive screen. There was a short delay as relays were established. In a moment more, the phone would create an untraceable and unbreakable encryption protocol. His smart phone and the THEATRES surveillance system were connecting. Once the hand-shaking protocol had finished, information displayed, with a menu choice at the bottom.

CRITICAL DATE:	JULY 22, 2008
DOCUMENT:	CAR LOAN LOGS
IDENTIFICATION OF PERSON:	JACK W. SEVERS

BANK NAME: BOLTON SAYRES

DIVISION: IN-HOUSE LEGAL

ALLOW?   DISALLOW?

He touched "DISALLOW", and sent the message back to the system. Whoever was trying to download the documents would not succeed until the matter was reported. Then, he tapped on his "contacts", and scrolled down. He found the phone number he was looking for, and dialed. A dialog popped onto the screen:

ENCRYPTED   NON-ENCRYPTED

He chose "encrypted," and the phone made its connection, synching its encrypted connection to another phone of the same type.

"Why are you calling me?" the voice demanded. "I told you not to contact me on this number..."

"This is Priority One." the blonde giant explained, in a slight Russian accent.

A pause.

"Priority One?" the voice questioned.

"Someone is downloading documents relating to July 22, 2008..." the blonde giant explained, confident that the other man would know the significance.

"Who?" the voice demanded.

"A person named Jack Severs." the big blonde man responded with a Russian accent. "He attempts to download loaner car index. I did background check. He 'vorks in Bolton Sayre' legal department."

"Jack Severs?" the voice questioned, surprised.

"Da." the blonde giant replied.

"What did you do?" the voice asked.

"Disallowed." the giant said.

There was a momentary pause.

"How many attempts?" the voice asked, slowly.

The giant blonde checked his phone, again, typing a few codes onto the touch screen.

"Seven." he said, finally.

"Interesting..." the man said.

"Should I find and terminate 'dis man?" the blonde asked.

"No." the man replied. "Wait exactly 10 minutes, and then let him download the document."

"Allow download?" the blonde asked, shocked.

"You heard me, allow it." the voice confirmed.

"But..." the huge blonde man began to object.

"Just do as you're told." the voice shot back, interrupting him.

"It's not good idea, I think..." the blonde warned.

"You're not paid to think. That's my job" the man said curtly, cutting him off. "If someone else requests that document, let me know immediately, before any further downloads are allowed. Is that clear?"

"Da." the big man confirmed.

"Good." the voice stated.

"Anything else I should do?" the blonde asked.

The phone connection ended abruptly, as the other man hung up without answering. The blonde giant slipped the phone back into his pocket. Then, after pressing a few extra keystrokes in order to follow his orders, he quietly continued his shopping trip, unperturbed.

Then, about 40 minutes later, another urgent Synod notification arrived, on the phone.

CRITICAL DATE:	JULY 22, 2008
DOCUMENT:	LOAN LOGS
IDENTIFICATION OF PERSON ATTEMPTING: SEVERS	JACK W.
BANK NAME:	BOLTON SAYRES
DIVISION:	IN-HOUSE LEGAL

ALLOW?   DISALLOW?

This time, his finger touched the button "allow", and he put the phone back into his pocket.

XI – SILICON ALLEY MAN

Silicon Alley is an affectionate term used to describe New York City's high tech industry. Unlike the real valleys near San Jose, California, there is no literal "alley." New York's high tech industry is scattered all over Manhattan and the boroughs. It can never compete with Sunnyvale, California in terms of hardware, telecommunications, game design, or any other segment of high tech industry. However, when it came to "FINTECH," the alley was the undisputed champion."

FINTECH means financial technology. Silicon Alley is the center of a universe consisting of money technology. Its software simplifies financial transactions, and is the backbone that supports bank machines, credit cards and money transfers all over the world. The physical closeness of Wall Street, and the biggest banks in the world, means that New York technology firms will always dominate the market for banking and e-commerce software.

Within every industry, there are a few brilliant men. In Silicon Alley, one such man was Jose Arias. He was a top computer development engineer, and a very old and dear friend. He was indebted to Jack, because it was quite possible that he owed him his life. They'd been friends since both men were 16, when Jack had rescued a nerdy teenager and his little sister from a group of gangland thugs.

Jose was not much when it came to socializing. He was no great lover or fighter. However, when it came to computer systems and related technical matters, there was no one with more expertise. Inside the realm of the FINTECH business, he was the "walking textbook." He'd received his UCLA Bachelor of Science in systems engineering, graduated summa cum laude, and followed that up with a master's degree a year later. Both men were the same age, but Jose had graduated two years before Jack. This was simply because computer engineering is a shorter course of study than law.

Unlike the law students, who were happy to get one job offer in an incredibly overcrowded field, computer science graduates were in demand. Jose had been face with a myriad of high paying jobs to choose from. He had finally been lured to New York City by the money. By the time Jack arrived, the man had already been living in Brooklyn for two years. So, when Jack had refused the free room at the Waldorf Astoria Hotel, offered to him by Laura's father, it was because he was going to bed down on the sofa of Jose's tiny flat, right across the river.

About an hour after Jack made the phone call, the two men were sitting together inside a Starbucks. Jose was what many people would call a "late bloomer." In recent years, though, he'd made big strides. Once gaunt and pimply faced, the pimples were gone and he had put on some weight. Instead of the thick black framed glasses, he now wore contact lenses.

Jack quietly explained everything he knew and suspected. He spoke not only about a wrecked apartment, but also about the case in upstate New York, and the THEATRES surveillance system, in spite of the fact that he'd given his word to his father-in-law and Admiral Stark. He was keen on keeping his word, but the issue was now one of life and death, and Jose could be trusted. So, he swore his friend to secrecy. Once he'd done that, it seemed, he was keeping his own promise to keep the secret safe.

"It's impossible to know who's listening on the phone." Jack explained. "They might be listening now, for all I know."

"That's sounds paranoid..." Jose said. "But, it's funny…"

"Why?" Jack replied.

"Because you're that much more like me now…" Jose said with a smile.

Jack smiled back.

"The truth is more outrageous than your wildest conspiracy theory..."

Jose was a big believer in conspiracies. He thrived on science fiction and the slippery slope from real science. Things like alien abductions, Illuminati and conspiracies appealed to him on several levels. He also liked to speculate about the reptilians from the center of the earth.

"The truth is out there, you know..." Jose said.

X-Files had always been one of his favorite television shows and he enjoyed quoting from it. Jack patiently ignored it, as he always did.

"What I need is the name of the dead guy." he stated. "That would lead me to the killers..."

"You're way too fixated on this." Jose commented. "Do you have any idea how dangerous it'll become if you actually do find them?"

"What else can I do?" Jack stated. "They invaded my home. I can't sit back and do nothing. They could try to murder me and my family, just like they did upstate."

"You might be increasing the chances by pursuing this…" Jose pointed out.

"I won't just wait to be victimized." Jack declared. "Somehow, this all traces back to Bolton Sayres Bank. That, I'm sure of."

"Isn't your father-in-law the CEO?" Jose asked.

Jack nodded.

"Why can't you just talk to him about it?" Jose asked.

Jack shook his head.

"Too risky."

"You think he's involved?" Jose asked.

"No, but who knows?" Jack stated. "I need more facts. That's why I need your help."

"What can I do?" Jose asked.

"I need your expertise with computers." Jack explained.

Jose nodded.

"I can do one thing right now." he declared.

He reached into his pocket, and took out a pair of ridiculously thick glasses. They reminded Jack of the black rimmed glasses the man had worn as a teenager. But, these were worse. They were thicker and even uglier. They had a piece of the clear carbonite sticking out from below the bottom frame.

"I thought you wore contact lenses now?" Jack asked.

"These aren't for me." his friend replied. "They're for you."

Jack's first instinct was to laugh, but he held back. It would wrong to ask for someone's help and then laugh at him.

"I don't need glasses." Jack declared.

"They're not for seeing." Jose said.

"What are they for?"

"Tricking."

"What?"

162

"To trick the computers, if you need to." Jose explained. "The glasses are designed to distort a person's facial features from the perspective of video cameras."

Jack picked up the strange-looking item and examined it.

"Did you know that my company designed part of the THEATRES operating system?" Jose announced.

"No." Jack admitted.

"Neither did I." his friend admitted. "I first realized it when you described the system. I think I've got a pretty good idea how THEATRES works."

Jack picked up the glasses his friend offered him and slipped them into a spot inside his backpack. He didn't quite understand how or why they would be useful to him in "tricking" the computer surveillance systems, but he would take that on faith.

"Where's the original diary, now?" Jose asked.

"I left it with the FBI." Jack answered. "Whether it's there now, I don't know, but they don't have a record of receiving it, anymore."

"You think the FBI invaded your home?" Jose concluded.

"That would be the natural conclusion." Jack answered. "Or, someone who has FBI agents on the take."

Jose maintained a grim look. He shook his head with utmost seriousness.

"If that's true, you're getting yourself into some dangerous shit..." he said. "If even half of what you suspect is true, you should run away as fast as you can"

"I can't run away." Jack declared.

"You never could, could you?" Jose mused. "I guess I might still be alive because of that..."

"I'm the hunted" Jack declared. "With your help, I want to become the hunter. But, first, I need to know who the dead guy was."

The other man nodded.

"The date they saw the body being buried was July 22, 2008." Jack said. "But, this all happened at night, so they could be talking about something that happened on the 23rd."

Jose got the gist of things immediately.

"You think the guy was killed on one of those days?" Jose asked.

"Yes." Jack confirmed. "Now, look, here..."

He flipped through a few pages he'd printed out from the scanned copy of the diary, until he reached the point he felt was important. He pointed out key words.

"BMW 528i?" Jose read.

"More than half of Bolton Sayres loaner pool consists of BMW 528i's." Jack noted.

"There are a few million more BMWs in the world..." Jose pointed out.

"But, Bolton Sayres gave this relatively modest farmer a huge line of credit." Jack explained. "It was a loan that should never have been made."

"We designed Bolton's database so that it's impossible to put anything into it, without listing a responsible person." Jose pointed out. "That might give you a lead..."

"It's not there." Jack said.

"It has to be there."

"But, it's not." Jack repeated.

"Then, someone's tampered with the programming." Jose insisted. "It can't happen the way we originally set things up. If the transaction is in the computer, there has to be a responsible person listed."

"It's in the computer," Jack said, "but no one is listed as having authorized it. There's no name there at all."

"Have you ever considered that the dead guy might have been sitting in the trunk of that car for two weeks, or even months?" Jose asked. "I mean, who knows?"

"Impossible." Jack explained. "Even a day-old corpse would stink to high heaven. There's nothing in the diary about any stink in the air. So, the man was killed that night."

"The body might have been embalmed or frozen..." Jose pointed out.

"Occam's Razor." Jack said.

"The simplest explanation is the right one?" Jose offered.

"Yes." Jack said.

"OK, maybe, you're right." Jose said. "Let's say they killed this guy that night. Why kill the farmer and his family so long afterward?"

"Witnesses." Jack said.

"More than a year later?" Jose pointed out.

"Somehow, the killers found out the kid witnessed the burial." Jack speculated.

"You say there's no authorization code?" Jose said. "When was the loan made?"

"Approximately 9 months after the body was buried." Jack answered.

"So, you think that the loan was a temporary payoff, to bridge the time needed to get kill them?" Jose asked.

"Yes!" Jack agreed.

"I guess that makes some sense..." Jose noted.

"I wouldn't blame you if you don't want to get involved." Jack said. "There's danger here..."

"If you thought I'd do that, why did you come to me?" Jose asked.

"I didn't know where else to go." Jack admitted.

"Well, you came to the right man." Jose stated. "I owe you. This is my chance to repay the debt. I might never have another chance. I won't let you down."

That was exactly what Jack had been hoping to hear.

"All right, then... as an expert at information science, tell me how I find out what I need to know?"

Jose beamed. He was proud that Jack Severs, whom he had admired since the incident near Long Beach, now described him as an expert. Not only that, but he needed his help, and he had so much faith in his ability to help that he had come directly to him. He resolved to make certain that faith wasn't misplaced.

"The first thing, as always, is to Google it." Jose said. "Did you do that?"

165

Jack nodded.

"I came up empty-handed." he said.

"Nothing at all?" Jose asked.

"Zero, zilch, nothing." Jack confirmed.

"Did you ever tell the FBI man you scanned the diary onto a flash drive?" Jose asked.

"No." Jack replied. "I did tell him that I scanned it to my computer."

"That's why they took your hard disk." Jose concluded.

Jack nodded. It made sense. Then, he suddenly had an idea.

"I'll give you copies of the loan documentation, and the loaner car logs." he said, after thinking for a moment. "If anything happens to me, I want you to send it anonymously to the media."

The other man nodded enthusiastically. Jack suddenly felt guilty for having involved his friend. The man loved conspiracies. But, this one wasn't like the ones he played with. This was for real. It could be deadly. He had to keep Jose's involvement to a minimum. Still, he desperately needed help.

"Here" Jose said, as he pulled out a 10 inch tablet computer from his carry bag. "I've got an idea."

A moment later, he had logged in. He tried doing all the expected searches on all the major database search engines. They were the same ones that Jack had tried earlier, and it ended the same. No hits.

"I could have told you that wouldn't work." Jack pointed out.

"I'm not searching for anything in particular…"

Jose seemed to be furiously typing new searches. For a person who wasn't searching for anything, he seemed rather intent on typing in a lot of search terms.

Finally, Jack couldn't stand it anymore and felt compelled to ask why.

"If you're not searching for anything, what are you doing?" Jack asked, finally.

"I'm trying to see how the search engines react." Jose replied.

"How they react?" Jack wondered aloud.

"Yes." Jose asked. "We're getting zero results from key words, relating to Bolton Sayres that almost certainly should give some results. That's not how search engines work. Bolton Sayres is one of the largest banks in the world. If you plug in the name of a huge corporation like that, along with a date, *something* should pop out. Instead, we're getting nothing at all. The total blank means that someone's tampered with the internet."

"Tampered with the internet?" Jack exclaimed. "Can they do that?"

"I wouldn't have believed it a moment ago. But, it's theoretically possible. To do it, you'd need extraordinary control over the underlying infrastructure. Only someone controlling the routing could do it."

"You mean Google is blocking the searches?" Jack asked.

"No." Jose stated. "The same thing is happening on Bing, Yahoo... even the Russian Yandex. They all come in blank."

"How can that be?" Jack asked.

"It can't be." Jose replied. "Whoever's done this might be altering the screen information that gets passed over the net. But, I'm using the https secured version, so that's unlikely. Or..."

Jose hesitated.

"Or, what?" Jack insisted.

"Or," Jose hesitated, "there are backdoors in the software or equipment that the search companies are using. Whoever is doing this has access and control over either the piping that connects the web servers or over the equipment itself."

"The government?" Jack noted.

"There have always been rumors about backdoors put in by the government, and some of it is true." Jose explained. "It was once rumored that the NSA was putting backdoors into American-manufactured routers."

"But, I think the Russian search engine, Yandex, wouldn't be using American equipment." Jack pointed out.

"That's a good point." Jose admitted. "And, it implies control over the piping, rather than the equipment itself."

"What about using a VPN to make everyone think we're in Russia?" Jack suggested.

"I've tried that." Jose said. "It doesn't work, probably because whoever is doing this knows the VPN URLs…"

"I see." Jack said thoughtfully.

"Another possibility," Jose speculated, "is that someone's infected the search engines with malware."

"Would that imply government involvement?" Jack asked.

"Not necessarily." Jose insisted.

There was a moment of silence as Jose went back to doing something with his computer.

"If I tell you a secret, will you also agree to keep it strictly confidential?"

"Of course." Jack replied.

"As you know, my company designed the basic software that all the banks use to power their databases." Jose explained. "Unknown to most of them, there's a back-door, through which they can be linked to external systems. Until you described THEATRES to me, I wasn't sure what it was for. But, theoretically, control over any bank's software can be passed to an outside entity without internal security clearance."

"You guys built that into the system?" Jack asked, shocked.

"We didn't do it because we wanted to." Jose pointed out. "The primary banks who bankroll us, including the one you work for, ordered it. It's a gaping hole. But, with access to Bolton's internal system, I can probably access THEATRES and even take it down."

"Interesting." Jack agreed. "I'll let you know if I ever need you to do that. But, let me add that I also searched Westlaw and came up dry."

"There's one place you haven't looked…" Jose noted calmly.

"Where?" Jack asked.

"The public library." Jose replied.

"You're joking..." Jack said.

"No." Jose explained. "Electronic data can be manipulated. The data may exist somewhere, on the web or on a backup tape, but you'll never be able to find it. With hard paper copies, they could destroy them, but they'd have to put a lot of man hours into doing that. They'd have to burglarized every library in the country."

"Brilliant!" Jack suddenly exclaimed. "They still print physical newspapers, even though most people use the web for news. An article about a missing person would get printed in a physical newspaper somewhere."

"Exactly." Jose agreed.

Jack glanced at his watch. It was getting late.

"The Main New York Public library is only open until 5 p.m.." Jack noted.

"What about Sunday?" Jose asked.

"From 1 to 5 p.m.." Jack answered.

"Then, let's go tomorrow." Jose said.

Jack nodded.

"Tomorrow, at 1 p.m...." Jack recited.

Jose nodded.

"See you there..."

After more a little more talk, on a variety of subjects, Jack insisted on picking up the check, and then he caught a taxi to midtown Manhattan. He returned to his apartment to gather a few last things, and with that, he packed everything he needed into a suitcase, and took a taxi back to the Stoneham penthouse. He spent the night with his extended family.

XII - THE PUBLIC LIBRARY

The New York Public Library houses the third largest collection of books, periodicals and newspapers in the world, behind only the British Library in London, and the Library of Congress in Washington DC. Most of the library, however, was of no interest to the two men. The periodicals section was the only place that interested them. Thankfully, the general librarian was available for a consultation without any wait.

"What can I do for ya?" the woman asked, with a strong Brooklyn accent.

"I'm looking for newspaper articles from 2008." Jack told her. "How do I find them?"

"The fastest way is wit' da' library database." she explained. "Dere' surchable..."

Jack interrupted her.

"No." he said. "I'm looking for physical copies. Do you store the physical newspapers?"

"From 5 years ago?" she asked, astounded that anyone would even venture to ask about physical copies in a digital age.

"Yes." he said.

"We got about a month and a half of da' New York Times." she noted. "About six months off-site on advance notice..."

"Nothing physical from 2008?" he questioned.

"Not that far back..." she replied.

"What happens if the internet breaks down?" he asked.

"We've got a local database on DVD that's updated every week." she replied, but as an afterthought, she added. "And, of course, we've got the microfilm."

"That's what I want -- the microfilm." Jack said.

"Reference Rm. 100." she advised, pointing.

"Thank you." Jack said.

The two men whispered to each other as they made their way to the target room.

"Is it possible to tamper with microfilm?" Jack asked.

"You can tamper with anything..." Jose conceded. "But, analog is harder to mess with, because it's arranged chronologically, like pure paper."

The microfilm room was empty. Several old readers stood unused. They picked two, side by side, and went about their business, busily pulled rolls of film out of the gray metal drawers. It was tedious work, and didn't pay off right away, but by 3:00 p.m., after intensively searching, there was a breakthrough.

"Jose!" he prodded his friend, excited. "Look!"

The other man turned to glance at Jack's reader.

"Here!" Jack pointed to the screen.

It was an article dated July 26, 2008.

BROOKLYN MAN MISSING FOR THREE DAYS

Manhattan Island, New York (KXAN) — The New York police are looking for a Brooklyn man who they say has been missing since July 23. Authorities say he expressed suicidal thoughts in the past.

Charles Bakkendorf, Jr., 32, worked for the well-known international investment banking powerhouse, Bolton Sayres, as a vault manager. He was last seen leaving work. His disappearance was reported by his landlord.

According to authorities, the man was wearing dress jeans, a white button down shirt with tie, and black dress shoes. He is a white male, 6-foot-1, with brown eyes and brown hair, and believed to weigh around 200 pounds.

The New York Police Department have conducted both ground and aerial searches in and around both the area in which Bakkendorf lives and where he works, but with no success.

Anyone with information of Bakkendorf's whereabouts should contact the New York Police Department at (212) 334-0742

"You've got your name!" Jose whispered, excitedly.

Jack nodded, smiling. Things were finally coming together. He looked at his watch, which the other man noticed.

"We've got 'till 4:45." Jose noted. "Then this section closes.

"We need to work faster." Jack concluded.

"I'm gonna' find the next one!" Jose declared, enthusiastically.

He turned his attention back to the reader machine, and both searched as hard and fast as they could.

"I found it!" Jose said.

This time, Jack leaned over to read.

> POLICE SAY BROOKLYN MAN SUICIDAL
>
> *New York, NY (KXAN) — The New York police have been looking for a Brooklyn man for over a week, since he was reported missing, but with no success. A police spokesman says that the man appears to have no immediate family. A co-worker, who wished to remain anonymous, disclosed that the man had become very depressed and expressed suicidal thoughts immediately prior to disappearing.*
>
> *The Brooklyn man, Charlie Bakkendorf, 32, was last seen leaving work on July 22nd with only his wallet and the clothes he was wearing. He was employed as an assistant vault manager at the well known international investment bank, Bolton Sayres. His disappearance was reported by his landlord on July 23rd.*
>
> *Authorities continue searching for a body, but assume that the man might have succeeded in his desire to commit suicide.*

"Who do you suppose that co-worker was?" Jack noted.

"Good question." Jose agreed, glancing at his watch. "We've still got a little less than an hour to find out…"

They'd found 37 articles, but still had no clue who the co-worker might be. Some were duplicates, published by different news organizations from the same generic news feed, but they'd accumulated articles from at least 10 separate sources. When the library lights flashed on and off, the signal it would close in 15 minutes, the two men wrapped it up. Jack gathered up the printouts, and stuffed them in his briefcase.

They made their way through the main reading room, back past the big stone lions at the entrance, and down the steps to the street. Thoughts were coming fast, one after another even as he walked. It was hard to concentrate on one thing at a time.

Now, it was becoming clear. The dead man was a vault employee who had once worked at Bolton Sayres. That meant the trail led back to the bank, as he had suspected it would. But, the existence of the physical newspaper articles had also highlighted something else. Someone with an enormous amount of power, and nearly complete control over the internet, itself, had managed to eliminate certain facts from almost every electronic database.

Who could do it? And, why kill a vault employee? It wasn't like someone had tried to rob the vault. The man had disappeared after going home from work. The only possible answer was that the man knew something he wasn't supposed to know. What did he know? What dark and dirty secret was so dangerous, if revealed, that keeping it a secret justified murder?

Jose's voice interrupted.

"Let's stop at Staples." he whispered. "There's one at the corner of 5th and 39th. We need to get this stuff scanned. Once it's in electronic form, we can potentially distribute it endlessly if we need to."

Jack nodded. But, suddenly, a chill ran down his spine as he realized that he'd missed something big. They were out in the open! Cameras were all over the city. Cameras had to be watching everything they did. The materials he'd read about the THEATRES program said that the cameras were watching everything, everywhere, all the time. They were bugging every public space, and monitoring all the streets.

Why not the library? Why not Staples?

The enormity of it was overwhelming.

Jose's now a target too...

Anyone sophisticated enough to mask the articles mentioning Bakkendorf's disappearance, could also have access to the THEATRES surveillance system. If so, there was nothing he could do now. Calling on a pay phone had been a fruitless effort. It was stupid. He'd brought his friend into a lion's den. He glanced in one direction, then in the other, suspiciously.

Could the murderers decide to kill again? He tried to put such worries out of his head, but it was impossible. Once they crossed 5th Avenue, toward 39th Street, he gently touched Jose shoulder, and both of them stopped. He whispered into his friend's ear.

"Remember that surveillance system I told you about?"

"Sure."

"It has tens of thousands of pinhole cameras and microphones all over the place. Some of them might be watching us."

Jose nodded, and adjusted the awful looking pair of black rimmed incognito glasses he had been wearing since they'd met.

"I'm sure they are." he whispered back, still smiling. "We'll talk about it when we get to Staples."

They arrived at the office supplies shop and walked through the door. Jose pointed toward the laptop sales aisle.

"Over there." he directed.

Jack followed him. A moment later, they were at their destination, among the laptops.

Jose examined the price tags as if he were looking for a new computer. A store clerk immediately appeared.

"Can I help you find something..." the man asked.

"No, thanks, I'm just looking." Jose replied immediately.

"If you need anything, I'll be over there..." the store clerk said, and then left the immediate vicinity.

"We can talk now." Jose announced.

"They know we went to the library." Jack whispered. "They probably know we're here, right now."

"No." Jose whispered back. "They know *YOU* went to the library. They know you went with someone. But, they don't know who you went with. Remember these?"

He pointed to the ugly glasses. Jack had an identical pair in his backpack from yesterday. His friend had given it to him and told him they tricked computer surveillance systems. He now remembered.

"They can't auto-ID me, so long as I've got these on." Jose declared.

"How can you be sure?" Jack questioned.

"You see these little lights?" Jose asked.

He pointed to the rims of the glasses. Jack noticed microscopic LED's. Some were lit but others didn't seem to be on.

174

"All the little LED's are on, by the way." Jose noted. "You just can't see them all. They run the gamut of the light spectrum. Some are in the near-infrared wavelength that human vision can't see."

Jack nodded.

"Electronic video uses infrared sensors to assemble faces for facial recognition. The software can't determine who I am when I wear these."

Jack relaxed. Jose had it figured out. He'd been wise to team up with his old friend. The only person in danger was him. It was a relief. He didn't like putting others, especially his friends, into harm's way.

"How do you know how everything works?" Jack noted.

"Partly, because you described it to me." Jose said. "But, partly because I realized that I designed part of it. I did the programming for their auto-ID program. I didn't know what I was working on or who I was working for."

"Are you sure about that?" Jack asked.

"Yes." Jose answered. "And, I'm also sure they've got no idea who I am, even if they've been watching everything we've done together. I simply faded out of existence, and got lost in the masses, a few miles past my home."

"Wouldn't they know just for the fact that no one normally wears glasses like that?" Jack asked.

"Once they get the system working well enough so that the ID failure rate is well below 1% that might be true." Jose admitted, "But, right now, that isn't the case. The error rate is more like 5 or 6%. Many people fade out of the system."

"Couldn't they figure out who you are by a process of elimination?" Jack asked.

"Not really." Jose answered. "Out of a population of 8 million people, 160,000 New Yorkers are off the grid at any one time, just because of the failure rate, and those who disappear change all the time. They fade, and pop back onto the grid, repeatedly. I'm lumped together into that 160,000. I've simply faded into temporary obscurity as far as the system is concerned."

"Couldn't they be watching and listening to us, right now?" Jack asked.

"It's possible." Jose said. "But, all the programming was based on the expectation that the cameras and microphones would be outside, operating in daylight and darkness, not interior lighting. There was no protocol for interior lighting, so, I don't think they're bugging the inside of homes, offices or stores."

Jack noticed a package of 4 USB sticks on the shelf and stopped to pick it up.

"Buy a pay-as-you-go Smartphone, too." Jose suggested.

"I've already got a mobile phone." Jack said.

Jose leaned over so his whispers could be heard.

"Every time you make a call on that one, the world knows who's making the call." Jose whispered. "You need a no contract phone so you can get lost in the signals. Buy it for cash, and invent some kind of name when you activate it. Buy the refill cards for cash too. If you need to make a confidential phone call, the computers won't know it's you. But, make your bland vanilla calls on your old contract phone. You don't want the algorithms determining that you're probably using another phone."

Jack walked over to a cheap prepaid deal, a low-end Samsung smart phone, picked it up, and, also picked up a recharge card.

"Let's do our scanning..." he suggested.

They walked over to the copy center, and the counter was empty of customers. They scanned all the articles into pdf files. Then, they downloaded copies into the four new USB sticks. Jack paid for everything in cash. After he finished, he slipped one of the USB sticks into his own pocket, and handed the other three over to Jose.

"Put them in different places," he instructed, "just in case..."

Jose nodded.

"I'll also post them online, in an encrypted envelope." Jose whispered. "That way, I can make them public, instantly, if I need to. "I'll walk out first. You stay here, browse the store for 10 or 15 minutes more, and then find a random person, preferably someone near my size, and walk out with him.

Jack nodded.

"I don't know how to thank you..." he said.

"You don't have to." Jose replied. "I still owe you."

"Not anymore..." Jack insisted.

Jose shook his head.

"You saved my life back then." he declared, quietly. "The debt hasn't been paid yet."

Then, he smiled, and then added something more.

"But, you may end up owing me, before this is over..."

Jack smiled back.

"Here" Jose said. "Take this."

He passed a CD ROM disk discretely from his jacket pocket into Jack's hand. Jack took the mirrored disk in hand, flipped it over, one side, then the other, slightly confused.

"Is it blank?" Jack asked.

"No." Jose confirmed. "It's got an encryption app on it. It something we've developed for the military. We call it Zambo. Pop it into your computer's CDROM drive, and follow the setup instructions. You can use it with WIFI or even on a smart phone. It'll allow us to communicate with each other in complete privacy."

Jack nodded.

"OK, thanks."

About 30 minutes after Jose left the store, Jack picked a man about Jose's height and build, and exiting the store with him. He tried to walk close to the unknown man. A few hundred feet down the street, they parted company, and Jack made his way back home.

XIII - COLLECTING MORE EVIDENCE

On Monday morning, Jack worked feverishly to complete all his assignments before lunch. At about 11:20 A.M., he dropped everything, and set off for the nearest police precinct. It was only a few minutes' walk from the Bolton Sayres building, and he arrived in minutes. The "information officer" on duty was a tall black woman, who practiced keeping a perpetual scowl on her face.

"What can I do for you." she asked.

"I need to find records on a missing person." he stated. "How do I do that?"

"Check the missing persons section of our website." she stated.

"I did that." he replied.

"Everybody who's missing is on the website, unless they've been found." she insisted.

"He hasn't been found." Jack stated.

"Then, he's on the website." she repeated, paused, and then concluded. "Unless his case is solved, but then he wouldn't be classified as missing anymore. But, if he were missing..."

"How do I know if his case has been solved?" Jack asked.

"Because he wouldn't be missing anymore, and he's off the website." the woman.

He couldn't help wondering whether the woman was part of a bad dream.

"I'm not trying to find out whether he's missing." Jack tried to explain. "I *know* he's missing. What I need is whether there's an investigation and, if there is, what's the status?"

"There would be a detective in charge of that." she offered.

"Who?" Jack asked.

"Who's your missing person?" she replied.

"A man by the name of Charles Bakkendorf." he said. "He went missing in 2008."

"The case is too old." she stated. "Unless there's a restriction on the file, you'll have to order it."

"Would there be an investigation?" he asked.

"Only if he's reported missing." she replied.

"That's what I'm trying to find out." Jack exclaimed, getting frustrated. "Can you to pull a copy of the file, please?"

"No." she replied.

"Why not?" Jack asked.

"It's not available at the precinct level." she insisted.

"Where is it available?" he asked.

"By mail." the woman insisted. "Only mailed requests are accepted."

"How long will that take?" he asked.

"A few days, maybe a few weeks... it all depends." she responded.

"Depends on what?" he inquired.

"On how many requests; how busy they are. I'm not in that department."

"Can't you just give me a case number?" he asked.

"No." she replied, dryly.

"Why not?"

"I'm not authorized." She replied. "You have to make your request by mail. Here's the form..."

She reached under the counter top, pulled out a piece of paper, and slid it toward him.

"Fill it and mail it." she said.

"To where?" he asked.

"To the address on the form." she replied. "Two copies, and a check or money order for $15. Cash isn't accepted."

He glanced at the document, titled VERIFICATION OF CRIME/LOST PROPERTY. It required a case number, the name of the reporting precinct, and more. It was all information he didn't have, and had hoped to gather.

"Can I just go physically to wherever this form is supposed to be mailed?" he asked.

"No."

"Why not?"

"Not open to the public." she reported.

"But, I don't have all the information requested by the form." he complained.

"Put in the information you have." she said. "They'll tell you if they need more."

"Do I get a refund when they don't find it?" he asked.

"No." she replied.

"Can't you just look up the case number?" he asked. "Just to see if there are some records. I'm not even sure it's been reported."

"We don't do that." she insisted. "There are many people behind you, sir. Please fill out the form and mail it in. Thank you."

It dawned on him that the imperious woman had just dismissed him. He glanced behind him. It was true that three people stood on the line behind him.

"Next, please..." she said.

There was no point in arguing. He simply turned and left. He looked at his watch as he exited the building. It was already 11:54 and Timothy Cohen would be waiting. He had to meet his friend for lunch at Marvin's deli. He flagged a taxi, and arrived only 10 minutes late.

Marvin's Deli is the most famous delicatessen in New York City. As he walked in, the door attendant handed him a printed, numbered ticket. They'd already warned him about the ticket. It was "mission critical." You walked around with it, had it stamped at the food bars, and provided that record, of what you bought, when you walked out. You settled the bill, using the ticket, as you walked out the door. If you lost it, the deli would charge you fifty bucks.

It was a strange system, but it was the Marvin system, and if you ate there, you had to follow the rules. He spotted his friend sitting at a table at the far end of the room.

"I was beginning to think you'd never get here." Cohen exclaimed.

"Sorry, Tim." Jack apologized. "I got held up by an idiot bureaucrat."

"Welcome to the lawyerly life, Jack!" Cohen said, smiling.

He told him the story about what had happened at the NYPD precinct. Cohen put down his can of celery seed soda for a moment.

"It's just city bureaucracy," he declared, "and the same reason the cops are always giving out petty citations for stupid stuff like J-walking. It's all about money. If you send in that written request, they'll write back, three weeks from now, and claim you didn't provide enough information. They'll say they can't locate the file, and demand you submit another form, with a new fee, for a new search. And, they'll keep doing it until you give up."

Jack threw up his hands in frustration.

"What am I supposed to do?" Jack asked.

"All is not lost, my friend..." Cohen said, holding up his index finger to make the point.

By now, they were both standing at the sandwich station. Before Jack could respond, his friend was off to the desserts station. With each plate of food, the little card got a stamp.

The sandwiches were huge.

Jack unwrapped his corned beef sandwich, and began to speak.

"You said all is not lost..."

"I just wanted to say you just need to get to the right people. You can get what you want in a few minutes if you do." Cohen replied.

"How?"

"We use a retired NYPD cop to get stuff out of NYPD. I can give you his contact information. He's a PI now."

Cohen scribbled something on a tiny piece of paper and handed it to Jack, who thought about using it. It might be exactly what he needed, except for one thing.

181

"Who is the 'we' in 'we use'?"

"The legal department."

"That's what I figured." Jack noted.

The answer meant that Cohen's private investigator was unacceptable. In some other case, someone like that might be perfect. However, the man's close connection to Bolton Sayres and other banks made him unacceptable now. If he hired an investigator, it would be someone with no ties to the banking industry, and especially no ties to his own firm.

"Thanks." Jack said, without revealing his thoughts. "Did you manage to get hold of Charles Bakkendorf's personnel file?"

Jack had enlisted the man in his search for evidence. He hated to do it, but he didn't have password access to the firm's personnel records. Cohen, in contrast, had a little romance going on with a girl in official records. If anyone could get the records, she could. She had access to the physical file storage rooms, and password access to the company's entire employee database.

"I had her do that records search." Cohen insisted. "But, I'm sorry, Jack... no one by that name ever worked at Bolton..."

"Did you have her do a physical records search?" Jack asked.

"I had her do exactly what you asked for." Cohen insisted. "She looked in just about every possible place. There's never been a guy by that name working for the company."

"But, he *did* work for the company. He's not a mirage." Jack insisted.

He reached into his briefcase, and extracted the prints of the physical articles from the microfilm collection, handing them, one by one, to Cohen.

"This is why I asked for the records." Jack said. "You still think he's a mirage?"

Cohen scanned through the articles quickly.

"I don't know what to think." Cohen said, shaking his head, nervously.

"There's a group of people, with an incredible amount of power, who've done everything they can to cover this up. This guy was murdered."

Cohen looked around the room searching for ghosts. Then, he turned to Jack and whispered.

"Do you know why?"

"Not yet." Jack replied.

"My advice to you is this." Cohen said, nervously. "Drop it! No good is going to come from it. Let the police do their jobs."

"I'd love to," he said, "but, the moment after I handed that diary over to our friend at the FBI, someone broke into my flat."

"Jeez, Jack..." Cohen exclaimed, "You've got a wife and a baby. Let it drop, for God's sake!"

Cohen knew Jack well enough by now, and had the distinct feeling he was wasting his breathe.

"I've got a ruined apartment and the privilege of living with my in-laws." Jack noted. "That's what your police, and specifically, your Agent Barkley gave me."

"Didn't you hear?" Cohen asked.

"About what?" Jack asked.

"Barkley is dead." Cohen stated. "He was in a bad car accident on Long Island."

The shock must have shown on Jack's face and he didn't respond for a moment.

"Wait a minute, Jack... don't even go down that road." Cohen said, anticipating the thought pattern of his friend, while holding up his hand as a sort of stop sign. "It was a *real* accident."

"How do you know that?" Jack said. "The accident might be a setup."

"Come on..." Cohen replied.

"It looks like I might owe Agent Barkley an apology, except that he's dead and I can't give him one. I didn't want to doubt him, you understand, but I didn't have any other explanation. I still don't..."

There was a moment of silence.

"That's it, then." Cohen said, suddenly, shaking his head.

"What?"

"Deal me out. I don't have a wife or a kid like you do, but I'd like to live long enough to have both."

Jack didn't know what to say.

"I understand." he said, finally.

"Drop this thing like a hot potato." Cohen urged.

Jack shook his head.

"I'm in too deep."

As Cohen finished his sandwich, Jack continued talking, but not about dropping the case.

"Let's say Charles Bakkendorf worked in the gold vault in the basement of the old Bolton Sayres' building."

"OK." Cohen said, hesitantly. He would have preferred not to discuss it anymore.

"Then, he gets removed from history, basically." Jack noted. "Removed, that is, to the greatest extent possible without having to physically burglarize every public library and physical records repository in America."

"Why not?"

"Why not, what?" Jack asked, confused.

"Burglarize every public library?"

"Well, I think it's obvious that they don't have enough physical people to mount an operation like that."

"A tiny number of people?"

"Maybe." Jack mused. "A few people, possessing high security clearance levels, could steal the guy's personnel file from Bolton especially if it's their base of operations. But, they must not have the work force necessary to mount a campaign nation-wide."

"What's your point?" Cohen asked.

"They can manipulate the internet, but they're still vulnerable." Jack replied.

"What about this guy's mother and father?" Cohen stated. "His relatives, friends… wouldn't they say something?"

"He doesn't have any close living relatives." Jack replied. "It was relatively easy to just make him disappear."

"I've got to go." Cohen announced, anxiously, and he stood up, ready to leave.

"Wait!" Jack begged. "Let me just bounce one more thing off you..."

Cohen closed his eyes in frustration. The whole thing was starting to scare him, and he wanted no part in it. But, in spite of that, he turned around and listened.

"What do you know about Marc Dunlop?" Jack asked, suddenly.

"Only that he's rich and a bit of an asshole..." Cohen said.

"Why were you hanging around with him?" Jack asked.

"I told you already." Cohen answered. "It was a networking opportunity. Nothing more. I haven't seen the guy since that night."

"OK." Jack said.

"Are you asking me about him because of the news?"

Jack shook his head.

"What news?"

"The President just appointed him to the Commodities Futures Trading Commission."

"What?" Jack asked, in disbelief.

"It's not official yet. In fact, it won't be announced to the public for a week or two, but everyone in legal knows."

"You mean Bolton Sayres' legal department?" Jack exclaimed.

"Yeah." Cohen assured him. "The Journal is already interviewing people for the story. He'll be the youngest appointee to the CFTC ever in history..."

"God damn that bastard!" Jack exclaimed.

"We should both make a stronger effort to get along with him, I think." Cohen noted. "It could be good for our careers..."

Jack shook his head in anger. Was his friend serious? Would he really pander to an asshole like Marc Dunlop simply because he had big enough family connections to get a position he wasn't qualified for? What a travesty!

185

"How can the President appoint the man like him to one of the most important regulatory commissions in the country?"

Cohen threw up his hands because he had no answer.

The whole place is a cesspool! Jack thought to himself. *Banking, government, New York City, all of it! It was a stinking rotting cesspool!*

He wanted out so badly that he could scream.

Instead of screaming, however, almost as a motor reflex, he took a bite out of the huge so-called "black & white" cookie he had bought for dessert. The so-called "Black & White" was a Marvin's specialty. As his taste buds savored the sweetness, it offset some of his anger. He stared at it for a moment.

In some sense, he decided, it was just like New York City and America in general. One side was black and other white. They were, of course, polar opposites, bad and good, the coexisted. Similarly, America was now an entirely corrupt place, but one that also happened to be filled with beauty, talent and wonderful food. That is always how things are with so many millions of people living together in one place. The city and the nation was the sum of its people and nothing more.

****

The giant blonde man seemed perplexed as he listened to the computerized voice that spoke to him, over his encrypted cell phone connection.

"Subject #1, identified as Bolton Sayres lawyer, Jack W. Severs, proceeded along with Subject #2, unidentified male, into the New York Public Library." the disembodied voice stated without elaboration.

"Identify subject #2." the giant blonde told the voice.

"Facial recognition impossible." the voice agreed.

"Why not?" the blonde asked.

"Failure of recognition software." the voice replied.

"What were they doing?" the blonde asked.

"Insufficient data." the computerized voice explained.

"Tell me, again, about ze' personnel office alert." the blonde giant demanded.

"Subject #3, identified as Bolton Sayres lawyer, Timothy Cohen, sought the personnel file of one Charles Bakkendorf. All inquiries on that name will automatically trigger an alert."

"Who is Charles Bakkendorf?" the giant asked, testing.

"Insufficient data." the voice replied. "Subject, Charles Bakkendorf, does not exist."

The last answer pleased the man. He had all the information he wanted, so he clicked the button to end the call. Then, he dialed another number.

"What do you want?" the voice on the other end of the call answered, with a Brooklyn accent.

"People in Bolton Sayres' legal department have been making inquiries about Bakkendorf." the blonde giant stated. "Yesterday, it was same man, Severs. Today, man's name, Timothy Cohen."

"Why didn't you erase Bakkendorf as you were told?" the voice stated.

"He has been erased." the giant replied.

"He should have been cremated. I should have handled it myself." the other man stated.

The giant squinted. He didn't like his judgment questioned.

"Using a crematorium would involve additional people..." he explained. "Should I take out Severs and Cohen?"

"Negative. Do nothing without direct orders from me. Do you understand?"

"Da." the blonde replied.

"The end goal, of course, remains the same."

"The same?"

"Yes." the voice said, and hung up.

XIV – A TOUCH OF GOLD

July 21, 2008 was almost a full 5 years before the fateful day, on April, 11, 2013, when Jeremy Stoneham went, hat in hand, to the President of the United States, begging for the opening of US gold reserves to save the banks. Things had changed a great deal from the state of affairs that existed in March of that year.

The automated trading programs that Marcus Dunlop used to manipulate markets were now concentrated upon the oil market, rather than the gold market. A few loud voices were declaring that both he and his bots had failed. They didn't have a clue. Such people expected miracles. When profits were late in coming, the investors got upset. The truth is that there are simply more and bigger players in oil than in gold. The players also have a greater capacity for pain.

The beauty of the gold market is that the main players, on the other side of the trade, are undercapitalized speculators. They panic easily, and the lack of capital makes it easy. They can be thrown out of their positions simply by running the price into pre-set stop-loss orders, where the computers would automatically sell them out in order to conserve cash. Since most of the speculators were also Synod bank customers, the banks knew exactly where those orders would automatically trigger.

The oil market is different. Alongside the usual undercapitalized hedge fund managers, there are well-capitalized state actors. They dominate the oil market, making it inherently more difficult to manipulate. The Iranians, for example, were already holding huge quantities of oil in offshore tankers parked in the Persian Gulf. That helped keep prices high, and made Dunlop's downside manipulation job harder. Most important, however, the most powerful single tool in his arsenal, which was the rock-solid U.S. government guaranty against losses, was usually missing when he undertook oil market manipulation.

Working within the limits imposed by the pool of Synod capital meant manipulating markets worth hundreds of billions of dollars a day with only a few hundred million dollars of seed capital. In a large market, with so many powerful players, that meant that the work was noticeably slower. Eventually, he would succeed. The fundamentals were solidly on his side. In fact, he was so sure of success that, if he had known about the Council's intention to crash oil prices, he would never have taken so much personal risk in the gold market. Huge sums of money could and would be made by simply by front running the oil price manipulation.

The fears of his colleague, Jennett, had put him into a real pickle, and led him to do a dangerous thing. He had been just shy of the full amount necessary to close on the Caribbean island. The prospect of losing a $500,000 deposit was frightening. It caused him to agree to a deal with Arthur Sansbury, the director of Bolton Sayres' vault.

Sansbury had claimed he'd done it many times before, in smaller amounts, and gotten away with it. His problem was a lack of contacts in the wider gold market. That was Dunlop's greatest strength. He knew plenty of people who would buy or sell without questioning the source of the material. He could move gold, quickly and efficiently, with no questions asked.

Unfortunately, the scheme was unraveling quickly and he deeply regretted ever becoming involved. Playing the paper game was clean, simple, and infinitely more profitable. Hapless hedge fund managers and individual gold traders were always easy to fool. Technical analysis gurus blamed the price movements on everything from the positions of stars and planets, to Elliot waves, computer based confidence models based on the number PI, Fibonacci patterns, and other nonsense. He got a good laugh whenever he read the half-wits who cited ridiculous explanations for the erratic gold price movements his bots caused.

The unraveling had started that morning. An employee had arrived in Arthur Sansbury's private office in a state of agitation.

"Charlie?" Sansbury had said, when he saw the man at his door. "What do you need?"

"It's the gold bars designated for Africa, sir..." Bakkendorf had replied.

"I'm glad you're working on that." Sansbury noted. "We've got to get them packed them up and out the door as soon as possible."

"I can't..." Bakkendorf responded.

"What happened?" Sansbury inquired. "Is it your back?"

Sansbury couldn't afford to have any more workers off work on worker's compensation. Lower back injuries were not common in the vaulting industry, but neither were they rare. When they happened, they sometimes resulted from moving many heavy silver bankers' bars. This was most frequent, however, when prices dropped dramatically. Delivery demand tended to spike into the stratosphere at such times, and it resulted in lower back injuries for the men who had to move the physical material on short notice.

He had two employees out on compensation already. Being understaffed, however, didn't relieve the vault of its delivery obligations or deadlines. It just meant that they could barely keep up. Another injured man would be a disaster…

"Don't worry, Mr. Sansbury, my back's fine."

Sansbury was relieved. What Bakkendorf said next, however, made him wish that the man had gone out on compensation.

"The problem is that the gold bars are all tainted."

Sansbury felt a surge of adrenaline. A foreboding of doom took hold and he felt sick.

"What do you mean, tainted?" he asked, trying to keep calm.

It was difficult not to panic. He tried to hide the slight tremor in his hand, and he hoped Bakkendorf didn't notice. How much did the man know?

"It's like I said, sir." Bakkendorf stated confidently. "The bars… they're, well, fake. Each one has a core of tungsten, surrounded by gold. By weight, there's more tungsten than gold in every single one of them."

A nasty pain was growing in Sansbury's belly. He had a long festering ulcer, and this news was causing it to act up again, or so he believed. He tried his best to control his terror.

"How do you know?" he asked as calmly as he could.

"The bars have been filled, sir." Bakkendorf insisted, proud at having discovered the anomaly. "No doubt about it. It's just a veneer of gold on the outside, thick enough to hide it. But, on the inside, most of the weight is tungsten, pure and simple."

Sansbury's heart raced.

"How can you possibly know it for sure?" Sansbury asked. "No one authorized you to drill into any of the bars."

"I used the ultrasonic tester." Bakkendorf explained.

"What ultrasonic tester?" Sansbury asked.

Sansbury was nearing 65 and retirement. His experience with gold was anchored in the 20th century, not the 21st. Testing a gold bar with great accuracy, in his mind, meant physically melting it down. No other test was 100% accurate. Because of the destructive nature of that type of testing, however, people rarely did it. Traditional vaulting practice relied upon a "chain of trust." If you could trace a bar from its original casting through known vaults, no one questioned its quality.

In recent years, ultrasound, which has provided physicians with pictures of the inside of their patients for years, was adapted to testing the content and purity of gold and other metals. It didn't boast 100% accuracy, like a melt test, but its 99.9% accuracy rating was good enough. In spite of that, no Synod associated gold vault regularly used ultrasonic testing, and there was a simple reason. For every 100 ounces of metal sold, the Synod member banks had no more than an average of about ½ of an ounce on hand.

Most investors thought their gold was safely stored in a bank vault, and they paid monthly storage fees for that. Little did they know that, in truth, little of it had ever even been purchased, or, if it had been purchased, that it was out on loan, or was sold to meet the liquidity needs of the banks in which it was held. Non-allocated storage contracts mean juicy storage fees, and no need to hold much real metal.

The major Synod banks have always maintained big stacks of bars that looks like "gold". These are on display in their vaults. Many or even most of those bars, however, are nothing more than bronze metal alloys, plated with gold. When the bankers hold tours for their best customers, and show them the bar stacks, they believe that investor confidence rises. They are right. However, the idea that an ultrasonic tester might get into the hands of an errant employee is enough to keep such devices at a distance.

"We don't even own an ultrasonic tester..." Sansbury said, trying to calm down.

His heart continued to race. This was close to the worst thing he could imagine. He was close to retirement. A scandal like this would get him in big trouble with Bolton Sayres, the Synod, and the Federal Reserve. It was an unmitigated disaster.

"Sir, if you follow me, I'll show you." Bakkendorf stated.

He led the old man to a pile of one-kilo gold bars. Sansbury didn't really need anything proven to him, of course, because he was the person who had tainted them.

A big batch of coin-melt bars had arrived well in advance of the delivery date, in an amount they had estimated would meet the deliveries. It arrived through the underground tunnel complex that led, back and forth, between the bank's vault and the Federal Reserve's vault at 33 Liberty Street. The Fed's rough and impure bars didn't meet COMEX good delivery standards, so they had to be remelted, refined and recast. Bolton was the US Treasury's primary agent in the gold market. Its vault was secretly equipped to do that. It could stamp bars, imprinting them with various brands to insure they appeared legitimate, including, especially, the imprimatur of the US Assay Office.

Creating new gold bars was something that few bank employees knew how to do, and almost none knew about. Sansbury did it personally after normal business hours. He used a specially ventilated room, and had assistance from shadowy people who were not bank employees. The identities of the people involved were as secret as the source of the gold, itself. But, for now, he wasn't interested in secrets. He just wanted to run back to his desk, where he had a bottle of Mylanta antacid stashed in the center drawer. He wanted to drink it like water.

He looked silently at the little contraption that would spell his doom. It lay next to the pile of gold on a small table, so simplistic in a new world dominated by tablet computers, smart phones, and other technical devices. Yet, this deceptively simple little device could prove to be his undoing. Would it be possible to refute the results? Was there enough time to recast the bars? Even if there were enough time, where could they find that much gold? Dunlop had already sold and delivered it all.

"Where did you get the device?" he asked, trying to appear nonchalant.

"It arrived yesterday." Bakkendorf noted.

"Who authorized it?" he asked.

"Nobody." Bakkendorf replied. "The manufacturer's rep says we've got it for two weeks as a tester."

Sansbury raised his eyebrow. Tight security surrounded the gold vault. The device shouldn't have been able to get through. The emphasis of vault security, however, was on stopping people from taking things out, rather than in. Security had probably x-rayed the device, but had seen no reason to detain it.

Damn the manufacturers! They'll do anything to make a sale!

"All right," he said, finally. "Show me."

Bakkendorf turned his attention to the pile of kilo sized gold bars. He picked up the first test bar, and smeared electrode gel onto it. Then, he attached the electrodes, and turned on the machine, pointing to the indicator dial.

"You see?" Bakkendorf pointed to the dial. "It's showing that there's a hidden core of tungsten occupying 4/5ths of the volume of this bar. There's only an outer covering of real gold."

"Maybe the test is faulty..." Sansbury suggested. "Only a melt can tell for sure."

"Well, we can melt it, of course, but let me show you another example." Bakkendorf said.

He picked up a different bar and testing it in the same manner. Again, 80% tungsten and 20% gold. More bars, again and again. Every one was tainted. Within minutes, he had tested fully 12 bars. All fakes.

"Maybe, it's a manufacturer's defect in the ultrasonic testing device?" Sansbury suggested. "Every bar is reading the same…"

"Let me show you what it does with a real bar I took from a different delivery set." Bakkendorf responded.

He picked up a small ten-ounce bar of gold, and tested it in a similar manner. The machine said that it was pure gold.

Bakkendorf looked up and spoke.

"We must have a record of where we got these bars from," he noted, "but, I checked the computer, and there's no chain of trust. They've got the imprint of US Assay Office, and they look brand new, but they've got an old date stamp. It's all inconsistent and suspicious."

Sansbury knew exactly where the gold had come from, but that didn't mean he would tell the young man. Instead of answering, he turned around and walked back to his office.

"Shouldn't we notify someone?" Bakkendorf asked, as he followed his boss for some distance.

"That's exactly what we're going to do." Sansbury agreed. "I'm getting on the phone, right now, and I'll get to the bottom of it."

Bakkendorf follow him, and spoke as they walked.

"What about the police?" he asked. "Someone sold us fraudulent gold bars. Shouldn't we try to follow the trail?"

Sansbury stopped, mid-stride, and turned around.

"Of course, but this is a sensitive matter." he explained. "We can't allow it to become public without going through the proper channels. Remember, banking is about reputation. This is obviously not our fault, but people will blame us. They could lose faith in our bank when we've done nothing wrong. We can't have this sprayed all over the newspapers. It makes us look bad. Understand?"

Bakkendorf nodded. He was still following a few steps behind his boss. Sansbury was desperate to get rid of him. He had to be alone.

"Charlie..." he instructed. "Go ahead, and remove whatever bars are already in the crates. I'm going to speak to higher authority and I'll tell you exactly what we're going to do as soon as I find out myself."

"OK." Bakkendorf replied instantly, and went back to the crates.

When he reached his office, Sansbury closed the nearly soundproof door and locked it. He walked to his desk, and opened the second drawer, taking out the bottle inside. Then, he uncapped the Mylanta antacid mixture and poured a long swig of the chalky fluid down his throat. The pain felt a little better after that. He grabbed the telephone with tremulous hands, and dialed the man he hoped could save him, if only to save himself.

Marcus Dunlop instantly recognized the name and number that popped up on his smart phone. Sansbury was calling from the vault. What was it this time?

"Marc..." Sansbury stated. "We've got trouble..."

"What trouble?" Dunlop asked.

"One of my newer vault employees found out the bars are fake." Sansbury explained.

Now it was Dunlop's turn to become nervous. His legs went weak, suddenly, and he collapsed into the chair beneath him. Sansbury told him everything, point by point. Dunlop's heart raced. His blood pressure rose.

"How could you not know this?" he exclaimed.

"I've always known of ultrasound testing." Sansbury insisted. "But, I never authorized using it."

"What if the Africans have one of these ultrasonic testers?"

"They don't." Sansbury said.

"Jesus Christ!" Dunlop declared.

"I didn't create the problem." Sansbury said, defensively.

Suddenly, Dunlop saw Sansbury for what he was; little more than a cave-dwelling ground troll in his opinion. The man spent his evenings, 85 feet beneath the bedrock of Manhattan, covertly melting coin-melt bars delivered by the Federal Reserve. His incompetence would drag both of them down a rat hole. The mess was giving him a headache.

He shook his head in frustration.

"How could you let something like this happen?" he suddenly exclaimed. "Fuck!"

Sansbury didn't respond.

"Why didn't you load that fucking gold yourself?" Dunlop exclaimed.

"I'm 64 years old." Sansbury stated. "I was up every night, overseeing the smelting and refining. Do you know how hot a furnace has to become to melt tungsten? "

"No."

"A lot hotter than for gold."

"Fuck the furnace!" Dunlop exclaimed. "It was a simple job. Just make the gold bars. Load the crate. Mail it out the door. That's all you needed to do!"

There was silence for a moment.

"Maybe, we can buy back the gold?" Sansbury asked.

"Are you out of your mind?" Dunlop replied. "There's no way we can buy that much gold in the time we've got. There would be a huge premium, and buying so much, so fast, would stand out like a sore thumb."

"Then, what are we going to do?" Sansbury asked.

He tried to clear his mind. He had to remain calm.

"I told him not to call the police." Sansbury added, hopefully.

"Oh, great," Dunlop commented, cynically. "that's really gonna' stop him. He's gonna' fuckin' report it to the police, for sure!"

There was dead silence for a moment.

"You'll never get your pension..." Dunlop added.

The mention of Sansbury's pension seemed to hit home. Dunlop heard the audible sigh of hopelessness. He liked that. The man needed to squirm. He deserved punishment, and it was always a pleasure seeing people in pain. The pleasure was reduced, however, because he felt miserable himself.

"Are we gonna' be arrested?" Sansbury wondered.

"By the police?" Dunlop asked.

"Yes." Sansbury stated.

He hadn't entertained that idea. Instead, his mind had occupied itself with the possibility that his father might find out. Stealing from the public was one thing. Stealing from the Synod was another. The penalties would not involve the official justice system. Any police investigation would end with one phone call to the right people. No bank could afford to have dirty laundry exhibited in public. Furthermore, a real investigation would reveal the government's involvement in gold price suppression, so highly placed government officials would put a stop to it.

"You think there's really a chance we'd be arrested" Sansbury repeated his question.

Dunlop shook his head, though the other man couldn't see him.

"No." he said verbally. "The matter would be dealt with internally."

"How?" Sansbury said fearfully.

"Likely, it would be referred to the Synod-wide RR." Dunlop warned.

"For one mistake?" Sansbury asked.

"It's a mistake that could cause enormous damage to the Synod." Dunlop pointed out.

None of it was true. His father would protect him and Sansbury would be protected as a secondary beneficiary. But, fear was fun to play with. The man had been in the business long enough to know the hidden face of the reputational risk department and what it could do. The official side of RR employed qualified security personnel on an open payroll. The hidden side dealt quietly with problems that had no other solution. It was staffed by "contractors for hire", suspicious looking men, with suspicious pasts, often having tight connections to agencies such as the CIA and MI6. Some still held "licenses to kill", issued by their respective governments, and were only moonlighting for the Synod. Others were in "retirement." All were potentially deadly.

When a newspaper article talked about a banker found hanging from a noose in his office, or splayed upon the pavement after jumping from a 40 floor office building, the cops ruled it suicide. The truth, however, was a bit different. The chance of Synod-wide Reputational Risk involvement was always there. However, that was something the cops knew nothing about.

"I'd swear not to say a word!" Sansbury exclaimed.

"Oh, I'm sure they'll take that into account, you stupid sack of shit!" Dunlop chided. "You stole millions of dollars worth of gold from the Synod!"

"You stole it too!" Sansbury insisted.

"Yes, I did." Dunlop admitted.

"What can we do?" Sansbury asked. "What?"

Dunlop was highly agitated, but knowing how agitated Sansbury had become was satisfying and made him feel better. The other man's expression of emotional pain was nice. He enjoyed watching people suffer, regardless of whether the person was a "friend", business partner or enemy. Sansbury's fear helped Dunlop calm his own mind.

"How old is he?" Dunlop asked.

"Early thirties."

"Married?"

"Not that I know of."

"Likes girls, though, right?"

"I think so." Sansbury said.

"Guys always need money for girls." Dunlop declared. "What does he make? $50, $60 Gs a year?" Dunlop asked.

"$65,000." Sansbury replied.

"The answer is easy." Dunlop concluded. "We'll bring him into the deal. Get it?"

"You mean offer him cash?" Sansbury asked.

"Exactly." Dunlop stated. "A cut to keep his mouth shut."

"Yes, yes, OK... yes…" Sansbury agreed. "Very good…"

It was a brilliant idea. Dunlop was proud of himself.

"What if he doesn't go for it?" Sansbury asked.

There was one thing that he knew. Every man had a price. The secret was only to find out what the price was. With income of $65,000 a year, a vault employee's price couldn't be too high. A million or two would be enough, he guessed. Once the oil manipulation was ongoing, he could make that money back in a half-hour.

"The money, uh..." Sansbury wondered aloud. "Where's it going to come from?"

"What?" Dunlop asked, disturbed from his thoughts.

"You know, we already have me, you and the black guy in Africa splitting the deal..." Sansbury complained. "And, I don't take home the kind of bonus you do..."

How did Sansbury know about his bonuses? What else did the man know? Did he also know about the side bets?

"This problem was created entirely by you!" Dunlop exclaimed, annoyed. "The whole thing is your fault!"

"No! I did everything I was supposed to do." Sansbury protested. "The ultrasound scanner wasn't my fault. I never authorized it."

Though the other man couldn't see it, Dunlop shook his head in frustration. It certainly was the man's fault! How dare he deny it? He toyed with making the man squirm again. He was so old and senile; it would be easy to fool him into believing whatever he wanted him to believe. By rights, since the screw up was Sansbury's fault, he ought to pay for it all.

Between the three men involved in the deal, they'd collectively clipped 12,860 troy ounces, with a market value of a little over $11 million. He had sold it on the black market for $9 million, with no questions asked. That meant that his share was only $3 million, and he didn't like digging into that, especially since he'd spent the money already.

Then, suddenly, the opposite half of his bi-polar personality took control. Instead of feeling vindictive, he began to feel magnanimous. After all, he concluded, Sansbury was nothing but a Plebeian. A common man. In contrast, he was a Dunlop, which meant he was a Patrician, a nobleman. Being noble carried certain responsibilities. Noblesse oblige, they called it, or more simply put, noblemen acted with generosity toward the common people. He was about to net tens of millions worth of additional dollars, from front-running the oil market. He didn't have any pressing need for the money, and there would surely be other manipulation events soon.

He forgot the pleasure derived from Sansbury's misery. As nobility, he had important matters that required his attention. One or two million dollars was chump change. Bakkendorf was a loose cannon who had to be silenced before he spiraled out of control.

"I'll pay 3/4s of Bakkendorf's fee." Dunlop announced, magnanimously.

That pleased the other man.

"Agreed." he replied, immediately.

"Keep the man there until I arrive." Dunlop instructed.

"What if he won't play ball?"

"He will. Has he seen the manifest yet?"

"No."

"Good." Dunlop said. "I don't want him to know where the gold is headed. There should be no chance of him talking to them, understand?"

"Yes."

"I'll have my own people pick it up and deliver it. Tell Bakkendorf that the bank will replace the bars with real gold, and that he'll be paid a big bonus for finding the problem. In return, he's required to keep his mouth shut, because the bank can't risk its public reputation by admitting that some of its gold bars were tainted. Any guy making $65K is going to jump at a big bonus, whether he believes the story or not."

"OK." Sansbury responded, enthusiastically. "But, hurry up!"

"I'll be there shortly." Dunlop announced.

The conversation was over. Dunlop hung up the phone. As usual, he was not as confident as he tried to sound. So long as Bakkendorf kept silent, everything would work out. The man would stay silent for the right amount of cash. That was very important. If the Synod Council discovered the theft, there would be hell to pay.

XV – LAURA REDECORATES

Delivery men were busy hauling new pieces of furniture up the stairs. Other men were frantically installing electronic gear. Three strategically placed burly security men stood guard; one outside the building entrance door, another at the stairwell and a third in the entry foyer. They were asking questions of everyone who walked in. The building seemed to be a fortress now.

The flat, itself, was still mostly in shambles. However, Laura had decided that new furniture would make a big difference. The few pieces in place already made the place look a lot better. She was eager to accomplish more.

"What's going on?" Jack asked at the door, once he made it past security. "What are you doing here?"

He had come to pick up the last few things he needed, and he was pleasantly surprised to see his wife. He tried not to show his surprise, and simply walked in and gave her a nonchalant kiss.

"You said you were never coming back." he continued. "What happened to that?"

"I changed my mind," she explained, with a smile, "and I bought stuff this morning, things that'll make the place livable again. Nobody will chase me from my home."

"You bought all this stuff this morning?"

"You can get same-day delivery if you pay for it." she explained, pointing to the side of the living room. "What do you think of the new couch?"

She seemed pleased with herself. He looked at the newly arrived French provincial style sofa. He had little interest in furniture, and couldn't get excited about it.

He nodded.

"Very nice." he said.

She seemed to dance around the room as she spoke.

"I've ordered new window treatments... new tile, new table, couch, a rocker-recliner, mattress, Persian carpets... new everything." she said, enthusiastically.

"I'm glad you're happy."

He was too busy worrying to become enthusiastic. He couldn't share those worries, however, with Laura. She was too emotional, and would react badly if she knew everything. It was better to leave her in the present state of elation.

"Most important is that we're going to have total security." she noted. "My Dad's men are here, wiring the place, and we're going to have a few guards permanently assigned by the building management."

"That's good, I guess." he responded.

"You don't seem to be enthusiastic." she noted.

"Well, I would have expected you to talk to me about this stuff, first."

"I wanted to discuss it with you." she explained. "But, I've been trying to reach you all day, and I can't. Did your battery die or something?"

Suddenly, he remembered turning off his mobile phone in a belief it might make it more difficult for people to track him.

"Darn!" he exclaimed. "This phone is so screwed up. It seems to turn itself off!"

He reached into his pocket, pulled it out, and turned it back on.

"It's getting hard to contact you." she noted. "It's either you're too busy, or your phone's off. What's going on?"

"It's not intentional." he said.

She shook her head, and continued.

"I'm throwing out that cheap crap you brought from California. It's ruined anyway."

"Okay, fine." he responded. "But, I thought you were afraid to come back here. You said it's too dangerous."

"My Dad says we're going to make this place totally secure. We're installing a full security system that covers the entire building."

"Did you ask the neighbors?"

"Why should I?" she countered. "They're getting free protection."

"Maybe they value privacy over protection."

She didn't respond and, instead, just looked around the room. Things were finally falling into place as far as she was concerned. With sophisticated electronic security and bank-supplied security guards paid for by the building's owners, new drapes, furniture, and carpets, the place would look better, be more secure, and even be more comfortable.

Suddenly, a walkie-talkie in her pocket buzzed. She slipped it out and pressed the button.

"Mrs. Severs, three more delivery men have arrived." a male voice said.

"Send them up." she replied.

A few minutes later, three strong looking men arrived, escorted by "Barry", one of the Bolton Sayres security guards, doubling as a building guard for the moment.

"Take this junk out, please." Laura directed.

About 45 minutes later, the men had removed most of the torn and broken pieces, and replaced them with a host of expensive-looking French provincial style furniture. A man approached her with the detailed invoice, and she signed on the line, signifying acceptance.

She handed the man a crisp new $100 bill.

"Thanks!" he said, enthusiastically.

"It's for you and your two friends." she said loudly so that all the men could hear.

Then, the movers left, and she turned to Barry, the bodyguard, who was still there.

"What do you think, Barry?" she asked.

The man surveyed the room and nodded.

"Beautiful stuff, Mrs. Severs." he said.

Jack interrupted.

"Excuse me." he said. "Barry? That's your name, right?"

The man nodded.

"If you don't mind, I need to speak to my wife for a few minutes." Jack continued.

The man, however, didn't immediately do as he was asked. Instead, he looked toward Laura for confirmation. Jack found that to be especially annoying. It seemed to him that a man ought to be King in his own house. But, here, he seemed to have no clout at all. In almost no time at all, however, Laura nodded, and the man obediently left, silently closing the door behind him. That left them alone together.

There was a moment of silence, and then, finally Jack spoke.

"I could have reupholstered that old recliner." he pointed out, annoyed more by the behavior of the guard than the loss of his old furniture. "You could have asked, before you trashed it."

"I want to be rid of everything that reminds me of what happened."

"Whatever…"

She leaned forward, hugged him, and then kissed him on the cheek, drawing him close. Then, she moved away, and took his arm, leading him around the newly decorated flat. She presented her workmanship with a florid wave of her arm.

"Ta da!" she said, with excitement. "What do you think?"

He shrugged his shoulders.

"It looks good. Why do I get the feeling that I owe a lot of money to your father…"

She shook her head.

"You know that my Dad never expects to be paid back for the money he gives us."

"That's not the point…" he insisted.

"It doesn't matter, anyway, because you don't owe him anything!" she exclaimed, proudly. "I paid for it myself, from my acting money, and the money from the insurance company. And, the management of the building is paying for the guards."

The run of the musical had been a short 2 weeks, but her salary was high while it lasted. Still, she was making a sacrifice. Buying all the new furniture had probably cleaned her out. But, he was relieved that her father hadn't paid for it. He was tired of being in debt to the man, regardless of whether he was expected to repay the debt or not.

"Thanks for the hard work." he said, and kissed her. "It's all nice, but… does this mean we're moving back in, because you said you never wanted to come back here."

Suddenly, there was a knock on the door. She gave him one final peck, stood up, walked to the door, and looked through the peephole.

She opened the door and a tall clean cut man, who looked like an aging US Marine Corp sergeant walked in.

"This is John Masters." Laura said. "He works for my Dad."

Jack stood up and the man offered his right hand in greeting. They shook hands.

"He's setting up our new electronic security system." Laura explained.

"Jack Severs, I presume?" the man said.

"Yes." Jack replied. "Nice to meet you."

"I'm glad we could finally meet." Masters said. "I've heard a great deal about you."

Jack looked at Laura slightly perplexed.

"Would you like a cup of coffee?" Laura asked.

"That would be nice, thanks." Masters replied.

"You want something, Jack?"

"No, I'm good."

She hurried to the kitchen.

"So, you work directly for Jeremy Stoneham?" Jack asked, trying to make conversation.

"Don't we all?" Masters said, with a laugh. "Technically, of course, I work for Bolton Sayres. But, Jeremy Stoneham IS Bolton Sayres, isn't he?"

"I don't know about that." Jack replied.

"Officially, I'm Vice President of Security."

"I see..."

"And, my job's simple." Masters explained. "We stop criminals, terrorists, what have you, from causing harm to our executives. That's our job. That's why we're here. We're installing one of the most sophisticated anti-burglary systems made in the world today. And, after we're finished, this building will be closely monitored 24/7 by my best men."

"I thought there was a guy named Navarro in charge of all that."

"He runs Reputational Risk, that's true." Masters explained. "But, I run security. There's an overlap but we're different parts of the company. I work directly for Mr. Stoneham, and, well, no one knows exactly who Mr. Navarro works for."

Jack smiled uneasily.

"The problem I'm having with all this is that nobody bothered to ask me."

"How could you not want to install a security system after everything that's happened?" Laura interrupted, as she returned with the coffee. "

"I didn't say I didn't want to install it." Jack insisted. "I said I wasn't consulted. No one's even bothered to explain how it's going to work."

"It's really simple." Masters explained. "We've installed video and audio viewing and listening nodes, and laser-based motion detectors. The motion detectors activate servo systems, allowing the cameras and microphones to track anyone and everyone moving in and out. Everything is fed into a central computer system."

"But, it's not only the criminals you'll be watching, it's us."

"We don't put cameras inside the apartment." Masters pointed out.

"Regardless..." Jack muttered. "I don't like being watched."

"We get that all the time." the man explained. "It's because you're unfamiliar with the technology. Once you're comfortable with it, you'll forget it's even here."

"Aren't there supposed to be hidden cameras and microphones already all over Manhattan?" Jack asked.

Masters looked surprised.

"How do you know that?" he asked.

Jack shrugged his shoulders.

"I know a lot of things."

"There are, yes." Masters admitted. "But, we'll be installing a denser cluster, and it'll be linked to a different computer system."

"If video monitoring is so useful, why hasn't anyone looked at the existing video and audio feed to find out who ransacked this flat?" Jack asked.

"We've tried that." Masters said. "But, it's blank."

"How could it be blank?" Jack asked. "I thought the system was on 24/7."

"It is." Masters agreed. "There was an outage. It happens from time to time."

"It seems like a convenient little outage." Jack stated. "There's a system, working all the time, and just when my flat is ransacked, it doesn't work. You don't think that's strange?"

"It's not my call to make."

"What if another outage makes these new cameras worthless?" Jack asked.

"This system is connected to a different network." Masters answered. "The two don't rely on one another. Nor do they trade data. We've also installed a more traditional alarm system. Anyone who enters this building without a proper pass code will set it off."

"But, everyone in the building has the passcode." Jack pointed out.

"That's true." the man admitted.

"So, in short order, they'll be giving that code to their friends, relatives, delivery men... everyone... and that means it's going to be worthless, very quickly."

"We can always change the passcode, and we do it on a regular basis." Masters pointed out. "Also, we've installed cameras and the computer-driven surveillance system."

"Tell you what, here's the deal." Jack said. "You can install the alarm, you can even have the armed guards on duty, but the cameras and the microphones... the ones inside the building... they've got to go. You can keep the ones outside, but no surveillance inside the building. Got it? I won't approve that. It's not the way I want to live."

"Mr. Severs, we're not trying to spy on you." Masters insisted. "We're trying to protect you."

"The way you've got it set up, the two things are the same." Jack declared. "You can leave the alarm and the guards, but forget about the rest."

"I'm sorry, Mr. Severs." Masters replied. "But, it's not up to you."

"The hell it's not up to me!" Jack exclaimed, angrily. "It's my place, and I'm telling you I don't want it. My wife agrees, right, Laura?"

206

He looked toward Laura, and she nodded, hesitantly.

"If that's what Jack says, then I support him." she said.

"So, that's that." Jack exclaimed. "Take the monitoring devices out."

"It's not up to you." Masters stated, again. "And, it's not up to your wife, either. You're just renters here."

"According to the law, during the term of the lease, we have the rights of the owner." Jack insisted.

"We haven't put one piece of equipment inside your apartment." Masters noted. "It's installed in the common areas; the hallways, the staircases, and outside the building; in all the public spaces. Liberty 19 has already given consent."

"Liberty 19?" Jack exclaimed. "What the hell is that?"

"It's the investment group that owns the building." Laura explained.

"Managed by Bolton Sayres, I might add." Masters added.

Jack stood up, and turned toward Laura.

"Did you know about this when we rented this place?" he asked.

"Of course I knew..." she answered.

"You didn't say anything..."

"Why would I?" she argued. "The apartment was empty. The price was right. I didn't want it. You did. I wanted the place my parents found for us, which was much nicer."

"Which they were going to subsidize..." Jack countered.

"So what?" she asked. "It would have been a nicer place."

"It was too expensive."

"My parents would have helped." she replied.

"I don't want any more of their charity." he declared.

"Fine!" Laura stated. "But, the bottom line is that you're the one who wanted to rent this place, and you're the reason we rented it. I don't see why it matters who owns the building."

Jack shook his head, annoyed.

"You didn't even tell me after the vandalism..."

"How is the ownership of this building got anything to do with vandalism?" Laura asked.

"Whoever vandalized us entered with no sign of forced entry." Jack pointed out.

"So what?"

"Who could do that without a key?" he asked.

She shook her head, flabbergasted.

"You can't seriously think the building owners, the bank, burglarized us?" she asked.

"We weren't burglarized, Laura. We were vandalized! We were ransacked. Someone came here to take something, not to steal. There's a big difference."

"What's the difference?" she asked.

"If you don't know, it won't do me any good to tell you!" Jack exclaimed.

He was unwilling to elaborate further.

If Masters hadn't been present, he might have tried to explain it all. But, already, in his anger, he had said far too much. He tried to take the conversation along a different track.

"Our privacy is being violated." Jack stated. "That makes a difference, Laura..."

The man took the bait.

"Mr. Severs," Masters said, "No one is trying to violate your privacy. This is all about your safety. You should be happy your landlord is interested enough in your safety to go to all this expense. Not everyone would."

"The investors in the land trust are paying for all this, aren't they?" Jack asked. "Isn't that right?"

The other man didn't reply.

"That's what I thought..." Jack said, sarcastically. "The bank does what it wants, and the investors pay for it all. They get the royal screwing..."

"Jack!" Laura exclaimed.

"I don't care who's paying for what." Masters said. "My job is to protect you, and that's it."

"Why don't you do your 'protecting' somewhere else?" Jack countered.

"You're being rude!" Laura blurted out.

"You're not the only person with an interest in this, Mr. Severs." Masters said. "You did marry a Stoneham. It was your choice to do that. You ought to think about your daughter, and not your personal feelings. Don't you want her safe?"

"Don't bring my daughter into this…" Jack warned.

He realized, however, that he had put too many of his cards on the table. It was time to back off. He had no way of knowing whether Masters was part of the conspiracy. Probably not, but no one at the bank could be trusted. He needed to speak with Laura alone, and he wanted no microphones on when he did that.

He had already done a great deal of reading on the details of how the THEATRES system worked, thanks to the voluminous materials sent by his father in law. Standard protocol there did not include placing microphones inside people's homes without a court order. Masters had confirmed that apartment interiors were off-limits. If the man left the premises, and they kept their voices low, Jack felt confident that he could speak to his wife with some measure of privacy.

"You've admitted that I've still got a lease on this apartment, don't I?" Jack asked.

"Of course." Masters agreed.

"Which gives me total control over everything that goes on inside it, right?"

"Right."

"Then, I'll ask you to leave the premises."

"Jack!" Laura exclaimed.

Masters spoke quickly in response.

"Don't worry, Mrs. Severs." he stated. "I'm not offended. It's his home."

He stood up, and walked to the door.

"Have a nice day." he said, as he walked out the door, and closed it behind him.

Jack went to lock it.

Laura turned to him.

"What's wrong with you?!" she exclaimed. "Can't you see he's trying to help us?"

"I'm not so sure. But, even if he is, I need to talk to you alone."

"You're making a mountain out of a molehill!" she exclaimed.

He moved close to her, and lowered his voice.

"It's not about the security system. I need to talk to you about the vandalism. The people who tore this place up... I believe they work for the bank."

She wasn't sure how to respond. It was an outrageous statement. After a moment, she smiled, but the smile turned into a nervous laugh.

"You're joking." she said, finally.

"Shh!" he whispered into her ear. "I'm deadly serious, Laura. Keep your voice down."

"You believe my father's bank burglarized our flat?" she whispered, skeptically.

"Not burglarized. Almost nothing was stolen."

She looked at him, no longer smiling. He looked deadly serious. It was pointless to argue with him when he got like that. Once he made up his mind, it was almost impossible to budge him. Time or evidence might prove him wrong or right, but no argument would dissuade him from taking whatever course of action he had decided on. It was part of what she both loved and hated about him.

She watched as he walked over to the window and looked out. The day was fading, and it wasn't easy to see in the dusk, but it was still possible. Master's team was busy fixing a multitude of tiny breaks they'd made in the mortar into which they'd slipped hidden cameras and microphones. It was just a matter of mortaring the devices into place.

He walked back, and whispered in her ear.

"The microphones outside may be sensitive enough to pick up our voices if we speak loudly." he explained. "So, keep your voice down, OK?"

"Let's go to my parent's house." she whispered.

Jack shook his head. He didn't really believe that her father played any part in the conspiracy fast taking shape in his mind. However, he could trust no Bolton Sayres' executive, let alone the man who ran the entire firm.

"There's no time for that."

"But, my Dad could get to the bottom of this."

Jack decided that he would have to choose his next words with great care. He didn't want to offend her. But, before he said anything more, she spoke again.

"He's the only one who can straighten this out, especially if someone from the bank is involved. I'll call him right now..."

"No!" he exclaimed. "Don't you dare do that."

Jack looked at his watch. It was 7:20 p.m. A few more minutes, and the sun would be down. It was better to wait, even though the darkness meant much less than it might have years before. There was once a time when darkness shielded men, but those days were gone. Night vision optics changed everything. Infrared CCDs are now built into surveillance cameras, and they see in the dark. Even if he avoided the guards in the dark, the cameras could still track him. It was impossible to know where all of the cameras were, and who was watching.

He picked up some books from the pile Laura had built up for their newly arrived French provincial bookshelves, and he walked back to her, handing her one and leading her to the sofa. They sat down, side by side, and he leaned over to give her a kiss.

"Pretend you're reading..." he whispered into her ear.

"What are you going to do?" she whispered.

"I've got work on my computer to do."

He reached over to the backpack that held his laptop and accessories, pulled out the computer, opened the lid and turned it on. It quickly came out of hibernation mode, and he pulled a CD from the bag, and inserted it. A screen popped up asking him if he wanted to install "Zambo." He clicked "OK" and then clicked through the questions on the setup routine.

When the installation was finished, a small icon on the top left hand side of the screen looked like a telephone embedded in a padlock. That indicated that he had successfully installed Zambo. Now, he had an encrypted method of communicating with his friend, Jose, which could not be traced. He created a new user ID, naming himself "Team Leader."

That left only one mystery. What was Jose's user ID?

"Occam's Razor," Jack reminded himself, silently, as he often did when he was trying to determine the answer to a hard question. The simplest answer was usually the correct one.

But, what was the simplest answer? Was there any simple answer? How could he find Jose's user ID on a highly secure communication system that didn't disclose usernames? At first, it seemed like a problem that could not be solved. But, a moment later, he had the answer. Jose was too smart. He wouldn't provide a method of communicating that could never be used. The answer had to be on the CD!

There was a tiny inconspicuous text file labeled "readme" on the disk, similar to many installation disks. He guessed, however, that this particular readme file was not from the software developer. When he opened the file, he found that his guess was correct. The file contained only one word: "Compumaestro."

That had to be it! He opened a chat window. At top, there was a little field, where you could type the specific user name of whomever you wanted to communicate.

He typed:

COMPUMAESTRO

Then, in the text box, he wrote:

HELP!!!

He clicked on the "send" button and the message was transmitted instantly. He hoped that his guess was correct. It was 11:10 a.m.. Would Jose be sitting right next to his computer just at the right moment? Then, he realized that it didn't matter. The man always carried a smart phone. Zambo was a tiny program that could easily run on smart phones.

He leaned over to Laura, again, while he waited.

"When it's dark, I'm getting out of here." he said.

"What about the guards?" she warned. "They'll know you've left. It's better for you to stay right here."

"They won't even know I've left, because I don't plan on telling them, and I'm not going downstairs..."

Suddenly, the computer beeped. Someone answered. He turned back to it.

Compumaestro – Hello! Who is this?

Team Leader – It's me, Jack.

Compumaestro – What's up?

Team Leader – Take down THEATRES, as we discussed...

Compumaestro – Now?

Team Leader – Yes.

Compumaestro – Any chance of doing it a few hours from now?

Team Leader – No. It has to be now.

Compumaestro – Give me 15 minutes...

Leaving his computer running, but putting it to the side, he pretended to read for the next 15 minutes while the sunset. Slowly, night fell. It was not entirely dark because it was still mid-town Manhattan, where lights shine 24 hours a day. They would not turn on the system just installed outside the building, until they finished mortaring in the cameras and microphones. It looked like they would work late into the night to finish the job. Meanwhile, if Jose succeeded in taking down THEATRES, the infra-red cameras that might otherwise track him would be useless.

He stood up, removed his work clothing, and put on a pair of comfortable jeans, a casual shirt and a windbreaker. He picked up the USB sticks, slipping them into their usual place in the upper right hand sub-pocket of his blue jeans.

Finally, the computer beeped again.

Compumaestro – Deed done!

Team Leader – Thanks!

He closed the lid of his computer, and stashed it back inside the backpack, put the bag over his shoulders, and turned off the lights. Other than the light coming out of windows and street lamps, it was dark, inside and out. He walked to the window, and Laura followed in lockstep.

"You're going out the window?" she whispered, incredulous.

"Yes." he whispered back.

"But, this is the fourth floor..."

"That's what a fire escape is for." he replied.

Then, he kissed her.

"It's crazy." she complained. "You'll fall…"

"No, I won't." he urged in a whisper, and gave her a final kiss.

"Where are you going?" she asked.

"Upstate." Jack whispered in her ear.

"Why?"

"To find the Mattingly girl."

"Why?"

"Because she's in danger and doesn't know it. There's no way to contact her by phone that won't be monitored. She's the widow of the man who wrote that diary. Everything he saw, she saw. She knows who the killers are…"

"Why do you always get involved with everything?" she declared. "It's not your business! Just call the police."

"I can't trust the police. I can't trust anyone…"

"How about me?"

"I just trusted you with my life." he whispered. "Don't repeat what I just told you, and don't let anyone know where I'm going, including your father. OK?"

Tears flowed from her eyes.

"No, it's not OK." she whimpered. "You're having an affair with this woman, aren't you?"

He wasn't having an affair, but he couldn't deny his physical attraction to the young widow. The intense attraction was memorable, though he didn't quite understand it himself. He felt an animal attraction to her that he no longer felt for his wife. The driving force was multifold. It was partly genuine concern for the woman, partly fixation on solving a mystery that intrigued him, and partly self-protection.

The woman upstate might have critical information about the identity of the people who had killed a lot of people already, and might even try to kill him. She knew too much and anyone who had read the diary knew that. He also might know too much. He could wait passively until they came for him, or he could go on the offensive. As he had told his friend,

Jose, he preferred playing the role of hunter, rather than hunted. He would go on the offensive.

It was also safer for both Laura and their little daughter if he did that. If the people who ransacked his flat were after someone, he was the target, not the two of them. Yet, if he stayed put, they might end up caught in the crossfire.

"This is about life and death." he explained. "Not about anything else."

"Then, I'm going with you." she insisted.

That was the last thing he wanted.

"You have to stay here to take care of Jenny." he replied, firmly. "Go back to your parent's house. You're safer there than you'll ever be here. Understand?"

The tears continued to flow, but she knew, in the back of her mind, that he was right. Besides, it was impossible to reason with him once he made a decision.

She nodded, amidst her tears, and he kissed her softly, yet again, whispering one more thing.

"The people behind the murders I told you about are the same ones who ransacked our apartment. The longer I stay, the more danger you're in."

"Then, you're never coming back?" she asked, through her tears.

"I'm coming back. I just need to gather the evidence to put these people away. While I'm doing that, I want you or Jenny out of harm's way."

He slid the window open.

"How about you?" Laura asked.

He said nothing in response. But, he kissed her again and turned to the window.

It was hard to ignore the tears, but he had no choice. He put on the ridiculous looking set of eyeglasses that Jose had given him, turned on the semi-invisible led display, and stepped onto the windowsill, squeezing through the open window. A moment later, he was on the metal grating. He hoped Jose succeeded in crashing THEATRES. If not, he felt sure that the killers would intercept, stop or even kill him before he got to his destination.

The evening air was cool but not cold. Still, if he hadn't worn the jacket, the sharp wind that blew between the buildings might have chilled him to the bone. The metal rods that formed the fire escape were also quite cold, but he ignored that, and carefully climbed down, step after step, on clattering metal. At the bottom, there was almost a ten-foot gap between the last grating and the sidewalk.

He maneuvered himself until he was hanging by his hands from the last grating, reducing the distance of the fall by the length of his body, which was almost six feet long. The final jump was only about 4 feet, and he did that as softly as he could. Hitting the hard concrete surface of the sidewalk, however, still stung. He felt around the bottom of his foot. It hurt, but nothing seemed broken, so he ignored the pain.

He was outside and so far, though it had only been a few moments, no one was rushing over to stop him! How long it would take the powers-that-be to undo the damage Jose would cause? Even when the system snapped back on, if he was careful not to trigger an alert, the computers wouldn't generate a report, unless one were specifically requested.

He glanced in both directions. The street was unusually quiet. That was almost suspicious itself. He shook his head. How paranoid he had become. In some sense, it was all for the good. Better to hope for the best, but expect the worst. The guards would be in the front of the building, just outside the main entrance. It wouldn't be hard, because he had to pass there if he wanted to take the shortest route to his destination. He could also follow a more roundabout route, but it would take a few minutes longer.

He turned and walked quickly down a side street, until he reached the main drag. Many other people were walking around, even though night had fallen. He tried to focus. About 5 minutes later, he saw it right in front of him. There was the mid-rise building where he rented a parking space for his car.

He fumbled in his pocket, found the key, and unlocked the steel security door on the side of the building. Then, he climbed downstairs. When he arrived on the fourth sub-basement, he exited the stairwell and looked around. There were rows of neatly parked cars. Only a few of the cars belonged to residents of the building. Many, however, had spaces that they'd gotten when they bought their apartments, but as city residents with no car and, in some cases, no driver's licenses, they were willing to rent their spaces to others. Jack rented his space from such a person.

The old beaten down 2002 Chevy Cavalier was exactly as he had left it. He had parked it there, months ago, and hadn't used it since. It always brought back vivid memories of when he had used it to drive Laura to the airport in Los Angeles. That was two years ago, and it seemed like another universe. Then, he'd driven it across the entire country, from Los Angeles to New York, on a long trip to be united with her that had taken 7 days. At the time, it had seemed like an eternity. The car had finally deposited him safely in Manhattan. It had always proven to be a trusty old hunk of junk, but especially because it had been sitting so long, he didn't really know whether it would even start this time.

He unlocked the door, sat down, and turned on the ignition. As feared, the battery seemed weak and the engine didn't catch. He tried again. A lot of pedal priming finally got the engine to start. Hopefully, the battery would recharge itself on the long trip he was about to take. He hesitated one last time. What he was about to do was, quite possibly, the most foolish thing he had ever done. Yet, it seemed like the only alternative. What else could he do? Sit by and do nothing? The girl was almost certainly the next murder target. Next, it might be his turn.

Once he drove out of the parking lot, he knew, there was no turning back. He released the parking brake, pulled out of his parking spot, and exiting the lot. By 8:10, he'd exited Manhattan through the Holland Tunnel. Then, he headed north through New Jersey, toward the New York Thruway.

And, then, suddenly, he realized that he'd done something that might turn out to be a disaster.

****

THEATRES Control Center was manned in three shifts, with 30-40 people on the job for each shift. In total, the command center employed some 110 people. An assistant manager supervised each shift, each specifically contracted to one of the four sponsoring banks. All reported to Adriano Navarro who was both the Director of Synod-wide Reputational Risk and the Chief Operating Officer of THEATRES.

Navarro was sitting in the living room of his home in Westchester County, when he felt a mild vibration in his pocket, and recognized it as the special rhythm that occurred when the phone received a call from THEATRES Central Control. He shifted his walking cane into his left hand, and balanced himself precariously, reaching into the pocket.

"Yes, Suzy..." he answered.

Bolton Sayres had once officially employed Susanna Maloney. Because of the inter-bank operating agreement, however, it was impossible to promote her to shift manager. Each operating bank was entitled to only one shift manager. That's why he had prevailed upon Christopher Dunlop, the CEO of W.T. Fredericks, and his strongest supporter, within the Synod, to hire her. She was now nominally a Fredericks' employee, and an excellent shift manager.

"Sir..." she said. "The system has been compromised."

"What? How?"

"A hacker came through the Bolton Sayres' interface, and introduced a virus that took us down."

"Isolate it, immediately!" he ordered.

"We're working on that."

"Where is Severs?"

"We're not sure. The last read we have is from his cell phone. He's in New Jersey, headed north."

"Where is he going?"

"North…" she replied. "The system crashed just before he left the city. So, that's all we know."

"Has the computer extrapolated his final destination?"

"There's still insufficient data. But, if you like, I could have the police stop his car, wherever it is, and question him."

"No." Navarro responded. "Just find out where he's headed. The moment he pops back onto the grid, let me know. We'll see how this plays out. How far outside the city can we track him?"

"We've got identity check cams at all the ticket booths on the Thruway, the rest stops, and throughout the toll payment system, traveling north and south."

"Good." he stated. "That should be enough. I need to know his coordinates on demand…"

"Yes, sir."

With that, the conversation ended. The problem would be resolved soon. When THEATRES snapped back online, assuming the boy was driving his own car, the tracking stations could detect it by the license plates. But, he had bigger problems. Who could have taken down THEATRES? There were three choices; an enemy nation, a terrorist group, or a rogue Synod executive…

****

Laura was just about to pack her things, when the apartment doorbell rang. She looked through the peephole. A well-dressed blonde woman stood there. It had to be someone sent by her father, she quickly decided. Otherwise, the guards would have notified her in advance of the woman's appearance.

She opened the door.

"Hello, Mrs. Severs." the woman said.

"Tell my Dad I have a few things left, but I'll be ready to go in, like, 10 minutes, OK?" Laura said.

"I don't work for your father." the woman stated.

That came as a shock.

"How did you get in here?"

"It doesn't matter." the woman replied. "I have something for you."

"I'm not interested." Laura replied, and tried to close the door.

The woman held the door open with her foot.

"I'm not here to hurt you, Mrs. Severs. I'm here to help."

"What do you want?"

"May I come in?" the woman asked.

"No."

The woman fumbled through her purse, even while continuing to block the door with her foot. Finally, she extracted a small device. It looked like a satellite navigation system. She handed the device to Laura.

"What's this?" Laura asked.

"It's a tracking device." the woman replied.

"I've already got a GPS."

She shook her head and tried to hand the device back to the woman.

"Does your GPS tell you exactly where your husband is, at all times?"

"What?" Laura asked.

"This one does."

"Who are you?"

"I've been sent by someone very concerned with your welfare. This is a gift."

"Who sent you?" Laura asked.

The woman said nothing more, and the door slammed shut, suddenly. Laura had continued to exert pressure against it even as the woman had edged her foot out of the way. She opened the door, and stared at the woman, who had her back visible, and was walking away, down the hallway, and had almost reached the elevator.

"Wait!" she called out.

The woman ignored her.

Laura thought about trying to catch her, but she had bare feet. By the time she'd managed to get her shoes on, it would be too late. She closed the door, and picked up a little walkie-talkie from the coffee table. She hit the send button.

"Barry?"

"Hello, Mrs. Severs." the man answered.

"There's a woman headed down the stairs. Detain her please. When you've got her in custody, let me know."

"Yes, Mrs. Severs."

Laura waited impatiently. But, after about 10 minutes, with no contract from the guard, she picked up the walkie-talkie and called him.

"Hello, Mrs. Severs." Barry answered, again.

"Well, did you stop the woman?"

"I'm sorry, but as far as we can see, no woman has come in or out of the building in the last two hours."

She stared at walkie-talkie speechless.

"That's impossible…" she exclaimed. "She was just here!"

Was she insane? Had she imagined the woman? She looked down at the device that sat on the table. There was nothing imaginary about that.

"Mrs. Severs? Are you OK?"

That startled her out of her stupor.

"Yes, yes, I'm fine." she replied, flustered, continuing to stare at the device just delivered.

XVI – ON THE RUN

By the time Jack arrived at the old yellow and white house in Paradise, it was about 11 p.m. Outside, there was a little lighted sign, mounted on a pole, and it read:

"Tagliano's Homestyle Bed & Breakfast – Your Comfort is Our Pleasure!"

Underneath that was a second sign announcing that there were still vacancies. Tourist season hadn't begun, and the place was probably close to empty.

He parked his car underneath the sign, and sat inside, doing nothing for a moment, but getting himself psychologically ready, and prepared for what lay ahead. It might not be easy to convince the girl of the danger she was in. He gritted his teeth, rolled up the window, got out of the car, and walked over to the door. There was no turning back. He had to do this.

It was ultimately his fault. The very possibility that she could identify the killers would surely bring them to her doorstep, and usher her to her doom. She had seen too much and, now, thanks to him, they knew everything. If they were as ruthless as they seemed, she was in mortal danger. He might also be a prime target. He had no choice but to do this himself. There was no one else he could trust that could do it for him. Someone had to let her know, and he had to find out exactly how much she knew.

The spring air of the Catskill Mountains is, on average, about 5-7 degrees Fahrenheit colder than in New York City, and that made him thankful that he'd brought the windbreaker. A gust of wind blew past him, as he exited the car, and the sharpness of the cold made him shudder. Then, a motion sensor, triggered by his movement, suddenly caused an outside lamp to turn on and illuminate the area.

He reached over to the doorknob and tried opening the door. It was locked. Next to it, however, was the "late arrival window" and a little button. He pressed the button. A moment later, he recognized the face of a young woman who came to the door, squinting slightly in the light of the door lamp. It was Sandra Mattingly, whose maiden name was Tagliano.

She unlocked the door, and ushered him in, robotically going behind the check-in desk and taking out a guest check-in slip, ready to fill in the form.

"You want a king or two queen beds?" she asked.

"Neither." he answered.

She seemed surprised.

"What do you want?"

"You don't remember me?" he asked.

She paused for a moment, squinting her eyes to look at him more carefully. Recognition seemed to come suddenly.

"The man from the bank?"

"Right." he replied.

"Why are you here?" she asked, perplexed.

"To talk to you…"

"In the middle of the night?"

"I've driven over 3 hours, up from Manhattan," he said, urgently, "and I'm here to help you."

"Help me? You're dropping the lawsuit?"

"I'm here to warn you that you're in grave danger."

The woman shook her head and laughed nervously.

"What are you talking about? How low will you people stoop to get hold of money?"

"This has got nothing to do with insurance money." Jack said, shaking his head.

"Then, what does it got to do with?"

"It's got to do with what happened on July 22, 2008." he replied.

Her face seemed to turn white, and she turned away, unwilling now to look him straight in the eye. She nervously picked up the pad of guest intake forms, and put them back underneath the desk. He could see a slight tremor in her hands as she did that.

"What about it?" she asked.

"July 22, 2008." he repeated.

"Why do you keep repeating that date?"

"Because it's the night you and Robert Mattingly saw two men bury a dead body."

She didn't respond, but was taking deep breaths and staring at the desk. Then, she finally responded.

"I don't know what you're talking about..." she said without looking up.

"You know exactly what I'm talking about, and I know exactly what you saw. But, they do, also."

"How would you know anything?"

"I read your husband's diary."

"You read what?" she asked, finally looking up again.

"His diary."

"He didn't keep a diary."

"You're wrong."

"Who do you think you are?" she snapped back. "Reading other people's diaries? If there's a diary, it's mine. It belonged to my husband!"

"Actually, from a legal standpoint, it's not yours." he explained. "It's the property of the estate, but, since you're the executor, I might have given it to you, except for the fact it describes a crime, which means it had to go to the police first."

"The police?" she asked. "You gave it to the police?"

"I tried to." he said.

"You just told me..." she started.

"I gave it to an FBI agent." he cut her off. "He was supposed to do an initial evaluation for federal jurisdiction. It was just an easy way to get it to the Verde County Sheriff while helping keep this FBI man, who's assigned to our bank, busy with something. I expected it to be forwarded to the Sheriff..."

"Then, why are *you* here?"

He paused, for a moment, and she waited for the answer.

"Because that FBI agent is dead." he said. "The original of the diary has been stolen. The FBI no longer even has a record of receiving it from me."

He could see her hand was trembling even at rest.

"I didn't see anything!" she exclaimed. "Bobby always had a good imagination."

"You don't need to be afraid. I'm just an innocent bystander, like you, caught up in this."

"What do you want?" she demanded.

"I want you to trust me."

"Why should I?"

"Maybe, because I drove three and a half hours in the middle of the night, just to warn you, and put myself and my family at risk to do that."

She shook her head.

"Why would you do that?"

"My apartment was ransacked a few days ago. They entered without breaking the lock. They tore apart everything. They took only three things; a printed copy of the diary, the receipt for evidence that I'd gotten from the FBI, and the hard disk of my computer. Nothing was stolen."

She stared at him, speechless. Then, after a moment, she spoke.

"I can't help you. Please leave."

He ignored that.

"I'm not the enemy." he explained. "The people who ransacked my place, the ones that killed that man who was buried, the ones who killed your husband and his family; they're the enemy. They wanted to find out what I know. But, you know much more than I do. You were there when it happened. You saw it. They could identify them, and they know it."

Tears flowed down her cheek, as she shook her head in denial. Then, she sat down to cry.

"No!" she insisted.

"Listen to me." he urged, taking hold of her shoulders across the desk. "You need to go into hiding!"

She looked up, shaking her head in disbelief.

"That's right." he explained. "You need to disappear, and so do I."

Suddenly, her face filled with anger.

"You stupid, stupid man!" she exclaimed. "Why did you do this? Why didn't you just leave it where you found it? Why couldn't you just throw it away?"

"How could I do that? Leaving it where I found it or throwing it away would be destroying evidence. I'm a lawyer. I did exactly what I was supposed to do. It just didn't work out the way I expected."

She shook her head, again.

"I know you're afraid." he said, softly. "That's why you stayed silent all these years…"

She didn't answer.

"You always knew there was no suicide, didn't you?" he said.

"I don't know anything!" she exclaimed.

"You knew that Thomas Mattingly never killed his wife or his son…"

"No!" she exclaimed. "I don't know any of that. I swear I don't!"

"You know." Jack said. "And, you kept silent all these years, because you're afraid."

Suddenly, she broke down, and collapsed into the chair behind the desk, crying.

"What about my son, my little boy…" she moaned.

225

"I also have a child; a daughter." he said. "I worry about her, also. But, for every minute I stay with her, I put her at risk. The same is true about your son. We both need to go into hiding, until we figure this out."

"And, how, exactly, are we going to figure it out?" she asked, skeptically.

"It all points back to the bank." he declared. "I think the body they were dumping was one of our former employees."

"I didn't see them murder anyone."

"But you saw them bury someone." he noted. "And, you could identify the men who did it."

"No." she insisted. "I can't."

"You saw their faces." he countered.

She shrugged her shoulders, but kept shaking her head and crying.

"It was a long time ago." she said.

"Did you get a good look?" he asked.

"I don't know." she replied.

"Did you or didn't you?" he asked.

"Why should I trust you?" she responded. "You work for the bank and you just admitted the bank was involved."

"I said that someone at the bank is probably involved." Jack clarified. "That doesn't mean that it's the bank's policy to kill people. But, listen, our lives are woven together now. We depend on the same thing. We depend on you telling me the truth."

"What good would it do?" she said. "They're all dead. My little boy..."

"What happened that night?" he interrupted.

She looked at him, and it might have been that she was resolving a conflict that had raged for a long time, inside her.

"I can't..." she protested.

But, suddenly, the memories she had suppressed for so many years came flowing out, and unquenchable desire to share it with another human being was too much for her. She told her story; everything, detail by detail.

"That night was really hot and humid." she began. "It's that way a few days a year, every summer. Neither of us could sleep. So, I left my house, and met Bobby, after my mom and dad fell asleep. It was almost 1 O'clock in the morning. It was cooler in the forest and I was always happy when I was with Bobby. I was only 17, and he was 19. We'd been seeing each other for about two months.

"The first 10 feet from State Road 23A is a wide grassy area, and the grass is mowed by the state, more or less, every month. Then, about 30 more feet is private property, but it's also mostly grass, and finally, there's the forest. His family owned the forest, and all the private land beyond.

"There's thick underbrush, and a tiny little glade that's hemmed in on four sides. It was one of Bobby's favorite places, and he was showing it to me, for the first time. No one from the road can see you when you're inside, but you can see out. You only need to pull aside some branches.

"It was beautiful that night, even though it was hot. The sky was clear and the moon was almost full, so it was even possible to see things in the moonlight, even though everything was in shadows of black and white. We were lying on a beach towel, when he kissed me.

"I'd never felt so close to anyone before. We were alone. There were only a few crickets chirping. Bobby kept pushing for sex, but I said "no", repeatedly. Still, he kept pushing and, eventually, I gave in. But, just before we finished, there was a loud rumble of a car coming closer fast. I was scared that, maybe, it was my parents, and the moment he finished, we both scrambled to get dressed.

"The engine stopped coming closer, but it was already so loud that it almost seemed like the car had parked right next to us. Bobby explained that the echo from the mountains expands the sound. The area is right between the two mountains, so it's kind of like one huge loudspeaker. The engine noise finally stopped though.

"We heard car doors opening and closing, and there were two male voices. Neither of them sounded like my father. For a moment, I was relieved about that. But, before long, I wished it was him. We went to the edge of the glade, parted the underbrush, and looked out. A dark BMW was parked on the grass.

"The trunk was open, and the two men were standing at the back. One was short, the other tall. The short one was black. The big one was white and blonde or maybe gray-haired. He was like a giant or something. I remember what they said:

"It's hot as hell..." the giant blonde man said.

"It ain't so bad..." the black man said.

"The giant finally unbuttoned his shirt, and went with the other one, over to the car trunk and opened it. They hauled out a narrow bag about 6 feet long. Something was obviously inside, and it seemed heavy, because they seemed to have a little bit of trouble lifting it. But, a moment later, they tossed it out of the trunk, and onto the grass.

"They took out shovels, and each man grabbed one end of the bag, and one shovel. Then, with two hands holding the bag, and the shovels lodged between their underarms and the bag, they carried the bag up the small hill formed from the sloping grass shoulder as it leads up to the woods.

"I turned to Bobby, and I was about to say something, but he put his finger to his mouth. I whispered to him. I asked him who they were. He said he didn't know. I also asked about the bag. It looked like a body bag. He didn't know. Finally, he told me we'd just wait them out, because they weren't moving in our direction. They were heading into the forested area, away from us.

"The black man stumbled over something, just before they got to the woods, and he dropped his half of the bag. Then, he cursed about having to carry a 'mothafuckin bag' and wiped the sweat off his forehead. The other one just told him to shut up, and said he was tired of listening to his bullshit. I don't think they liked each other very much. But, the man kept talking.

"We shoulda' burned him, man!" he complained. "Why the fuck didn't we burn this motha'"

"Just do vhat you're told, and shut up!" The giant blonde men replied coldly, with a Russian accent.

"My fuckin' hand hurts..." the other man complained again.

"Just pick up your side, and shut your trap!"

"The smaller man didn't say anything more for a while. He just did what he was told. I think he was afraid to say anything else. A moment later, they disappeared into the underbrush, and we couldn't see them.

Bobby told me he was going to follow them. I begged him not to do it. I just wanted to get away. We could have left, but he wouldn't listen. He said it was his land. The two men were trespassing, and he insisted he had to find out what was in the bag. He followed them. There wasn't anything I could do to stop him."

Tears formed her eyes again, and she flicked them away with her fingers, and went back to the story.

"I don't know exactly what happened when Bobby was in the woods, except what he told me later. All I know is that I was alone and scared. But, he told me it was much harder for them to walk than it was for him, because they were carrying this heavy bag. He managed to sneak around and secretly watch them. Finally, they dropped the bag with a loud thud, and caught their breath."

> *"This mothafucka' weighs a ton." the smaller man complained, as he dropped his shovel into the ground, next to the bag. "We shouldn' burned it!"*

> *"And, how ve going to do zhat, huh? Put on show so dat' zey vatch us on grid?" the giant asked.*

> *"Fuck the grid, man... we coulda' just taken it out! Just like we did when we got him!"*

> *"You don't know shit." the giant stated. "Shut up, and dig!"*

The other man grumbled something but he began digging again. They were both digging, but the smaller man was slower, and the giant blonde man seemed to resent that.

> *"Dig faster, you lazy fuck..." the giant said. "A voman can dig faster zan you."*

> *"Fuck your Russki ass, man!" the other man exclaimed, as he threw down the shovel.*

> *"Vhat you say?" the giant asked, coldly.*

> *"I said fuck your Russki ass, man! I ain't afraid a' you no more."*

> *"You're not going to dig?" the giant asked.*

> *"No, mothafucka'! I ain't gonna' dig until I feels like it!"*

> *"Good, because I tired of listening to you." the giant said, shaking his head.*

"According to Bobby, the giant blonde man showed no emotion. He just reached behind his back, and pulled out a semi-automatic pistol that had a silencer on it. Two short pips later, and the black man had two holes in the middle of his forehead. He fell into the hole, as dead as whoever was in that body bag. The other man grumbled something in Russian, and then, he started complaining, in English, to no one in particular, since no one was around, that "dey all useless pieces of shit" or something like that, and he dragged the dead black man's body out of the hole. Then, he just continued digging.

"When the hole was big enough for both the bag and the dead black man, he tossed both of them into it, as if they were nothing but rag dolls, and he started covering it up with dirt. Bobby didn't wait for it to be finished. He left and made his way back to the road. When he got to the BMW, he found a pen and an old 7-11 receipt in his pocket. The car's trunk was still open, and there were several different license tags in there. So, he jotted them all down, along with the one that was hanging on the car. He came back, from there, to the glen where I was waiting. When I saw him, I was so happy that I collapsed into his arms.

"He said we had to get away and he led me out. We both kept our heads down, heading in the direction opposite to where the giant blonde man was. It took us a little time but we finally reached the cultivated section of the farm. I felt safer then. Bobby said he was going to wake up his Dad to tell him what happened. That was the last thing I wanted him to do. It would have only been a matter of time before my own parents found out..."

There was a momentary pause in the narrative.

"And?" Jack asked.

"And, I decided it was some kind of mafia hit. Bobby didn't seem to care that we would be the only witnesses and targets if they ever found out what we knew. He said it was even more of a reason to tell his Dad. I told him that if he told his father, he'd never see me again. So, he promised not to tell."

She paused for a moment. This gave Jack a chance to ask a few questions.

"Your father passed away in 2010, didn't he?"

"Yes." she replied.

"What did he die of?" he asked.

"Cancer." she answered.

"I'm sorry..." Jack said. "Is your mother still alive?"

"Yes."

"Where is she?"

"In Albany, visiting relatives." she replied.

"How about your son?" Jack asked.

"With my mother in Albany." she said.

"Did you see the giant's face?" Jack asked.

"Yes." she quickly replied.

"Clear enough to identify him?" Jack asked.

"I think so." she said.

"I'm fairly sure that whoever buried that body also killed the Mattingly family."

"There's more. I didn't finish yet."

"What else?" Jack asked.

"A while later, in spite of promising not to say anything, Bobby said that he'd told his Dad. He told him everything, except that he left out the part about me. According to his father, we were now felons, for not reporting it to the police when it happened. We'd both go to jail if we ever did."

"That's not true." Jack commented.

"I know that." she agreed.

"Who told him that?"

"His Dad said he talked to the local attorney."

"Failure to report a crime isn't a crime in New York State."

"I know that now." she said. "But, Bobby believed it. He gave his father all the plate numbers from every tag he'd found in the trunk of that car."

"How do you know that?"

"Mr. Bennington told me."

"Is he the same lawyer Bobby's father supposedly spoke to?"

"Yes."

"You ask him directly?"

"Yes."

"And, what did he say?"

"According to him, he told him that it wasn't a crime in New York State."

"So, he lied to his son?"

"I think so." she agreed.

"What do you mean when you say he gave his dad 'all the plate numbers'? How many were there?"

"A lot." she said. "I don't know how many."

"You think his father traced the tags?"

"I know he did. An old high school football buddy of his works for the DMV. That's where he went."

"Hmm..." Jack mumbled, beneath his breath.

A picture was beginning to gel, as she continued to tell the story. Getting it all out seemed to be therapeutic for her.

"A few days later," she said, "his dad announced he was going down to New York City for a few days."

"Did he mention why he was going?" Jack asked.

"He said he had to talk to investors about his ski resort." she replied.

It was just as he had suspected. The elder Mattingly must have tried to blackmail someone at the bank. Whoever approved the loan must have done it to shut the man up long enough to kill him. There was no other answer.

"Less than six months later, Bobby's whole family was dead." she continued. "I was a widow, but with a little boy still in my belly, about to be born an orphan."

Her eyes were red and filled with a heavier rain of tears than before. She seemed to be sobbing uncontrollably. The truth had been suppressed so long that she'd forgotten how frightened she was. Now, having had the catharsis of telling all, she was deathly afraid, more terrified than ever before.

"We'll call the Sheriff's Office." Jack stated. "They'll provide protection."

"How can the Sheriff protect me? The FBI couldn't even protect its own agent."

"We don't know he was murdered..."

"You don't think it's too convenient for the intake record of the diary you gave them to be gone, along with your evidence receipt?"

She was right.

"They know who you are." he stated the obvious.

"Which is your fault."

Jack nodded, but explained the reality of the situation.

"It doesn't matter now whose fault it is. I had no way of knowing."

Suddenly, his attention shifted to the television set, suspended from the wall, above the desk. It had been continuously playing, but on mute. But, it was now displaying a photo of his wife!

"What the..." he exclaimed.

He seized the remote control, lying on the table, clicked the un-mute button, and adjusted the audio volume upward. The newscaster's voice became audible.

"...Mrs. Laura Severs, the daughter of financier, Jeremy Stoneham, CEO of Bolton Sayres Bank, has been reported missing, tonight. Mrs. Severs was last seen in the company of her husband..."

His own photo filled the screen.

"Police say that her husband, Jack Severs, is being sought for questioning about the disappearance of his wife."

How could this happen? When he'd left, her father's people had built a virtually impregnable fortress around her. He'd told her, specifically, to go to her parent's house. A pang of guilt swept over him. Why had he left. He should have stayed with her. He hadn't protected her. Could he risk calling the Stonehams? No, that was impossible. What good would it do? A phone call would simply reveal his location. It wouldn't help to locate Laura.

The TV said he was wanted for questioning. Why? If the police had spoken with the Stonehams, they would surely know he had nothing to do with her disappearance. Was it a trap? Were the killers creating this scenario to get him to call? If they found out, would he pay with his life? The Stoneham's would have the finest investigators working on it. There was no useful help he could offer.

The wisest course of action would be to find a trustworthy member of law enforcement, preferably someone far from New York City, in a place where banks had little political influence. Then, he could turn over the evidence he'd developed. With a few perpetrators in custody and her testimony on tap, he could go into a witness protection program, along with his wife, child and Sandra Mattingly. The chain of evil doers might be unraveled all the way up to the top.

"What's going on?" the girl asked, noticing both his unease and his photo on the television.

"I don't know."

"Who is that woman?" she asked.

"She's my wife." he replied. "We need to get out of here, right away!"

She shook her head in disbelief.

"You're married to an heiress?"

"She's not an heiress. Her father and mother are very much alive."

There was a pause. Then, the girl spoke again.

"I'm not going anywhere with you. How do I know you didn't hurt your wife? How do I know you won't hurt me?"

"If I wanted to hurt you, I could have done it already."

"Even so, you've got too many of your own problems. I think I can do better without you..."

"It's only a matter of time before they come for you." he warned. "You you won't stand a chance alone. I know how they operate, now, and I've got people who can hack their systems. You'd be better off with me."

"What, exactly, do you intend to do?" she countered.

"First, I'm going to run so far, so fast, that they won't know where I am. I'm off the grid, now, and I've got a good idea how to keep it that way. I'm going to hide, and while I'm hiding, I'm going to figure out what the hell is going on. I'll choose the time and place to go back onto the grid. I'll choose the people who get the information I put together. Finally, I'll go into a witness protection program until the people who did this are arrested and put behind bars.

He waited for a response, but she stayed silent for a moment. Then, suddenly, she spoke.

"You're not inspiring me with confidence."

"You're putting yourself and your family in incredible danger if you stay here..." he warned.

Before she replied, however, the front door buzzed. The young woman checked the video feed to see who was there. The closed circuit camera gave a clear view of the man's face on her computer monitor. She turned back to him, and her face was white.

"It's him!"

"Who?"

"The giant... from the woods!"

The buzzer kept going off, repeatedly. The man was pressing the button, repeatedly. When it was clear that no one would answer, the doorknob began to rattle.

Tears filled her eyes. Jack looked desperately around the room. He had to find something to use, and fast! Suddenly, he spotted something. A three inch paring knife lay on the inside lower counter. He grabbed it, and even as he did, a loud clang echoed through the house. It was the sound of a speeding bullet crashing against the hardened steel of the deadbolt! Clang, again! Another clang! The walls vibrated with each shot.

Finally, the lock broke off, along with a piece of the door itself, and the whole assembly fell onto the floor. The man on the other side, kicked, and the rest of the door swung open, crashing heavily, half against the

235

floor, and half against the sidewall. The huge man entered, with his right hand outstretched, and his semi-automatic 9mm pistol trained in their direction. He had to look downward for an instant, however, as he bowed his head to pass through a doorway too short for his mighty frame. That gave Jack his chance!

As the man came into view, Jack desperately threw the little knife, giving it everything he had.

XVII - STONEHAM GETS THE MESSAGE

Jeremy Stoneham sat quietly at his expensive mahogany desk. The library of his penthouse was a large decorated room he used as both a home office and a retreat. The furniture was lavish but it got little use. No one regularly visited the room except him. When he was there, he used the black leather executive swivel chair to sit on. There were also two armchairs in front of the desk, waiting silently for someone to sit on them, but, after 7 years, they had gotten little use. He could count on his hands the number of times people had sat in them. There had been a few times by his wife and daughter. There had been that one time when his future son-in-law, Jack Severs, sat down in one, and he had tried to bribe the boy to stay away from Laura. That was it. They looked almost brand new.

Deep stained mahogany shelves color-coordinated with the desk, and lined all four walls, neatly stacked with books of all types. The books were covered in the finest bindings and the subjects concentrated on finance and banking. Many were relatively new, but all were gold embossed like classic works. There was one real mint classic among them; one of the few remaining copies of the first edition of Adam Smith's "*Wealth of Nations*." His wife had picked that up at a Sotheby's auction.

Mrs. Stoneham and her interior decorator had decorated the library and had selected the books like everything else in the penthouse. They weren't there for reading. No one ever bothered to read one, least of all Jeremy Stoneham, who had never been much of a reader to begin with. They were there to lend "atmosphere" to the room. Therefore, the books themselves remained closed. Stoneham did make heavy use of the room, however. It was his office away from the office, a sanctuary and escape.

There was no true escape from the pressure of being CEO of one of the largest investment banks in the world. Kicking back and relaxing wasn't an option. He was on call 24/7. His fat compensation package included millions in salary and tens of millions in year-end bonuses. Beyond the money, there was the power. It could intoxicate. He hobnobbed with the most important people in the world. He controlled the lives of over thirty four thousand employees worldwide. He affected the lives of millions of other people with each choice that he made.

The bank's business model was simple. Make money at low risk by using government connections to trade the markets and to issue lucrative derivative bets like interest rate swaps. The bank also made a lot of money by underwriting stock and commercial and government bond sales, and by running an active clearing and retail brokerage house. It was an international business, and some of the richest clients were overseas.

Telephone calls might come at any hour of the day or night. That was OK because he was often available in the middle of the night. He didn't sleep more than 4 hours at a time. Being an insomniac made him ready and eager to take calls in the wee hours of the morning. Therefore, when the phone suddenly rang, at about 1:30 a.m., he wasn't shocked or surprised. As soon as he saw the caller ID, he picked up immediately, because he knew who it was.

The meat of the conversation came a moment later, however, and it left him agitated, annoyed and breathing hard.

"How could that happen?" he demanded.

"It's your son-in-law." Adriano Navarro explained. "His ID and password were used to access Bolton's intranet. He introduced a serious virus into the system and it's infected everything."

"I find it hard to believe." Stoneham stated, flatly. "He wouldn't do that, and even if he would, he doesn't know how. Where is he, anyway?"

"I don't know." the other man replied. "The virus was coordinated with his car leaving the city. We triangulated him, for a while, through his cell phone, but he turned it off. He's managed to crash everything, including all video and audio feeds, throughout the greater metropolitan area. We're basically blind."

"You and I both know that Jack doesn't know how to hack computers, let alone a system as complex as THEATRES." Stoneham insisted.

"I'm not saying he did it alone." Navarro insisted. "But, whoever did it, took out multiple layers of security. And, they got into the system by using his login ID. Where would they get that from, if not from him?"

"It could have been stolen. I presume you've plugged the leak?"

"We're in the process of plugging it. To stop it entirely would mean shutting everything down, which we can't do. But, we've isolated the virus, limited its ability to affect other parts of the system, and are eliminating it node by node."

"What about Khasan?" Stoneham asked.

"It's confirmed on Khasan." Navarro noted. "He's back in the picture."

"Could he be responsible?" Stoneham asked.

"You mean working with Jack Severs?" Navarro asked.

"I mean stealing his credentials and hacking into the system."

"It's remotely possible, of course." Navarro said. "But, although he knows a little bit about computers, to do this, he'd need to be an encryption specialist. We're working on identifying those who might be working with your son-in-law."

"How do you know Khasan is back in action?" Stoneham asked.

"Because THEATRES identified his height and body shape before it went down."

"Where?"

"We don't know. We've only got partial functionality. But, wherever he is, he's one of the most dangerous men alive, as you know."

The former agent of the Russian Federal Security Service, code-named Fyodor Khasan, was the product of a Chechen father and a Russian mother. He'd spent many years in the FSB perfecting his skills. Later, he'd been brought to America by the Synod's collective Reputational Risk division. That was back in 2006. His formal purpose was to deal with security threats in Eastern Europe.

The man had quickly discovered the luxuries of the western world didn't come cheap. His salary wasn't enough to support the lifestyle to which he wanted to become accustomed. A skilled assassin could always find wealthy people willing to pay juicy fees for private jobs. Often, however, the personal agendas and goals of these individuals ran counter to official policy, which is why Khasan was an outcast.

Some of his activities included the outright killing of high-level executives, without authorization by the Council. The collective Synod-wide RR had tried, several times, to take him out but, so far, it had not succeeded. Khasan always seemed to be one step ahead. Many people believed he was getting help from the inside. It was impossible to determine who was behind it. About two years ago, when his pursuers had gotten very close, the man had simply disappeared from the grid.

The fact that Khasan might be alive and well, and back in active operation was frightening. The man could kill in a thousand ways, appear and disappear without a trace, and murder without remorse. Not even the most sophisticated surveillance systems had been able to nab

239

him. Until the people responsible for shielding him were identified, the man would be nearly impossible to catch.

"When did you first identify him?" Stoneham asked.

"We don't have a definite ID, but we spotted what we believe to be him at 7:45 p.m. this evening." Navarro reported. "We had our net out, with everything set to catch him, until this computer virus took us down. If not for that, I think we'd have him in custody."

Stoneham shook his head, doubtful.

"You've never been able to catch him before." he said. "Why should it be different now?"

Navarro wasn't prepared to answer the question. In truth, nothing had changed. There was a good reason he couldn't catch Khasan. He didn't want to. Of course that was something he could never admit to. Therefore, he changed the subject.

"Which brings us back to your son-in-law." he said, finally. "We know he drove north, and disappeared. Just before he left, someone using his credentials crashed the system. It's a rather suspicious set of events, wouldn't you agree?"

"All these fancy and expensive electronics, and you can't even stop one simple lawyer from leaving the city?" Stoneham asked, smiling, enjoying the rare opportunity to taunt the man.

"That virus was designed to take us out, just when your son-in-law wanted to disappear."

"As I said before, he couldn't possibly create such a virus."

"With the system mostly offline, now, we'll need to resort to some old fashioned intelligence tricks, like questioning witnesses." Navarro noted.

"Good luck..." Stoneham said.

"In Jack's case, the most important witness would be your daughter, Laura." Navarro revealed.

Was the man suggesting that he intended to interrogate Laura? Navarro was as nasty a Dego as they came!

"She's not a witness to anything."

"She is." Navarro insisted. "But, it doesn't really matter anymore. She's gone too."

That hit Stoneham like a ton of bricks.

"What? Where is she?"

"We don't know. I was hoping you did."

"What the hell is that supposed to mean?" Stoneham screamed into the phone, standing up.

"It's supposed to mean exactly what I just said. We have no idea where she is."

Stoneham thought about his granddaughter. She was safe in Nanny Isabel's room, sleeping soundly, right down the Penthouse's main hallway.

Thank God for that!

"The ransacking of their apartment was a bad sign. As I warned you, you should have allowed my experts to deal with it."

"Masters dealt with it just fine. The whole place is wired, and we've got three armed guards."

"Your man doesn't have a clue where she went." Navarro pointed out. "He just let her go, and no one followed her. He designed that system to stop people from coming in, but he did nothing to track people going out. Of course, he also didn't bother to build a link to THEATRES, as I suggested he should."

Stoneham had instructed him not to link to THEATRES. As far as he was concerned, the less Navarro knew the better.

"I want every system diverted, immediately, to finding Laura!" Stoneham ordered.

"You know I can't do that."

"You'll do it, or else!" Stoneham exclaimed, but he knew he had no cards to play.

"Or else, what, exactly? You have no direct control over me anymore. I'm under direct orders from the Synod Council."

Navarro had always been a Bolton Sayres employee, at least officially, even Stoneham recognized the near impossibility of firing him because of the waves it would cause among other Council members. But, the man was implying that his relationship to the Council had become something more than before...was something different now? That was impossible because the Council hadn't met in full.

"Since when?"

"Your authority has always been more theoretical than real, and you know that. But, now, it's official. I work directly for the Council."

"That would require a special meeting and there hasn't been one." Stoneham objected.

"That's where you're wrong. There was an emergency meeting tonight. You were recused because of multiple conflicts of interest."

"You son of a bitch!" Stoneham exclaimed in a raised voice.

He was livid, but he knew he had to calm down.

The matter required careful thought, but for the moment he was so angry that he couldn't help but raise his voice. Had he have lost so much influence with his colleagues? Just a short time ago, he'd saved their collective asses by using his influence with the President. Navarro was unscrupulous and he had too much information about too many people. Had the dirty Dego threatened other Council members with the disclosure of deep dirty secrets.

"I'd suggest that you treat me with some respect from now on." Navarro said.

"I'll treat you the way I see fit."

"That would be unfortunate, given how badly you may need my help to find your daughter. Otherwise, she won't be found until she wants to be found and that might be a long time."

"You son-of-a-bitch!" Stoneham grumbled, and slammed the phone down.

The revelation that his daughter was missing was like stabbing a knife into his gut. Was she gone because she wanted to be? Or, was she kidnapped? Could it be Navarro's doing?

He tried to clear his mind. How to find her? He didn't know the first place to look. She might not even need rescuing. It was found it hard to believe, though, that she would voluntarily leave little Jenny. Still, it was possible that she'd left the apartment because she wanted to. That was especially likely if Jack had taken off to parts unknown. She might just be traveling with her husband, but if that were the case, why hadn't she told him in advance? Khasan was out there too…

There were several potential paths to follow, at this point. He could use his political connections to take control THEATRES by force. He could make use of the system to find her. It wasn't something he particularly wanted to pursue. Taking the control center would be messy and complicated. It would be better to get voluntary cooperation. Much as he disliked Navarro, no one understood the system as well as he did.

He spent a moment wondering about Jack. Was it even remotely possible that he was capable of introducing a virus powerful enough to collapse the network? If he was capable of doing that, didn't that prove his fitness to serve as Navarro's replacement. It would take time to groom him for the job, and to convince enough other minds on the Synod Council that he was the man for it. But, it wasn't an easy prize. All the CEO's had to agree. Jack had to want it badly enough to make that happen. So far, his interest level had seemed luke-warm.

There was no time to dwell on Jack's future employment. He had more immediate problems, most notably the whereabouts of his daughter. He had telephone calls to make, and would be calling in some favors. In the end, he also had to strengthen his political position. He had to find out exactly what had happened in the Synod Council. This was certain to involve another big internal political struggle.

Finding Laura was the priority. Everything else had to be on the back burner. His wife was fast asleep. The baby and her Nanny were sleeping in another room. It was better to let all of them sleep. Having them stay up all night worrying about Laura would be no help. By morning, the whole affair might be over. Thankfully, the library was noise-proof. No matter how much noise he'd made as he shouted at Navarro, no one could have heard any of it.

He slipped into the master bedroom, for a moment, and taking great care not to wake her, gave Erica a light kiss on the forehead. Then, he closed the door silently, walked into the kitchen, picked up a pen, and tore off a little slip of paper. He wrote a quick note and left it on the kitchen countertop.

> *"Sorry, honey, I had to leave. The firm has pressing business abroad. You know how the time zone differences cause problems, sometimes..."*

A few minutes later, he was out the door. The night was silent.

XVIII - FYODOR KHASAN

After driving several hours, the giant blonde man finally arrived at his destination, determined to do the job. The woman had to die. The only question left was the manner of her death. Staged suicide was a customer favorite, but he preferred the garrote. On the other hand, a simple breaking, entering and quick murder could also work well.

Even as a petty criminal on the streets of Moscow he'd only been caught once. That was long before the FSB had trained him as an assassin. He knew how to kill in hundreds of different ways, from poisons like ricin and radioactive polonium to a simple muffled shot to the back of the head.

He hadn't killed many young girls. It wasn't because he had qualms about doing it. It was simply a matter of supply and demand. The major demand was for assassinations that focused on business and political competitors. Young girls rarely fit that bill. He figured, however, that it wouldn't be particularly difficult. She was likely to freeze up like a deer in the headlights, making her an easy target.

He glanced at the car's built-in satellite navigation system, which told him he was almost there. The pleasant voice told him to go straight, and, finally, when he arrived at "Tagliano Bed & Breakfast", it told him to stop. He did that, and he parked his Jaguar next to an older 2002 Chevy Cavalier. It was the only other car in the front parking lot.

Inside the glove compartment, he had stashed a pair of black gloves and a Taurus 9 mm semi-automatic handgun. The gloves would insure no fingerprints. The gun was a throwaway he'd picked up at the black market in Miami. Originally manufactured in Sao Paulo, Brazil, it had been stolen in Rio and quietly shipped it to the United States. He would rid himself of it after the job. If police found it, they'd be able to trace it back to its original Brazilian owner.

He slipped on the black gloves and picked up the weapon. There was a silencer in the glove compartment, and he screwed it onto the nozzle. The handgun would emit nothing more than a short pip when fired. He pulled the photo of Sandra Tagliano out of his pocket, stared at it for a moment, and committed the face to memory. Then, the photo went back into his pocket, and he exited the car.

He reached the front door, which was locked. He rang the doorbell. No one answered. He tried his best to jimmy the lock, but the well designed deadbolt couldn't be triggered without better equipment. In frustration, therefore, he shook the knob violently. It didn't help. He didn't like making a lot of noise, but speed was more important than silence. He pointed the 9 mm semi-automatic directly at the deadbolt and fired several times.

Each time the bullet met the bronze there was a loud clack. The silencer provided no benefit, of course, when the bullet noise was from an impact on a metal deadbolt. It made a lot of noise. After a few more shots, the entire lock assembly, including a piece of the door itself, broke off, and with the door still in place, he kicked heavily, and it fell open.

Instantly, he spotted the woman in the photograph at the front desk. The figure of a man was standing by her side. There was no time to figure out who he was. Collateral damage was undesirable, but often unavoidable. The rule was to leave no witnesses behind. The client would understand. The man was in the wrong place at the wrong time. The doorframe was too small, and he stooped down in order to pass through. He lifted the gun to take his first aim at the girl first.

Meanwhile, the other man waited patiently. He hadn't thrown a knife in years, and this was a light one; a cheap blade, poorly balanced and difficult to aim. Yet, he hadn't forgotten what he'd learned. He knew how to throw. Having trained long and hard in his youth, he had to rely on instinct now. The training would determine whether he would get it right, so many years later, even with an inferior blade.

That little unbalanced blade spun through the air like a tiny bolt of lightning. It didn't exactly hit the mark, which was straight to the heart. It hit very far from target. In fact, he was lucky to have hit anything at all. But, luck was on his side, and the knife sliced into the huge man, deep into edges of the meat on his chest, clipping a minor vein, but one capable of emitting enough blood to make quite a mess. There it sat, the handle sticking out, as blood gushed out of the wound, like red-dyed water spraying out of a fountain.

The big man roared in pain, even while shooting at the same time. The shot went wild, hitting the floor several feet in front of the girl. In the next moment, he was clutching his damaged leg with his free hand. He grimaced in pain. Meanwhile, the smaller man jumped forward and kicked his gun out of his hand, and away to the side on the floor. Following up, Jack kicked it far enough to prevent the man from recovering it.

Then, he landed another kick to the big man's face, and a heavy blow to the solar plexus. Both blows connected perfectly, and if he had been dealing with any normal man, it would have either knocked him senseless or killed him outright. However, Khasan was no ordinary man. A knife might slice through his flesh as easily as that of any other man, and it happened that he was acutely sensitive. His pain threshold was very low. The giant was able to dish it out, but incapable of tolerating it himself.

The mere blunt impact of a comparatively tiny flying foot and fist, however, was another matter. Khasan was almost 7 feet tall, and weighed in at over 420 pounds. Every bit of that prodigious mass was whalebone and muscle. In contrast, Jack was slightly less than 6 feet, and 168-pounds. The big man was more than 2 ½ times his size. It was something like a 5 year old child fighting a full grown man. His kick and punch, well targeted though they were, had little effect.

The sad reality was that he'd lost a critical element of surprise. The man flicked the second kick away like a feather with one huge paw. Then, he grabbed Jack's leg, and pulled him down hard, onto the floor, where he landed on his back, onto the slippery coating of bright red blood that had pooled up near the big man. If the huge man had his senses about him, he almost certainly would have finished him off. Thankfully, for Jack, he didn't.

With extreme sensitivity to the searing pain of the knife in his side, the man focused on staunching the bleeding, and controlling the pain. He grabbed the hilt of the blade, pulled it out quickly, and howled in pain. There was a gusher of blood, for a few seconds, before he could staunch it, but a moment later, it had stopped. This momentary preoccupation gave his opponent a chance to get away.

Jack had been convinced that a hand-to-hand battle was unwinnable. It was too dramatic of a mismatch. Against such a huge opponent, no amount of skill, speed or training would be able to compensate for the difference in size. He needed a gun, or a well balanced knife, and he had neither. The big man's gun was too far away to grab. He couldn't get to it without passing within reach and, if he did that, it would spell catastrophe. There was only one alternative. Run!

The woman still stood transfixed behind the front desk, paralyzed like a deer in the headlights, exactly as Khasan had expected. She was staring at what unfolded in front of her, but seemed unable to react. Jack jumped up, ran toward her, and grabbed her hand. He pulled her after him, urging by whisper and gesture for her to follow. She did.

They could no longer go forward, because the giant blonde man lay between them and the front door. If they tried to pass him, he'd surely manage to grab one or both of them. Then, they would be doomed. They had to go backward, and Jack, his shirt and pants still partly wet and stained red with the big man's blood, fled deeper into the house, toward the back door.

Meanwhile, with his moment of disorientation passing, Khasan was coming to his senses. He picked up the knife that had wounded him, and cut a wide piece of cloth from his shirt, and tore it off after ripping it the rest of the way. He wadded it up, put it in his right hand, and pressed it hard against the wound, staunching the bleeding, at least for the moment.

Almost in the same instant, he turned and picked up his gun. He could hear the whispers, deeper in the house, and even though he couldn't make out what they said to one another, he knew it was the man and the woman. He only needed to follow the sound.

"Come on!" Jack urged, gesturing for the girl to follow.

She no longer needed any convincing. They passed through the sitting room, and she pointed to the right.

"That's the way to the back door?" he asked, anxiously.

She nodded, unable to voice sounds from her mouth anymore. He pulled her along after him. A moment later, they were out the back door and in the back parking lot. Around them was the unpaved gravel.

"There!" she exclaimed, finally regaining the power of speech, and pointing to an old Ford Ranger pickup truck.

They ran toward it and got in. She fumbled in her purse to find the keys, and handed them over. He frantically turned the key, trying to start the ignition. The engine turned over, started, and then stalled. He continued to turn the key, stepping on the accelerator pedal, periodically, to prime the pump. The same thing happened, several times.

For an instant, he saw the giant man barreling out of the back door with his gun raised. Then, like a miracle, the small pickup truck's engine roared to life. Even as the giant stopped to take aim, Jack released the brake and shifted into reverse, almost instantly slamming down on the accelerator pedal, causing a sudden surge backward. The man had expected him to go forward and not back, so his shots went wild.

Then, Jack put the transmission into drive, and sped forward. The man continued to shoot, but the loss of blood, the shock, the pain and the need to apply continuous pressure on the wound with his right hand, combined to make him a very bad shot with his left. He aimed at the tires, but missed. Then, he fired directly into the rear glass window, hoping to hit one or both of the people inside, but only succeeded in shattering the glass into pieces.

Despite the silencer, the shots made a loud racket as they crashed against sheet metal and glass. The old Ford Ranger, now bearing a selection of bullet holes and a shattered rear window, sped into the night, and was soon out of sight, its occupants shaken, but unharmed.

Jack's foot pressed the pedal down to the metal of the floor. The little Ranger had little in the way of an engine, but with what it had, it sped up to what seemed like light speed, and they fled as fast as the car would go, their final destination unknown. Fyodor Khasan stood, like a giant statue, continuing to silently hold his gun in one hand, while applying pressure to his wound with the other. He watched as the vehicle left the range of his sight and pistol, a bit shaky on his feet from the blood loss.

He had additional weaponry, more precise and with greater range, but they were still inside his vehicle. There was no time to get them. The pain was bad, and he knew it would get worse. The blade looked dirty, and the wound was probably infected. He thought about his next move.

Should he pursue the man and woman without delay? His Jag was much faster than a crappy old Ranger pickup. If they stayed on SR 22, he would be sure to catch them, but there was no guarantee that they would. There were plenty of side roads for them to take. It was far too dark to follow the trail, even if he used night vision goggles, and he was badly hurt. His blood was everywhere, a genetic marker that could prove his guilt if he were ever arrested.

The operation seemed cursed. Once again, it had ended in disaster. He looked down at his leg. If he didn't get antibiotics quickly, it might become badly infected. He had never encountered a situation where he had been unable to get rid of the evidence barring a drastic remedy. This would be a first. The drastic action he was now contemplating would attract an enormous amount of unwanted attention that the client wouldn't be happy about it, but he had no choice.

The boarding house was isolated, and far enough away from other dwellings. It was possible that no one had heard the racket. But, that was certainly not a given. The place seemed empty now. If there were any guests sleeping in the bedrooms, upstairs, they probably would have woken up and he would have known about them. It didn't matter. Anyone there was a potential witness, and he would have to kill them anyway. There was no time to waste. He made his way back through the house, to the other side of the parking lot. There, in the trunk of his car, he retrieved two 5-gallon cans of gasoline and limped back to the house carrying them in one huge hand.

He poured the gasoline as he walked, catching all the surfaces where his blood might have dripped. Then, he continued throughout the house, saturating the floor, carpets and furniture. He continued the process as quickly as he could. Finally, he made his way out to the back parking lot and dribbled what was left of the gasoline along the path he'd taken there.

When the gasoline was gone, he discarded the cans and moved into the kitchen. With a quick twist of a small wrench, he expertly opened the propane gas tubes that led to the oven and heating system. The uncontrolled leak would quickly vent gas all over the house. Thankfully, it was a rather chilly night, and all the windows were already shut. That saved time and effort.

He made his way back to his car as quickly as he could and drove away. Then, he heard the faint sound of sirens come closer. Someone had already reported the incident! He had acted just in time. A safe distance from the house, he drove off the little road, and quietly climbed out. He opened the rear door to the vehicle, and pulled up the back seat cushion.

Underneath, in a specially designed compartment, was what he was looking for. He snapped the parts together. In less than a minute, the portable grenade launcher was set up and ready to go. Three Sheriff's cars sped past, their sirens blaring, but none noticed Khasan, who had carefully parked in the shadows of the berm.

The house was clearly visible in his scope. He mounted the device onto the hood to stabilize it, and took careful aim. Then, he fired. The small rocket-grenade made a screeching whistle as it careened toward its target. It seemed to strike almost immediately. A massive explosion was the result, as the gas leak and the gasoline combined to blow the house to pieces. The flames licked everything, and finally, the entire building imploded, falling into itself in a viciously burning pile of rubble.

Fyodor Khasan nodded his head, satisfied, but he was angry and in pain. The explosion had accomplished nothing more than covering up the mistakes he'd made. He had made sure, now, that his tracks could not be followed. The blood was incinerated, his DNA no longer identifiable. If there were any guests upstairs, they would be but ashes, and would tell no tales.

The implosion would also keep the local Sheriff's deputies busy, while he dealt with his next task. Feeling increasingly ill, he disconnected the grenade launcher, and limped back to the rear door, replacing the parts into their holding position underneath the seat. It wasn't easy to open the driver's side door. He had some antibiotics in his first aid kit, but proper medical attention was critical. He'd seen soldiers with festering wounds who never recovered.

He found and opened the little medical kit under the passenger's side seat, and cut off a long piece of gauze bandage. Then, he dribbled hydrogen peroxide onto the wound and it stung like hell! The kit also contained a bottle of Kyostat, a special product designed for the US armed forces that coagulated blood on contract. He dusted some of it onto the wound. Then, he painted the whole thing with povidine iodine, wrapped it in gauze and sat back.

It was time to open his favorite beverage, so he took one of the cans of Coca Cola he always kept in the car and washed down a capsule of amoxicillin. He needed something more powerful than the tiny amount of caffeine contained within the cola bean. There was another vile, in the first aid kit, and it contained a white powder that looked something like Kyostat.

The other white powder, however, was about as similar to the instant coagulant as iodine is to morphine. He poured a tiny amount onto his hand and snorted it up a small tube. The sudden rush gave him what he wanted. Cocaine was his drug of choice. He bought the finest, and he'd been taking it so long it now seemed to affect him not much more than a strong cup of coffee. It helped clear his mind, and made him feel less dizzy.

He still had a lot of work to do. To insure there was no trail to follow, he had to rid himself of one of his most prized possessions. The girl and her male companion were still alive, and they might be able to describe his car. Jaguars are unusual enough to allow some level of identification even if he changed the plates.

He drove to the little downtown area, a small drag of pavement a few minutes away from the Tagliano Inn by car. When he reached it, he surveyed the area quickly, and spotted an older 2006 model Ford Explorer parked in front of the local hardware store. There were a few newer vehicles, but none of those would be suitable. The newer ones took too long to hot wire. An older Explorer would be quick and easy.

He pulled parallel to the Explorer, and painfully climbed out, the wound throbbing. He limped a foot or two over to the other car. It hurt to touch it, but it wasn't bleeding anymore. He quickly jimmied the lock on the front driver's side and opened the door to the Explorer. Maneuvering carefully into the compartment, he sat down slowly, trying to avoid touching the injured leg.

A small wire cutter and electrical tape was more than enough to jerry-rig the ignition assembly. It took only 60 seconds from the moment he entered to the moment he held the two hot wires together, starting the car by bypassing the ignition interlock. The engine roared to life. He looked at the gas tank meter, and noted, with satisfaction, that it was almost full. He carefully exited, stood up, and limped back to the

Jaguar. Then, he gathered his things, including a collection of fake VIN placards, license tags, night vision goggles, and an ultra-secure Russian-built tablet based on the same modified derivative of Android, RuMos, that powered his phone.

There was one last thing. He pulled a simple shoebox out from under the seat. Inside, there were stacks of currency. There were several hundred $100 dollar bills and two hundred fifty €500 Euro notes. It amounted to more than $155,000 when converted to dollars. He carried the box in one arm as he limped to the rear seat. He lifted it up to reveal a special compartment, filled with pallets of C-4 explosive.

The job of molding and positioning that putty in the key points of the vehicle didn't take long. Finally, he wired it and connected the car's battery, setting a timer for 15 minutes. He closed the door and made his way toward the Explorer. There was plenty of time. At the rear of his new vehicle, he unscrewed the existing license tags, and replaced them with new tags from his collection.

Later, he'd access the New York State DMV database. The SUV would be properly associated with the plates, and then, registered to one of his many alter egos. The VIN wouldn't match the registration right away, but that was a mere formality. He would affix new VIN placards soon enough. Once finished, the only way of knowing the truth about the car would be to look into the engine compartment. Short of that, not even a police officer giving him a speeding ticket would realize the truth.

About fifteen minutes passed, as he drove down SR 23, toward the New York Thruway. By the time the fireball lit up the night sky, he was many miles away. Even at that distance, the explosion was large and powerful, almost like lightning and a clap of thunder landing right next to his car. That made two massive explosions about 30 minutes apart. One had imploded a local guesthouse. The other left a crater downtown, collapsing a nearby brick wall, and shattering the glass windows of just about every building on Main Street. For a few weeks, it would look like a war zone.

XIX - HACKING

Jack wanted to get away far and fast. But, he was exhausted. It was just a matter of time before fatigue would cause collapse. For the moment, however, his mind and body were still functioning. He pulled into a motel parking lot at almost 3 a.m., opened the door, and stood up outside. Stretching his legs was just about the most beautiful feeling in the world.

He reached into the right hand pocket of his jeans, and confirmed that the envelope was still there. He felt more secure after that. It was the same $3,000 he'd stashed in the top dresser drawer, and recovered after the ransacking of his flat. Under no circumstances could he risk the use of an ATM machine to withdraw additional cash. If he did that, anyone who might be tracking him would immediately know where he was. It wasn't much and it wouldn't last too long. He had to get the information before it ran out.

He glanced at Sandra Mattingly in the passenger's seat. She was fast asleep. It was late, but he was still surprised. Many people wouldn't be able to fall asleep under these circumstances. He wondered if he could sleep, regardless of how exhausted he might be. He was tired enough but he thought it was impossible to relax. Still, there was a point at which even the most anxiously over-stimulated nervous system would give up.

The girl was young and pretty, but that was old news. Bearing a child hadn't ruined her looks as it had ruined Laura. Why did women react so differently to pregnancy and giving birth? Genetics couldn't explain it all. Eating too much was the key to obesity, and both his wife and her mother had become fat because of their eating habits. If genes were involved, it was only in the propensity toward excessive food intake, and nothing else, he decided.

Since the girl was sleeping, unless he woke her up, he'd have to go into the motel lobby himself. It wasn't something he relished. The news media had splattered his face all over the airwaves. He feared being recognized. Making matters worse was the fact that his shirt and pants were extensively stained with blood. As he opened the door to leave the vehicle, the squeaking of the old door woke the sleeping girl. She yawned, and stretched. It was just as well, because he would have had to wake her, anyway.

"What time is it?" she asked, eyes still half-closed.

"A little past 3 a.m." he replied.

"Where are we?" she asked.

"A motel near Albany." he explained. "Maybe, it would be better for you to get the rooms..."

"Why?" she asked.

"Because my face was on television." he explained. "And, look at my shirt and pants."

She nodded, finally understanding. He handed her two hundred dollars.

"Go ahead, and get us two rooms." he said.

She shook her head.

"I don't want to be alone." she said. "Can we rent one room with two beds. Is that OK?"

He nodded.

"The sign says $49.95..." she noted, and she handed one of the hundreds back to him.

"Remember, if they ask, tell them you don't have any ID." he told her.

"OK." she agreed.

The carpet in the entry lobby was threadbare beige, and it sported some large visible stains, the biggest of which was almost a foot wide. The other stains were smaller but scattered all over the place. One thing good about fleabag motels was that they tended not to ask many questions. Even Motel 6 would demand a driver's license. A no-name motel wouldn't care, as long as you paid cash.

An elderly Indian man sat behind the check-in counter, dressed in a traditional off-white collarless shirt. The shirt was open and hanging over his trousers. On top of a small utility table, there was a cup of tea he sipped occasionally. With his eyes glued to the television set, the man didn't seem to notice she had just walked in. That's when she noticed another photo of Jack on the cable news channel.

As she came closer to the counter, the old man suddenly awoke from his television induced "coma" and noticed that a potential guest had arrived. He stood up and walked over to the reception desk, speaking with a strong East Indian accent.

"Can I help you?" he said.

"I need a room." she replied.

"For tonight?"

"Yes."

"How many people?" the old man asked, as he took out a reservation form.

"Two." she said.

"One king or two queen beds?" the man asked.

"Two queens, please." she answered.

The man glanced at his watch, and handed her a registration slip.

"Please fill this out and I'll need your driver's license or photo ID…"

"I lost my license." she replied.

"You don't have other ID?" he asked.

"Not with me." She replied. "I left it at home."

"What about your husband?" he asked.

"He's sleeping in the car."

"You're driving without a license?"

"I have a license." she explained. "I just don't have it with me."

He looked at her suspiciously, then smiled and nodded. She filled out the form, complete with fake name, surname and an address invented on the spot. Then, she handed the completed document back to him.

"How will you be paying?" the man asked.

"Cash." he replied.

"OK" the man said. "That will be $159.60."

"Excuse me?" she asked, surprised.

"$159.60 please." the old man repeated.

"It says $49.95 on your sign." she pointed out.

"That's for one person." the man insisted. "But, you have two. There's also the tax."

"For that kind of money, I could stay at the Hyatt." she argued.

"Yes, but you'd need photo ID." the man said in his strong East Indian accent.

Sandra shook her head, turned and walked away.

"Where are you going?" the man asked.

"I'm leaving." she declared.

"No, no, no," he insisted, "don't worry. I can make you a special deal... and this only for you... it can be two nights... $79 per night... no problem!"

The old Indian man, who she first thought to be senile, was anything but. He was a conniving crook.

"It says $49.95 per room on the sign." she said, again.

"But, you are two people." he complained.

"I'll have to talk to my husband." she agreed.

Without giving the old man time to respond, she walked quickly outside, got into the car, and told Jack the story. He pulled out the second $100 bill and handed it to her.

"Just rent it." he told her.

About 10 minutes later, she returned with the room keys. He started the engine, and they drove quickly over to the other side of the motel. After surveying the parking lot carefully, he found a secluded spot. Shielded by a thick evergreen hedge and the motel's ugly metal dumpster, the branches of a large tree, newly green with young leaves, shielded the small pickup from view.

The room was as musty as the lobby. The drapery wasn't big enough for the windows. There was an unrepaired hole in the bathroom, where several ceramic tiles had broken, and several other things were in disrepair. The towels seemed clean enough though and the two queen-sized beds weren't uncomfortable.

The room was fully equipped with a small desk, several sitting chairs, and a big chest of six drawers. There was a lot of room into which they could stuff clothing. Regrettably, neither of them had any clothing. They had only the clothes on their back.

"This room is disgusting," she grumbled and yawned.

He walked to the window and lifted the curtain slightly, just to look out, for no particular reason.

"You're welcome to do what you want." he quipped. "As for me, I'm going to get some sleep in the bed."

Then, he turned around. The young woman was laying on one of the beds, her eyes closed, already sleeping. He turned his own attention to the other bed. He removed the bedspread, and opened up the underlying layer of blanket and secondary sheet. Then, he got under the covers, and closed his eyes. Within moments, exhaustion overcame him and he was sleeping too.

When he woke up, it was early the next morning. The girl had already taken a shower, and was putting on makeup in the bathroom.

"I'll go buy us some food." she said, as she exited the bathroom, and noticed he was awake. "Give me the keys to the truck…"

"They're in my jeans' pocket…" he replied.

He pointed to the pair of jeans he'd left lying on the floor.

"But, it would be better to lay low."

"Lay low and starve?" she mocked. "There's a McDonald's right around the corner. What do you want?"

He rubbed his eyes, still tired.

"Egg McMuffin, maybe, some juice. If you see a drugstore, or something like that, buy two hair dye kits. If there's a place to buy clothing, buy me a pair of jeans and a new shirt. But, use cash-only. Don't use your credit card. Understand?"

She looked confused, so he explained.

"We'll be safer if we change our hair color, and we should also do anything else that might make us look different. As for the shirt and pants, do I need to explain?"

She looked at his clothes, now stained brownish with dried up blood, and nodded.

"What size?" she asked.

"For the pants, 36 waist, 32 length." he replied. "The shirt should be a large, or a 34 sleeve."

"OK."

Then, she left the room, leaving him alone. The room was silent. It was so quiet that although he had intended to wake up, when he closed his eyes again, for what he thought would be a few seconds. Soon, he was sound slept again. An hour and a half later, he woke up to find Sandra and the smell of bacon and eggs filling the air.

The aroma made him realize how desperately hungry he was.

"There's a big WalMart Super Center down the street." she explained. "I bought everything there."

He saw a brand new shirt and pair of pants sitting on top of the chest of drawers. She opened the small refrigerator that came with the room, and pointed to a stack of frozen TV-dinners.

Microwave food had never tasted very good. Now, half-starved, it seemed like gourmet fare. He gobbled it down quickly. As he ate, he tried to think of the last time his wife had cooked anything, even with a microwave. Breakfast at her parent's penthouse or in the Hamptons getaway, always included a choice of bacon and eggs, cereal, pancakes, lox and bagels, and several other items. All prepared by the Stoneham's cook. For privacy reasons, he'd refused to hire a cook or a live-in maid. That meant that, in their own flat, breakfast normally consisted of boxed cereal and milk.

He looked at his watch. It was almost 10:00 a.m. After eating, the girl went into the bathroom with her newly purchased box of hair dye. Meanwhile, he opened his laptop and connected to the motel's WIFI. Following the instructions given to him by Jose, he double-clicked on the Tor browser icon.

Tor is a high-security browser developed by the US Navy, then placed into the public domain, and now maintained by a group of volunteers. It makes it almost impossible for snoops to track users of the internet back to a particular IP address.

The US government has a case of schizophrenia regarding its use. On the one hand, the NSA hates it because it shields users from their spying operations. The U.S. State Department and various propaganda arms of the US government love it, because it allows dissidents in unfriendly nations to listen to America's point of view without their governments knowing.

He used Tor to navigate to the Bolton Sayres' website and then logged in. With signals bouncing through a multitude of Tor nodes, the browser slowed down the overall process, but it kept your location a

257

secret. Finally, however, the system gave an error message consisting of two words.

"ACCESS DENIED!"

He couldn't understand what he'd done wrong. He could do nothing further without help. He clicked on the now familiar Zambo icon, and hoped Jose would be available. As he waited for a response, the girl walked out of the bathroom wrapped only in a towel, her thick head of hair now nearly the color of a carrot.

"What do you think?" she asked, modeling her new red tresses.

She looked funny, because her eyebrows no longer matched her hair color, but the red hair definitely changed the way she looked, and that was the point of the exercise. Meanwhile, the outline of her breasts and hips, underneath the towel, was as sexy as he could imagine, and he felt something stir in his groin at the sight of her.

"Do you like it?" she inquired again.

"Yeah." he said, enthusiastically "You look great!"

She turned on the television to watch a morning talk show.

"Could you turn it down?" Jack asked.

"What are you doing?" she asked.

"Trying to save our necks…" he replied.

It was a cryptic answer, but she didn't inquire further, so he didn't have to explain. Instead, she rummaged through her purse, and extracted a pair of ear buds, which she plugged into the television jack. The sound died.

"Thanks." he said, and he went back to work.

A few moments later, a message popped up on his screen.

Compumaestro – What's up?

Team Leader – I've got serious problems...

Compumaestro – I know. I saw the news. What's going on?"

Team Leader – We're on the run.

Compumaestro – Where are you?

Team Leader – Upstate.

Compumaestro – What do you need?

Team Leader – I'm trying to access Bolton's intranet using Tor, like you said, but I can't get in.

Compumaestro – You can't do it like that...

Team Leader – Why not?

Compumaestro – No one can log in without using the VPN software. It's designed to protect the system from third parties. Problem is that, the minute you use it, they'll know your IP address, and that will tell them where you are.

Team Leader – So, did you bring down THEATRES?

Compumaestro – Yes.

Team Leader – How?

Compumaestro – I used your VPN, user name and password. It was the only way.

Team Leader – I thought hackers didn't need stuff like that.

Compumaestro – You thought wrong. There always has to be a point of entry. I ran spoofing software before loading the VPN, so they still don't know it was me. They'll never know.

Team Leader – No, they must think it's me! That's why my face is all over the news!

Compumaestro – Sorry about that... but there wasn't any other way... You can just claim that someone stole your credentials.

Team Leader – Tell me about the spoofing program? Can I use it?

Compumaestro – Yes. I'll send it to you now...

A moment later, a little icon appeared, allowing him the option of saving the small executable that Jose had just transmitted. He saved it to his download folder.

Compumaestro – While I was inside Bolton's intranet, incidentally, I changed a few things...

Team Leader – You brought down THEATRES through the Bolton Sayres?

Compumaestro – Yes.

Now he understood why the police were looking for him. They wanted to question him about his entry credentials. That was something they obviously couldn't broadcast. These events, he decided, would guarantee that the job his father-in-law had offered him would not be available when he got back on the grid. He consoled himself, though, with the thought that he didn't want the job anyway.

When he'd asked Jose to break the system, he hadn't thought it through. He hadn't realized that because Jose would have to use his credentials to do it, everyone would assume that he was involved. But, had he known, it wouldn't have mattered. He would have asked Jose to do it anyway. With killers highly placed inside the banking industry, and with the banks running the surveillance, bringing down THEATRES was essential. Otherwise, he might have never have been able to get out of New York.

It was true that the blonde giant had shown up, in spite of it all. However, if THEATRES control center had known his exact destination, perhaps the man would have shown up earlier. Perhaps, the girl would have been dead before his arrival. Or, perhaps, he would have been intercepted on the way. They might have delayed or even killed him too.

Team Leader – If you used my credentials, they'll have me blocked from access by now. How am I supposed to log in?

Compumaestro – I set up several fictitious executives with even higher level access codes than you have.

Team Leader – How could you do that?

Compumaestro – I told you before, there are a lot of gaping security holes in the system that can be exploited if you know how.

Team Leader – So, what do I have to do?

Compumaestro – First, remember to use the spoofer software before you run the VPN. It'll fool the VPN into thinking you're at a different IP address. Then, you can always piggyback with Tor. No one will know who you are, or where you are.

The little Zambo file transmission icon appeared, again, on the screen. Another file, containing Jack's brand new login ID and password, was delivered a moment later. He opened it in his word processer.

Team Leader – I've got them. Hang on...

Compumaestro – :)

The installation window appeared once Jack double-clicked on the file. He followed the prompts, installing the tiny spoofing program that made tiny but critical changes to the Windows operating system. Then, he ran the VPN, and, finally, logged on. A little blue icon lit up at the bottom left hand side of the screen. The connection made, he logged on with the new credentials. It had all worked perfectly.

Team Leader – I'm in!

Compumaestro – Great! I'll stay on the line...

Team Leader – The name of Marcus Dunlop, a scumbag I've run into before, is the most likely one that appeared on the list of cars borrowed from Bolton Sayres' on the night of Charles Bakkendorf's murder. I want to pull up all records with his name on them.

Compumaestro – Try to access his trading records and emails, if you can.

Team Leader – OK.

He typed the name "Mark Dunlop" into his search window and received references to thousands of emails on his screen. The total size of the files added up to over 345 gigabytes. The emails, alone, amounted 176 megabytes. That was too many pages to review.

Team Leader – It's an enormous file. How can one man generate so many records?

Compumaestro – It could only happen if he's doing a lot of light-speed computerized trading, and those trades list his name as either the broker or the principal customer.

Team Leader – I'm not sure what to do next. There's no way we have any hope of making a serious dent in all those records. The download, alone, would take days based on the speed of the WIFI here, and I wouldn't even have enough room on my hard disk.

Compumaestro – Maybe, we don't need all the trading records. How about just the 176 megabytes worth of emails?

Team Leader – OK. That makes sense.

Compumaestro – Didn't the dead guy, Bakkendorf, work in Bolton's gold vault?

Team Leader – Yes.

Compumaestro – I'm figuring his death must have something to do with gold. Did you know that there's a vast government conspiracy to control gold prices?

Jack knew nothing about that. As far as he was concerned, it was just another one of Jose's conspiracy theories, akin to the reptilians from the center of the earth.

Team Leader – I remember you telling about that at some point, yes.

Compumaestro – Well, it's true and scientifically proven. The price movements in gold and other precious metals are impossible to explain by anything other than active price manipulation.

Team Leader – So what?

Compumaestro – Well, this missing guy, dead guy, I thought we agreed that they murdered him because he knew something…

Team Leader – Yeah…

Compumaestro – They've been covertly manipulating gold prices since 1980. There's a pattern to it. They sell more paper claims in a few months, than the total amount of physical gold ever mined in the world. They also sell it in sudden bursts, a few seconds or minutes at a time, using computers, all carefully designed to torpedo prices at selected points in time.

Team Leader – What does that have to do with this?

Compumaestro – His place of work has every probability of having something to do with his death. The big bullion banks carry out the manipulations and Bolton Sayres is one of them.

Team Leader – I don't see the connection.

Compumaestro – Maybe, he was killed for that.

Team Leader – For what?

Compumaestro – For learning about the conspiracy.

Team Leader – The hole in your theory is that, if they wanted to torpedo gold prices, the US Treasury could just sell gold. They've got over 8,000 tons of the stuff.

Compumaestro – You're wrong. They don't have enough gold to overwhelm the market anymore. They've printed so much paper money that the only way is to covertly manipulate gold prices. If people knew they were doing it, it wouldn't work. People would just buy the gold and wait for the price to rise. The only way they can control prices, now, is by using trickery.

Team Leader – Who care about the price of gold, anyway?

Compumaestro – All the big shots do. The US Treasury cares and so do all the other central banks that produce paper money. So, do the banksters. They need to keep conservative investors and foreign governments buying bonds and stocks. If people turned back to gold, for example, instead of government bonds, it would be all over for the statists. The whole system would implode.

Team Leader – What's a statist?

Compumaestro – It's someone who believes in the power of the state over the individual. They support deficit spending, soft money policies, and limiting economic liberty. Statists hate gold because it protects people's wealth from covert taxation through inflationary policies.

Team Leader – The system is corrupt without even talking about gold.

Compumaestro – Sure. But, Bakkendorf must have gotten in the way, and the government killed him!

Team Leader – You mean the US Treasury or Federal Reserve is going around killing people?

Compumaestro – Why not?

Jack didn't want to get into a discussion of conspiracies, especially considering the number of them that his friend believed in. So, he laid down what he believed was the single most critical fact for discussion.

Team Leader – The burial on the Mattingly's farm happened in 2008.

Compumaestro – If we concentrate on certain key dates, if my theory is right, it won't take long to find your answers.

Team Leader – What key dates?

Compumaestro – The dates they bombarded gold futures with short positions. We concentrate on those dates, together with the date you just mentioned.

Team Leader – July 22, 2008 is the most likely date of death. It is one of your key manipulation dates?

Compumaestro – No. But he worked in Bolton's gold vault, not trading futures. Every time the conspiracy torpedoes gold prices, physical demand skyrockets. Paper manipulations and physical delivery are two very different, but related things. What happens in the futures markets gets reflected in the physical market, but always with a significant delay. The man worked in a gold vault, so I assume his disappearance involved physical gold somehow.

Jack was skeptical about Jose's gold conspiracy theory. However, he didn't have any better ideas, and he'd still be reviewing the same records he needed to review, specifically Dunlop's emails. So, he decided to play along.

Team Leader – I get what you're saying.

Compumaestro – Here's my idea. After a big price attack, more physical gold is delivered, but the deliveries won't happen until a few months later.

Team Leader – Then, we need to correlate the futures trading dates with the approximate dates that deliveries would normally take place, right?

Compumaestro – Yes!

Team Leader – I'll physically download the files just in case someone cuts our access, so we can work with them, offline.

Compumaestro – Good idea.

Team Leader – OK. I'm downloading all the emails and every record of every gold piece that's ever gone in or out of that vault. So, give me some of those dates...

Compumaestro – Try the week of March 18th, 2009. It was just before the Fed first announced its multi-trillion dollar "QE" money printing program. That morning, they mercilessly attacked the price of gold.

Team Leader – Bakkendorf disappeared on July 22, 2008. That means 2009 is too late. Instead, let's first review all emails 10 days before and 10 days after each of your big manipulation dates, but make sure all the dates are before July 22, 2008.

Compumaestro – OK. Wait a second... let me review the historical price information.

A few moments went by as Jose searched. Finally, a message popped onto Jack's screen.

Compumaestro – We can start with March 17, 2008. Just after the collapse of Bear Stearns...

Team Leader – OK.

Compumaestro – Let's share whiteboards... so we can each do half of the work, OK?

Theoretically, by allowing Jose to assist him, and in penetrating the Bolton Sayres' intranet, he was in direct violation of his lawyerly duty toward his client. He was not keeping his client's secrets confidential as lawyers should. But, with life and death in the balance, the possibility of disbarment paled into insignificance. He clicked the button that allowed them to share whiteboards.

Compumaestro – Thanks!

Team Leader – Remember... you can't release anything unless I give approval...

Compumaestro – What if something happens to you?

Team Leader – If I'm dead, then do whatever you want. If I disappear or I end up in custody and you can't contact me, give it 30 days. After that, do what you want.

Compumaestro – Agreed.

Jack felt secure. Jose was a man of his word. Once he gave a promise, he would keep it.

Team Leader – You review 10 days after March 18th. I'll review 10 days before, and on the 18th itself.

Compumaestro – OK.

Jack read through each of the emails and instant messages, page by page, starting from March 7th upward, but quickly passed over any messages that didn't seem immediately relevant. Suddenly, one particular email caught his eye.

Team Leader – Check this out!

The email displayed on the joint whiteboard.

Subject: Time for a bigger short!

From: marcus.dunlop@boltonsayres.com

Date: 3/13/2008 4:35 a.m.

To: michael.jennett@boltonsayres.com

Mike!

Do everything you can to build our gold and silver short in London. But, sell slowly, so we don't push down prices right away, and let's not raise the cost of the puts. I'll be working my end, here in NYC. In a few more days, we'll sitting pretty, ready for the big take down!

Best,
Marc

Team Leader – I would have thought he'd keep something like that secret from the firm. Why didn't he separately encrypt this?

Compumaestro – He did. But, I hacked the system and the virus infected both Bolton's intranet and THEATRES. The moment this guy typed in his password to read one of his separately encrypted emails, all his emails were globally decrypted for us.

Jose's efficiency was impressive.

Compumaestro – Look at the date!

Team Leader – When would the manipulations have happened?

Compumaestro – They would have started shortly before March 17th. These guys know in advance. They're selling short based on the government's positioning.

Team Leader – It's called "front-running" and it's illegal.

Compumaestro – The guy gets up early, doesn't he?

Team Leader – Here, I found another one. Check this out!

Another email appeared on the whiteboard.

Subject: profit is a beautiful thing!

From: michael.Jennett@boltonsayres.com

Date: 4/28/2008 6:35 a.m.

To: marcus.Dunlop@boltonsayres.com

Marc...

Beautiful, baby, beautiful! We're cleaning up! How much cash is left to move the price?

Best,
Mike

Compumaestro – I knew it! Conspiracy theory becomes a conspiracy fact!

Another email appeared on the whiteboard.

Subject: re: profit is a beautiful thing!

From: michael.Jennett@boltonsayres.com

Date: 04/28/2008 6:40 a.m.

To: marcus.Dunlop@boltonsayres.com

Mike!

Not enough gold to keep the game going. Fed is cutting us off. They've got another game in mind for Sept. Don't know details yet. Cover the shorts on May 1st & 2nd. Get ready to go long...

Best,
Marc

Compumaestro – These SOBs must have sold short somewhere in the high $900s...

Selling "short" means promising delivery of something in the future that you don't have today. The rules don't require a seller of gold, for example, to actually own any real gold. All he needs to do is promise to deliver it. He puts down a small cash deposit called a performance bond. Sellers speculate that they will eventually be able to buy back short positions by buying a long position. That is, they expect to buy someone else's promise to deliver gold, which cancels out their own obligation.

If the paper price goes down between the time they sell short, and the time they must buy back, they pocket the difference in cash. The one thing almost no one ever does is actually fulfill the original promise to deliver. Every few months, a series of futures contracts matures, and a tiny percentage of the long buyers force delivery, but it rarely amounts to more than 0.5% of the futures contracts. If a large number of short sellers were ever actually required to deliver the gold they promise, the whole system would come tumbling down.

Team Leader – How much did they pay to buy the positions back?

Compumaestro – They covered on May 2nd and 3rd, which means they bought back in the mid-$800s... and pocketed a profit of $130-140 on every ounce. You know this guy?

Team Leader – I know him. He's an asshole and, obviously, a crook. He's a member of one of the richest banking families in America. I'm sure his ancestors got rich the same way, by breaking the law. Officially, he's a managing partner at Bolton, and believe it or not, he's about to be nominated by the President to the CFTC!

A loud scream suddenly interrupted Jack's concentration.

"Oh, my God!" Sandra exclaimed. "Jack, come here…"

He turned to her.

She shook her head, and her face seemed to have lost color. He typed a few words into Zambo to let Jose know he would be gone for a few moments. Once he walked over to her, she pulled her ear bud connector out of the television set. The speakers came back to life. He could see the cordon of State Police surrounding what appeared to be a building that had collapsed into a large crater. The police were preventing the news cameras from getting the best photos, but something terrible had happened.

Tears were streaming down the girl's face.

The television news reporter spoke from just outside the imploded building that had once been the Tagliano Inn.

> "Police do not know whether the two blasts are related, but are investigating. A man from New York City, identified as a Mr. Jack Severs, was seen in the area just before both explosions. Severs, a lawyer from New York, is also wanted for questioning concerning the disappearance of his wife, New York City socialite, Laura Stoneham. Neither her whereabouts nor his are yet known. Police say the remains of the man's abandoned vehicle were found in the parking lot of the now-destroyed Tagliano Inn. A warrant has been issued for his arrest."

Jack's photograph displayed onscreen.

> "Anyone with knowledge of the suspect's whereabouts should report it to the police immediately, and should not attempt to take matters into their own hands. Severs may be armed and dangerous."

A moment later, a photo of Sandra Mattingly displayed on the screen.

"Sandra Tagliano Mattingly, an owner of the inn is feared dead. The Verde County Sheriff is attempting to contact closest family members."

Jack closed his eyes for a moment and shook his head.

"This is total bullshit!" he exclaimed.

The nightmare was growing worse. He looked at Sandra, who was still very much alive, mostly thanks to his intervention. Only his timely arrival had saved her and she knew it. He wished he could shout it out so loud that the TV announcers would hear it. But, announcing his innocence was, of course, impossible.

"Maybe, I should contact my mom, and tell her I'm alive and well?" Sandra suggested. "I can tell them everything you did, and that you're innocent."

He shook his head.

"No." he said, firmly.

"But, my mother and son might think I'm dead." she countered.

"Would you like the man who tried to kill us, yesterday, to finish the job?" Jack asked.

XX – CONSPIRACIES!

Fyodor Khasan lay quietly in a hospital bed in Westchester County, alone in a private room. The injury was nasty, but not as bad as he had feared. The doctor had cleaned and sewn it up. The man came highly recommended and was well paid to keep the secrets of questionable patients.

Khasan had safely buried his valuables, including his money box, license tags, VIN placards, multiple ID documents, night vision goggles, guns, knives, and other things, in a box in a wooded area not too far from the hospital. The spot was well marked in the memory chip of his satellite navigation system, and he could find it again on a moment's notice. The anesthetic was wearing off, and the chest hurt even though, for the most part, it was just a surface wound. Still, it occupied most of his thoughts.

Before the pain had begun, again, however, he'd had some time to reflect on the events of the last few years. He'd accepted the job of killing Charles Bakkendorf almost 5 years before. Amazingly, there were still loose ends. It was incomplete. The failure hurt his ego so much that it bothered him almost as much as the pain. The contract had called for only one killing. The three additional killings, however, had been necessary tasks.

He wasn't good with pain, but it wasn't entirely new. He had a healed wound in his shoulder from a bullet fired by a Chechen rebel. It was satisfying to think about killing that man slowly, with his bare hands, by squeezing his skull into mush. The bullet wound had left an ugly scar. The knife wound would probably be worse. He didn't like scars. He promised himself that the man who had hurt him so badly wouldn't get off easy. The woman would get a bullet to the brain. But, this man…if he had the opportunity, when the time came, he would make sure he crushed the skull of the man who'd stabbed him, just as he had done to the Chechen.

The hospital had unquestioningly accepted his identity documents. Of course, only the doctor knew he was not who he claimed to be. The intravenous drip of saline solution and antibiotics were for "Leon Gray", a resident of Clifton Park, New York. There were a few whispers, among the nurses, concerning the how stupid a man had to be before he would mistakenly stab himself. But, no one suspected the truth.

His smart phone sat on a small table next to the bed. Like his tablet, the phone was powered by RuMos, the modified version of Android created by Russian intelligence. American programmers had later modified the Russian work further, just as they had done on his tablet computer.

He placed a tiny blue tooth ear bud and microphone over his ear, reached over and dialed the phone. A very similar phone instantly buzzed on an oak topped desk, inside a large red brick home in Scarsdale, NY. The crippled man with a cane noticed the buzzing, and picked up the phone. Adriano Navarro had been waiting for the call ever since hearing the news reports.

Khasan had once been his most reliable agent. Now, he was the biggest screw-up. He placed his thumb in the square marked off for it so that the print could confirm his identity. Then, the two devices synchronized. The nearly instant process was very different from the clumsy process used just a few years before, in the 2008 models of the Zephyr Cypherphone.

"What the hell did you do up there?" Navarro exclaimed, immediately, without waiting for the other man to speak.

"Collateral damage." Khasan explained.

"You weren't there to blow up an American town!" Navarro declared. "The mission was simple. Eliminate one girl. Nothing more. You've made a holy mess out of things!"

"There were complications." Khasan admitted.

"Complications?" Navarro said, deeply irritated. "The whole state is in an uproar. They're calling for creation of a special task force to investigate the explosions. What the hell were you thinking?"

"There was an unexpected third party." Khasan said.

"What are you talking about?"

"He threw a knife."

"A knife?" Navarro asked.

"Yes." Khasan stated.

"What kind of a knife?" Navarro inquired.

"Kitchen knife." Khasan said.

"A kitchen knife?" Navarro repeated, amazed.

"Paring knife." Khasan explained.

"A what?"

"A paring knife…"

Navarro shook his head, disgusted.

"Idiot!" he exclaimed. "You arrive at a house armed with a gun, you've got gases, poisons and other weapons stashed in your car. But, some man throws a little paring knife at you, and the whole operation falls apart?"

"The man is an expert." Khasan reported. "A trained assassin. No doubt sent by someone in the Synod."

"How could anyone in the Synod even have known you'd be there?" Navarro asked.

"I don't know." Khasan replied.

"Did you identify him?" Navarro asked.

"Yes." Khasan stated.

"Who is he?" Navarro suggested.

"His code name is Jack W. Severs." Khasan reported. "The same individual who downloaded the car rental records. According to zee database, he's a lawyer, employed by Bolton Sayres. He supposed married to daughter of Jeremy Stoneham. I believe that job and relationship fake. Cover story, but he probably does verk for Jeremy Stoneham."

Navarro leaned on his cane, speechless for the moment. Then, he broke down and laughed uncontrollably, shaking his head.

"Jack Severs?" he said, unable to stop laughing.

"Code named." Khasan insisted. "Ve don't know real name."

For a moment, Navarro considered the seemingly ridiculous theory that Jack was a covert operative. Someone had introduced a virus into the databases. Someone had used the man's credentials to do it. The hacker had jumped from the Bolton Sayres' intranet into THEATRES, and compromised the entire network. All those things were facts.

He stopped laughing. Could Jack have always been more than what he seemed? Could he really be one of Jeremy Stoneham's agents? Could the marriage be fake? No. He'd investigated Severs and uncovered things that couldn't be fabricated. It was impossible. Also, Stoneham would never allow his daughter to marry such a man, and the marriage was very real. Severs' was a young man running scared, and nothing more.

Khasan's interpretation was that of a lunatic who had outlived his usefulness. One positive thing had come out of it. He now knew where Jack had gone the night that THEATRES went down. From that, it might become possible to extrapolate the young man's current whereabouts.

"What do you want?" Navarro asked, suddenly.

"THEATRE link not verking." Khasan complained. "I can't get tracking informatsia."

"A minor glitch." Navarro explained. "It'll be back online shortly."

Information about the virus was on a need-to-know basis and Khasan didn't need to know.

Because of the issues with THEATRES, Navarro wouldn't ordinarily be able to find Khasan's location. But, during the process of removing the back doors installed by the Russian government, Navarro's New York team had installed a few of their own. One was a locator tracker. He could track the giant man through his phone or tablet computer anywhere in the world.

Navarro tapped on a little icon on the screen. It asked for codes, and he typed them. A map appeared, and he zoomed in. The locator button narrowed down the man's address. Khasan was in White Plains Hospital. Navarro smiled. Young Jack Severs could throw a knife well enough to put a people in the hospital? The boy was full of surprises.

Going to rescue a damsel in distress was foolhardy, but it fit into Jack's personality profile. People never really change, and this was yet one more example. He was a super-hero want-to-be. He'd done something similar at 16 years old, by single handedly fighting off three armed gang bangers. The problem, now, was simply that Jack's fixation on playing hero was interfering with Navarro's plans.

Or, was it? Could he use it to his advantage?

"Where is he now?" he asked.

"I lost track dem." Khasan replied. "Need to use system to find. When I find, dey die."

There was a short pause. It would be a shame to terminate the boy, Navarro thought, but he said nothing.

"Need target location information for complete mission." Khasan continued.

"You intend to blow up more small towns?" Navarro quipped.

"No." Khasan insisted. "But, if you want job done, I need target information."

He thought about that for a moment. Did he want the job done? Did he even need it done? So far, all the secondary killings benefitted Khasan but didn't benefit him. He'd been willing to go along with it to a point, because he considered the man useful. But, the girl had seen the blonde giant, and had never laid eyes on him. All the risk was through the one man who had become a liability. If he happened to suddenly disappear, the risk disappeared with him. No one would suspect anything. Most would simply be glad Khasan was gone. There would be no way to link them.

He kept those thoughts to himself.

"The system is being repaired as we speak." He said, finally. "I'll notify you when it's back online."

Without waiting for the reply, Navarro tapped on the "hang-up" button, and the connection ended. There had been a time when Khasan's work was valuable. That had changed. He was now a liability, not an asset. The latest fiasco was his last chance. There would be no others.

Only sheer panic would cause an operative to blow things up the way he had. Dramatic explosions attracted too much attention. Attracting attention was the last thing a covert operation needed. The man deserved to be caught and jailed. It might be worthwhile to help that process along, if not for the fact it was too risky. The potential exposure of his role, in the staged suicides and assassinations, was too far too great.

Suddenly, the regular landline phone rang. He answered.

"Navarro speaking..."

"Sir, there's a new log-in ID, one created by the hacker." a woman's voice reported. "It's being used to download data from the Bolton Sayres' intranet."

The information intrigued him.

"New credentials created by the same hacker?" he asked.

"Yes." she said.

"What kind of data are they trying to get?" he asked.

"Trading data, gold vault data and email records." she replied. "Many of the records involve Marc Dunlop. Some are emails are encrypted with his personal passcode."

"Any other records?" Navarro asked.

Such downloads didn't worry him too much. He was confident that no one could access the Synod's secrets records, even with newly created high-level passwords and usernames. Such documents needed not only the system password, but document specific passwords. Only he and the members of the Council possessed the document passwords.

What he didn't know was that he was at a disadvantage. He had designed the system in broad strokes. But, when it came to implementation, he was no computer scientist. He relied upon others. Implementation of his ideas required expertise he did not possess. He didn't fully understand the backdoors, or the technical process by which passwords could be lifted directly off microchips, or the full depth of the danger posed by Jose's virus.

"Did you trace the IPs?" he asked.

"We managed to trace one IP out of two dozen the hackers are using. It's the same IP that tried to use Jack Severs' old login credentials."

"Where did you trace it to?" Navarro asked.

"A cheap motel, near Albany." she replied.

The location fit in with the young man's appearance at the Tagliano Bed & Breakfast. It was only an hour or two away from there. He was willing to bet it was Jack. This would present excellent opportunities, if he played his cards right.

A plan began to form in his fertile mind. He could kill two birds with one stone. If Dunlop's recklessness could be channeled, and Khasan could be led to the slaughter, the result would solve all his problems. The scheme would take careful planning to pull off.

"But, there's something else, sir." she noted. "Even as we've been speaking, I've received a report from our programming staff that they've detected the hacker using yet another identity."

"Is he attempting to penetrate THEATRES again?"

"No. He's been trying to hack into the transfer system of a bank."

"Bolton?"

"No. It's not even a Synod member. The bank is in the Bahamas…"

"What his IP address?" Navarro asked.

"We can't find it." she replied. "He's very careful, much more so than the other one, and he's proving to be impossible to track."

There it was. It was proof positive that there were two people involved. One was Jack Severs. Who was the other? What was the connection between them? Why was the other hacker trying to penetrate the system of a non-member bank? But, since the Bahamian bank wasn't a member, did it even matter?

"Whose transfer system is it?" he asked.

"I just pulled the SWIFT code on it. If you give me a few seconds, I can get you the name…" she replied.

Navarro was familiar with all the major Bahamian banks. It was common for Synod member bank executives to kept secret accounts there. Some accounts were used to transfer money invisibly without the knowledge of US tax authorities. Others held the proceeds of illegitimate business done inside the USA. Still others held money arising out of legal business done overseas.

The IRS doesn't impose tax upon money from legitimate overseas operations until it reenters the USA and enters the balance sheet of the American mother corporation. Therefore, there is a real tax benefit to keeping money abroad. The Bahamas are particularly convenient, because they are merely a speedboat ride away from the Port of Miami. Strict secrecy also inhibits the IRS, and prevents the American court system from attaching money to pay off legal claims.

"Is he targeting any one particular account?"

"Yes." she stated.

"Whose account is it?"

"Officially, we can't access that information..." she replied.

"Then, don't do it officially." he ordered.

To join the international payment networks, all banks installed certain software systems. That was just as true of banks in tax haven jurisdictions as of banks based inside the USA. The interlink software was a vulnerability. At the urging of the government, and with Synod Council approval, the designers had programmed numerous back doors into all the necessary systems. Few people had the sophistication to detect them. Fewer still had the means to close them. The keys were stored in a secret database. But, if you had the key, the account information was easily obtained, regardless of security measures.

"It's Marcus Dunlop's account." she announced.

That was interesting piece of information. Jack Severs was trying to download the man's trading records, and the other hacker was breaking into a supposedly secret account held at a Bahamian bank. Who had the level of expertise capable of doing all these things, and helping Severs? He had to concentrate some resources on resolving that question. The name list would be relatively small.

Navarro wasn't particularly worried about the gold trading records. Almost every reasonably intelligent person already knew that the banks controlled the price of gold. On top of that, the key documents could never be read, because of the double encryption, and the rest of the documents would implicate Dunlop, but not the Synod as a whole. Beyond that, they could always claim that the documents were forgeries. Expert witnesses came at a price, but they could always be hired to testify to anything you wanted them to say. If worse came to worse, a host of Ph.D.'s would swear up and down, and under oath, that the documents were fake.

Events were beginning to move at a frantic pace, faster than his comfort level. His plans needed to dynamically mold themselves to the situation, as it developed. That wasn't easy to do, and now it might include allowing Jack to disseminate some sensitive documents in order to achieve the greater goal. The trick would be to continue to link Dunlop to all the crimes, and to lure him into going after Severs. If he could get Khasan there at the same time, all the pieces would fall into place. He would deal with all his problems at once, with plausible deniability because of the circumstances.

He made a quick decision.

"Let Severs have the documents."

"What?" she asked, not believing what she was hearing. "Did you say give him access?"

"Yes." he replied.

"There's one more thing..." she noted.

"What?"

"Just a second ago, someone put a trace on him." she noted.

"Who?" he asked.

"The tracers are coming from Mark Dunlop's system interface." she replied.

"That was fast..." Navarro noted.

Dunlop's trace attempts would play right into his quickly developing plan to get rid of his problems.

"Can you make it look like his Bahamas account was hacked from Severs' IP instead of by that hacker's IP?" he asked.

"Of course." she replied.

"Then do it..."

Occasionally, he had wondered about Dunlop's Bahamian bank accounts. Up until now, there hadn't been enough reason to borrow the back door keys, but he knew the boy was up to no good. He was nothing but a greedy self-dealing slime ball. His only fan was his father, Christopher Dunlop, who was willing to pay a lot to protect his son.

As far as Navarro was concerned, the younger Dunlop's claim to fame arose mainly out of being born into the right family. Thousands of people could take his place. He was a common thief. Charlie Bakkendorf had reported the fake gold bars to the reputational risk division. He had done that because he was blissfully ignorant of the fact that Dunlop was running a private operation, and he had believed that his two million dollar bonus had come from the bank.

Navarro had informed his patron, Christopher Dunlop. The elder Dunlop had immediately decided the man's fate. Bakkendorf's willingness to talk was intolerable. It could bring down the Dunlop dynasty, destroy Marc's standing within the Synod, and damage the Synod itself. The old man had offered $10 million to cover it up. It was a lot of money, and eliminating one low-level bank employee had seemed simple enough, at the time.

Fyodor Khasan was an experienced assassin who had done jobs for him before. He was well known for getting jobs done right. A former agent of the Russian FSA, he was ruthlessly efficient. In spite of his impressive reputation, however, he had screwed up badly, and repeatedly, making mistake after mistake. There was no room for error in the business of murder. As a result of Khasan's choice to bury Bakkendorf in a rural area at night, farmer Thomas Mattingly had come knocking on the door with blackmail threats.

The blackmailer had to be kept happy while arrangements were made for his death. He wanted a lot of money. He was given a line of credit amounting to $25 million dollars for a hare-brained scheme to open a ski resort. No high-level bank executive could be trusted enough to approve it. So, instead, with the help of a few of his most trusted programmers, Navarro changed the Bolton Sayres' system protocols to allow hundreds of thousands of dollars to be funneled to the farmer while his death was being arranged. At just $1.4 million, the transaction was lost in the system.

At Navarro's request, Khasan had staged what appeared at the time to be the perfect murder and subsequent suicide. He had even made sure that the man's hand contained gunpowder residue. The case was deemed a murder followed by a suicide, and closed by the police. Everything seemed fine, until the foolish young super-hero-want-to-be, Jack Severs, appeared. He'd somehow stumbled upon a lost diary with enough information to blow everything to hell. The Sheriff's office was bound to reopen the investigation the moment that diary was delivered. The trail would certainly lead back to Khasan, and possibly to Navarro himself.

The remaining witness, Sandra Mattingly, had to die. Khasan's incompetence, however, showed itself again. The enormous secondary damage he'd caused in upstate New York was now putting everything at risk. The police would ask questions. The man was a serious liability. There was no choice anymore. The mess had to be straightened out even if he had to take care of things himself.

"Keep watching Dunlop." he ordered. "As soon as he locates Severs, and leaves his office, I want to know about it, right away."

"Yes, sir." she replied.

He hung up the phone, with his new plan coalescing in his mind. If he executed the plan with skill and care, his problems would be over...

XXI – FOLLOW THE MONEY

Jack sat at the edge of the bed, his computer in his lap. He was becoming more paranoid by the moment. Who was he really up against? A handful of crooked bank employees? The entire bank? The entire banking industry? Or, was he up against an out of control government? Could it be all four?

He was working against time and enormous odds, and he felt overwhelmed. He glanced at the girl in tight jeans and a pullover top. Was she the reason he'd come so far, at such a high cost? The pants were so tight he could see the outline of her labia. The curve of her hips and the mound of her breasts fit together in a perfect picture. When he looked at her, as usual, he felt something stirring in his groin.

He tried to shake himself free. There were more important things to think about. Imagining sex with a woman he barely knew was foolish and distracting. He had a wife and a little daughter. He had to get that out of his head? But, it seemed impossible. Why did he want her so badly? He was staring at her too long because she looked up and noticed. Their eyes met. She got up and crawled over to him, touching his shoulder softly.

"Is there something you want?" she asked.

"No, not really." he said, lying.

"Are you sure?" she asked.

He thought, for a moment, about how to best respond, but before he could, she was speaking again.

"Put the computer down..." she urged, softly.

"I can't... I'm right in the middle of something..."

She put her hand on the computer and, with some gentle pressure closed the lid. There was a faint scent of lavender about her, and it overwhelmed his senses. He was hard as a rock already, and when he glanced down, it was overtly obvious. It would have been impossible for her not to notice.

She slid closer. She was young, thin, beautiful, and inviting. Her lips were waiting, and she was obviously waiting for him to kiss them. The desire was too strong to fight. Making matters worse, she seemed to want the same thing he did.

Who knew when such an opportunity would come again? In a few more hours, a day, a few days, a week, whatever... they might both be dead. In this moment, he was alive and a man in the prime of life. She was a beautiful woman, and she lay next to him in a bed.

He made the fateful decision against his better judgment. While he could still live and breathe, he would live and breathe as a man. He turned and kissed her, deeply, and pressed her lithe body down onto the bed, running his hands along the curves of her body, and the silky skin of her arms.

Jose might be online, and they might be in the middle of a critical moment, but all of that was lost for the moment. He couldn't think of anything but the woman. Moments later, her blouse and bra came off. Then, she squeezed out of her skin-tight jeans, and he slipped off his own clothes and her panties. He became lost in a unity and rhythm of movement. He kissed her on every part of her body, and she responded with the natural ecstasy of a female to a male. The matter soon reached climax, and he spilled into her as naturally as an April shower falls from the sky.

Afterward, the two lay together on the bed. He felt more relaxed than he had in a long time. He leaned over and kissed her again, then laid back and stared for a moment at the ceiling lamp, with nothing on his mind. He was satisfied and fulfilled. Suddenly, it came to him with a start. He'd left Jose hanging on the line right in the middle of their joint investigation.

He sat up. Was his friend still there? He hoped so. The computer was where it had been moments before, but the lid was closed. He opened it, and reactivated the machine from hibernation mode. He wrote an instant message and transmitted it.

Team Leader – Sorry, for the delay... I'm back.

There was a pause, but soon the little animated pen that showed that Jose was writing back moved. Thankfully, Jose was still on line!

The response came a second later.

Compumaestro – I'm still here! I've been hacking deeper into the system.

Team Leader – Let's double down on getting this information quickly.

Compumaestro – I found a whole chain of emails and replies, between these two guys, starting May 28th...

Another email came up on the joint whiteboard.

Subject: Hulk says smash!

From: michael.Jennett@boltonsayres.com

Date: 06/28/2008 6:01 a.m.

To: marcus.Dunlop@boltonsayres.com

Marc,

What's the deal? We could easily do another smash. I thought you told them????

Best,
Mike

Subject: re: Hulk says smash!

From: marcus.dunlop@boltonsayres.com

Date: 06/28/2008 6:05 a.m.

To: michael.Jennett@boltonsayres.com

Mike,

I did. Physical demand too strong. Soared in March. Fed's vault very low on gold. They want to try something else...

Regards,
Marc

Subject: re Hulk says smash!

From: michael.Jennett@boltonsayres.com

Date: 06/28/2008 6:11 a.m.

To: marcus.Dunlop@boltonsayres.com

Marc,

Should we go longer?

Best,
Mike

Subject: re: Hulk says smash!

From: marcus.dunlop@boltonsayres.com

Date: 06/28/2008 6:13 a.m.

To: michael.Jennett@boltonsayres.com

Mike,

I got WORD!!! Big gold smash planned for September!!!! Equity boys selling too. Should be a rout!!! Build short. Target accumulation between July 10 and 21. Cover in Oct. If you can get any repo loans out of the BofE, do it!!! Use them. Build up as big a loan window as you can. My contact is waiting for your call...

Regards,
Marc

Subject: Hulk says smash!

From: michael.Jennett@boltonsayres.com

Date: 06/28/2008 6:15 a.m.

To: marcus.Dunlop@boltonsayres.com

Marc,

What about NY futures? Loans from the fed???????? :-)

Best,
Mike

Subject: re: Hulk says smash!

From: marcus.dunlop@boltonsayres.com

Date: 06/28/2008 6:17 a.m.

To: michael.Jennett@boltonsayres.com

Mike,

Forget the futures. Gold bugs follow every single trade there. NY is the pricing machine. I want London. I want to take all our shorts, from this

284

point on in forwards and options on forwards. Is that agreed? Nice,
confidential, no disclosure... perfect!!!

Best,
Marc

Subject: re: Hulk says smash!

From: michael.jennett@boltonsayres.com

Date: 06/28/2008 6:21 a.m.

To: marcus.dunlop@boltonsayres.com

Marc,

Ok. Lots of counter-parties want to be long gold. Shouldn't be a
problem going short on as many forwards as we can.

Best,
Mike

Another email popped up on the whiteboard.

Subject: Bots rock!

From: michael.Jennett@boltonsayres.com

Date: 10/13/2008 6:33 a.m.

To: marcus.Dunlop@boltonsayres.com

Marc,

Wow! Beautiful bots baby!!! Your bots rock! Friday's action was
spectacular! $70 swing! Everyone's talking about it. You're a master
craftsman!

Best,
Mike

Team Leader – OK, I'll grant you, we can prove they're manipulating gold prices. But, how do we prove murder?

Jack moved his mouse to the download button and clicked. Files transferred to his computer. He clicked, and clicked again, on the date July 22, 2008, until he came to the vault records. There should have been a long list of receipts reflecting gold bars arriving in the vault. But, there were very few. He worked his way backwards. The first receipt, nearest to Bakkendorf's disappearance, reflected delivery of 4 tons of

285

gold on July 16th. Jack popped the image up to the top of their shared whiteboard.

Team Leader – What's the "undefined location"? What about bar numbers, manufacturers, and purity?

Compumaestro – Did you know that President Franklin Roosevelt seized all gold in America in 1934, and melted it all down into what they call coin-melt bars?

Team Leader – No.

Compumaestro - Only America has bars like that, with a huge percentage of cheap base metals. The commercial standard is different. We're talking 1 kg. gold bars 99.99% pure versus 300-400 ounce coin melt bars only about 89% to 91% pure. My guess is that the raw material comes in as coin melt, then they refine it and recast it into new bars. That's why there aren't any bar numbers…"

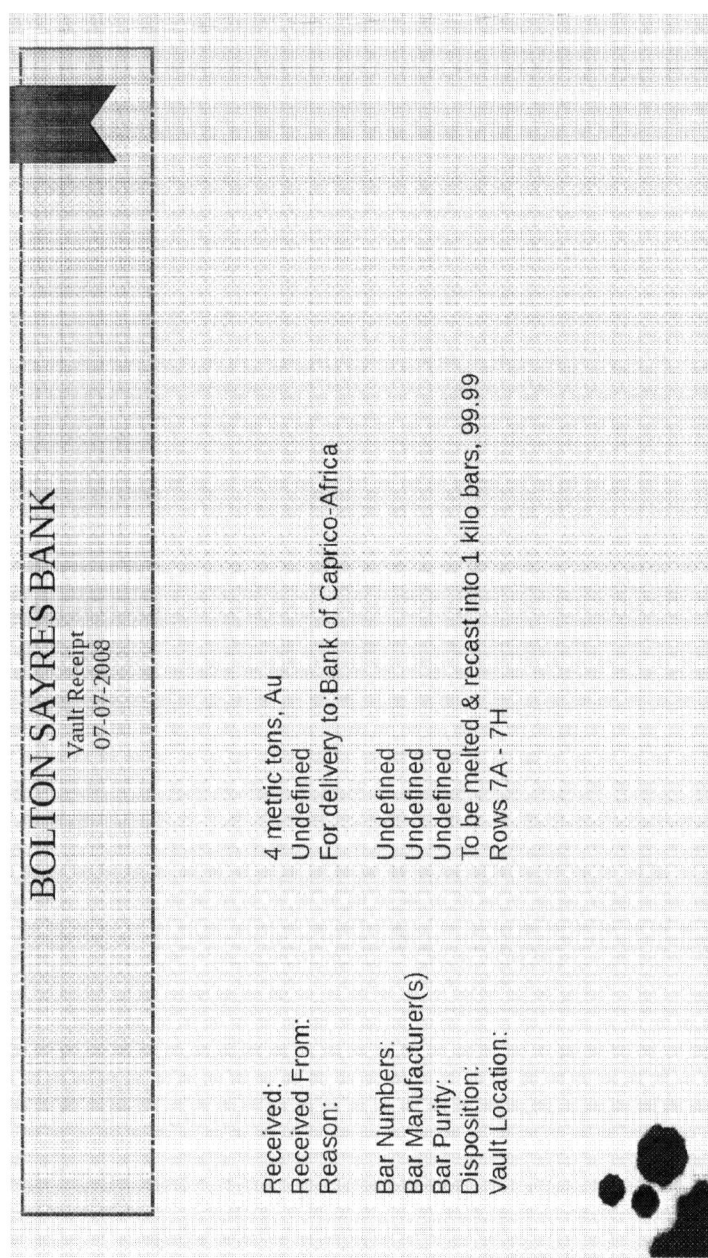

BOLTON SAYRES BANK
Vault Receipt
07-07-2008

Received: 4 metric tons, Au
Received From: Undefined
Reason: For delivery to:Bank of Caprico-Africa

Bar Numbers: Undefined
Bar Manufacturer(s) Undefined
Bar Purity: Undefined
Disposition: To be melted & recast into 1 kilo bars, 99.99
Vault Location: Rows 7A - 7H

Team Leader – That's pure speculation. There's nothing to support it. Let's follow the vault receipts, one by one, and see what we find.

Jack tried to identify the fate of the raw gold described on the vault receipt. He took nearly 5 minutes and, finally, he found something. The

287

spreadsheet popped up on the whiteboard. On July 23, 2008, the records showed that 400 one kg. gold bars shipped to the same African central bank noted on the vault receipt.

Team Leader – That's a day after the body was buried at the Mattingly farm. Look at the name of the "responsible person"!

The shipping spreadsheet read "Charles Bakkendorf"

Compumaestro – Didn't Bolton's H.R. department says there never was an employee by that name?

Team Leader – Yeah.

Compumaestro – The word "undefined" is a blue hyperlink! I'll click on it...

Jose clicked on the hyperlink, and the message was instantly displayed on both of their screens.

"ACCESS DENIED! INSUFFICIENT AUTHORIZATION. LEVEL 1-A CLEARANCE REQUIRED"

Team Leader – What the hell is "1-A clearance"?

Compumaestro – There isn't any level 1-A. Not the way we designed it. There should just be level 1.

Team Leader – The user name and password you created, apparently, aren't enough for this.

Compumaestro – Maybe. But, I think I can solve that problem. Bolton's mainframe runs 24/7, which means it is never turned off, and people at the top of the company's totem pole access it frequently. Some must have 1-A access.

Team Leader – So what?

Compumaestro – Well, if someone accessed the system today or yesterday, or anytime after it was last physically unplugged and rebooted, the password is still in the computer. And, someone with top level clearance would have had to access it, to clean up the damage my virus did. Until the computer is turned off, the RAM chips will keep an image of the passwords and user names. It's one backdoor required by the NSA and it's used to access foreign bank computer systems. Our primary customers agreed to it, and the others, mostly overseas, get it by default.

Team Leader – That's fantastic!

The command prompt window suddenly popped up on the white board. Codes and numbers flashed across the screen. They appeared and disappeared so fast they were impossible to follow, as Jose's favorite hacking tool accessed the memory buffers. It took about 20 seconds and it was over.

Compumaestro – Try clicking now...

Jack clicked, and the information hidden was now displayed. A message flashed onto the screen.

"Federal Reserve Vault, 33 Liberty Street, NY, NY."

There was a moment of unexpressed elation, and electronic silence, because neither of them was sure of exactly what he wanted to say. Finally, Jack wrote the first chat message.

Team Leader – I guess your conspiracy theory is now conspiracy fact.

Compumaestro – I always knew it! But, as you said, it doesn't explain why Bakkendorf was murdered.

Team Leader – He's listed as the responsible person.

Compumaestro – You think he would spill the beans?

Team Leader – I can swallow the Fed's suppressing gold prices, but murder?

Compumaestro – Why not? Did you know they have an internal police force. It's bigger than most city police departments.

Team Leader – I just can't believe it. If it's true, I suppose, I'd must join the terrorists, and go to war against my own government.

Compumaestro – Look, check this out!

Another vault receipt popped onto the whiteboard.

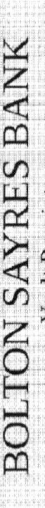

BOLTON SAYRES BANK
Vault Receipt
07-23-2008

Delivered Out: 4 metric tons, Au
Received From: Bolton Sayres Mint
Reason: For delivery to:Bank of Caprico-Africa

Bar Numbers: 40 one kilo bars numbered 24331 through 24370
Bar Manufacturer(s): BSM
Bar Purity: 99.99
Disposition: Airlifted to Caprico
Vault Location: N/A - Physically Delivered to Customer

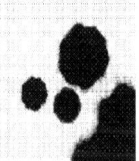

290

Team Leader – It shows they made the delivery.

Compumaestro – There's an identical receipt showing another 360 bars being delivered to the same central bank. You want me to pop that one up?

Team Leader – Just save it. Let's go on to something else...

After cleaning herself up, Sandra Mattingly returned from the bathroom to the bed, but saw that Jack was preoccupied. She didn't disturb him. Instead, she replaced her ear buds and busied herself listening to music.

Jack keenly focused on figuring it all out. Having exhausted the physical urge that had been distracting him, he could now concentrate all his energy on the task at hand. The two men worked feverishly. One after another, they reviewed many pages. Finally, a message came in

Compumaestro – Take a look at this one...

Another vault receipt was on display on the shared whiteboard.

BOLTON SAYRES BANK

Vault Receipt
07-23-2008

Delivered Out:
Received From:
Reason:

Bar Numbers:
Bar Manufacturer(s):
Bar Purity:
Disposition:
Vault Location:

3 metric tons, Au
Bolton Sayres Mint
For delivery to: FIRST BAHAMA BANKCORP ACC 3429910022287

300 one kilo bars numbered 24370 through 24399
BSM
99.99
Airlifted to Nassau, Bahamas for credit to Acct. W7429-118334112
N/A - Physically Delivered to Customer

Team Leader – Did that also come from the Fed's vault?

Compumaestro – There's no receipt for incoming delivery. I checked and double-checked.

Team Leader – It could have already been in the Bolton vault...

Compumaestro – Impossible. I checked the stock records. There's hardly any gold in Bolton's vault. All the gold they've been shipping from New York has been coming from the Federal Reserve. The rumor is that the gold they ship from London is from the Bank of England, backed up by location swaps with gold from the Fed. It looks like the coin melt bars arrive a month or two ahead of major deliveries. Then, they must refine it on site and, later, deliver it. It's a closed system. But, there's no record of this batch of gold coming into the vault.

Team Leader – It must come from somewhere.

Compumaestro – That's my point.

There was a long pause. Then, Jack sent another instant message to his friend.

Team Leader – Is it possible to manufacture a gold bar that isn't 100% gold and pass it off for real?

Compumaestro – There are loads of stories about bars filled with tungsten. It's got almost the same molecular weight as gold and a similar density. The match isn't exact, but it's close.

Team Leader – Let's look through the incoming vault receipts for other metals!

It didn't take long. A few moments passed, and he found what he was looking for. There was another vault receipt for 3 metric tons of tungsten rod, dated April 16, 2008 that popped up on the whiteboard.

BOLTON SAYRES BANK

Vault Receipt
04-16-2008

Delivered Out:
Received From: 3 metric tons, Au
Reason: Tungsten Forge, Inc.
Fabrication

Bar Numbers: Rod – No numbers – 3 metric tons.
Bar Manufacturer(s) Tungsten Force, Inc.
Bar Purity: N/A
Disposition: For permanent storage
Vault Location: New York, NY

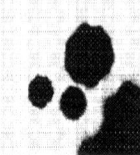

Team Leader – What else is tungsten used for?

Compumaestro – Light bulbs, tungsten carbide, which is almost as hard as diamond… it's used for cutting glass and grinding stuff, not much else…

Team Leader – Why would a precious metals vault take delivery of 3 tons of tungsten?

Compumaestro – To create fake bars!

Jack did quick calculations, and then wrote another chat message.

Team Leader – If you were making new bars, you could just melt it the tungsten first. According to Wikipedia, it has a higher melting temperature. You would fabricate a tungsten core. Then, over that core, at a lower temperature, you'd pour the melted gold. A tungsten core of about 24 ounces each, coated with 8.15 ounces of gold, would create a near-perfect fake 1 kilo gold bar. If you got 4 tons of gold from the Fed, and then you created these fake bars, you could pilfer 3 tons of pure gold.

Compumaestro – That batch of gold bars, the ones Bakkendorf was working on just before he disappeared, was tainted by tungsten fill.."

Team Leader – That's a relief, because it means it's probably not the Fed going around killing people.

Compumaestro – We've got enough proof to put these two guys behind bars...

Team Leader – Yeah.

Compumaestro – There's enough to put Bolton out of business and the Federal Reserve, maybe, too!

Team Leader – Keep it under wraps, until I give the word.

Compumaestro – It's too big. We've got to let the public know! They're ripping people off every day. They're using gold that belongs to the People of the United States in schemes to enrich a few bankers. I say jail and bankrupt the bastards.

Team Leader – If we release all this stuff, we could both end up assassinated. We need to think about it carefully.

Compumaestro – Fine. Let's think… OK, I'm finished thinking. Let's release it anonymously.

Team Leader – That's impossible. Everything points back to me. Here, look at this…

A compensation log popped up on the whiteboard.

Compumaestro – It says Bolton earned $145 million from trading gold in the 2nd quarter of 2008.

Compumaestro – They took short positions in early March...

Team Leader – And, covered the shorts in early May which gave them $81 million in profits. Look at the compensation log!

Jack hit a few buttons on his end of the white board, and a summary of compensation paid to Marcus Dunlop appeared on both screens.

Compumaestro – He got a $10.5 million bonus that quarter! That's on top of stealing the gold, and making money on his side bets! It's motive to kill.

Team Leader – Look where he deposited the money…

The records showed a wire transfer of $10.5 million to Dunlop's account at First Bahamas Bancorp, Ltd.

Compumaestro – The same bank that took delivery of 3 tons of physical gold.

Team Leader – Yes. But, the account number is different.

Compumaestro - W7429-118334112

Team Leader – He's got at least two accounts. One he discloses and uses to transfer funds openly. Another is secret. Too bad we can't get all the records. No one's ever going to get those records, you know. The Bahamas have strict banking secrecy.

Compumaestro – The hell with that! We know two of his numbers. That's all we need. Tax haven banks also allow people to access money through various electronic money networks. They use our interlink software. Their top level user IDs and passwords are still going to be in memory, like at Bolton. I can penetrate that network.

Team Leader – How long would it take?

Compumaestro – Not long.

Team Leader – Go ahead, and do it, then! Save everything onto redundant storage including DVDs, flash cards, or any other storage device we can easily hide but be ready to use at a moment's notice.

Compumaestro – OK.

Team Leader – Do you need me along for the ride?

Compumaestro – I just need you to leave your computer running. I'll need your VPN turned on. I'll piggyback from Bolton Sayres, through the card systems, and into the bank in the Bahamas.

Team Leader – OK. I'll leave it online and running.

Jack changed the settings so the laptop would continue to run even after he closed the lid. Then, he closed it and looked up from his work for the first time in an hour. His heart jumped.

Sandra Mattingly was gone. He'd been so involved in chatting with Jose that he hadn't even noticed her leaving. It was dangerous. She'd changed her appearance with the hair color, but her face was still the same. It was foolish to take chances by going in and out of the room unless it was necessary.

Then, he remembered the little box of hair dye that still sat on top of the chest of drawers, and his new clothes. His own hair color remained unchanged. He glanced down at his shirt and jeans. He was still wearing the bloodstained ones. There was nothing left to do anyway, while he waited, so he picked up the clothing, and the hair dye kit and walked to the bathroom. Twenty minutes later, he was finished. He walked out, and looked in the mirror above the chest of drawers.

Someone he didn't fully recognize seemed to be staring back at him. His hair was now yellow. With his dark brown eyebrows, it looked a bit ridiculous, but he definitely looked significantly different. It felt good to wear fresh clothes, and it was a pleasure to get rid of the bloodstained ones.

He had no way of contacting Sandra, and she was still gone. Both of their cell phones were off, at his request. They had to stay turned off to avoid being detection. He could do nothing but wait. He turned on the television and clicked to the cable news channel. The same stories repeated on a twenty-minute cycle, as usual. The disappearance of his wife was still a hot story, and his photograph was on-screen yet again.

XXII – A GOLDEN SCAM OF GREAT PROPORTIONS

When he wasn't cavorting with prostitutes or adjusting the programming of his trading bots, Mark Dunlop spent much of his time staring at his bank balances. He checked his Bahamian bank account balances several times a day. There was nothing more gratifying than to see the money grow.

By mid-2008, he had fully paid for and acquired title to a Caribbean Island. By June 2009, he had finished the sea walls, the mansion, and dredged a small harbor for his yacht. By 2010, he finished the helicopter pad, tennis courts and other final additions. Proudly showing off the new tropical paradise had been great fun. He was elated with the process, and continued to show it off to anyone from New York that he could manage to import there. This had continued for several months, much longer than normal, with his usual toys.

Unfortunately, there was now no one left to impress. He'd spent a lot of time there, but had grown tired of the heat and humidity. He was now spending almost all his time in New York City, in spite of his plan to make the tropics his permanent home. In fact, he was even spending the winter up north. It had been nine months since he'd even set foot in the tropical getaway that had cost so much in money, time, death and destruction.

He was especially excited about the newest government subsidized gold operation. It would be the biggest haul ever! In April 2013, after getting access to 1,300 tons of government gold, he had orchestrated the largest attack against rising gold prices in history. He had the full support of financial institutions worldwide, some even outside the usual Synod member cabal. By investing a wad of his own money, in March, he'd already collected a profit of almost $35 million, just by liquidating a portion of his put options. There was a lot more money on the way. His Bahamian bank balance was now swollen to over $145 million dollars.

As he logged in, and began the habitual practice of staring lovingly at his bank balances, however, he could see at first glance that there was something very wrong. The ledger showed less than $1 million remaining on deposit in the account. The more he stared, the faster his heart began to pound. Where was his money? For a moment, he sat stiffly, in his black leather swivel chair, staring in disbelief.

The transaction roster showed wire transfers totaling about $144 million. The ledger notation claimed that he had "authorized" the last occurring transactions over several months. He hadn't. Just a day before, he'd looked at the same ledger, and all the money was safely there. Now, a vast majority of the money seemed to have been wired to an unknown bank in the former Portuguese colony of Macau. That little city is a former Portuguese colony, now a self-governing province of the People's Republic of China that has both a thriving gambling industry and a bevy of banking institutions.

His hand trembled as he pressed the special communication icon on the touch screen of his phone. The icon created an encrypted connection to the private banking division of First Bahamas Bancorp. The face of a beautiful young blonde woman appeared immediately on the screen. Ninety five percent of the population of the Bahamas was black, but the private bankers to high net worth customers were all European. Often, the females among them were model-quality.

The woman spoke with a carefully studied British accent, but he knew she was Swiss.

"Can I help you?"

"I'm looking... at my bank account..." he stated, stumbling over the words, finding it hard to speak. "The transactions roster shows multimillion-dollar transfers to Macau."

"Before I can discuss this any further," she began, "I need to confirm your identity. I know we've talked before, but our bank's regulations require me to ask you to place your registered fingertip into the box on your touch screen."

"OK." he replied, and did so.

"Thank you, Mr. Dunlop," she noted, "your fingerprint is confirmed. I'll now need you to answer a few challenge questions."

She quizzed him on his account number, user name, telephone access code, secret question, mother's maiden name, street address, mailing address, email address, nationality, passport number, and prior addresses. When he correctly answered everything, she was ready to discuss his account.

"I see that $144 million was wired through online banking to a brokerage house in Macau over the last few months."

"I never gave those instructions!"

"When you made the transfer, your fingerprint was checked, and you correctly answered all the same questions I just asked." she noted.

"I never gave any fingerprints or answered questions!" he insisted. "I never authorized any transfers! It's a fraud! You need to reverse the wires, immediately!"

"Let me put you on hold for a few moments, sir..." she said.

Calming music played, but it didn't calm him. He was angry and anxious. After a few moments, a new face appeared on the screen; a middle-aged man with dark brown hair and blue eyes.

"Mr. Dunlop..." the man said, with a strong German accent. "My name is Axel Dietrich. I am Vice President of First Bahamas Bancorp. It is my understanding zhat you claim you didn't authorize a transfer to your account at our branch in Macau?"

"I don't have any accounts in Macau!" Dunlop screamed.

"Please calm down." the man said. "Ve' vill do everything ve can to resolve zis problem, okay?"

He nodded. Since it was a video phone, the man could see everything he did, and vice versa.

"How can you allow $144 million to be transferred without a personal confirmation?" Dunlop screamed again.

The other man didn't flinch.

"Vhen you opened your account, you authorized instant transfers in any amount vithout verbal confirmation." Deitrich explained. "You chose biometric authentication and challenge qvestions. Zese transfers vere subjected to ze most rigorous biometric confirmation and every vone of our challenge qvestions vas ansvered correctly."

"I don't give a shit!" Dunlop screamed. "I don't have any accounts in Macau."

"Our records show that the Macau account was opened 2 years ago, zrough ze inter-bank hypernet. The IP address zat vas used to open ze account corresponds to ze Bolton Sayres Bank." Deitrich pointed out. "You still verk dere, do you not?"

"Yes, I work there." Dunlop admitted. "But, I NEVER OPENED ANY ACCOUNT IN MACAU!"

"I see." the Swiss banker went on. "But, ze account vas opened over two years ago. And, it shows substantial transfer activity throughout zis entire time period. It also shows a number of very large transfers, to and from your account here."

"I'm telling you I don't have any such account and I never transferred any money, now or in the past!" Dunlop declared. "God damn it!"

"Zhat's not vat our database shows, sir." Deitrich insisted. "It shows extensive activity, all of vhich vas initiated, during ze entire time period, from ze same IP address of Bolton Sayres Bank, vere you verk. You see, if zat vas not ze case, such a large transfer might have been qvestioned. But, ve look at ze history, and ve see similar transfers, done on a regular basis, many times in ze past."

Dunlop shook his head virulently.

"No! There's never been any activity like that!" he insisted.

Each breath came faster, one after another, until it almost seemed like he was panting like a dog. But, now, he was feeling like throwing up.

"Ve show substantial activity." Deitrich insisted, nodding his head.

"What kind of activity?" Dunlop asked.

"Vell, Zhere's a $7 million transfer to ze Macau account on July 9th, 2012." Deitrich answered. "One for over $3 million on August 22nd. Another for $35 million on October 6. Zhen, a transfer back to the Bahamas branch on December 15th in the amount of $10,465,000. Another for $14 million on January 7, 2013. And, the final one from Macau was for $10,535,000, and that took place on February 1st 2013. Of course, we zhen have the more recent transfers you are complaining about. But, all of zhem show za same pattern."

Dunlop wrote down the numbers as the man rattled them off. Then, he swallowed hard, and his mind raced.

"It's a fraud!" he screamed, again.

"I understand you say dere's a fraud." Deitrich stated. "But, vhen ve have extensive historical activity, along vit a vaiver of verbal confirmation, there is no reason for us to suspect anyzing out of ze ordinary."

Dunlop was speechless. He busied himself adding up the numbers on a little sheet of paper. Suddenly, he understood.

"Can't you see it?" he exclaimed. "All the transactions, prior to February 1st were fake. When it's all said and done, $35 million was transferred back and forth, leaving no net change to the balance! They're all fake transactions. They never happened!"

"But, our records show you've logged into your account every day, a minimum of 4 times, sometimes 8 times per day, every day, for the last

2 years." Deitrich stated. "Vhy vouldn't you report such activity, if you didn't make zese transfers?"

"They were never in my transactions register, until now." Dunlop insisted. "Don't you see? Someone's tampering with your computers!"

"Ve have multiple security measures." Deitrich replied. "Frankly speaking, zhat is impossible."

"Your so-called security measures aren't worth shit!" Dunlop screamed. "Someone broke into your system!"

"Zhere is no need for foul langvige." Deitrich insisted. "And, again, let me say zhat zhere are multiple security measures zhat vould prevent zhat."

"Just take the money out of the Macau account and put it back." Dunlop demanded.

"I vould if I could." Deitrich stated. "But, unfortunately, zhe computers in Macau are physically separate. Ve have already contacted zhat branch. According to zhem, the money has been transferred to another bank in Singapore."

"I want my fuckin' money back!" Dunlop screamed. "You understand me, you fuckin' kraut!"

"Mr. Dunlop." Deitrich said, ignoring the ethnic slur. "If I could reverse zhese transactions, I would do zhis. But, I cannot. I vill advise our board of your problem."

"When do I get my money back?"

"Official inkvyories' vill' be made. Unt, ve vill do all in our power to help."

"What, exactly, are you going to do?"

"First, ve report to za central bank." Deitrich said. "I'll need your permission to transmit za information, of course."

"And, after that?" Dunlop asked.

"Ze financial crimes unit vill take over…" Deitrich explained. "It is verking now, closely, vit you FBI. Dey vill take statements. You vill need to give statement about your account. If a fraudulent transfer vas made, ze authorities can zhen get a varrant to investigate."

None of that cooled him off. The process the man spoke about might take months. By then, the money would be long gone. More important, it was mostly black money, made from illegally front-running the market. He had paid no taxes on his winnings for years, and that meant would end up a loser. He might even be arrested."

"I don't want all that." Dunlop said. "I just want my money back!"

"I'm sorry sir. Ve don't have your money now. You transferred it."

"I didn't transfer it!"

"Somevon vit your credentials transferred it, zhen. You are responsible, of course, for keeping za credentials."

"You fuckin' incompetent idiots have been fucking hacked!" Dunlop screamed, and slammed his phone so hard onto the desk he broke the bezel. The LED screen then flickered on, one last time, and died.

"Crap!" he exclaimed, and threw the phone in the garbage.

He was seethingly angry. He could never accept the cynically polite offers to enlist law enforcement and they knew it. No one put lily-white money into Bahamian banks. It was always dirty money. Dirty in one way or another. Sometimes, it was the proceeds of illegal activity. Sometimes, no taxes had been paid. A Bahamian bank customer could ill afford to have losses reported to his own government.

He anxiously considered the next move. He would have only one option. Private action! Tough people could be hired; private enforcers who knew how to do their jobs. He needed the identity of the thief. As uncooperative as the Swiss banker had been, he had provided a precious tidbit of information. The transfer requests had all come from a Bolton Sayres IP address. That narrowed things down. He could trace it back to the source.

He logged into the Bolton database, and typed feverishly on his computer's keyboard. Speeding from one section of the underlying framework to another, he used his high-level password to bypass most of the system's security protocols. Within a half hour, he had his answer, and it was as irritating as it was surprising. It was that same son of a bitch he'd run into before. Jack Severs, of all people, had raided his accounts!

Where was the bastard? He logged into THEATRES, using a private set of credentials given to him by his father. Within 15 minutes, he had his answer. The picture fit together perfectly. The multiple entries into his account at the National Bank of the Bahamas all had a common origin in Severs VPN. There were attempts to mask it, but the THEATRES computers knew his location. Now, he knew exactly where to find the man.

Severs had, apparently, engineered the whole theft out of a fleabag motel near Albany, New York. The audacity of it all was astonishing.

But, one thing made sense. It figured that trailer trash would choose a fleabag motel. His anger was almost uncontrollable, and in his fiery temper, he failed to consider how his rival could have suddenly gained such hacking brilliance.

Severs had stolen his girl. Now, he'd stolen his money! How could he think he could get away with that? He didn't need extra muscle to deal with Severs. He didn't need a third party enforcer. He'd deal with the man personally. Not hand to hand, of course. Severs was too good at that. However, no amount of Karate would stop a speeding bullet. The guy wasn't superman.

He reached into his pocket to take out his phone. Then, he remembered. His cell phone was dead. He'd broken it, just a short time before, and thrown it into the garbage. He felt momentary regret about that, but then he simply picked up the landline phone and made the call.

"W.T. Fredericks Executive Services..." some girl answered.

"This is Marcus Dunlop." he said. "I need a helicopter at Bolton Sayres Tower in ten minutes!"

"I'm sorry, but we don't have any choppers available..." she replied.

"The hell you don't!" he raged. "Do you know who this is? My father's Christopher Dunlop, understand? I want a chopper here in 10 minutes."

"But, I can't..." she tried to explain.

"No fuckin' buts!" he screamed. "You want to explain it at the unemployment office? Cancel somebody. Give me that chopper, and quick!"

There was a momentary pause.

"Where do you want to go?" she asked.

"Albany." he replied.

"We can have it there in 15 minutes..." the girl replied.

"Fine." he said, and slammed down the phone.

He reached down, and opened the second drawer of his desk. At the bottom, there was a Ruger 9mm semi-automatic pistol. Such guns were illegal in New York City unless you had a permit to carry. A few bucks slipped into the right pockets always produced results. It was easy to acquire such a permit, and he had one. He slipped the weapon into his pocket.

The blood rushed to his head. When he was this angry, he found it hard to think straight. Whom did that son-of-a-bitch think he was dealing with? No one would steal his money and get away with it! He would teach the man a lesson he'd never forget. He'd shoot him full of holes if necessary, not to kill, but just for the fun of it. He wasn't afraid of prosecution. A guy like Severs had no clout. A few dollars in the right pockets would buy his way out of anything. He'd force the bastard to put the money back, regardless of what it took to do so.

He stood up, opened the door and walked out, slamming the door to his office behind him. When he reached the elevator, he typed the pass code into the control panel. A few moments later, he was standing on the top of the building, next to the helipad, waiting. Then, a helicopter arrived in a swirl of wind, dust and noise. He climbed in, and it whisked him away.

Adriano Navarro was driving to a heliport in White Plains when the phone call finally arrived. He'd agreed to work with Jeremy Stoneham on finding the man's daughter. There was no point to having an open war. It was simply good business to cooperate, and it fit into his overall plan of action.

That pitiful man had been flying around in a Bolton Sayres company helicopter, trying in vain to find his daughter. Doing that without a tracking device was like looking for a needle in a haystack. Navarro knew exactly where she was, thanks to the transponder she was using to track her husband. He'd given it to her through his agent. It sent out a continuous tracking signal.

The girl was driving upstate, following instructions offered by the special satellite navigation system. Since Jack was back on the grid, Laura's GPS would know where to find him. It would have been easy to tell Stoneham where she was. However, that didn't fit into his plan. Besides, giving such information might implicate him in her disappearance. It would also disrupt a few critical elements in his carefully concocted scheme to end his troubles.

Navarro's mobile phone had an electronic link to the hands-free speaker system of the car and it rang.

"Answer." he spoke into the air.

It was enough.

"Hello?" the woman's voice said.

"Navarro speaking." he said.

It was Susanna Maloney again.

"You told me to tell you when Mr. Dunlop began to follow our trace to Jack Severs." she noted. "He's doing it now."

"What's he doing exactly?"

"He's ordered one of W.T. Fredericks' company helicopters to pick him up at the heliport on top of the Bolton Sayres' Tower."

"Excellent."

The younger Dunlop had taken the bait. Things were falling into place perfectly.

"Where is Jack Severs now?" he asked.

"Same motel as before."

"Keep me informed if anything changes."

"Yes, sir!"

"End call." he stated, and the hands-free system hung up.

Navarro was feeling quite satisfied. His plan was now moving along perfectly. Khasan had checked out of the hospital an hour earlier. If he wasn't in Albany already he'd be near. His exact arrival time would be imperative. The timing and coordination needed to be perfect.

Navarro pulled his car onto the side of the highway. Parking for a moment, he removed the smart phone from the car's hands free. Then, he tapped on the interface icon. That would connect it to THEATRES. There was a code number, a fingerprint to scan, and a few codes and commands to input. Soon the super-computers understood. He would now receive continuous reports on the exact whereabouts of Fyodor Khasan, Mark Dunlop, Laura Stoneham and Jack Severs every minute.

Finally, he reconnected the phone to the car interface, and looked at his watch. Jeremy Stoneham would be anxiously awaiting him. He smiled and put the car into drive, pulled back into the road, and rapidly speeding up to full highway speed. He had to get there quickly, to make sure he arrived with Stoneham, at the very moment that Khasan reached the motel.

XXIII - THE LAST MEETING

When Sandra Mattingly returned, about two hours had passed, and Jack was very frustrated.

"Why didn't you let me know you were leaving?" he asked. "Where did you go?"

She held out open hands.

"I just went to the store to buy some makeup." she replied. "Can't I do that?"

"No!" he barked, "that was a completely foolish thing to do."

"I can't stay locked up in this little room." she argued. "There's nothing to do."

"Someone might identify you." he explained.

"But, my hair's red now." she reminded him.

"You still have the same face," he explained, "and anyone who looks carefully can see that. Your photo has been on the news. The media may think you're dead, but that blonde giant, and whoever sent him, knows you're still alive. There's a good chance that these people have control over what is the most sophisticated surveillance system in the world, and they've got tentacles everywhere..."

"I think you're going totally paranoid..." she said.

"Do you not remember getting shot at?" Jack exclaimed. "Do you not remember almost being killed? Do you know what's going to happen if they find us?"

She suddenly cried, shook her head and then collapsed into his arms.

"I'm so sorry..." she said, while crying.

His heart melted, and his anger abated.

"It'll be all right."

He touched her arm gently, trying to calm her.

"What are we going to do?" she said, shaking now.

She was beautiful but shallow and entirely unpredictable. That made her different from Laura, who was completely predictable. Both engaged in emotional outbursts, of course, but so did most of the other women he knew. His wife, however, had a good head on her shoulders. It wouldn't have been necessary spell things out for her. She would have understood right away.

"It'll be all right," he said, stroking her hair.

"I don't think anyone can recognize us now." she said, hopefully. "Have you looked in the mirror?"

He hadn't looked very closely. She was partly right. He looked ridiculous with the bleached blonde hair. But, he definitely didn't look like himself.

"I just can't stand this anymore." she continued.

If she were so frustrated after only a day on the run, what would she be like after a few more days or weeks? It would be a problem.

"We won't stay here much longer," he said, "I just need to find some prosecutorial authority that isn't compromised. When I do, I'll hand them a rock-solid case."

"But, the police are after you…"

"We don't know all the facts about that," he replied, "but there's might be more than appears on the surface. I know that there are still some honest prosecutors out there."

Finding them, however, he thought silently, wouldn't be easy.

"If you want," he offered, "we'll risk getting something to eat."

There was a Denny's restaurant not far away. The food would be satisfying enough, and it would feel good to be out of the room. There was still the recognition problem. However, with a change in hair color, and the absurdly nerdy glasses Jose had given him, along with almost 2 days worth of stubble on his chin, he didn't look much like the picture they were spreading on the news.

Sure enough, when they got to the restaurant, no one recognized them. By 8:45 p.m., after the short meal, they returned to the room. He inserted the key, and opened the door. Fumbling for the light switch, he finally found it, and switched the lights on. That's when his heart rate and blood pressure jumped into the stratosphere.

Sitting silently in the armchair, waiting for them, was Marcus Dunlop, who was the last person he'd expected or wanted to see. The man had a 9mm Ruger semi-automatic pistol in his hand, aimed straight at Jack's chest.

"Hello, Jack." Dunlop said with a smirk. "Come in. If you don't, I might have to shoot you. Come in, that's it... don't be shy..."

He motioned with the gun, and they silently complied.

"Now, shut the door behind you." he demanded.

The girl shut the door.

"What are you doing here?" Jack asked.

"Don't even dream about trying that Karate crap, today, Jack." Dunlop said. "If you do, I'm gonna' blow a huge hole in you, understand?"

"Who are you?" Sandra asked in broken tones.

Tears streamed down her cheeks.

He didn't answer, but, instead, turned to Jack.

"Who is this little slut?"

When there was no answer, he kept talking.

"It doesn't really matter, but, frankly, Jack, I'm shocked. Positively shocked! You, a family man! Cheating on your wife. What our poor Laura has to put up with... shame on you!"

"What are you talking about?" Sandra Mattingly asked, haltingly.

"Shut up, slut!" Dunlop exclaimed, and turned back to Jack. "You've been a naughty boy, haven't you?"

"The police are on their way." Jack offered. "If I were you, I'd get out of here as soon as I could..."

Dunlop laughed.

"It's you, who need to run, isn't it?" he said, wryly. "Here you are, in a broken down crappy hotel room, with a floozy."

"What do you want?" Jack asked.

Dunlop ignored the question.

"I must punish you, you know…" Dunlop stated. "For your naughtiness… your infidelity to my dear Laura, and for the theft, of course, among other things…"

"You'd better do what Jack says." Sandra warned, in a wavering voice.

"Where did you find this dumb slut?" Dunlop asked him, shaking his head. "Did she grow up in the same trailer park as you?"

There was a pause of about 15 seconds.

"You know exactly who she is." Jack stated.

"I really don't." Dunlop stated, smiling. "But, actually, what I care about is getting my money back."

"What are you talking about?" Jack replied.

"You know exactly what I'm talking about." Dunlop warned. "I *will* shoot you full of holes, unless you cough up the cash."

Suddenly, there was a loud knock on the door. Jack turned, but Dunlop shook his head sharply, and held up his index finger. He shook his finger in the negative. Then, he held the finger against his mouth, in a gesture to keep quiet. The knocking continued. Finally, it became a pounding. Dunlop was the first to break the silence.

"We're busy…" he called out. "Come back later…"

The voice that spoke back, through the door, was very familiar.

"Mark Dunlop?" a woman asked, confused.

The owner of that voice was unmistakable. It was Laura Stoneham. She had used the tracking device she'd been given and had finally found her husband. Dunlop laughed, uncontrollably, and then, he finally spoke.

"Ok, you… slut," he said, speaking to Sandra Mattingly, "open the door and let her in. She may as well see what you've been up to, Jack…"

Sandra Mattingly opened the door and Laura appeared. She entered without bothering to notice the surroundings, and immediately embraced and kissed Jack on the lips.

"Sickening…" Dunlop commented.

A moment later, she noticed Dunlop's gun, still aimed at Jack.

"What are you doing?" Laura demanded, fearlessly.

"I'm going to turn your thief of a boyfriend back into an honest man." Dunlop said calmly.

"He's not my boyfriend. He's my husband!"

"Whatever..." Dunlop answered.

"Put the gun down, and get out of here, now!" Laura insisted.

"Oh, please, Laura, I'm the one who gives the orders, haven't you noticed?" he replied, motioning to the gun.

"You'd better get out of here, now, or I'm going to tell your father!"

"Shut up, Laura!" Dunlop said firmly. "You used to be pretty and smart. Now, you're fat and dumb. But, there is one thing I want to know..."

"I don't care what you want to know!"

"No, wait, this is a good question." Dunlop insisted. "Why did you choose him over me? I mean, he's a poor slob; trailer trash. And, now, take a look at this little slut he's fucking..."

He pointed toward Sandra Mattingly.

"Yeah, that's right, he's fucking her," Dunlop continued. "But, you know that, don't you?"

She glanced over at the other girl, and for a moment, jealousy welled up in her eyes. She tried to hide it, and spoke again.

"If you shoot that gun, everyone will hear it for miles around, and the police will be here less than a minute." she snapped.

He ignored her.

"He's cheating on you." Dunlop stated, and then he pointed again to Sandra Mattingly. "She's the other woman. This motel is their little love nest. A perfect place for the trailer trash crowd."

He gestured with the pistol barrel, toward Sandra Mattingly.

"Who's the fool now?" Dunlop asked, amused.

She turned to Jack, with a hint of anger on her face.

"Who is she?"

311

There was a pause, as Jack didn't know what to say. Although the man couldn't possibly know it for sure, much as he hated to admit it, Dunlop's claims and taunts were true. It hadn't been intentional. The circumstances were beyond his control, at least in his mind. But, even if he had a quiet place to explain it all, could he possibly make it a convincing explanation? That was neither here nor there. There was no time to explain anything, and this was not the place to do it.

A moment later, and he found his wits, and spoke.

"She's the eyewitness to the burial of a corpse, a man named Charles Bakkendorf. One of Dunlop's goons tried to kill her last night."

Then, he pointed in the man's direction.

"This is the man who murdered her husband!"

Dunlop seemed genuinely surprised by the accusation.

"What are you talking about?" Dunlop exclaimed. "Bakkendorf? The guy from the vault? She should thank me for making her husband rich. But, I always thought the guy was a total loser. Surprising that he had a little whore of a wife stashed up here?"

"Who's Charlie Bakkendorf?" Sandra Mattingly asked. "My husband was Bobby Mattingly."

"He claims he didn't murder anyone," Jack noted, accusingly, "but look who's aiming a gun, threatening to kill me."

"You stole my money, a lot of it, and you won't get away with it." Dunlop declared.

"You shoot that gun, and as I said, everyone in 5 miles will hear it." Laura warned again.

Dunlop simply laughed.

"You really should stick to putting on diapers," he said, finally, "because you don't know what you're talking about."

Then, he turned toward Jack.

"You know what this is, don't you?" Dunlop continued, pointing to the gun's barrel. "Why don't you explain it to your wife?"

"Why don't you explain it?" Jack replied.

"I will." Dunlop replied instantly. "You see this, Laura? It's a silencer. No one is going to hear this gun go off. No one!"

She bit her lip.

"You won't get away with it." Laura snapped.

"I'll get away with whatever I want to." Dunlop insisted. "But, all I really want to do is to put a few bullets in him to teach him a lesson. I won't actually kill him, so long as he gives me back my money…"

Then, he turned toward Jack.

"Give me my money! A few bullet holes will heal. Then, you can go on trying to steal the Stoneham's money, if you want. I don't care about that."

"I can't give you back what I don't have." Jack insisted.

"Liar!" Dunlop snapped, and then, shaking his head, he turned toward Laura. "Can you believe what a liar he is? This is who you want to be with?"

He turned his attention back to Jack.

"I know you've got the money. I traced it back to you!"

"You're the thief, Dunlop." Jack retorted. "You killed Bakkendorf because he found out, and then you killed her husband and his entire family, because they knew you killed Bakkendorf!"

"Ridiculous crap." Dunlop said. "I want you online, now, putting out wiring instructions that replaces the cash in my account. If you don't do it, I will shoot you, one hole at a time, until you're like a sponge. Got it?"

"Like you killed Bakkendorf and the Mattingly family?" Jack asked.

"I didn't kill Bakkendorf." Dunlop insisted, shaking his head. "And, the others… I don't even know who you're talking about. But, I *will* kill you, if you push me too far."

"If you touch him, I'm a witness." Laura noted.

"So am I." Sandra Mattingly added.

"So, I guess that means I'll kill both of you, too." Dunlop said. "Get online, Jack, and put money back. My trigger finger's itchy."

Jack's mind raced. He had a few suspicions about what might have happened. Jose had said he would penetrate the Bahamian bank. He assumed that meant gathering data. However, once the man had successfully penetrated the bank's security system, theoretically, he could do anything. Perhaps, he had transferred the man's money. Unfortunately, he didn't have the faintest clue on how to put it back.

Dunlop was doing a lot of talking. That was good. Talkers, he knew, tended not to be doers. The man wasn't ready to shoot anyone. It was important to keep him talking. The only other alternative would be to contact Jose. If he did that, however, he would be compromising the other man's identity. He'd then become a target too. There had to be another way.

His best hope was to disarm Dunlop. The man was slow, and didn't know how to fight. However, if he managed to shoot that gun, the bullets would do his work for him. No one is faster than a speeding bullet. Surprising the man might be difficult. However, the longer he could delay, the more likely that an opportunity would present itself, and better his chances would become. He needed an element of surprise, and he didn't have one.

The laptop was in the pickup truck. He'd put it there when they'd left the motel to eat dinner. That gave him an excuse for delay. In the time used to fetch the computer, an opportunity might open up.

"Obviously, I can't do anything without my computer." Jack said, finally.

"Where is it?" Dunlop demanded.

"In the pickup." he replied.

"Then, get it!" Dunlop demanded.

Jack nodded, and headed out the door.

"Stop right there!" Dunlop demanded. "You think I'm an idiot? You're not just going to walk out the door..."

He got out of the arm chair, and stood up.

"You two!" Dunlop addressed the women. "Get moving! Don't get any ideas, because I'll shoot at the slightest provocation."

Laura shook her head.

"I'm not going anywhere!" she insisted.

"Even a glancing impact from a bullet leaves a very nasty scar, my dear..." Dunlop warned.

"You wouldn't dare!" she replied, defiantly.

"Don't bank on it." he responded. "But, if you were smarter, you'd encourage me to shoot that little slut over there. Maybe, your cheating hubby too. We could be together after that and nobody has to know anything. How about it?"

"Go to hell!"

"You always were too squeamish." Dunlop commented.

Laura looked at Jack.

"Just do what he says." he said.

"That's right." Dunlop added. "Even your dumb husband is smartening up."

The two women moved into position in front of Dunlop. The moment that the Mattingly girl was within reach, however, he grabbed her, and pulled her around, forcing her to walk at the point of his pistol. He pointed it directly into her back, near her heart. From an outside view, however, the pistol was invisible, hidden from view by the angle of sight.

"Now, let's just get moving quietly, Jack." he warned. "If you're thinking about trying anything, a bullet goes into her. Understand. Nobody's going to miss one more little slut, and I guaranty you that I'll buy my way out of any prosecution even easier than it would be with you. She's nobody squared."

Jack walked forward, and opened the door.

"You'll walk outside, go to that truck, and get the laptop..." Dunlop ordered. "I'll be right here, just inside the door, with Laura and your little friend. Try to get away, and your little friend buys it. Understand?"

Jack nodded.

A moment later, Jack was outside. Several burned out lamps that should have lit the parking lot were out. He walked toward the pickup truck mostly in darkness. A moment later, he was walking back to the room, carrying the backpack that contained his laptop. Dunlop and the two women continued to wait just inside the door of the motel room.

Unknown to the others, hidden behind the cover provided by a stand of newly blossomed rhododendron, a blonde giant was crouching down, watching everything through night vision goggles. He focused on Jack for a moment, anger piqued by the memory of the continuing pain of the knife wound he had inflicted on him. There was a momentary compulsion to pull the trigger, but if the man suddenly dropped, it would alert the others to the danger. That might negatively impact his ability to terminate his primary target. He reminded himself that he was a professional. His primary target was still the girl, so his attention shifted to the door of the motel room, where she was standing in front of Dunlop.

It was uncomfortable to crouch and aim the sniper rifle, given that the wound was still raw. It almost felt like the stitches slowly torn out in the most painful way possible. He bore the pain silently, however, and took careful aim. The girl's forehead was squarely in the center of his scope. He pulled the trigger. A flash of light and a small muffled pip came from the barrel. A millisecond later, and the girl slumped to the ground, shot through the head. Then, there was another pip, and a second bullet, which came from a different direction, which entered Mark Dunlop brain.

Both Sandra Mattingly and Marc Dunlop crumbled to the ground as blood welled out from gaping holes in their foreheads. Deeper in the room, hidden behind the wall, Jack could hear a woman screaming. It was unmistakably the voice of his wife. He turned toward the direction of the pips and could just barely made out the giant's blonde hair slightly above the bushes, silhouetted against the light from one of the working parking lot lamps. Instinctively, he dropped to the ground, to get out of the path of what would likely be the next bullet.

Sure enough, there was another short flash of light and pip as a bullet meant for his heart entered his shoulder instead. The searing pain was almost unbearable, because it caused an involuntary contraction of the muscle there, and he fell hard to surface of the tarmac, his head hitting the concrete curb. Already in shock from the wound to his shoulder, he was bleeding from two places, the shoulder and the head.

Suddenly, the air was shattered by the loud clap of three unmuffled bullets. They slammed into Fyodor Khasan's head, one after another, turning his blonde hair into a bloody mess of brain and pieces of bone. He collapsed into the bushes, his skull and brain now pulp.

Jack felt weak and cold. He could hear the screaming coming closer. He lay prone on the ground, an ever-growing puddle his red blood welling out from his body. It was warm and wet as it dribbled out onto the pavement. A small dark skinned man was suddenly at Jack's side, attending the wounds with a portable medical kit. His shoulder was quickly wrapped with a tourniquet and gauze bandage.

He could see that Laura's father was there too, holding Laura as she sobbed on his shoulder. The sirens wailed as the ambulances arrived. The outside world had become a foggy mist. He was still half-conscious, but he didn't exactly know what was happening. Soon, he could sense he was inside an ambulance, and his half-open eyes could sense the outline of his wife by his side, crying. The tears streamed down her cheeks.

Was this the way it would all end?

He drifted off quietly, and as Laura hovered over him, he realized, through the fog, that he loved her. Then, he finally drifted into the fog completely, and unconsciousness overtook him. The outside world disappeared.

XXIV - REST & RECOVERY

Jack awoke five days later at Albany Medical Center. The drugs that had kept him in a medically induced coma hadn't worn off. The world still seemed blurry. He was tired and both his head and shoulder still ached. He tried to shift position in the hospital bed, but the sharp pain that streaked through his right side stopped him. He glanced upward, and noticed that he was connected to a network of tubes. His shoulder was entirely bandaged up, and the arm looked somewhat like that of a mummy.

With his eyes open, he stared at the ceiling, and then he could hear his wife's voice.

"He's up!" Laura called out.

Almost instantaneously, two Lauras hovered above him. Both kissed his cheek and forehead, with double hands sifting through his hair. He turned his eyes slightly to the left, and there were also two nurses, standing next to each other and the bed, adjusting two IV hoses that connected a double set of left arms to two bags of saline solution hanging above the bed.

How did I get an extra left arm? he wondered.

He closed his eyes, and tried to shake himself free of cobwebs. Then, he opened them again. He was still seeing double, but when he squinted, things came together, as the second image would fade into a shadow of the first. The last thing he remembered was the warm blood dripping down his arm, and someone tightly wrapping gauze bandages around it. He experimented, and tried to move the arm, but stopped instantly. The pain was too great.

Laura sat down on the armchair next to the bed. She continued to hold his left hand, and spoke to him in reassuring tones.

"Don't try to move, Jack." Laura said, planting a kiss on his forehead. "Relax. You caught a bullet in your right shoulder. The doctors pulled it out and sewed you up. They say you'll be almost good as new once it heals. You'll just have a tiny little scar."

He smiled though the ache.

"What about you?" he asked. "Are you okay?"

She nodded.

Things were slowly coming back into focus. It didn't take as much effort to stop the double images anymore. For a moment, he just stared at her. He was tired, but it was good to see her smiling face. She was a good wife, he decided, standing by him and being there for him, despite the fact that she must now suspect his activity with Sandra Mattingly.

What of the Mattingly girl? Her fate was horrifying to think about. He felt deeply saddened from remembering the bullet hole in her head. After having gone so far and done so much to protect her, he'd failed miserably. It was better not to question Laura about it. The girl was dead. No one could have survived that bullet.

The nurse finished adjusting the IV, and headed toward the door. That drew his attention toward the door itself. A uniformed police officer stood there, guarding it. The man opened the door for the nurse, and she walked out. Then, he took his position again.

Jack turned back to Laura.

"Who is that?" he asked.

She took a deep breath.

"A police officer." she said softly.

"Why?"

"He's protecting us." she replied. "Partly, anyway…"

"And, the other part?"

She paused for a moment, trying to collect her words.

"They've charged you with possession of a deadly weapon…" she said, quickly.

He closed his eyes for a moment, and nodded.

"What deadly weapon?" he asked.

"They say you stabbed somebody with a knife." she replied.

"I stabbed the guy who killed Dunlop and the girl." he said, immediately. "It was self-defense."

"I'm sure we'll get it all straightened out." she said, hopefully.

"What about the blonde giant?" he asked.

319

"He's dead. My Dad and Mr. Navarro saw to that. They shot him." she said, proudly.

That was a small comfort.

"What about Dunlop?" he asked.

"Also dead." she replied.

"And, Sandra Mattingly?" he finally asked, taking the chance.

"She's dead, too." she replied.

That final revelation cut deep. Did he love Sandra Mattingly? It didn't matter anymore. She was gone. Until that moment, as unrealistic as he knew it was, he'd entertained a ridiculous hope she'd survived the bullet in her head.

"Who was he?" he asked.

The giant's identity was an important piece of the puzzle, because it put his theory into question. He had once concluded that the man worked for Marc Dunlop. However, that now seemed impossible. If Dunlop were the employer, he wouldn't have shot him dead.

"He was some kind of assassin, I think, but I don't know..." she replied.

Someone had hired the man. If it wasn't Marc Dunlop, who was it? The last witness was dead. Marc Dunlop was dead. The blonde giant, one of two men identified by the girl, was dead. Every potential witness was dead. The people behind the killings, whoever they might be, were probably still very much alive. No one would ever find them now.

Two well-dressed men wearing suits and ties interrupted his thoughts. Jack recognized one of them. It was Laura's father, but the other one was unknown to him.

His father-in-law maintained a broad smile.

"Ah," Stoneham spoke to his daughter, as he moved closer. "Our young man has awakened!"

Laura smiled.

Jack stared expressionless.

Jeremy Stoneham turned to his daughter.

"Laura, might we have a word in private with Jack?" he asked.

"You mean, without me?" she asked, surprised.

Her father nodded.

"If you don't mind... just for 10 minutes..."

She didn't like the idea, but assented, anyway, kissing Jack on the forehead. She pressed her hand into his, and whispered.

"I'll be back in 10 minutes, sweetheart..."

Once she had left the room, Stoneham motioned to the much younger man who stood by his side.

"This is Special Agent Felix Martin, Jack." Stoneham said. "He's with the Federal Reserve Police."

"The what?" Jack asked.

"Federal Reserve police, Mr. Severs." Martin repeated loudly. "You realize that you've been arrested for possession and use of a deadly weapon?"

"So, I'm told..." Jack stated. "Can I ask you something... what the hell is the Federal Reserve police?"

"It's an in-house police force that protects the Federal Reserve, Jack." Stoneham interjected.

"That's right." Agent Martin agreed.

"The Fed has its own army?" Jack asked.

The two men ignored the comment.

"We need to know who falsified the credentials that allowed you to break into the high security intranet." Martin insisted.

"I have no idea what you're talking about." Jack answered.

"This is not a game." Agent Martin stated, firmly. "You entered your credentials, created new credentials, and then completely compromised computers belonging to a number of banks and the Federal Reserve. You understand that sabotaging a computer system is a felony? I want answers!"

"I don't have a clue what you're talking about." Jack replied.

"I think you do." the man insisted.

"I don't." Jack replied. "And, I'm tired and dizzy. I need to sleep."

He closed his eyes, for a moment, but opened them, again, as the man continued talking loudly.

"Are you aware that tampering with a federal computer is a Class C felony, carrying a penalty from 3 to 15 years in a federal prison?" Agent Martin warned.

"Am I charged with tampering with a computer?" Jack asked.

"You're involved with a conspiracy to tamper with a computer, yes." Martin declared.

"Am I charged?" Jack asked, again.

"Not yet…" Martin warned.

"Then, go away." Jack replied.

"I could have you hauled out and put in jail the moment you recover." Martin exclaimed, waiting a moment to gauge the effect. "You want to spend the rest of your life in jail? We know what you did, and we know you didn't do it alone. You can tell me who did it, and we can do something about the charges against you."

"If you're going to charge me, do it." Jack replied, calmly. "And, by the way, I've got a constitutional right to counsel."

"You're a lawyer yourself!" the man exclaimed.

"It doesn't matter." Jack noted. "A man with himself as a lawyer has a fool for a client."

Agent Martin stared at him with visible annoyance. Stoneham interrupted the escalation.

"Let's calm down…" he said, quietly.

The man turned to Stoneham.

"Cyber terrorism is a serious crime!" the man exclaimed.

"You're charging me with cyber terrorism?" Jack asked. "I thought you said 'tampering with computer systems'? Don't you know that they're two different crimes?"

The Federal Reserve man was becoming red in the face, and looked almost ready to physically attack him. Instead, he spoke again, in even tones.

"You're a smart ass." Martin stated. "But, that's not going to save you. You downloaded sensitive materials; US government secrets, using falsified credentials. We could prosecute you for treason!"

"Treason?" Jack asked, smiling. "Wouldn't you agree that it's a lot more treasonous to sell off our national treasure without the consent of Congress?"

"You like to twist things, don't you?" Agent Martin stated.

"And, by the way... why is the Federal Reserve storing documents on private servers belonging to private banks?"

"It's not your business where government secrets are stored!" Agent Martin declared.

"Wait a minute..." Jack noted. "There's a whole series of cases where the New York Federal Reserve tries not to comply with "freedom of information act" requests by claiming it isn't part of the government. How, then, can any of its secrets be government secrets?"

"I'm asking the questions, not you, Mr. Severs." Agent Martin insisted. "I'm going to ask you, one last time, who helped you break into the computer systems?"

"Direct your questions to my lawyer." Jack replied.

"Who's your lawyer?" Agent Martin shot back.

"I don't know yet." Jack promised. "But, I'll let you know when I'm charged with something and have to hire one."

The man was enraged.

"You'd better tell me who you're working with, or you're going to face serious charges, very serious jail time..." Agent Martin warned.

The antics of the brash agent of the Federal Reserve were adding to the headache Jack was already suffering from.

"Who are you working with?" Martin continued.

"I just told you to direct questions to my lawyer." Jack said. "But, you keep asking questions. That's a violation, you know. Even if you manage to get something out of me, at this point, you couldn't use it in court."

"Then, you admit it!" Martin said, triumphantly.

"I don't admit to anything." Jack insisted. "I'm just pointing out how clear it is that you couldn't care less about admissibility. That means you don't intend to charge me with anything. The Fed is deathly afraid of having its dirty little secrets aired in public, isn't it? That's what this is really all about, isn't it? What are you afraid of? Revolution?"

The man glared at him with intensified hostility. Stoneham put his hand on Agent Martin's shoulder and gently nudged him toward the door.

"I'll deal with this..." he said, softly.

Agent Martin seemed to acknowledge his failure and the other man's authority by nodding. Still, before he left, he turned back toward Jack, and the one more thing.

"Unless you enjoy the idea of sitting in jail for a decade or more, you'd better talk..." he said as loudly as he could.

Then, he left the room. Stoneham turned toward the uniformed police officer at the door.

"Could you guard the room from outside the door, please?" he suggested.

"Yes, sir." the man replied immediately, taking the suggestion as an order.

A moment later, he was gone. Stoneham walked back to the bed, and sat down in the chair vacated by his daughter.

"I'm on your side." Stoneham assured him.

"It sure doesn't seem like it." Jack stated.

Stoneham nodded with a serious face.

"I'm sorry I've given you the wrong impression." he said. "But, this is sensitive."

"Where are the *real* cops?" Jack asked.

"They're all real cops." Stoneham replied.

Jack shook his head.

"No they're not." he said. "First of all, the Federal Reserve police can't charge me with possession or use of a deadly weapon. You know that just as well as I do. Not even the NYPD would have jurisdiction upstate. If it happened, it happened in Verde County, and the only entity that can charge me is the Verde County D.A."

Stoneham shrugged his shoulders.

"OK, you've got me." he admitted. "But, we had to come up with some excuse for police being here. Obviously, somebody's killing people, and you need protection."

"You lied to your own daughter?" Jack asked him, accusingly.

Stoneham shrugged his shoulders, again, and adjusted his trousers upward, so he could sit more comfortably for a longer while.

Jack was in no mood for long conversations.

"The things you looked at in the archives are highly sensitive." he said, finally.

"As I've said, over and over again, I don't know what you're talking about."

"OK. You don't know. But, theoretically, if someone like you saw something that, maybe, they didn't agree with, it would still be a complete violation of attorney-client privilege to say anything about it. If this theoretical person ever disclosed the content of any pilfered documents, he would end up disbarred, at minimum, and, probably in jail for a long time."

"So what?" Jack said.

"We're talking about matters of national security."

"National security?" Jack smiled dismissively. "You've got to be joking."

"I'm not joking at all." Stoneham said.

Jack laughed, but he stopped when each laugh brought streaks of pain.

"Protecting fraud, front running and market manipulation are now matters of national security?" he asked, facetiously.

"That's a naive way of looking at things..." Stoneham commented.

"Naive?" Jack shook his head. "It's a sensible way unless you're benefitting from the fraud..."

"Do you know why the Federal Reserve has a 1,400 man police force?"

"The Cosa Nostra mafia also has soldiers, so I figure for the same reason. It's a criminal organization..."

"This isn't the time for sarcasm, Jack."

"I wasn't being sarcastic."

"The Fed police exist because there are people out there who would like to attack the U.S. financial system. I'm talking about terrorists, enemy nations; Russia, China, you name it... all kinds of people who hate us."

Jack switched the subject.

"You filed a report with the New York State police saying I kidnapped Laura."

Stoneham shook his head.

"I never said you kidnapped her." he insisted.

"You claimed I was responsible for her disappearance." Jack said.

"She disappeared and you disappeared. The connection was a natural one to make. It was for your protection and hers. With Khasan out there, you were both in terrible danger. You saw what happened to Marc Dunlop and Sandra Mattingly? It could have been you or Laura."

"They were claiming I was behind the bombings in Paradise." Jack protested.

"That had nothing to do with me." Stoneham insisted. "They found your car up there, and made the connection. You were already wanted for questioning..."

"How about the giant?" Jack said.

"What about him?"

"Who was he?"

"Fyodor Khasan."

"Who?"

"A former Russian spy." Stoneham replied.

"Why did he kill Sandra Mattingly?" Jack asked.

"I don't know."

"A private job to cover up a murder?" Jack wondered aloud.

"Perhaps…" Stoneham agreed.

"Well, it's a murder that involves someone working for our bank." Jack insisted. "I thought it was Dunlop, but it's someone else. What are you going to do about it?"

"I don't know where to start." Stoneham said.

"Why did Khasan kill Marc Dunlop?"

"I don't know."

"Tell me the truth!"

"I don't know." Stoneham repeated. "What other truth do you want?"

"There's only one truth." Jack said.

"Your truth?" Stoneham asked.

"The shooter was one of yours, wasn't he?" Jack declared.

He watched Stoneham's face carefully. There was no reaction, except what appeared to be minor irritation.

"No." Stoneham declared. "I don't employ mercenaries."

"But, you know who he worked for?"

"I only know who he used to work for."

"He used to work for Bolton Sayres, right?"

"No." Stoneham shook his head.

"Who, then?"

"A shadowy group that interferes in politics, banking and world affairs." he noted, truthfully, without disclosing his own relationship to the Synod.

"Who is this shadowy group?" Jack asked.

"I can't say." Stoneham responded.

"Is it the same shadowy group that puts the Federal Reserve at your fingertips? Is this some kind of an intra-bankster war?"

Stoneham shook his head in exasperation.

"Don't use that stupid word, 'bankster'...it's for the idiots on the blogosphere."

"Interesting that you don't like being called a bankster." Jack noted, "Why don't you want to answer my questions?"

Jack was getting excited. Maybe, the answer was right in front of him. It was almost enough to make him forget about his injuries. When he moved, however, the sharp searing pain that shot down his arm reminded him. He lay back.

"I really thought you were a clever boy." Stoneham declared. "That's why I let you marry Laura. But, now I'm not so sure..."

Jack stared at the wall for a moment and then turned back to his father in law.

"You didn't 'let' me marry Laura. We were in love, and she was going to give birth to my child. There was nothing you could do about it."

Stoneham smiled.

"Maybe. But, I can do something now."

"What." Jack challenged him.

"I can let them put you away for a long time."

"And, leave your daughter and granddaughter without a husband and father? Not to mention having all your dirty secrets aired in the media, along with the documentation to prove everything."

The pause in the conversation lasted almost 30 seconds.

"Perhaps, we can reach an understanding." Stoneham said, finally. "What is it you want, Jack?"

"I want the truth. I want honest markets. I want an end to the manipulations. What do you want?"

"I want loyalty." Stoneham said. "To me, to Bolton Sayres, and to your country..."

Jack raised an eyebrow at that.

"Loyalty?"

"We don't manipulate markets for personal gain." Stoneham insisted.

"Looks to me that there was a hell of a lot of personal gain going on."

"Not everyone follows the rules, but that's not why it's done."

"Why is it done, then?"

"Our country isn't blessed with an endless supply of gold."

"So what?" Jack asked.

"The economic strength of a nation should be based on the hard work, productivity and genius of its people, not how big a pile of gold it has."

"That's a false narrative." Jack insisted. "If you're hard working, productive and brilliant, you'd end up collecting gold from all over the world, as people buy the stuff you've got to sell."

Stoneham said nothing for a moment.

"Things would have fallen apart years ago, if we hadn't stepped in." he said, finally.

Jack shook his head.

"Look at silver." Stoneham stated. "It's an important and strategic industrial commodity that for years was wasted on coinage. There's not enough silver for that. If we return silver to coinage, we price it out of the reach of the industries that need it most. That wouldn't improve the lives of people."

"How about gold?" Jack asked. "What's your excuse there?"

"It's an arbitrary thing, gold..." Stoneham mused. "Why should the wealth of nations be determined by an arbitrary thing?"

"Better to determine it based on the capricious decisions of Mandarins on a Federal Reserve Open Market Committee?"

Stoneham shook his head.

"Why should some country that has the good luck to have the most gold mines control the world?"

"That's bullshit." Jack insisted. "Countries that have more resources are always richer than ones that have less. It's no different for gold. It's just a false narrative. The gold will always flow to the nation that is the hardest working, brilliant and creative."

"You sound like a gold bug." Stoneham stated.

"Does that bother you?" Jack asked.

"Not particularly." Stoneham replied. "But, our job is to protect the value of the US dollar and nothing else."

"So, gold competes with the dollar, and you've got to manipulate it, is that what you're saying?"

Stoneham shook his head.

"Gold competes with nothing. If it were money, we wouldn't be able to manipulate it, would we?"

"You can lie, cheat, and steal, and covertly use the full faith and credit of the United States of America, to manipulate anything. It's all about fooling people and scaring them."

"Which proves that the paper is mightier than the gold, doesn't it?" Stoneham quipped.

"It doesn't prove anything. Nothing but the fact that you're abusing the trust people put in you."

"The instability from a collapse of the US dollar would put the entire world in chaos." Stoneham countered.

"It wouldn't be in danger of collapsing if not for the fact that you and your friends at the Federal Reserve keep printing endless numbers of dollars."

"Nonsense." Stoneham countered, without addressing the point. "Our nation's power, wealth, and influence, in spite of what people think, isn't based on tanks, ships or fighter jets. Ultimately, the soft power of the dollar and its role as the world's reserve currency makes us strong. The Pax Americana is the first of its kind in history. The Romans ruled the world based on the success of their legionnaires. We rule the world based on economics. We destroy rogue nations by cutting off their money. We've kept the peace that way since WW II. We've avoided the needless death and destruction that comes from war."

"That's pure bullshit!" Jack commented. "We've had lots of wars. And, then there's the question of who decides what other countries are rogues?"

Stoneham didn't reply immediately.

"The President and Congress decide." he said, finally.

"But, you control the President and Congress." Jack insisted.

"Not true." Stoneham said.

"You control the money and money controls the elections." Jack countered. "You and your friends manipulate the price of stocks, bonds, commodities, currencies, gold, you name it, all based on how much money the Fed creates at any particular time, and how much it takes back in. You control when and how the Fed prints money. So, you make or break Presidents."

"You read too many conspiracy blogs." Stoneham insisted.

"Do I?"

"The truth is more subtle than that. We do everything possible to keep markets orderly, that much is true. Some of that involves price management. Is it wrong to give people stability?"

"You're damn right it's wrong! It's bullshit! Just as bad as sending tungsten filled gold bars to Africa!"

"That was the work of two foolish and greedy men." Stoneham said. "One of them just paid the ultimate price. The other will be fired. We're in the process of correcting that shipment, by the way, even as we speak."

Jack shook his head in disgust.

"So, you knew all along about the Tungsten filled bars, didn't you?"

"No." Stoneham insisted. "I'm aware of them because we've reviewed all the records you pilfered."

"Why didn't you review them before?"

"There was no reason to."

"They were always in the database."

"Maybe." Stoneham admitted. "But this is a big institution. It's not as tight a ship I would like it to be. There's room for improvement. We've got governance problems, compliance problems, and a whole host of other problems. That's why we need men like you. You can help change things. It's the only way, Jack. You've got to work within the system. Otherwise, they'll destroy you."

"Who, may I ask, are 'they'?"

"Leave it at 'they' for the moment." Stoneham responded.

"They killed Charles Bakkendorf, didn't they?" Jack asked.

"I don't know who killed Charles Bakkendorf."

"But, you admit that he was one of our employees, right?" Jack asked.

"Yes. He was."

"Who staged the murders at the Mattingly farm?"

"Khasan." Stoneham replied. "I'm almost sure of that."

Jack shook his head.

"Who paid him?"

"That, I don't know. And, that's the truth."

"Them?"

"I don't know." Stoneham repeated.

"Who killed Sandra Mattingly?"

"Fyodor Khasan, but, now you're going to ask me who hired him again, and I'd have to say, once again, I don't know."

"Who killed Khasan?"

"Adriano Navarro, one of our security people." Stoneham replied. "He's also the current supervisor of THEATRES; the man I'd hoped you would someday replace. Oddly, he saved your life."

There was pause.

"Laura thinks it was you." Jack said.

"She thinks a lot of things, not all of which are true." Stoneham replied. "But, the big question, right now, is about you."

"If your people kill me, every document you're worried about will go viral." Jack warned. "They'll go to the newspapers, the internet blogs and other media around the world."

Stoneham laughed, and shook his head.

"We're not killers, Jack." he said. "We're bankers, for God's sakes!"

"Same thing happens if I rot in jail." Jack warned. "All the dirty laundry gets washed publicly."

"Do you realize that you'd be causing chaos? There would be untold suffering. People would lose faith in America, and the value of the US dollar would probably collapse. Is that what you want? Do you want to destroy your country and impoverish millions of people, all over the world, who are keeping their savings in dollar bills because they trust America?"

"Maybe... it should all collapse. But, I don't think it would happen. I think it would renew the country. In the end, the most suffering would be right here on Wall Street, and most specifically, at Bolton Sayres."

"Are you blackmailing me? I don't like being blackmailed."

"I don't like being threatened." Jack retorted.

"Well, it looks we've got a Mexican standoff." Stoneham stated. "So, let me ask you, again. What do you want? And, don't ask for things I can't give you."

"First, I want all claims to the life insurance policy in the Thomas Mattingly Estate waived by the bank. All that money goes to Sandra Mattingly's son, and gets administered by his grandmother. And, the bank gives back the proceeds from the sale of the house, too."

"Done." Stoneham agreed.

"Second, I want an annuity, providing at least $30,000 per year for the boy to be raised and educated, adjusted to inflation each year." Jack continued.

"Done." Stoneham agreed.

"Third, I want the lawyer, James Hunter, fired permanently, and prohibited from doing any more work for Bolton Sayres.

Stoneham hesitated for a moment on that one, but finally, he spoke.

"Agreed."

"And, finally, I want Bolton Sayres to cease and desist from further stock, bond and commodity price manipulation." Jack added.

"Agreed." Stoneham answered quickly.

Jack wondered why Stoneham didn't object to the last demand. He had told him not to ask for things he couldn't give him. How could he make such a huge concession so easily? Why hadn't he at least put up a fight? Before he could come to any conclusions, however, the other man spoke again.

"What do I have to secure your side of the bargain?" Stoneham asked.

"You have my word." Jack noted.

Stoneham knew Jack's word was his bond.

"Done!"

Actually, the last condition hadn't been difficult at all for Stoneham to agree to. With Marc Dunlop dead, Bolton Sayres was certain to lose its place as the leading manipulator in financial markets. Beyond that, Stoneham had felt, for a long time that manipulation on the bank's own balance sheet was too risky, even with a Federal Reserve backstop.

Off-balance sheet hedge funds and private equity groups were more suitable for such activity. People tightly connected to the bank controlled all the key funds. Many had been bank officials at some time in the past. The funds could get indirect borrowing status at the Federal Reserve by working through one of the banks. In theory, the Volcker Rule of the Dodd-Frank Act would eventually prohibit employed bank executives from running such hedge funds. However, the rule wasn't going to take effect until 2017, and there were a million ways around it. Stoneham kept those caveats to himself.

XXV - OVERLOOKING THE ADRIATIC

The modern city of Tivat is on the Bay of Kotor, in the tiny nation of Montenegro. It is named after the Illyric Queen Teute, a long-time patron of piracy, once known as the "Terror of the Adriatic." In 229 BC, she was foolish enough to murder a Roman emissary and the Roman Republic declared war. It invaded her lands with an army of 20,000 men, defeated her, and deprived her of all territories. After the conquest, the city became a tourist destination, and it has been catering to tourists ever since.

In the foothills of the Black Mountain, overlooking the city and its sparkling blue bay, stood a mansion-like villa, originally built by a Russian oligarch. Recently, however, a man reputed to be a wealthy American tech entrepreneur had bought it. There were several different cars parked on the circular driveway outside. The most conspicuous one was a Lamborghini Veneno Roadster.

In the back of the Villa, with a view of the sea, there was a small white marble table. The serving staff had carefully set the table for three. Jack sat across from his friend Jose Arias. They hadn't seen each other for a while. Sitting next to Jose was his girlfriend of the moment, a 19 year old green eyed beauty from Ukraine, Olga Tamchenko. Each man was dressed in a t-shirt and a pair of light shorts. That was about as much as anyone would want to wear during a hot June day on the Adriatic. The thermometer was nearing 89 degrees Fahrenheit.

The girl was also lightly dressed, in a light yellow flowered summer dress. She couldn't speak much English. One thing she could, do, however, was smile. The beautiful smile was as attractive as the rest of her. Suddenly, she stood up and slipped off the dress. A toned and tanned body was hidden underneath. There wasn't a drop of fat on her. Despite that, her breasts were ample, and her hips wide. She wore a little string bikini top and bottom, which hid almost nothing.

She looked somewhat like he remembered Laura in her heyday, before she'd become fat.

"Ya zbirausa pirnuti v bacein." Olga said, smiling.

Jose laughed, and translated.

"She's going to jump in the water..." he explained to his friend.

"She doesn't speak much English, does she?" Jack commented.

"No, but she understands a lot, and what a face and body, eh?" he said.

Jose was right. The girl was attractive. Since gaining fabulous riches, Jose had also developed a fine taste in women.

She ran to the pool, giggling, and then dove in on the deep end, splashing around when she came out. With the girl busy, and no longer listening to them, they felt free to talk frankly.

"Where did you find her?" Jack asked.

"She found me." Jose explained. "I spent 3 months in Odessa, Ukraine, studying Russian."

"Really?"

"The girls there love Americans, didn't you know?" Jose noted. "At least, they love our money."

"Since you've got so much money, she should love you a lot."

"She does."

"Did you learn Russian there?" Jack asked.

"Sure. I'm not fluent... but I get by." Jose replied. "The language in Montenegro is Serbian, which is very similar to Russian, and probably half the residents here, in Tivat, are Russian or Ukrainian."

Jose seemed to have found his place in the world. Jack was happy for him. It was nice to see his friend enjoying life. It got annoying, though, when he brought up the same subject that had been a point of tension between them.

"When are you going to quit that bullshit job?" Jose asked, finally. "Remember, your share is $72 million, which is more than either of us can spend in a lifetime. It's sitting in Singapore, waiting for you."

Jack smiled, and looked at the table for a moment. He didn't answer, right away. Then, he looked up.

"It'll sit there forever." he said, finally. "I have absolutely no intention of ever taking it."

"You really are nuts." Jose said.

"I'm surprised you haven't spent it already?" Jack noted. "This new lifestyle, including the girls, must cost a fortune."

Jose laughed.

"Not really." he said. "I can't even think of enough ways to spend my half of the money. This villa cost me $2 million. I pay the servants twice what everyone else in the neighborhood does. But, they still cost only about $900 bucks a month each. Its chump change..."

"Hmm..." Jack stated.

"Yeah, you should take the money, drop the rat race, come here, and enjoy yourself."

"I am enjoying myself." Jack insisted.

"No you're not. Get out and live like a human being, not like a drone ant in a disgusting city. Take Laura with you, if you want. If she won't go, leave her behind. You see what's in that pool? You can have one, too! It's all here. You just need to reach out and take what's yours!"

Jack just shook his head.

"That's just the problem. It's not mine."

"Sure it is."

"No, Jose, I'll never take the money."

"Well, then, you're dumb." Jose said.

Jack shrugged his shoulders.

"Maybe, but I'm telling you the facts."

"You'll take it someday."

"Never."

"Why not?" Jose asked.

"It's stolen money." Jack answered.

"It's NOT stolen!" Jose exclaimed.

He had said the same thing many times before.

"You stole it from Dunlop."

"It was never his to begin with!" Jose insisted. "He stole it himself! Besides, he's dead, so he can't use it anymore. I can, and so can you..."

"Give it to charity." Jack suggested, sipping wine.

"No." Jose stated, and pointed to the pool. "Look. There's no girl back in the States better than the one I've got in the pool. This kind of girl is only in magazines back there. And, even if they did exist, they'd never give me a second look."

"You're fixated on women." Jack pointed out. "There are other things."

"Like what?" Jose snapped back.

Jack shrugged his shoulders, and shook his head slightly.

"If you don't know, it won't do any good for me to tell you." Jack stated.

He looked at Olga's nearly naked body. She climbed up to the diving board, and was just about to take another dive into the swimming pool. She was beautiful. Looking at her made his groin stir as much as it had when he'd first met Laura, and then, later, Sandra Mattingly.

"She's hotter in the sack... believe it or not." Jose whispered, when he noticed Jack staring. "You want her tonight?"

That last statement shocked Jack.

"What?" he asked.

"I can see you want her." Jose said. "You're my best friend. I don't mind sharing."

"I don't think she'd be so keen on the idea."

"She'll do whatever I tell her." Jose said. "That's 'cause she loves me. If I tell her to sleep with you, she'll do it."

"I wouldn't call that 'love'..." Jack pointed out.

"Call it whatever you want. But, the bottom line is that if I tell her to do it, she'll sleep with you, guaranteed."

It was a tempting offer, and he toyed with it for a moment. Just thinking about it raised the intensity of his desire.

What would happen if he accepted the offer? Would the girl really sleep with him just because Jose told her to? That was crazy. He tried to put sleeping with the beautiful foreigner out of his mind. Jose's new lifestyle could be contagious. Why was he so eager to pull him into it? He wanted no part. He'd sworn never to cheat on his wife again. Still…

"What do you say?" Jose asked.

Jack shook his head, and took a deep breath. Both the money and the girl were temptations that were difficult to resist. The girl was as beautiful as any girl could be. The weather was ideal. Multicolored floral hedges surrounded the Olympic sized pool, and pleasantly scented the air. There was a sound of chirping songbirds in the air. It sure beat the gray ugliness of Manhattan. The lifestyle was amazing.

There was one thing wrong with the whole setup. It wasn't honest, and it wasn't real. If this girl, Olga, would sleep with anyone Jose told her to sleep with, common sense should have told him that she didn't love him very much. The man was operating on dangerous delusions. He'd sucked himself into a false reality. Jack would not follow.

"I don't understand you, Jack." Jose finally declared. "Here you are, lecturing me on stealing money, but you're working for those fucking banksters. You're gonna' end up being one, someday."

"I've been cleaning the place up, actually." Jack explained. "Since I've taken over the compliance department, we've put a lot of scammers out of business."

"Are you still being groomed to take over THEATRES?"

"Nothing more has been said about that." Jack admitted.

"As I remember it, you once said that entire operation ought to be closed down."

"I did say that, once." Jack admitted. "But, there's a huge threat from terrorism. It's a dangerous system, but if someone with integrity is in charge, it can work, I think."

"And, that someone is you?" Jose asked.

"Maybe."

"What about the manipulation?" Jose asked. "You made a deal to stop it, but it hasn't stopped."

"Bolton Sayres isn't involved anymore."

Jose shook his head, irritated.

"Now their hedge funds do the dirty work." he pointed out.

"By 2017, the Volcker rule will prohibit bank executives from using bank money to finance hedge funds." Jack countered.

"A lot can happen between now and then."

"You're right." Jack agreed. "But, in the meantime, I'm making a lot more changes at Bolton."

"It's a pipe dream." Jose insisted. "You'll never make banksters honest men."

"They're just greedy like everyone else."

"You're doing it because of Laura and the kid. That's the real truth. Otherwise, you'd be here with me."

"And, what if that's true? What's wrong with that?"

"You're not even attracted to her anymore." Jose noted. "What was it you said? Oh, yeah, 'having sex with her is like making love to a walrus'?"

"I'm sorry I said that. I shouldn't have."

"You should have! Because it's how you feel."

"I don't feel that way anymore. And, she's the mother of my child."

"So what?" Jose asked. "Leave the woman and visit the child. Live like a man again."

"You make it sound so easy."

"It is easy!" Jose insisted. "It's as easy as doing it."

"If you came back to New York, you could help me a lot."

"I'll never go back."

"We could work together and make a big difference. For example, right now, I need compliance software that can monitor employee misconduct and generate alerts automatically, to stop stuff like what Dunlop was doing."

"You're suggesting that I go back to programming?" Jose asked in disbelief.

"I'm suggesting that you return to New York." Jack urged. "Bring your Russian girlfriend, if you want..."

"She's not Russian... she's Ukrainian..."

"Whatever... But, come back and form a company. Develop this software and market it all over the world. You'll end up with more money than you have now, and it would be honest money."

Jose laughed.

"Don't take this the wrong way, but sometimes I think you're a better comedian than a lawyer."

"I'm not joking." Jack insisted.

"I don't want to go back to New York or even to America. I like things exactly the way they are."

"I need your help."

"You're spinning your wheels, and going nowhere. Sooner or later, you'll realize it."

"What you're doing makes you no better than Dunlop." Jack countered.

"I'm much better than him." Jose insisted. "He stole the money by cheating innocent people. I stole it from someone guilty as hell..."

Jack watched as the girl dried herself with a towel. She walked back, toward them, at the table. Jose said one more thing in a whisper.

"Remember, your money's waiting for you."

"I'll never take it." Jack insisted, yet again.

EPILOGUE:

High on the 29th floor of the W.T. Fredericks building, Adriano Navarro's expansive personal office had one of the best views of New York Harbor. The Statue of Liberty dominated the skyline. He no longer noticed the view. There were too many other things to occupy his attention. He sipped on a cup of espresso as he thought about everything that had happened.

Christopher Dunlop's son was gone. The trouble he'd caused was gone with him. Best of all, no one was the wiser. No one was left to tell the tale. It was a nice clean finish to a messy mistake. It had even resulted in some new advantages. The W.T. Frederick's CEO believed his son was assassinated. He would look long and hard for the people he believed were behind it. However, he would find only what Navarro wanted him to find. The old man was easy to twist around his little finger.

Dunlop's frantic attempts to find his enemies didn't worry him. No one would ever suspect that the bullet that killed the son of Christopher Dunlop had come from a sniper rifle, held by a hidden operative charged with the job of making sure that both Fyodor Khasan and Marc Dunlop were dead. The local town police department had even closed the case, without even so much as a ballistic test. The town didn't want to spend that type of money on an open and shut case, and neither did the state.

Navarro smiled at the irony. Christopher Dunlop was now one of his strongest supporters within the political structure of the Synod. Yet, he had killed the man's son. The killing, of course, was entirely justified. Marc Dunlop was a bad seed. The world was a better place without him. Meanwhile, Jeremy Stoneham was also looking for his enemies. The only question left was how to capitalize on all these anxious fools flailing about? It was a prime opportunity.

The Stoneham insurgency had once come close to ending Navarro's control over THEATRES. He'd castrated that movement. It was hard for the man to continue actively opposing him, in light of the fact that he was led to believe that Navarro had saved his daughter and son-in-law.

A profound idea was taking shape in Navarro's mind. He'd been taking orders his entire life. Other people had always set his agenda, his goals and his limits. That had all changed. Now, he would take no more orders. With THEATRES in his pocket, he didn't have to. With the government's help, his power would soon span the entire globe.

He had access to the deepest secrets of every executive in the Synod, and every powerful person inside the government. The lives of ordinary citizens, powerful businessmen and public servants were all in his hands. His power would increase as the network expanded throughout North America. In time, he would watch everyone, every day, everywhere.

Knowledge is power, and everyone has a skeleton somewhere in the closet. He would use it to find those skeletons and use them. He would make and break bankers, businessmen, politicians, even Presidents. The world was within his grasp. He needed only to reach out and take what was rightfully his.

END

HOW TO LEAVE A REVIEW

Thank you for reading this novel. If you enjoyed it, please consider leaving a positive reader review. The author would like to get feedback from readers. Also, leaving a review is the single most helpful thing you can do to share your enthusiasm. Positive customer reviews are the social proof needed to get more people to read the book.

GO HERE TO LEAVE A REVIEW!

myBook.to/TheSynod

This same URL will take you to the correct Amazon.com site wherever you may live in the world. In addition, the book is sold elsewhere, such as at Barnes and Noble, Kobo, Apple iBook, etc. You can also leave your review at the relevant URL at other booksellers' websites.

KEEP UP WITH THE LATEST BOOKS, ARTICLES AND EVENTS BY JOINING THE MAILING LIST!

http://www.averybgoodman.com/myblog

Printed in Great Britain
by Amazon